All that Malue Is

Malue:

The plants and the animals lived in a world that was blue. The sky was blue and the sky told the sea to be blue, so the sea reflected the sky and the world remained what it was. The animals knew not the color blue, so though the sky spoke to the sea and the sea spoke to the shore, the plants and animals did not speak at all.

But born of blood was the ame, the ones from the red. They were man and woman. They spoke to animals and the animals did not hear. So, they spoke to the plants and the plants did not hear. Finally, they spoke to the sea and the sea heard them. The sea commanded the ame to breathe with fish, but they would not. The ame commanded the sea to part and the sea was forced to listen.

Using their language, they gave the sea and the sky names. Because they named the sky and the sea, what the sky and the sea had created was theirs. What was two was now one, and that one was Malue. They summoned fire from their burning blood. They believed themselves the most potent in blood, but they were mistaken. Dragons came with their words, and with their words came law. The law was written in spirit. A dragon breathed power and named the ame human, and it owned the human.

But the dragon did not name Malue, and Malue took pity on its former master. The human took from within themselves their souls and sealed the dragons away. The land flourished and the people built cities and created borders and boundaries. Over time, they no longer asked of Malue and only took what they knew to be theirs. So without knowledge of what they once were, they were human forever more.

The Northern Kingdom:

The Northern Kingdom was a monarchy in the far north that occupied a large portion of the central continent. The area was too large to be controlled by one ruler, so it was divided into five provinces: Goldenhill, Ironforge, Witshore, Dimfir, and Icebreaker. It bordered The Anarchy to the east and Drasil to the south. The northern and western borders were coastlines.

Geographically, the Northern Kingdom was generally cold and dry, with Icebreaker being the coldest and driest. Most of the five provinces were self-serving, functioning as their own mini countries. But only together could they hope to stand as a world power. One king or queen ruled at a time and there should have been four dukes. In practice, there were usually three.

The king or queen originated from any of the five provinces and came to rule based on the strength of his or her bloodline. To prove their bloodline's strength, the royal families of each province named their children after themselves. They often cheated and lied to make their family's seem older, leading to ludicrously long lines of lies.

Goldenhill: Ruled by King Richard the 540th since he, in one way or another, proved the strength of his bloodline. By having his family name their children, even girls, "Richard" for hundreds of generations, he secured the throne by birthright. Goldenhill owned little land that is not already taken up by Goldenhill City, the capital of the Northern Kingdom. Rocky terrain on the eastern side of the Whitegold mountains broke into a valley, and in it laid Goldenhill City, adorned with glittering gold.

Ironforge: Ruled by Duke Arthur the 539th, Ironforge borders The Anarchy in the East. Rich mountains crawled across the stone-ridden landscape of Ironforge, and in those red mountains, iron was used to create weapons to defend against the dangerous pirates to the east. The iconic Iron Wall stretches from the coast to the border. The wall is made of black stone and reinforced with iron.

Witshore: Ruled by Duke Charles the 537th, Witshore laid farthest to the west and possessed docks full of fish that they exported all over the world. The wet area had some of the highest populations and were previously far wealthier than any other province. However, King Richard the 540th of Goldenhill, their neighbor over the Whitegold Mountains, taxed Witshore's exports immensely, causing the inner lands to thrive while Witshore lies less than prominent.

Dimfir: Ruled by Duke Alexandria the 538th, the woodlands were south of the Half-Thawed Mountain Range, which acted as the border between Dimfir and Icebreaker, and east of the Whitegold Mountains, barring them from access to the western coast. Lush and green, Dimfir was sparse in cities and towns, but even so, it housed hardy individuals willing to work their way to the top. Dimfir had the ability to be completely self-sustaining, and for the common necessities, it was most useful. The people of Dimfir had a fearful respect for the woodlands and chose not to completely chop them down, instead farming trees in specific orchards. Many residents believed that the woods were infested with beasts of gruesome power. They treaded lightly while hunting game in the wild.

Icebreaker: Icebreaker broke the trend of the other provinces. Icebreaker never housed a king of the Northern Kingdom, instead relying on its own government system. The hearty land valued the strength of soul and muscle over blood. It was ruled by Chief Janmar, a ruler who believed in the eye-for-eye philosophy almost to a fanatical level. Icebreaker was the province furthest to the north, past the Half-Thawed Mountain Range. The Northern Kingdom claimed dominion over Icebreaker, but any good Icebreaker nomad would have said that Icebreaker was its own country. The rugged terrain was mastered by the nomads that wandered the frozen tundra. Chief Janmar was an ironfisted ruler, but he was also fair and compassionate, which is more than could be said for most of the Northern Kingdom.

The Anarchy in the East:

Despite its name, the Anarchy in the East—or Anarchy for short—was not a true anarchy but instead was ruled by several pirate gangs that roamed the wastes and dunes. People living in Anarchy worked completely out of self-interest. Laws were a disliked idea, and gangs that enforced them too strictly often ended up worm food. No one could argue that the people of Anarchy weren't clever; their technology was unrivaled in all the world.

Drasil:

More of a place of life than a country, Drasil was a disorganized mess of wildlife. South of the Northern Kingdom thrived a massive tree, its roots shaping the contents themselves. The ground of Drasil was wood and all life lived on the tree. The people that lived there could read the will of the tree and its nature granted them power unfamiliar to the Northern Kingdom.

Aerokite:

Aerokite was the land across every sea. Every waterway, every current, went to or through Aerokite. The Northern Kingdom was trapped by the Aerokitian Empire. Yet, still with all this power, their navy was only suited to sink pirate vessels. The Aerokitians had a miniscule army in comparison to their vast population. Their power came from the Aerokititan Crest: their currency and their king.

Ardelamor:

South of Aerokite, Ardelamor lived in envy of the posterity of their northern sister. While Aerokite flourished, Ardelamor was trapped in a dark age that they couldn't seem to escape. With a crippled economy, they resorted to the evils of slavery and dark magic unseen by other countries. Their feudal shamans conducted heretical rituals that manipulated star and sky. For that reason, they were Aerokite's sworn enemy.

All That Malue Isn't

Liax was a world view much broader than the idea of Malue.

A history much different in nature.

Only fools would call the world Liax, but some of those pagans existed.

To these false prophets there was a world below others.

Dessees, hot and dry.

A complex layout of labyrinthian caves where water was the hardest prey.

These caves were unlit, but they smolder with power.

In places where the rock was weak, one could feel the heat of magma through the wall.

The cave never ended and great underground cities were abandoned as the residents followed the water into infinity.

But the great lie of Liax did not end there.

The pagans were so foolish that they believed the sky itself to hold a secret—that the dragons who were long gone lived on land that floated in the sky like islands float in water.

But only a fool would believe such a thing, for how would one not be disillusioned when they looked to the clouds and saw no land?

They called this place Disus and claimed to be able to see it between the clouds.

But when the clouds parted, there was no land and no winged beast.

But perhaps these myths should have been taken more light-heartedly.

Children were filled with wonder looking for the Skylands, and they feared the caves that led to the supposed Underworld.

In reality, it is of no harm to tell a child a lie.

Is it?

Hera and Aaron

Aaron wrinkled his nose. "I'm getting tired of wearing this every day."

Aaron was a tall, lanky boy. He was built like a climber with his forearms the strongest part of his lean body. His mop of hair was a mess, dark blonde, and knotted. It was long enough to reach his shoulders—or would be if he ever ran a comb through it to detangle the knots. His features were broad, his skin fair, and his eyes narrow. What Aaron wore was of little importance to his figure, as he was quite tired of wearing it every day.

"I don't know. I like the armor. It makes the guards mistake me from a distance," Hera answered.

Aaron's friend, Hera, strode next to him. They were in an empty street an hour before sundown. By now, all the people that lived in their small island village of Great Neighbor were finishing up their day.

Hera was dressed as she had implied, wearing guard armor. She dared not imitate the full livery of a guard. That was illegal, and Hera would never dare do anything illegal. Her hair and face were cleaner than Aaron's in almost every way. Her hair was not knotted except into a bun, which was evidently on purpose, though Aaron had no clue why. Her hair was brown and only slightly longer than Aaron's, and her face was much sharper than his.

"Come to think of it, you do smell horrible," Hera added.

Aaron wasn't quite sure if she was joking or not, so he laughed. His pace quickened ahead of her, and he looked over his shoulder to talk to her. They passed houses, and as Aaron passed them, he pointed interesting objects out.

"We can take that," Aaron said, pointing to a beautiful flower pot.

"We don't have a house," Hera sighed.

"Fine, fine, how about that?" he pointed to a small apple tree.

"The apples?" Hera asked.

"Yeah, they look tasty."

The apples from the apple tree did not look particularly tasty, but they did look expensive. There was a woman on the island who was capable of selling an apple from that tree for an exorbitant price of five goldenteeth, enough to buy a full meal. That was ten Aerokitian crests and fifteen eastern betevils. The money wouldn't make anyone rich, but it was a lot for an apple.

"I wouldn't mind one, but it's too late to eat," Hera said.

A devilish grin crossed Aaron's mouth. "Exactly. So, if we won't steal the flower pot and we won't steal the apple, we might as well steal some clothes, right?"

Hera shook her head in exasperation. "Fine, but I get to choose the next thing we snag."

"Deal!"

The King

"Rose! Rose!" A shrill shout danced through the castle.

The King kept much to himself, as per his advisors' requests. He was mad, no doubt, finding odd books in odd languages that filled his head with tales of magical genies sailing the seas. This was one of those unfortunate times when he was out and about.

A lowly advisor happened to be the one unlucky enough to be in the general vicinity of the King when he escaped from his study. The King waved down the advisor and angrily told him to come over. The advisor stopped in his tracks, said goodbye to the late afternoon snack he had been hoping for, and turned to the King.

"Yes my—" the advisor got out before the King interrupted.

"That's King to you," the King said quickly, "and I'm not li*king* your attitude."

The advisor sighed. "That's what I was going to say," he muttered under his breath.

The King made sure to prove his status by announcing the word "king" in any word unfortunate enough to have the four letters side-by-side. Though most kings had their name following the title, the King insisted his name was just King and that his original name should be forgotten. Which it was… rather quickly.

"No, it's not," the King protested. "The word liege was actively being formed on your tongue. I could tell by the inflection of your previous word and the shape of your lips."

The advisor turned slightly red with anger. The King was right, of course. How was the advisor supposed to know that the King wanted to be called King today? My liege would have been fine yesterday.

The King of Great Neighbor was no fashion expert, but he was still adorned in kingly attire. Purple being the color of wealth, he had it, in cloth form, imported to his location. He had the expensive cloth used to make his kingly robe, which was far too big for his short stature. He tugged on the edge of his robe, impatiently expecting the advisor to answer his question before he even asked.

"What is required?" the royal advisor asked.

The King cocked his head to the side, causing his crown to slide off of the thin wires the man called hair and down past the uneven stubble the King insisted was a clean shaven face. He looked down at the crown now on the floor, and his eyes widened in panic. He darted down to all fours to pick it up and placed it forcefully on his head, causing it to plunge far down his forehead and stick there.

"Where's Rose?" the King spat.

The advisor breathed in deeply. "Rose is at home, sire-King. She has taking the day off."

"Unlike her..." the King pondered.

"Not really."

"She once stayed awake for two weeks straight," the King noted.

"No, she didn't."

The King scowled up at the advisor. "You're fired."

The advisor sighed. "No, I'm not."

The King did not fire the advisor.

Rose, Mouth of the King

Rose stood at the doorway, ready to leave. She had already adorned the armor that she wore in honor of her guard captain. Her cleaver leaned against the wall. She doubted she would need it today, but even so, she looked at it longingly.

"You were supposed to have the day off," her husband called to her.

Rose responded over her shoulder, "You can spend some time with my parents."

Her husband was still sitting in the dining room, finishing dessert. He was always a late eater.

"What makes you think I want to do that?" her husband asked.

Rose rolled her eyes. She was fairly short for a guard. The red hair, for which she was so named, was tied tightly in possibly the most disciplined bun any on the island had ever seen. Her eyes were tired, and her skin was burned from long hours in the sun. But still, she had a job to do for the King. One didn't become the Mouth of the King by slacking off.

"Shush," Rose said.

Her face was not visible, but her scowl could be heard through the door.

"You wanted to see your brother, didn't you? Why do I always have to beg you to stay?"

"I have a duty to this island."

Her husband chuckled slightly. "There are two kids on this island that cause trouble. You are hardly crawling in crime."

"What about Hal?" Rose smiled. "Hal sucks."

"I went drinking with Hal," Rose's husband said.

Rose laughed, "You suck, too."

Her husband imbued his voice with mock rage and said, "Take that stinking cleaver with you; I don't want it in my house!"

Rose smiled dimly and crossed the room to pick up the cleaver. The handle was fairly normal, with a normal hand guard. The sword's specialty was that the blade extended out to the tips of the otherwise normal handguard, creating a heavy weapon. Rose was attuned to the clumsy tool and renowned for its usage.

"Yes, sir," she called one last time.

The door shut behind her, and her face immediately fell into a blank stare. She was infamous for her calm demeanor, and this moment was no different. She had no idea what compelled her to go to work that day, but something in her gut told her she had to go to the castle. She wasn't one to ignore her intuition.

Viner and Fredrick, Hand of the King

"Ah-ha!"

Two guards were fencing in the castle courtyard, one being Fredrick, the captain of the guard himself. He swished his rapier into his brother Viner's armored stomach, barely giving him any time to deflect the blow. Viner was able to parry, but just barely. He knew that if this had been a real fight, he would be dead.

"That's what I like to see. That's faster than last time," Viner roared.

Fredrick stood slightly shorter than his younger brother, but his spiky red hair almost made up for the difference. He looked like a fire, with his sharp goatee splaying wildly in every direction but down.

The guard captain laughed and flourished his rapier in the air, pointing it at Viner with a confidence that no one in the entirety of Great Neighbor could replicate. Viner was a broad-shouldered man with a bald head and stubble beard. In place of hair, line tattoos dotted the peripherals of his head, each two inches in length. The black lines were only faintly visible, showing just how tan Viner had become working in the sun.

Viner went for a flick into Frederick's chestplate. They both wore identical armor pieces even though Fredrick was the captain. It was a sign of respect that each member of the guard wore the same armor. That armor was Fredrick's pride and joy; he couldn't bear to keep it to himself.

The armor of the guard depicted a turtle shell in all its metallic glory. As far as the people knew, the insignia had been chosen to represent strength and protection. However, the real reason why the majestic turtle was chosen was that Fredrick liked turtles. Rose and Viner had devised the design as Fredrick's birthday surprise.

Fredrick parried the flick with ease and started up a friendly conversation. "Calessa is proving to be a good fighter."

Viner knew his brother was trying to talk him into submission and was of half a mind not to respond. But as he parried the next blow and noticed it was off, he decided he could play his game.

"Aye, she's disciplined."

"Disciplined?" Frederick laughed.

"Aye, yes." Viner nodded without a glimmer of humor.

Fredrick's face turned solemn. "I suppose she would have to be. Some of our guards are on the precipice of losing their jobs because they continue to attack her iron defenses."

"She is good with that shield," Viner agreed.

Frederick shook his head. "That's not what I meant."

"I know."

Calessa

Calessa, her sister, and her father were the only Aerokitians on the island, making them rather unpopular. Calessa's mother was also unpopular for marrying one. Calessa's father had been born on the island. His parents were two traveling Aerokitians that decided to settle down in Great Neighbor. Who could blame them? It was a beautiful place. What they did not expect was the general dislike from the populace. They had been under the impression that the people of the Northern Kingdom would be used to Aerokitians by now, but Great Neighbor was rural and was not big on international trade, even with Witshore.

Calessa's grandparents were not especially rich, but the people of Great Neighbor would have told you otherwise. This, among many other foolish reasons, added to the blatant racism. Her grandparents could have fled, and often Calessa resented them for not doing so, but they took it as a point of pride to stay. Calessa's father met her mother and continued his life, starting a family. Calessa's grandparents had died of natural causes some years ago, so now it was just the four of them against what felt like the world.

Not everyone in Great Neighbor was cruel. Calessa's sister had many friends who were far more open-minded. It was really the guard that was harshest against them. Calessa was determined to prove them wrong, so like her grandmother and grandfather, she joined the guard who would not accept her.

Frederick was not one of the cruel men, and he made certain that she would someday adorn the armor that she was rightfully owed. That day was approximately six months ago, and she had proven herself a bulwark. She was one of the best shield and spear fighters Great Neighbor had seen since Lieutenant Viner.

"Did the guard treat you well?" Calessa's sister asked.

Calessa let loose her long black hair after a long day of work. "Like always."

"Always isn't well," Calessa's sister said fearfully.

"They get more used to me day after day. I just keep to myself," Calessa said.

Calessa's sister was younger than her but that didn't stop her from sharing her sage wisdom. "They are not going to just 'get used to you'. They haven't gotten used to us after forty-five years."

Calessa changed the subject, "What did you do today?"

"I applied for a job with Diane," her sister responded cheerfully.

"You're going to be selling fish?" Calessa asked.

Her sister was almost bursting. "Hopefully to Witshore."

"Witshore! You mean you are going to try to leave the island?"

"Yes!"

Calessa's sister was trying hard to not jump up out of her seat.

"And dad is okay with this?"

"It took a lot of convincing."

It would also take a lot of convincing to sell fish to someone from Witshore. Calessa knew it was a starter job, but she was glad her sister had gotten one at all. Calessa was worried her sister would never leave the house. She would miss her though. The journey from Witshore was not a long one; hopefully, she would be back often.

Tython, Emissary of Dimfir

The sea splashed against Tython's face. At first, the young emissary was filled with wonder, but after an hour of standing at the end of the ship with saltwater constantly making its way into his nose, the blue sea lost its allure. He spluttered for the last time, deciding it was best if he didn't stand at the tip of the ferry.

Tython attracted eyes from those taking passage on the ferry. Not many outsiders made their way into Great Neighbor and less looked like Tython. He was from Dimfir. Someone from Dimfir was either excessively short or excessively tall with excessively few exceptions. Before Tython was born, he had had a fifty-fifty shot for either one. His father was excessively tall and his mother excessively short. He had drawn the short end of the stick, as they say in Dimfir. But only in jovial spirits as it was not looked down upon to be shorter than average. At least any more looked down upon than a short person often is.

His height was not exorbitantly strange. Many people on the boat were short. What no one else on the boat had was a bow on their back, a lantern on their belt, and a wrench somewhere in between. His pants drooped to his knees, his overcoat had flourishes on the shoulders, and he wore a green feathered hat. In short, he looked like a poor man who had just come into wealth. Or, he looked like he was from Dimfir.

Tython paid no attention to the stares. He jovially greeted many of the ferry's passengers as he walked across the ship. The boat was small and filled with fewer than a dozen passengers, not including the crew. It was made out of an agreeable wood that looked out of place sailing the sea.

Tython was familiar with wood. He had worked as a logging machine mechanic back in Dimfir. But he was no longer a logging mechanic; now he had been sent to represent his people. It was a great honor. He had been tasked by not only the Duke of Dimfir but also the King of Goldenhill to travel to Great Neighbor and convince the people there to join the Northern Kingdom from which they seceded so long ago.

By his count, he was the fifth to attempt this. But he had something the others didn't. He had a lute. Tython's belief in the power of song could not be overstated. The simple string instrument that weighed him down, along with his bow, lantern, and wrench, provided him with a sense of security that even his arrows could not. His sense of security was not unfounded. A man walks onto a ship with a weapon and people become afraid. But a man walks onto a ship with a giant wooden turtle shell that supposedly plays dulcet melodies and suddenly people are much less so.

Why Tython had brought a bow to Great Neighbor was a mystery to everyone except those from his hometown. Pick out anyone from Trihearth and they too would have brought a bow. In the woodlands, you could never be sure of what lurked in the dark. But what Tython failed to realize was that in the rest of the world, the dark is the least of their problems.

Filius

With the clinking of glasses and the smell of ink, a tall, lean man in dark, ragged clothes slaved over the writing of knowledge better not known. He drew two figures mirroring each other. They were sleek and slender with little detail added to either of their bodies. That fact was not a flaw of the drawing but an actual accurate depiction.

The first was humanoid, but winged and horned. It was covered head to foot in white, sleek, feathers, even in the face. Its feet and hands were taloned like a hawk. The being had a long grinning mouth and one single penetrating eye. The second was a depiction of the first, but had no wings and its feet and hands were more human-like. However, this being still possessed the same horns as the other. Instead of being covered in white feathers, it seemed to be made out of black metal. Most disturbing of all, it was lacking a face. The lean man had done some digging and ruined some books, but he had finally pieced together their names—the seraphars and the tevnal.

He was Filius, and he wove a tapestry of knowledge through the underground. He was an observant man, so when he observed the disappearance of people to whom he told his secrets, he thought it high time to flee. Now he, a spider-like figure, crawled through the sewers of Goldenhill, fearing the eyes of those who would harm him. He did not know who was an ally and who was not, so he feared the powerful most of all. The Great Warrior was his greatest fear, the man who protected Goldenhill. They say that the warrior commands nature itself. The wind rose when he jumped, the land flooded when he needed a drink.

Filius's purple eyes were oddly beautiful, framed by the black hair that covered his scalp and face, but the beauty did not cover the fear in his eyes. His nerves got the better of him, and he slammed his book closed while the ink was still drying. He packed it away in his bag and started to make his way down the dampened path.

Several steps in, he stopped and took a look around. He knew no one was there, but that was a moment ago. He needed to be sure that no one was watching *now*. Without removing his eyes from the survey, he delicately removed the knife from the scabbard on his hip. A purple gemstone functioned as the pommel of the blade. It glowed the same color as his eyes. When viewed in just the right light, the metal of the blade radiated a similar slight purple glow out of the otherwise iron forging.

He etched the wall with the knife and tore down on the stone, sparks flying as he did so. He recoiled at the sudden light, but after a moment he regained his bearings. The only thing that could be done was to live to learn another day.

"Fleeing festering foaming with fear, Filius what has happened to you?"

Chapter 1
Meddling

"My Love, It would have been Saturday, if we still kept track. Yes, I know, I still keep track."

An old man sat at a desk in a white room writing a letter in black ink and soft handwriting. His back was hunched from years of gravity, but his face had nary a wrinkle. He dipped his quill in ink and clumsily spilled a good helping of it on his white coat.

"It is noon, anyway," he wrote. "You like to know that, and the clouds are looking spectacular with the sun, as they always do this high up. It is a blessing that our divinity allows every man and woman to see this view. How the folds of red gush over every blue stretch. How they reflect on the face of our child, Liax. See, I can still be romantic."

The coat he wore was made by a masterful hand. It detailed, in extravagant embroidery, two giant hands spread like wings. But upon closer look at the coat, one could not make out anything but golden spiderwebs sewn clumsily through the white fabric. A thick hood covered his head making certain that his hair—if he had any other than his short beard—was contained in many folds of fabric.

"Ah, but I have something important to tell you. If you would ordain it under your power, I would like to call a council meeting. I'll be blunt; it's about Hiver. I, too, thought we were finished with him. The damage he has done is irreparable, although not wholly unnecessary. Still, I question whether we should have cut the string sooner. Perhaps it is time to right an old wrong? Yours, Calm."

Calm looked up from his writing. He had little more to say. Perhaps he could dip his pen in the ink and add a few more pleasantries, but perhaps not. It was important that he gathered his fellows to Castle Ame as quickly as possible.

He glanced out the window again to observe the view he had penned. Although he did not notice it previously, a thin glimmer of ice overtook what little he could see. Perhaps his memory had made the clouds look more appealing. With a sigh, he rose to his feet and noticed the large ink stain on his right sleeve. He blew onto the splotch, and the ink retreated from his breath, diving into the darker folds of his cloak and leaving the white cloth spotless.

He turned to walk down the stairs. He had been lonely in this castle, wordlessly watching the people below for such a long time, but soon, he knew, he would come to miss the bliss of boredom. His shaking legs stretched stairs as he moved down the ramparts of Castle Ame.

The castle was made of stone bricks that would have looked white had they not been contrasted to the noon-lit heaven. The structure was intricate in design and absurdly gargantuan. It took ages for Calm to walk across the entire castle, which would have been impractical, but people like him rarely needed to walk. It was evident that the castle's sole purpose was to look pleasant to the eye, the colors soft and palatable. The rounded stone bricks almost made one forget the sharp aluminum rigging that decorated the tops of the spires. The castle was multicolored—the base was comprised of giant blue stones, transitioning then later into white and finally at the top was glossed over with a painted coat of pinkish red that looked like the rays of a sunset.

Below the ramparts was a rounded room which featured eight thrones in a disheveled circle. One of the thrones was made of quartz and sported several feather pillows inlaid into the white material. Rose-colored gemstones were pressed into the spotless stone, and immaculate hieroglyphic tales were engraved on the throne's base.

One might assume that tales adorned on such a rich

quartz throne must be about brave warriors and their adventures against evil—but that would be incorrect. In fact, the tales told were very boring. Calm hobbled forward to the throne and took a seat. One might also assume that the old man who sat atop boring tales would be a boring man, but that, too, would be incorrect.

He pressed his fingers against a hieroglyph about the first person he had ever tutored. A gentle smile pushed aside his beard, and he shifted his weight to sit comfortably on the uncomfortable throne, cushioned by the memory of life thousands of years ago. His eyelids started to droop. Despite his conquest against sleep, after some time he fell into a slumber while waiting for his companions to arrive.

***

"Your Lordship?" said a voice.

Calm snapped awake to see the golden face of Lady Love smiling at him from across the room. Her skin twinkled with a radiance of beauty and power. Calm could have looked at her smiling pink lips for the next eon, but Lady Love was quick to turn serious and put on an expression of worry.

"You had me call this meeting?" she asked.

"Yes." Calm nodded. "I see everyone is here."

He looked around to address all his compatriots. Of his court, there was Lord Calm, two ladies of equal rank, one freiherr a seat below, a marquess and a marquis below that, and one thane at the lowest level of the court.

Lady Luck spoke loudly enough for all to hear. "I would rather not be…"

The other members of the court spared her their disapproving looks, except for Marquess Euphoria, who eyed the floor sarcastically. The most visibly offended was Fear, who frowned at the crystal ball held idly in his hands.

Calm wasted no time quelling the irritations of the young royal and preceded the procession with a proclamation. "I would be embarrassed if you did not see this meeting coming. So, have you seen what I have seen?"

The old man looked around at his compatriots, waiting for a response. His clean white cloak swished softly with a wind that was not there. Calm had a well-trimmed white beard. Other than that, his hair was completely contained—quite convenient for reading. Even in his old age, his beard was thick, if only an inch or two long, and his skin perfect. He was old, not in an aged way, but in a powerful way. It was undeniable that he carried an authority with him that could only result in age. Even with authority, his eyes were astoundingly soft, as if he had learned all he could from sharp eyes and switched to a softer pair. Those soft eyes surveyed the room, but no one responded save for some nods here and there.

"Alright," he continued. "Lady Love has permitted me the first words. I shall be direct and decisive. I have good reason to believe that Dessees is under siege."

A slow, weak voice made itself known in response to Calm's outrageous claim, "No, no, that can't be. I've been watching death, you see. And death has only decreased."

What looked to be a heap of rags laid on the floor next to an iron throne. Upon closer inspection, one could make out an old, shriveled man clothed in those rags. He was the Knowledge Keeper and Thane of Castle Ame. His name was Despair. It was his duty to watch death. He sat on the floor, slumped against an iron throne. The throne looked painful to sit on. Metal spikes jutted out from the seat and back. It would have even been a lethal trap had the spikes not been filed down.

"When was the last time you set foot in Dessees?" Calm asked.

Despair fondled the tip of one of the spikes and tried fruitlessly to draw blood. His crippled neck turned to look pensively up at Lord Calm like a crow eyeing a dead carcass.

"Dessees is the neighbor of my paradox; the Inbetween is thin there. I can look into it any time I please."

Thane Despair was an old, shriveled man with lines under his eyes. He was hunched over to the point of appearing crippled. Gray stubble lined his wrinkled mouth, growing with the patchiness of a teenage boy and the coarseness of a rottweiler. His hairline was thin and retreating revealing a wrinkled and tanned forehead.

Lord Calm continued the interrogation, "How often do you receive souls from Dessees?"

"Death," Despair said slowly, "Has decreased."

"Yes. It has. Is that odd?" Calm asked.

Thane Despair was silent for a moment, seemingly lost in thought. He looked questioningly at Calm, not quite understanding what he meant. How could a war decrease death? He stopped to rub his shriveled eyes for a second or two. Calm wondered why the others still subjected themselves to human discomfort, like the itch of an eye, when instead they could just remove the issue entirely. He considered removing all feelings then and there but stopped himself and decided to not rush into a hasty decision. Losing a humanity was not a simple matter after all.

"My lady, if not the Well of Dessees, have you received any dwarven souls?" Calm asked.

"Not since Liax divided," Lady Love said.

Lady Love sat atop a golden throne, similar in shade and texture to her golden skin. The woman was also aged but far more beautiful than any other in the room. Her lips glowed with a soft pink radiance and the same shade enunciated her pale blue eyes. Golden wings sprouted from her back, folding to cradle her body. She radiated power. She pursed her lips and looked down at Despair, commanding her thane to admit any findings.

"I have not received a Dwarven soul for several years," Thane Despair surrendered. "To my recollection," he added hesitantly.

"Why is that?" Lord Calm questioned.

"Dwarves live long," Despair reasoned. "It could relate to the birth rates one hundred fifty years ago. Perhaps there was a spike in population, one that caused this fluctuation."

"It could..." Calm contemplated, "The Inbetween has put us in a difficult position with Dessees being so hard to see in the first place. Between that and the introduction of the Inbetween and our enemy's active pursuits of denying us observation of the area..."

Lord Calm took a solemn look around the room. His presence was ever commanding and dark. Within moments, he completely usurped the meeting with his gaze alone. He strode to the center to turn and look at his fellows.

"Thane Despair, you have never received... Hiver?" He said.

Despair bowed his head to the ground, "No, my lord."

"And you, Freiherr Mayhem, he was not your follower? He does not battle in your paradox?" Calm double-checked.

"He would have won by now if he had been." Mayhem chuckled.

Lord Calm turned to Fear, "He was a dragon. You did not..."

Marquis Fear shook his head.

"Lady Luck? You wouldn't have?" Calm said.

"No, I didn't even notice him when he was alive, truly," Lady Luck stated absentmindedly.

Euphoria didn't wait to be asked, "Not my thing, Calm."

"I doubt I even need to ask my lady..." Calm glanced at Lady Love.

"No, I did not," Lady Love said.

"I was wrong," Lord Calm grimaced, "it is impossible that Dessees is under siege."

The other sorcerers looked shocked. A glimmer of hope in the darkness. But it could not be so. Calm continued.

"It has already fallen."

If the court had been shocked before, they were fried to ash now. Thane Despair looked offended by the notion that Calm presumed. None of this made any sense. Had Calm finally cracked after all these years of loneliness?

"This is illogical," Despair huffed. "I told you, the dwarves of Dessees are afflicted by very little death. Why would that not indicate prosperity?"

"The prosperity is Hiver's. If Hiver were to rise to attack Dessees, he would need all the power he could muster and would deny the dwarves a peaceful passing. What point does Hiver have in attacking Dessees if not to plunder power from the dead?" Calm answered.

"I suppose so, yes," Thane Despair pondered, "Let me see..."

The fellow members of the court waited for Despair to say more. Instead, the creature took a book from his folds of rags and started thumbing through it. The pages were stained with red, and the cover was stitched together with seemingly no skill in tailoring.

"Here," His lips moved through the sentence slower than a valley forms through stone. Every word was conjured from the stars, struggling to glimmer through the veil of the night sky. "A single time in which a human reportedly met death at... the hands of a dwarf." He thumbed through another page of the book. "Intriguing... that's impossible. The Inbetween makes access from Malue to Dessees taxing. And while dwarves are trapped... in Dessees, humans live in Malue."

The sorcerers heard all of this over the course of a full minute as Thane Despair pulled words from the air and fashioned them in possibly the slowest way he could.

"Why on Liax would we not know where humans and dwarves live!?" Interrupted a booming male voice.

Lord Calm looked angrily in Mayhem's direction, but he bit his tongue, knowing the freiherr could turn violent in a moment. With a broad, brutish figure, Freiherr Mayhem towered above all the other sorcerers. It had been him who had dared interrupt a fellow of the court. His entire body was covered in thick black hair, like a mane more than anything. His eyes resembled those of an ox, and he wore a ring through his nose to cement the similarity. His hair and beard were clumsily braided to keep them more under control. Mayhem had failed in that. Unlike all other royalty, Freiherr Mayhem was covered from head to toe in black plate armor. The steel plates clinked loudly at the rivets whenever he shifted, which the impatient man did often.

Freiherr Mayhem's throne was made of blackened stone that melded into the ground like a mountain overlooking a savannah. Forged into the stone were skulls. These skulls ranged from human to lizard skulls, with the crowning jewel being a dragon skull that was used as a canopy, casting shade over the grand seat of the throne.

Thane Despair began to insist, "Confusion should be avoided-"

"I don't see what's confusing about it!" Freiherr Mayhem said. "Why don't we go down to the Middlelands and see what's going on ourselves?"

The thane struggled to rise to his feet, showing a completely uncharacteristic demeanor in his posture. Not only was he taller than expected, his tongue was sharper and faster than it first appeared. The rags he wore threatened to tear under his malnourished muscles as he stretched. This wasn't the first time the toga had been close to tearing; the many folds of gray cloth had already been punctured by several small rips.

Despair quickly stammered, "I would avoid calling it The Middlelands. Its residents call it Malue-"

"So you can speak quickly," chuckled Mayhem. "Tell me again. Why do I care if it's called Malue? It's the Middlelands!"

Mayhem, too, was starting to rise. He would quell any sense of defiance shown by this weak old thane. The Freiherr outranked Despair by two chairs. If the sniveling pile of bones thought he could stand against the might of the strongest sorcerer in all of Liax, he was mistaken.

"Shut up, you oafish brute," a shrill voice commanded from across the room. "You are getting sidetracked with the wrong questions."

"Shut up, Fear!" Mayhem replied stupidly.

The throne room was circular, but Marquis Fear still managed to place his throne in just the right orientation to look like it was off in the corner. At a glance, it appeared like he was sitting in the carved-out stomach of a dragon, one half the size of the skull that Freiherr Mayhem used as a parasol. After looking at the dragon for more than a moment, it was easily discernible as a replica. The guts of the dragon were not spilling on the floor, but instead were transformed into a comfortable red cloth chair where the marquis sat.

Marquis Fear himself was skinny and tall, with a long nose and a pointy hat. It was a shame that the mortals just so happened to choose him to model their legends after. Fear's eyes sank into his gaunt flesh. Combined with the additional shade cast by his hat, his pupils expanded to adjust to the dim conditions of his gaunt face. His greasy hair fell neatly around his shoulders and his long beard was tucked into his belt, making him look rather silly to anyone that got past the dragon he sat in.

The dragon's scales were made out of black metal, but the teeth looked like real ivory. The dragon was effectively chair-ified, with leather straps holding the complex structure together. A black mist perpetually spewed out of the dragon's mouth. The mist looked like smoke, but it did not rise. Instead, the black smog fell to the floor and dissipated shortly after. Whenever Marquis Fear breathed in, he had to be extra careful not to sputter or he would look even more foolish than he did already.

Even while insulting Mayhem, Marquis Fear goggled at a crystal ball held in his hands. It was filled with what could only be blood. He licked his cracked lips, revealing a mouth filled with yellow teeth and several empty canals.

"This. Do you see it?"

Everyone's eyes followed those of the marquis. No one responded to his question. They waited for him to continue, but he did not. He looked up from his crystal ball of blood, but his eyes struggled to tear away from it. It was as if the blood in his veins wanted to unite with the blood in the ball. A second reddened pupil manifested at the corner of one eye to keep a lookout on the glass ball of blood allowing his primary set of eyes to scan the room.

"I asked if you see it!" He yelled.

Spit flew from his mouth and caught on his beard. A tirade of unhinged anger was evident on his face. He visibly grew older in seconds. His complexion reddened and wrinkled from the yelling.

Euphoria had no patience for the otherwise intimidating man, "Yes, we see it. Can you move on?"

Fear seemed to shrivel at being belittled. He sank down into the multiple layers of cloth he wore over his body. The outer layers were a deep black, while the inner layers a crimson red. His hat was bent at the tip, but not by design making it the most ragged of all he was wearing. The belt he wore was made of dark gray cloth embellished with silver skulls stitched into place with red leather. Most sinister of all was the moon-tinted whip attached to his belt. He moved his hand down to it as if he would dare take scarlet retribution for the insult. The court knew he was far too cowardly to try.

"In this ball is Mordecai and Hiver's blood. It has served us all for generations."

Lady Luck interjected, "It has served you, Fear. And Freiherr Mayhem. For me, it has done little."

"The point stands," Fear continued, "All attempts to replicate this ball have failed. Only dragon blood can have enough potency to sustain itself after the soul link has ended."

Luck rolled her eyes and stared forward. She idly fiddled with one of the many gold and emerald rings on her delicate fingers.

"Don't-" Fear started to say.

The powerful voice of Lady Love rang out before Fear could interject, "Why is this relevant?"

"Or so we thought," Fear said.

He raised his hands in the air as if he had just stated something very controversial. The other sorcerers were not as impressed as he would have liked.

"Or so we thought?" Calm asked.

"What if the soul link never ended?"

Despair's head perked up at this. An interesting thought to be sure. His previous experiments hadn't attempted to capture near lethal amounts of blood while the donor was still alive. And with an active soul link, it was possible that the potency of two powerful beings could be fed by one.

"That's-" Euphoria started to say.

Despair finished. "Completely logical."

Fear began, "So if we-"

"Find Hiver and..." Despair stuttered.

A grin spread across Fear's face as he watched the malnourished man fumble through the outcomes of this new discovery. Mayhem looked at both of them repeatedly and huffed a large plume of cinder-filled smoke out of his nose and mouth.

"Kill him," Mayhem said.

All the sorcerers turned to look at the bull-like Freiherr, frankly astonished that he was following along at all.

"What?" Mayhem asked. "That's what we all do, isn't it? There've been years when I'd go out and challenge a man to a duel every day. For the good of House Ame. But now you are saying that if we eliminate the Hiver threat once and for all and regain our soul well in Dessees, which we think is in jeopardy, we will lose our draconic blood."

"By the powers of mortals all united, I can't believe an old ox can learn new tricks," Fear said.

Mayhem looked like he didn't know how to react. "Now what's that supposed to-"

Calm sensed the tension between the two and chose this moment to end any possibility of conflict. "The proof that Hiver is still alive is becoming overwhelming. I dare say that this is a time of emergency. That we must do something which we have not done for many lives."

He stood there, at the center of the court, all eight thrones facing him. Two sat empty, one being his own and the other being a silver mirror of his own directly opposite his. But unlike his own throne, the engravings were of heroes. They were grand and powerful. They told of ambition and adventure, of love and loss, of the world as it turned from chaos, and how it folded with the waves of all races coalescing into a vortex of power. The excitement, the drama, the heartbreak, the triumph. The tales, they bled onto the floor, engraving the very place where Calm stood. A beautiful mosaic of the three worlds—Disus, Malue, and Dessees—came together in one great world, Liax. Dragons flew to the stars while seraphars handed down tevnal ambassadors to the ranks of man so that the knowledge of magic could flow. The dwarves and monki fought great wars with fire. It was nauseatingly horrible and phantastical all at the same time.

Calm's eyes darted across the rivets of white stone, memories of war plaguing him. He looked up again at the silver throne, and now a man sat on it. His face was the same as Calm's, but his hair on his head was gray, uncontained, and wild. Unlike Calm, his beard was neatly trimmed into a goatee, contrasting with his hair that looked like it had been struck by lightning. The suit and pants he wore were flamboyantly purple. He smiled, an electric glimmer in his eyes.

He looked questioningly at Calm and spoke, "Aren't you a little behind, old man? Go ahead. Make the order. Break the rule. It's worth it. Or have you become the god of lollipops?"

Calm had no clue what lollipops were, but he had enough sense to be insulted. He thought for a moment about the consequences of his mirror's manifesto. Calm knew he could not trust him and his confidence in his original claim was shaken. But he could not allow this evil to sway what was right. He was Calm. He governed reason. But in his actions, he was not torpid. A king needed clarity to make decisions; a warrior needed serenity to carry them out. The court was a coin, and this room had two sides. While he sat on tales of peace, he was and would always be Calm, God of War.

"We are gods!" he announced.

The room had not seen what he had seen. It shifted back into motion like a wind suddenly blowing again. All members of the court flinched at his exclamation, but Lady Love was pleased.

"We change the flow of life with our very hands! We craft and sculpt what is to be with the loving embrace of a true artist." Calm slowly turned to gaze at his fellow Gods of Ame each in turn. "We have been scared. Scared of our own creation. We have watched what we created condense itself into twisted renditions of the truth. It is time that we walk the world again. It is time that we take a conduit again. It is time to place our hands unto Malue, to preempt Hiver's next course of action. I say, my fellows, we take a champion."

The wizards sat in silent contemplation. Marquis Fear was holding his breath. Well after his lungs started begging for air, he breathed out a great sigh and inhaled deeply, but what he inhaled was a puff of smoke. He coughed and sputtered, trying to regain himself, but this humiliation was the last straw.

"You come to me with sky and sky, I know," he growled, "but I have no such duty to protect the lands of men. They are ruled by tyrant kings and horrid pirates in the east. What do we owe them?"

Calm looked back. "If you owe the isles of men nothing, then do it for the dragons. Hiver might have been defeated once, but he still intends to regain control of the clouds. No greater dragons are left to contend with him. Mordecai died of exertion before he could overpower him. I do not believe that he would die in the caves under our lovingly created world, Liax. In fact, I am certain he didn't. The place that is his prison forever shall fuel his rage and increase his power. The evil in all the paradoxes is ever-growing and we are almost powerless to stop him."

Lady Love rose. The ground trembled with the force of her motion. She again regained control of the room, and Calm gladly surrendered it.

"In all of our glory, all of our magic, what has divinity left us now? A dwindling supply. All of our energy bent on keeping our withered bodies alive."

"Our bodies would be easier to keep alive if you didn't focus so much power on keeping yourself young!" Marquis Fear spat.

Tendrils of spectral energy trailed from Lady Love's fingertips. Her head snapped to look at Fear faster than a darting hare, and her arm rose at the same pace. Tentacles of magical energy, pink in luminescent glory, crossed the entirety of the circular chamber, seeking to enthrall Fear in their grasp.

Fear jumped off his seat, and a tendril bore into the velvet, leaving a gash on the dragon. The next tentacle went for another attack. Fear tugged his coat away and was able to dodge the grapple. Both chain-like tendrils bent backward and tangled themselves around Fear's arms before he even knew they were still attacking him. They lifted him from the ground and slammed him against his own throne. His hat fell to the floor, revealing his balding head with smatterings of greasy hair. The tendrils retreated, allowing Fear to get to his feet again. A stain of blood was left where his head had collided with his red cloth throne.

Fear stumbled upwards, regaining his shaky footing. He scrambled down to all fours and fumbled around on the ground for his hat. Instead of finding his hat, he found another torrent of pink magical energy. It hit him in the stomach and forced him over his throne and onto the ground behind it. He cradled his inflamed stomach like a wounded animal, roaring like a dragon.

"Go!" Lady Love commanded. "Thane Despair, stay with me. You and I will have to compare death analytics. Calm, garner a champion. You're the only one I trust with the task. Marquis Fear and Freiherr Mayhem, you must protect Calm with your immortal life. Listen to his wisdom; you know that he is my voice."

Chapter 2
What Keeps the King Awake at Night

Great Neighbor sat atop three islands just off the coast of Witshore. The climate was tropical, as it lay to the southwest of the humid and cold country of the Northern Kingdom. The King of Great Neighbor was bent on preserving Great Neighbor's independence. He was not one to be controlled. By making certain Great Neighbor was independent, he ensured his own independence as well. For this purpose, he halted all trade with the Northern Kingdom. But to his dislike, the embargo did not stop the people of Great Neighbor from looking for work on the mainland. But the embargo did accomplish something—rarely would someone from outside Great Neighbor come into the archipelago.

The largest of Great Neighbor's three islands was located to the west. This island was used for agriculture and was vital for keeping Great Neighbor self-sustained. With an orchard on the north side of the island and a cow barn on the south, the western island was a super farm where several farmers worked in close proximity. Further inland, the land was terraformed to be as flat as possible and used to grow wheat and barley. The grain was in turn used to feed both the livestock and the people of Great Neighbor.

Most of the population of Great Neighbor lived on the center island. The center island was significantly smaller than the farming island and slightly larger than the third island to the east. It was important to the residents of Great Neighbor that their homes looked clean and smelled fresh. Flowers were planted at the doorstep of most, if not all, residential buildings. The flowers left a mess of petals across the roads. The roads themselves carved through the ground as if they were streams of water.

Few houses had more than one story, but the few that did looked almost upside down, with the top floor much larger than the bottom. The shade cast by the top floor made the doorway of a home a great place to feel the breeze without the sun in your eyes. Some houses in Great Neighbor were log cabins made of thin light-colored wood gathered from the orchard. Other houses were much more solid with a base of stone and walls of terracotta, using the thin orchard wood to provide structure and stability to the house. Roofs of straw were popular among Great Neighbor and were often used to dress wooden ceilings.

The easternmost island was used as a keep for the people of Great Neighbor. In that keep, lived the King himself. For a place that was supposed to convey wealth, the keep was messy. Massive slabs of stone were stacked haphazardly atop one another, grout clearly visible and protruding like pus from the masonry. The stones themselves were deep gray. The edges of the slabs looked like they had been shattered by the hands of a giant rather than mined by the tip of a pick.

On this island lived the ever-expanding guard force that the paranoid King had ordained. The guard, led by Captain Fredrick, ran the city almost as much as the King. When one chose to be a guard in Great Neighbor, not only did they take on the duty of enforcing the law, they also took on the duty of writing it.

Frederick, as the Captain of the Guard, was tied for second most powerful individual in the city, beneath only the King and equal to Rose, the Mouth of the King. Luckily for the people of Great Neighbor, Frederick was closer to a knight than a guard. He was bound by honor in any and all actions he committed, causing him to be a great captain and a good man.

In a small study of the castle, tucked away from the politics of Great Neighbor, was a little man who hardly looked like he was worth a scrap. He wore royal colors, it was true, but they were hard to see in the dim light of this library. He decorated the interior of his manor in gold and silver. The support to his great hall was made of rich mahogany. Still, he chose to spend most of his time in this musty little alcove. He was the King of Great Neighbor, a mad man hunched over a book in a paranoid room hidden behind his throne. His name had been forgotten long ago; his time as a morganatic pseudo-noble in Goldenhill had kissed his aged face goodbye. Now, he was lost in a world of fantasy where he read about ancient legends filled with ancient beings. Clutched in his hands was a scroll containing his personal favorite myth, *The Genie of the Woods*. The King squinted down at the words scrawled across the parchment...

***

The Genie of the Woods

Perhaps the greatest hunter to ever live was Razor-Exen. Over the years of his life, Razor-Exen had done many deeds, not least of which is outlined in this scrawl. And a scrawl these pages are, as they do no justice to the true tales of the Hunter of Werewolves—Razor-Exen—a name that would do well to be remembered in years to come.

How Razor-Exen became so powerful is conjecture. Some say he was a werewolf hunting werewolves, others say he was a man born with four limbs, and still others say he was a god of the hunt. But perhaps the story that hushes the noise of night is the most accurate. The story of *The Genie of the Woods*.

Razor-Exen was born in Dimfir, that much is certain. But upon meeting him, one would have sworn he was from Ironforge. Everything about the young man resembled a grizzled veteran of Goldenhill's iron military. Most of his adult life was spent on the prowl. It sounded like a lonely life and it was, but there was no greater comfort to him than hunting the beasts that plagued Dimfir.

Even before he was a legend, he was a folk hero who drove out the wild dogs of Dimfir that attacked horses and men. But what made him legendary is that he used a sickle and a scythe to do it.

Yes, Razor-Exen started his fanatical slaughter with nothing but farming tools. He was just a boy, never handed a bow in his life. He had barely seen a sword out of its sheath. One day, his farm was attacked by wolves and his family grotesquely strewn across the furniture, and Razor-Exen took to his hands the sharpest tool he could acquire—a sickle from the wall.

He raised his sickle towards the sky, and legend tells that it was struck by lightning, sharpening the tip with crackling energy. Unswayed, a wolf leapt for his chest. In a panic, Razor-Exen reached out with his other hand and found it closed around the handle of a scythe.

Dual weapons in hand, Razor-Exen ripped the wolf in two, from stem to stern. The wolves began to surround him. None dared to get in his way, so Razor-Exen made the first move. With a spin, he began to dispatch the wolves one by one, and when they were all dead, he dragged their skulls across the floorboards.

He fell asleep next to his dead family, using the hides of the canines as blankets and their flesh as bedding. When the boy returned the next morning to the village of Fur, he was still drenched in blood, dragging behind him no less than a dozen dead wolves. Some say he was also shirtless and handsome.

With no one else to blame, he went to the keep to complain to the countess. He slammed the bodies of the wolves to the floor in front of Lady Freya the 72nd, the countess of Fur. The military was under her command, but more important to her were her nights spent drinking. She looked down her nose at the dead wolves and let out a great scoff, completely unimpressed. She told the boy that she had seen children younger than him take down bears in this number. She was lying, of course, but Razor-Exen fell for the bluff.

Razor-Exen's blood lust could not be satiated, but the countess tried. She sent out the boy alone into the woods to hunt down the wild dogs that had been disrupting her trade. It was not a day before the boy returned to her, dog tails clutched in one fist. This deed has been recounted in great detail but is not the main focus of this story. If you desire to see exactly what transpired, look no further than *The Wolf Who Slew the Dog*, a children's tale not suitable for children.

When Razor-Exen returned to the countess, she was shocked at how quickly the boy had finished the impossible task. Still, Freya was quick-witted as ever. She knew that this boy would not stop until he died. The countess stroked her fat chin, thinking further about what could be done. Her paranoia made her suspect that Razor-Exen would usurp her if given the chance. Instead of congratulating him for the hero he was, the countess kept the story of his feat hushed behind closed doors and covered lips. But Razor-Exen's tale was too great to be kept locked away, and later that day it was told to every ear that could listen.

The countess needed to remove Razor-Exen before he became a threat. The countess conjured an excuse for sending the boy back into the woods. She thought for only a moment before it crossed her mind. The thought not only crossed her mind but crossed her face in an upside-down crescent shape. She sent the boy out into the woods again, this time on the mission to hunt down and kill every wolf that he met on the path.

Razor-Exen gladly took on the task, ready to vanquish anything that walked on four legs. He ventured out into the woods when the sun was at its highest in the sky, ready to kill any wolf that showed itself. He knew that wolves hunted in the night and thought it better he found them while they slept, but no den was visible in the brush. Razor-Exen searched and searched, but all he found were deer. He searched more, and still, he found no wolves.

His blood-frenzied search was fueled by the carcasses of animals he killed and ate raw while hunting his prey. He had never felt more exhilarated in his life. He searched relentlessly, blood running down his mouth like a salivating bulldog. At this point, the boy was more akin to a wendigo than a man. But nightfall was soon and after that, he was as good as the elk he killed. He dreaded and longed for the time when he would turn from hunter to prey. He knew now that only then would a true predator show its face, and he was ready for that time.

Soon the moon began to rise. The sky must have been on his side as the moon was full and bright, allowing him to see as well as any man could. Unfortunately, that was not well at all. Someone mimicked a wolf's howl somewhere behind him. The person's voice cracked as he desperately howled toward the sky.

When Razor-Exen rounded on the noise, he saw a wolf standing on grotesquely long arms, with skin hanging off the bone. The beast was foaming at the mouth. When it looked into the eyes of Razor-Exen, it saw an opponent equal to itself.

Razor-Exen knew immediately that this was a werewolf and remembered his vow to the countess. He would slay every wolf he saw. Razor-Exen tightened his grip on his scythe, waiting for the werewolf to make the next move.

The werewolf lunged at him, and their battle was legendary. Razor-Exen shrugged off the first strike as if it was nothing and adopted the posture of the beast that stood before him. He went first for the lengthy arms that the beast used to attack.

With his sickle, he pulled the leg of the beast, forcing it to bow to him. He commanded the beast kneel, and the werewolf only growled in response. It went for his neck, not fearing the blood that now dripped freely from its open wound. Razor-Exen blocked the strike with his arm, but at a cost.

The werewolf's great mouth engulfed the hand of Razor-Exen, cracking the arm at the bone and ripping it off. Razor-Exen's scream of rage could be heard from Aerokite, deafening the wolf. The countess smiled sinisterly in her chamber and sipped a glass of wine.

Razor-Exen bared his teeth. He opened his own mouth and clasped his teeth against the neck of the wolf. Still entangled together, they tussled in the long grass like two cubs play-fighting, the difference being the visible wolf blood streaming from both bodies. After an hour of gruesome combat, Razor-Exen exacted revenge for his cracked limb and used his bare hand to rip the werewolf's arm clean off from the shoulder socket.

He left the wolf there to bleed out and die, but Razor-Exen's fate was already sealed. He had not bound his amputated arm and was going to share the same fate as the wolf. Razor-Exen fell to his knees and closed his eyes to die in peace.

I implore you to remember the title of this scrawl, for only now does it become relevant. With Razor-Exen meditating, kneeling, on the ground, he heard a crackle of electricity gathering above his head. The sound of thunder drowned out the howls of the wolf. Rain started falling on the face of Razor-Exen, clearing the blood from his eyes and mouth.

From the sky came a being that looked like a man, a being so muscular and so handsome he commanded the eyes of all the animals in the forest. His hair waved wildly around his clean-shaven face, the rain glistening on his dark skin.

He looked at Razor-Exen and proclaimed, "I am Balbai! Genie of the woods!"

Razor-Exen could not bear to look away from the magnificent man. He witnessed lightning strike Balbai. The genie did not react. It was as if he summoned the lightning to do the deed.

Balbai swaggered forward in a self-righteous manner. "You are a great hunter, but even you cannot defeat the werewolves that pillage the woodlands."

Razor-Exen growled, "Have I not just slain the greatest beast in the woods?"

"No," Balbai replied with a chuckle, "because there were two, and with two comes more."

"It is impossible," Razor-Exen cursed.

"It is so!"

Even Razor-Exen did not dare to stand against Balbai, even if he had the strength to do so. Balbai was the greatest thing he had ever witnessed. The storm grew and swirled around them, its cold embrace touching Razor-Exen's arms and leaving goosebumps where the rain dropped.

"I can grant you the power to stop them all, but you must trade what you have never had!" Balbai's voice boomed like lightning.

Razor-Exen's eyes lit with determination. "And what is it I trade?"

"You're humanity-"

Before Balbai even finished the last syllable, Razor-Exen interjected, "Yes!"

Balbai put his chin on his chest and smirked down at the hunter. Whether or not he was surprised by the sudden outburst was unclear, but he was pleased, that much was certain.

"Then I shall grant you three gifts," the genie said. "I grant you the storm at your back, propelling you forward and your enemies toward your hunting grounds!"

Lightning clapped in the sky.

"I agree!" Razor-Exen felt the thunder of the storm shift at his touch, bending with his motion.

"I grant you an extra set of arms, allowing you to duel with four wolves at a time, so that the one can stand against the many of the pack!"

The muscles contracted in Razor-Exen's body, and he struggled not to keel. He felt his broken bone start to contract and mend.

"Grant them to me!"

A searing pain traced under the arms of Razor-Exen, like his ribs were splitting apart, and that they were. He doubled over in pain and howled like an animal.

"I grant you the curse of wolfblood, so that it may consume only your body and not your mind!" cried Balbai.

"What?" Razor-Exen stammered, "N-n-" But his stammer grew to a growl, which grew to a howl.

The man's body sprouted the gray hair of a wolf. He began to foam at his mouth. He bit his own lips, not of his own volition. His teeth were growing into them. To avoid injuring himself, Razor-exen opened his mouth in a bestial bark.

His vision turned red and his hearing became acute, allowing him to hear the countess laughing safely in Fur. He smelled the wine on her breath and knew that the countess was not fit to lead. The wolf of six limbs started leaping toward the town of Fur, pouncing on the dirt like the ground was a deer ready to kill. With hunger in his eyes, the wolf and man were one. In his hands, he held a sickle and a scythe.

***

The King of Great Neighbor had sucked up every word of that fairy tale and made it his mission to stand in the presence of that great genie. The King would give everything to just witness the face of Balbai. The small man had spent many a night in his magnificent fir-wood bed, dreaming of one day going to Dimfir and meeting the Genie of the Woods. If it were not for his distrust of the people that lived there, he would have already been on his way.

Perhaps the only people who were different from the entirety of Great Neighbor were Hera and Aaron, two individuals of minor importance who drifted around in Great Neighbor. The two miscreants were responsible for the ever-growing guard. Hera and Aaron would have liked if the guards acknowledged that it was thanks to them that they had a job. It wouldn't be a leap of logic to say that they deserved a little gratitude. But unfortunately, the guards did not agree. They knew Hera and Aaron were master thieves.

It was common knowledge to those close to Captain Fredrick that Hera and Aaron were the mysterious thieves on the island. The real mystery is why they were never caught. Occasionally they would be pinned for a minor crime and given the maximum sentence, but it was never for more than a few months. Frederick was far too honorable to arrest them without a crime to their name, but it was obvious where the supplies were going. How else would a pair of unemployed adults in their early twenties be wearing fine clothing and look so well-nourished?

It wasn't that there were no jobs available; Hera and Aaron were two able-bodied workers and quick-witted. Merchants and loggers alike would've killed to have either under their wing. Instead, Hera and Aaron stole for the thrill. They were merciful as far as thieves went. They had no desire to hurt anyone and wouldn't steal things of too great a value. In their naive minds, they fancied themselves similar to Viner, tax collector and brother to Fredrick. All they did was take a little off the top.

They were not the only miscreants on the island, but they were the only full-time thieves. Hal, the pig farmer's apprentice, would get drunk the occasional night and start a fight with one of the younger boys, but he was not a serial burglar. Ironically, Hera and Aaron were far more liked than Hal was.

It was deceptively pleasant, sighting the two walking and talking gleefully down a not-so-crowded city street. Petals limply compressed under their work boots. With each step, a pink blossom lying on the floor was kicked up and carried an inch or two with the wind. To this, the two paid no mind, but the old man watching them amused himself by observing the beauty of the scene.

Sullivan, the bookseller, sat still, eyes squinting, watching the two pass. His store was warm and inviting, and no less inviting with him sitting comfortably on a padded chair outside of it. An aspen wood sign hung lazily on the doorknob proudly stating that the store was open and bidding passerby to visit. The old man's long stark white hair was pulled back by a sweatband so that he could better read his books and better peruse each and every doorstep with his eyes. He had a book in his hands at that very moment titled "From Devil to Tevnal Daemons are Real". Ask anyone and they would have said Sullivan was a recluse who had lived in Great Neighbor for quite some time. But ask any further and they would realize just how little they knew about him.

Sullivan observed the two young adults walking down the street. With his old eyes, he was able to notice much more than most, even if the vision was slightly blurred. He noticed how Hera and Aaron wore almost identical shirts and equally similar pants. Even though Aaron was taller than Hera and broader too, he wore the same size as she. Even so, the way they wore the clothes was distinctly different.

Hera seemed to prefer to be neat and tidy. Her light brown, almost blonde hair was tied up in a bun with a loose piece of thin barreling rope. A similar thicker rope tightened her pants around her waist and kept her shirt tucked in place. At her arms and legs, the cuff was folded back to calf and mid-forearm, making the clothing look baggier while still holding in place.

Aaron, on the other hand, seemed to prefer the route of least maintenance, slipping on his clothes and being done with it. Even his hair matched that description. It looked like it had never been styled in his life. It was not horribly knotted, however. Hera had insisted on combing it every once and a while. Even so, at the moment, it was fuzzy. The cuffs of his pants were covered in mud like he had been stepping on them repeatedly.

Sullivan was able to surmise the event that happened beforehand. These two had come across a clothing rack, a man's by the looks of it, and decided that they wanted to wear his outfit. Sullivan chuckled to himself, like a parent watching a toddler do something mischievous.

Sullivan's face fell like he had just spotted something very wrong. The moment after, a glistening shape appeared in the ocean to the south. Out of the corner of his eye, he could see it peeking over the top of an oak shack. As if light had blended to form it, a giant square white shape materialized sitting gently atop the waveless water.

The square object appeared to be made from marble, polished so fine that it reflected the entirety of Great Neighbor back at its people. Slowly, naturally even, vines of metallic gold snaked and curled over the edge of the marble block. They settled at just the right point to become an ornate framework. The mirror would look delicate if it could fit in one's hand, but it could not fit in one's hand nor an army of hands. It was taller than the castle, extremely huge, a marble marvel to be sure.

All this in less than a minute, but a minute is all it took for Sullivan to react. The mirror did nothing for a long time. It sat at the foot of the island while islanders flooded out of their houses to gawk at the spectacle, followed by even more islanders to investigate the commotion. And before they knew it, a good flood of population was on the shore. Nothing exciting aside from the scuffles of Aaron and Hera had ever really happened before in the southern marketplace, so naturally, the residents jumped at any chance for stimuli. It was not exciting. All that followed was horror and decay.

Chapter 3
Horror and Decay

In the moments where the mirror and the crowd were beginning to form, in that precious minute, those slipping seconds, two things happened that would be vital to the survival of Great Neighbor and her people.

The first of the two things involved Sullivan. As soon as the weak old man saw that glimmer of magic on the horizon, he sprung up from his seat faster than a cat, dropping his book. Immediately, he turned to walk down the stone and mortar street in the western direction. He was only a few paces away before he turned back around. He stopped for a few seconds. He didn't have the time, but still he returned to the front of his bookstore. For a moment, it looked like he had changed his mind and was going to stay there, wait out whatever was happening, and peacefully read a book on his nice porch. Instead, he spotted the aspen wood sign on the door and flipped it over. Turned around, it read, "Saltwater".

As fast as his old legs could carry him, he made his way a few houses down. An overwhelming sense of dread made it feel like he couldn't lift his feet to walk another step. He forged down the street, each push forward like he was wading through a river. He metaphorically waded until he was at the foot of what was possibly the ugliest shack in town. If not the ugliest, it stood out the most. It was made from darkened rotting wood and green, malodorous flowers grew at its step.

The door blended perfectly with the wall. Above it was a sign fashioned out of iron and nailed to the rickety boards of wood. The bent metal flimsily made the shape of a flask. The iron looked as if it was crafted by a child, making the flask shape difficult to discern. Attached haphazardly to the flask were extended wires of malleable metal spelling out the phrase "Curious Drinks".

A metal knocker protruded out of the door, silently begging not to be used. It was rusty iron at best, rust formed in a circle at worst. Sullivan reached out his smooth hand. Its perfect shape contrasted the gnarled door. He gave the knocker a good knock, and the strike nearly disintegrated the poor handle.

After a short delay that was too long for Sullivan, he heard the clinking of gears, the noise of several locks being undone, and metal mechanical parts being loosely twisted. It took an agonizingly long amount of time for any progress to be made on the door and still it barely budged. It did not help Sullivan's mood that he was already on edge. The sum of the equation equaled one very upset, very feeble man not-so-feebly banging on an ugly door.

"Fear, hurry up," Sullivan begged, "Now is the time. It's happening."

The metal clanging became noticeably more rushed, followed by pounding on the door.

"Almost... there..." The door hissed.

Fear had been adamant about not wanting visitors, but his stubbornness seemed to be second to the door's. It refused to open even for him. Fear was not young by any means, but the chances of breaking a bone did not stop him from crashing his shoulder into the ashen door.

Sullivan became impatient, "Now, Fear, now!"

A sizzle hissed through the door and a second later was trailed by a quick crack. The door came flying off its hinges. It lay smoldering on the ground past Sullivan's feet, sufficiently fried. Fear loomed in the empty doorway, full black garb and all. His silly hat was resting on his head, just barely covering his eyes. The hat still showed his gaunt eye sockets, creating a menacing visage. A small smile creased his pasty lips, moving aside his thin inky beard, and revealing his rotten teeth.

***

The second thing that happened was less fantastical in nature but important none-the-less. A crowd rushed toward Hera and Aaron, causing their jovial smiles to falter. Aaron quietly tapped Hera on the shoulder and moved his head to point at an alleyway on the side of the street. Hera nodded back silently and followed him.

Aaron casually pivoted to enter the alleyway, not quite running but moving fast enough to vacate the area efficiently. They made sure to keep their footsteps light and agile. With their roguish expertise, they were able to slip into the alley like a mouse into a crack well before the first person leading the crowd got even remotely close to them. They tried their best to meld into the wall, but the sun shone directly on them and they had little cover. They were lucky their long shadows looked less like people and more like the scaffolding of a building.

The first person walked past their hiding spot and Hera and Aaron held their breath. The citizen didn't pay the alleyway any attention and continued sleepily walking. Then came the next and the next. None of them moved faster than a walk and all of them were fixated on what was happening in front of them. Not a word was uttered by the thieves or the folk. It was only after they passed that Aaron spoke.

"They missed us," he whispered in Hera's ear.

"I don't think they're looking for us," Hera said quietly.

"That's what I said."

Hera looked him in the face, eyebrows furrowed. "No, it's not."

"That's what I meant," Aaron grinned sheepishly.

It was unclear whether or not Aaron was joking in the first place or just covering up his mistake. All that Hera knew is that those people were gathering for something and that she wasn't invited.

"What are they doing?" Hera whispered slightly louder.

Aaron slipped to the edge of the alleyway. The motion rubbed his shirt against the terracotta wall. The shirt caught the wall a few times, but not for long. He hesitantly peaked his head outward. Down the road, he was able to see the general shape of the marble mirror. He put two and two together. The people were looking at the marble mirror in the ocean.

The mirror was like nothing he had ever seen. If it had been handheld, he would have been too intimidated by its flawless cutting to steal it. He cringed at the ocean waves lapping against the smooth stone, but the waves did not leave a stain on the faultless carving.

"I have no clue how to describe this..." Aaron began.

Hera was already shoving her way past him to look out herself. She did so in a far more deliberate but admittedly less suave fashion. She poked her head out horizontally, a little hair getting in her eyes. Ready to tell him what it was, the words caught in her throat.

"I don't blame you," she was finally able to say.

"What do we do?" Aaron asked.

Hera scratched the side of her face. "I have an idea," she said.

Hera surmised that if most people were distracted by a shape in the water at the southern side of the island, then fewer people would be left on the north side where the King had given luxurious housing for emissaries from the Northern Kingdom. Because of the distraction, it would be significantly easier to burglarize the house. The current emissary wouldn't suspect he had been burglarized. By the time he figured out what happened, he would be on a boat back to Witshore. It was the perfect crime and the perfect time to do it.

Aaron shook his head sourly. "Why don't we just go check out the mirror?"

Hera's grin fell at the sight of the less than enthusiastic Aaron.

"Come on," She begged, "It'll be fun! You said I got to choose what we steal next."

"What would we steal anyway?" Aaron asked.

Hera grinned. "Have you seen that Tython boy around? He wears the funniest clothes. He has a fancy lantern on his belt and a bow strapped to his back, too. What if he has extras?"

Hesitantly, Aaron returned a nervous smile. "I do like that stuff…"

"Then let's go!"

They sprinted on their toes down the street, avid on making sure they had as much time as possible during the distraction. The emissary's house was on the stone beach to the north, ostracized from the other houses. It was designated for visitors on the island, esteemed visitors to be precise, so it was extravagant in decoration and well taken care of by servants of the community.

Great Neighbor Island had an inn where a traveler could feasibly spend a night or two, but it was dusty and small with only one room available. Few people visited Great Neighbor for a tour. The inn was only able to stay afloat on the backs of locals who liked to go there to have a drink. Usually, it was frowned upon to have to stay the night after an outing, but it could happen. Instead, emissaries used this house.

It was lavish in size, probably the tenth or twelfth largest residence. The windows glowed with warm firelight dancing over the lightly dusted clay walls and the dark and sharp wooden rivets that held the building up. The front door was mounted atop three stone steps that looked like they had been placed there by the tides of the wind and breezes of the water.

It was humorous how pathetically easy it would be to burglarize this house, so easy in fact that they could simply walk through the front door. Both thieves were grinning madly. They gawked at the house for a moment before approaching the inviting door, observing the easily twistable handle. It might even be unlocked.

Hera tentatively reached for the handle before she heard a blast of fire in the distance, like a barrel of Anarchy gunpowder had just exploded. She jerked her hand back like a small dog about to be stepped on. Her eyes widened as she looked around for what had made the noise. Her gaze rested on Aaron who had jumped back a good foot. His face was white as snow.

***

And so simultaneously, when Hera reached for the knob of a door and Fear broke down a door, horror and decay ensued. It is ironic how often things of intricate beauty can be so unfathomably dark. Unfathomable, not because something is initially too complex to understand, but because the addition of factors hidden in shadow adds to the complexity. The mirror was beautiful, but in the many folds of that frame, a sinister depth loomed.

Through the mirror, thin augmented shapes started to form, vague at first but soon defined. One of these shapes was extremely tall with what seemed to be thick arms.

Behind the tall creature, bipedal yet animalistic shapes limped forward.

Captain Frederick, Hand of the King, narrowed his eyes to understand what was happening. He saw himself in the reflection, just what one would expect to see in a mirror. He attempted to look at the shapes but failed, resting his gaze again on his own face instead. He was pale, with fire red hair and sunken eyes. The soldiers might have thought he would die soon if he had not proven himself the most capable warrior on the island even in his late age. Streaks of gray darted through the red hair that reached toward the sky. Though it would at first appear that the gray told a story of agedness, in reality it was one of stress. One of honor. One of duty. Again, he looked past himself and this time was able to make out something more than a mirror.

He saw a bigger picture. He saw the grand picture. He saw a figure of shadow blurrily come into focus, seemingly getting closer to the edge of the mirror. The frame of the mirror extended backwards, creating a marble platform for the shadows to stand on. With each step, the short bodies behind the tall one tilted forward. Too late, Fredrick saw a plank of wood being heaved up. It pointed vertically to the sky before starting to tip forward. It fell, touching the edge of the mirror and seamlessly sliding through. A large wooden plank bridged the mirror in the ocean and the island. Several other wooden planks followed. And through it all, the tall figure lumbered forward.

He was nothing; He was Horror. This... Horror that had come through the mirror was much more grotesque in the, what some would call, flesh than as a silhouette. What looked like two thick arms through the blurred image of the mirror was actually four thin arms tied closely together. The creature that was Horror possessed the humanoid shape of a man but truly only mimicked the appearance of a man in an unholy way. A thin layer of tar skin stretched across sharp human bones. One could count not only the ribs but the rivets of the spine and neck. When he opened his mouth to curse the townsfolk with the image of his blackened teeth, his tendons popped out of his jaw.

Rusty chains were lazily strewn across his shoulders, weighing his body down to Dessees, the underworld, itself. They hunched him forward like a weak old man. When he walked, they rustled beneath his feet, catching on the wooden planks set out before him and making an ear-wrenching screech when he yanked them forward.

Slowly, methodically, he stepped onto the makeshift bridge. Before the eyes of the horror-struck crowd, the bridge looked like it had aged a thousand years. It began to rot and curl, black and green, and an acrid scent filled the air. Seeing his approach, the frightened residents of Great Neighbor cowered back a few steps.

Horror shambled onto the shore. The sand compressed beneath his feet like he weighed hundreds of pounds. The fumbling figure stumbled forward, using his four long arms to balance himself. A piece of cloth draped the entirety of his body, revealing most of his chest and his boney upper thigh. A crown made of golden and black thorns protruded from his deformed skull, attaching itself grotesquely to his bone. A rotted wooden plank was tied tightly to the back of Horror.

With a sudden lurch forward, Horror fell to his knees, finally escaping the decaying sand and meeting flora. Where his hands touched the grass, it died almost instantly. He gagged his neck forward, dry-heaving on the floor and spitting out ink saliva.

Fredrick made a motion with his hands, commanding his fellow guard to surround the tevnal in front of them. He led by example and was the first to meet the tall slender figure, positioning himself right in front of Horror. He drew his maul and tightened his shield before getting ready in his battle stance. Behind him, several soldiers followed, their nerves ever so slightly eased by the action of their respected captain. Slowly, one by one, the Great Neighbor guards drew their swords, the turtle shell embroidery on their chest plates glittering in the setting sun.

This was soon shown to be a mistake. Horror had the first guard grasped in his long fingers before he even stood upright. The poor guard's flesh started to decay beneath the iron hold of the invader. Cold gray steel morphed to brown, salt-colored flesh morphed to gray, and white bone morphed to black before succumbing to an empty cavity thrust into the ground. The civilians in the crowd tried desperately to scatter, tripping over each other and getting in one another's way, cursing their curiosity all the while.

A spear from Horror's left pierced the air whistling in the wind, but too late. Before it made contact, the skeletal figure caught it in his secondary left arm. The spear turned to dust in his hand, falling to the ground as if it had always been two molded sticks.

Next, he leaped to a group of guards and with all four of his hands, touched some part of their bodies. Whether it be their chest, neck, or head, they died unnaturally quickly. The more heavily armored guards were able to last longer under the decaying touch, but not much. After finalizing his four victims, Horror straightened himself. A second later, he received a strong blow to the right side of his lower back. He was sent sprawling on the floor, face first, cradling the place where he had been struck. He tried to rise but was struck again, this time in the back of the head by a heavy metal blunt object.

Finally, Horror was able to roll over, his mouth agape. Above him stood a man in shining armor, helmetless, with his fiery red hair and beard accented by the red glow of the setting sun. In his hand, Fredrick held his trusted maul, now with a large, rusted hole in the side of it from where it had twice struck the monster of decay.

A horde of zombie-like figures swarmed over the bridge and began to raid the village. They were short and gray in flesh. Most held an axe in their hands, waving it wildly above their heads as they charged the city. Others were completely unarmed and grappled with any citizen they could find, dragging them, screaming, down the rotting wood bridge and into the marble mirror. In a quick assault, the horde of horrid creatures struck as fast as lightning, preferring to capture rather than kill. Their faces were filled with the fury of the ocean as they belched their mighty war cry in deep and bellowing voices.

The city guard had much more luck fighting back against the footman than they did fighting Horror. The brutal axes of the invaders could tear through the defenses of a shield, even one made of metal, but the attack would often leave the warriors open for assault. Even so, the invaders were mad, often sacrificing themselves in an attempt to drag even a single soldier into the mirror.

***

Sullivan heard screams in the distance from the soldiers being attacked by the ravenous army. Fear made eye contact with the man and spoke to him.

"Aren't you supposed to keep calm?" He asked

Sullivan frowned. "I am calm; I just needed to make sure you lived up to your name, too, so you would hurry up."

Fear growled and bared his teeth at the man. "Let's go get that stinking oaf!"

The light from the sun bent around Calm, and the darkness from the shack eloped with Fear, causing both the white wizard and the shadow sorcerer to be consumed by air, disappearing. When they re-emerged, they were significantly farther from the point of destruction than they had been before. Though the screams of combat and kidnap could still be heard in the distance, it was far less distinct and could be mistaken for a rowdy get-together held by a disliked family.

The dirt beneath their feet was softer, the grass greener, and the air smelled like compost after a rainstorm, not pleasant, but not unbearable. Calm, who no longer tried to pretend to be Sullivan,bent to look at the white sandals. Brown soil crept under his shoes and between his toes. He frowned vehemently.

Fear was already on the move toward the farmhouse, not afraid to let his cloak drag on the ground and track up nearly invisible mud on the already dusty black cloth. Each step inlaid the soft dirt into the traction on his boots. The shape of his shoes was unusual. They were riveted on the bottoms in a strange pattern that allowed for more traction than even the highest quality mortal footwear. As soon as Fear reached the farmhouse, a gargantuan figure covered in black hair and metal burst out of the door.

"I can hear the sweet cry of combat from here," announced Mayhem.

Calm kept his face straight. "Mortals are dying; we must act quickly."

"What is the death of mortals to a god?" Mayhem swung his Mourning Star lazily around his bulking shoulder.

"Placate yourself." Calm pushed his hand forward in the air like he was taming a raging bull. "We have a job to do. We are under attack by those who would see the throne of the gods empty. Earth and sky save us now."

Chapter 4
Earth and Sky

With Hera's hand on the knob, she heard several sharp shouts from the distant shore. She and Aaron both turned to look behind them, fearing that they had been spotted by some stroke of uncommonly bad luck. Relief was not what flooded their souls.

Moments before, a shamble of armor shuffled down the street. A tall, broad figure walked alone. It wasn't the job he wanted, but it was the one he had. Frederick had known the city was in danger as soon as the mirror appeared. He had sent his most trusted man to make sure that everything was secure. This soldier was not the only one sent, but he was the only one sent alone.

In the distance, small figures bounced against each other, like flies against glass. Hera tightened her eyes to try and make out what was happening but could not distinguish the events unfolding. Her eyes widened when she saw the wooden rotting planks coming from the mirror to the island and the black scarred path it left.

"Are we..." she puzzled, "Under attack?"

"Great Neighbor?" Aaron scoffed. "Who would attack Great Neighbor..."

He trailed off, still trying to comprehend the confusing sight in the distance. Aaron tried his best to convince himself that his sarcastic remark was correct. No one would attack Great Neighbor. Why would they? But he couldn't help feeling an overwhelming sense of dread creeping into his consciousness. He began looking around, planning out a place to run. He turned to his left, then his right to see the engraving of a metal turtle just below eye level. He jumped back another good foot. The turtle shell insignia would be enough to scare any thief if thrust a few inches against their face. Aaron looked up to see the scowling face of Viner, brother of Fredrick the Hand of the King. Viner pulled his stubbled cheeks back in a fearsome snarl, veins in his tattooed bald head popping out.

"You worthless dogs! How dare you waste my time with this nonsense while we are under attack! Haven't you fools learned anything after years of being on the island? I suppose not, you wouldn't be vagrants if you had!" he rapidly hollered at them.

The pair were so surprised at this loud babble that it took them a few seconds to register what had been said. They both cowered away in fear, Aaron further back than Hera, as he had been closer to the screaming man.

Finally, Hera managed to stammer, "Wh-what are you doing here? What's happening down at the beach? Is it... dangerous? Are we in danger?"

It was true that Hera was afraid of what was down at the beach, but she was significantly more afraid of the giant standing in front of them. Hera had spouted a series of questions, but Viner only answered the first.

"It is my job as a guard to make sure that all citizens are safe!"

The guard stepped forward, not making eye contact with either of the thieves. He proclaimed to the sky in a proud bombastic manner, making sure his presence was seen, heard, and felt. His head was tilted up. So proud and noble was he that even the birds stopped their song to gaze at the exclamation of the guard. His fibrous arms looked like they held up the sky in their mighty arch.

"Even you good for nothing scoundrels," he boomed. "Though I would like to see nothing more than you useless scum dragged into Dessees prematurely, I am honor-bound to protect you."

The officer's heavy armor did nothing to weigh down Viner's broad shoulders. He looked like a gorilla, tall and huge. The armor was too small for his arms, with plates struggling to contain his mass. Viner's build was the polar opposite of his brother's. Where his brother was lean yet strong, Viner was pot-bellied and had arms sculpted from fatty muscle that made him all the stronger. It looked like he could headbutt down a door and laugh about it after.

"That hurt a lot, Viner," Aaron said.

His voice wavered slightly. He sounded somewhere between mock hurt and genuinely upset. Even Aaron didn't know where he landed on the spectrum. Viner detected the tone. His face fell from the sky, and he looked down at Aaron. A frown stretched over his huge mouth. He removed his hands from the air and placed them on his hips.

"I am stressed," he said in a half-hearted apology. "Just... stay with me and after all of this is over, we can discuss your trespassing."

Discussing their trespassing was the second to last thing that Hera and Aaron wanted to do, the first being dragged into a giant marble mirror by small men wildly wielding axes. However, at this moment in time, they did not know the latter was a possibility and were still confused as to what was happening around them.

"You said invasion?" Aaron said.

Viner's response was cut short by the first glimpse of their invaders. Six maybe seven stout berserkers marched down the street. They crawled in a disorganized pattern, using both their feet and occasionally their arms to propel themselves forward in bizarre lunges. Almost foaming at the mouth, their faces looked barely human under mats of brown and black hair. The hair was inconsistent in both color and density. It spread across their pugnacious faces like a wild boar's. They looked similar to wolverines, treating their chainmail less like armor and more like fur.

"What are those?" Aaron asked awkwardly.

Viner kept his eyes forward while drawing his spear from his back. He slid his shield down his arm, resting it in the ready position. The petals of pink flowers retreated away from his sliding foot as his stance turned into one ready for even the largest wave to come crashing over the rock shore that was his fury. He opened his mouth wide, his face becoming chiseled at the motion. His semblance to an ape became uncanny as he shouted his mighty war cry.

"I have no idea!"

It was most definitely the strangest war cry Hera and Aaron would ever hear. Yet astoundingly, it wasn't the strangest Viner had ever uttered.

Viner set himself on the defense, holding a kite shield in front of his face and positioning his body to protect the young man and woman. His spear was ready to impale any stubby attacker that got too close. He had a significant range advantage against their short axes, and if one was able to get past optimal striking range, his shield might just be able to shrug off a blow or two before his defenses were broken. Hopefully, by then, his shortsword would be drawn.

A short attacker reeled forward like a charging boar. Viner's teeth were borne as the animal sprinted with its axe dragging behind it. Viner was lucky that the warrior practically impaled itself on his spear. The attacker did not immediately die. Death on the battlefield is hardly ever immediate. But, he was most certainly incapacitated. Viner quickly yanked his elbow back, but the body was stuck firmly to the spear. The spear had gone all the way through, and without the proper leverage, Viner would struggle to get the body off.

Another invader raised its axe over its head on Viner's left. Viner saw the attack out of the corner of his eye and awkwardly tilted his arm to block with his shield. The axe of the warrior came crashing down against the metal. It landed on a tilt and scraped off with a loud scratch. Viner jutted his shield forward with all his strength, striking the warrior in the nose. The soldier recoiled just far enough for Viner to angle his spear in a way where it impaled the berserker in the side. The only problem was that his spear was already occupied. Still, Viner stabbed his spear into the side of the berserker.

For a moment, Viner entered a stoic calm. He wondered how he had gotten into this situation so quickly. It was impressive, really, that he had reacted so quickly to the invasion, but still his fastest wasn't enough. He had been swarmed in moments.

So...

He would swarm back.

His spear split the small man's flank, failing to completely impale the ugly creature. He tried to pull the spearhead back out, but it was stuck fast. The invader wasn't quite dead, but out of commission, no doubt. Resolve came over Viner and he dropped the spear. He reached for his shortsword. His hand clasped around the hilt. With a slash of steel, he drew it just in time to elegantly dispatch another attacker.

The soldiers regrouped and gathered around Viner. Viner took a quick glance over his shoulder to see if Hera and Aaron were still safe. He looked back and did not see them. He cried a mighty bellow and heaved his sword in a circle around him. The attackers gnashed their teeth, but they did not fear the blade's razor. The invaders had multiplied; it would be impossible for anyone to escape. But escape wasn't Viner's only motivation.

He retreated backward, making sure that he kept his shield held high, or at least chest-high. The enemies he fought were three-quarters his size, after all. They only got more aggressive as he backed away. The invaders' combat tactics were lacking. Usually, a soldier would focus on staying alive. These soldiers, on the other hand, were constantly on the offensive, often finding themselves with a new slash in their neck, a gift from Viner.

The original six or seven that attacked at first had now grown in number, adding a dozen more to their ranks. They scoured the city and burned it to the ground all around Viner. The guard was forced to watch citizens be dragged out of their homes, powerless to do anything about it. He fought not only for the citizens' lives but his own. The enemy was smaller and less trained, but their ranks were unrealistic. They swarmed like wolves, all with a pack tactic in mind, not caring for their own lives.

Viner's eyes surveyed the area. He couldn't save those who had already been captured, they were too distant, but he could save two particularly troublesome individuals. His eyes focused like a hawk, seeing Hera pulling Aaron into an alleyway. He smashed his shield into the face of an enemy. How could those two be so foolish? They would get swarmed within seconds!

Viner set his face strong. He straightened to full height, making him look goliath in context to the attackers. With a grunt, he trudged forward, calm and collected. The great swipes of his sword tore swaths through the invaders like a scythe through a field of grain. He pushed onward with his shield, moving aside the torrent of arms like water. His legs took the most brutal assault. He staggered forward, the single man trampling anything in his path better than a rampaging herd of buffalo.

He was beaten bloody, but by looking at him it would have been impossible to tell. The biting axes of the berserkers only made contact from his chest down, slashing at the armor. Viner thanked the forge that his armor was holding so well against such abuse. He knew he would be bruised and cut in the morning, but he was focused on making sure that as many people as possible saw tomorrow's sunrise.

It felt like hours before he made any headway to the alley. But with sheer grit, he made it. Hera and Aaron were already shuffling up a wall to their right. Viner was glad they had a plan, but he knew it wouldn't protect them for long. He reached out his gauntleted hand and clasped it firmly against Hera's forearm.

Hera tried to shake him off, but Viner held the grip adamantly. He pulled her toward him, ducking behind his shield to block a blow from yet another attacker. Taking initiative, Aaron latched onto the wall with a firm grip. He pulled his torso up and brought his boot down on Viner's hand. It was one of the more acrobatic feats Aaron had accomplished, but he had no time to marvel. His foot loosened Viner's tight hold but did not completely shatter the bond. It was all Hera needed. While Viner was distracted, she wriggled free from him. As soon as Viner's grip slipped, he reached out again like a cat trying to catch a fly, but Hera had already started scrambling onto the roof.

Aaron pushed off Viner's hand, propelling himself upward and then proceeded to use the face of an attacker as another foothold. Not so gracefully, he pulled himself onto the roof and reached his hand out to help Hera up. Quicker than a hare, Hera was holding Aaron by the wrist, just barely missing Viner's second swipe, as she was pulled onto the roof. Invader soldiers started filing in from the other end of the alleyway, getting ready to surround Viner. He looked up at Hera and Aaron, anger and fear mixed in his face, but most of all, determination.

"Like it or not, I swear to you—you will live to be happy again, and I—" Viner smashed his shield into a hairy face, "keep my promises."

***

Frederick knew his mace would be of no use soon. It was decaying with every passing moment. He prepared himself, if need be, to switch to the rapier at his side, and, if need be still, to take the utility knife from his boot and strike the horror with it. Horror was on the ground before him, spiteful as ever, and Frederick had no intention of letting the black skeleton get back up. He brought the mace in his hand crashing down on the monster. The creature lay motionless on the ground, but still it was ready. The head of Horror snapped to the face of the mace. Quicker than gravity, a black hand emerged from its mouth and caught the spherical weapon.

The hand was made of a fleshy, tarry liquid that looked disgustingly like tongue tissue. Frederick recoiled. That very recoil saved him from the slithering arms that made a lunge for his chest. Horror had attempted to finish him quickly, but Fredrick was one of the greatest warriors Great Neighbor had ever seen. The prodigy would not go down without a fight. Horror got to his feet, rising like he had just woken from a long sleep. He poised himself, ready to kill the annoyance that had struck him.

"To me, you are a wasp!" he hissed.

He spoke in a hushed, yet audible voice. It was raspy and trailed the p in wasp with strong pronunciation.

"To me, you are nothing," Fredrick responded.

It was true. He was nothing. He was Horror. Frederick feared that nothing, and he would not let it spread across the island. He looked down at his mace. It was rusted and destroyed. It wouldn't be worth another strike. This creature's powers seemed to have unfortunate effects on his weapons. He dropped his prized mace and whispered it a hurried goodbye before drawing his rapier with a slash. He would have preferred to use the weapon properly and whip the monster, but he hardly had the time to line up a flick when drawing the weapon.

"Nothing but a pest on my island that I have to squash!" Frederick bravely spat.

He whipped forward with the rapier and made contact, but not where Fredrick had aimed. The dreaded monster had caught the blade. Horror cocked his head, examining the rapier in his two right hands. He bent his top arm, and the blade of the rapier crumbled to dust. He opened his mouth, and out of his throat spewed black mist. The smog condensed in the air, clouding Fredrick's vision. Horror started to speak through the darkness.

"You talk more than the others."

Against his will, Frederick inhaled the black smoke spewing from Horror's mouth. It smelled like molasses and coated his mouth like molasses, too. He could still breathe, but shallower and more labored. He gasped for air, but all that filled his chest was panic. Quick as a falling branch, something darker than the fog pushed forward. The movement displaced the fog and, for a moment, dispelled the darkness. Fredrick's eyes widened just before the open black hand of Horror struck his forehead.

"I don't like that," Horror spat.

Frederick keeled onto the ground. His hand cradled the place where his flesh was beginning to blacken. It felt so dry, so cold. Dying skin. He turned to the sky to see not the sun, but Horror standing above him.

Crimson turned to darkness in the heavens as night fell.

***

Mayhem swung his prized flail, a weapon he had humorously named Mourning Star. Bloodshed was foretold by the ground under his feet. The cattle beside him lurched at his excitement, partially against their will... but what was their will to his own? He was a god and they, stock.

"You two, go to the keep. The citizens will rendezvous there in time of need," Calm said. "Make sure the way is clear. I will deal with the defiled sorcerer."

"Sorcerer?" Mayhem asked

"Yes, there has to be a sorcerer, I told you the underworld was clouded. Only a powerful sorcerer could bridge the Inbetween and cloud our vision."

"Is it Hiver?" Fear questioned.

"This is soul magic. Hiver is adamant on blood magic," Calm surmised. "It is possible, but not likely."

The wizards had no need for walking. Again, Fear slipped into shadow, and Calm bent into light. Mayhem was somewhere between the two, with a little blood mixed in for flavor. It wasn't like his massive body didn't have a few drops to spare. Besides, his own veins weren't his only source.

They each teleported a few meters east to the residential island. Then, the triumvirate split off, each to accomplish the task Calm had laid out. The beach was closest to their confluence with the island, so Calm arrived at site zero first. He took a moment to admire the magical handiwork involved in making the mirror. His eyes darted from the golden frame to the decaying planks of wood that bridged to the island. He found the contrast exceedingly distasteful. He continued his examination and noted footprints in the decay leading to the shore. Only then did he notice the nine-foot-tall skeletal figure standing above a cowering red-headed guard surrounded by raging combat.

His eyes narrowed. The valiant knights of Great Neighbor fought the dwarves of Dessees—an unorthodox sight to be sure. The bravery on the battlefield was admirable, but futile. They had never seen an enemy like this before. The strange shape of the enemies' bodies was enough to stun a soldier for a moment, let alone their vicious fury. That was not to mention the Horror that commanded them. If their brave captain did not duel Horror without any hesitation, the chances of the guard even attempting to put up a fight would have been low.

But what could have happened was no matter to the guard nor to Calm. Now, the guard fought tooth and claw against a surprise invasion. The eerie, unnerving conjured by the invaders was only bolstered by the mad ramblings that left the blood-soaked mouths of the blasphemous creatures. When they spoke, they spoke in a raspy voice, like an animal trying to mimic human speech. Their commands were in what sounded to be gibberish, but certain words could be made out. Namely "blood" and "death" which, for whatever reason, were in clear Northern.

Few soldiers were given the blessing of hearing one of their faceless invaders do something as even remotely human as speak. Most died in some way or another before that could happen. But they fought. They fought with swords and shields and everything in between. Some fought to survive, and some fought to protect their families. A will to live is an impressive character trait, and a retired guard named Traya had that will more than any other.

"Traya, good you're here!"

Traya nodded to her comrade, but she had little time. One of the berserkers was hot on her trail. Despite her attempts to get the little creature off her scent, the monster was adamant on hunting her down in particular, which was why Traya was now cowering behind one of her fellow guards.

"What are you doing?" the guard asked.

They were still jovial, a little out of place for the situation. Still, they seemed glad to see Traya, a feeling they would soon take back. Traya unsheathed a sword from her belt. The type of sword was called a xiphos. It was slender and sharp, more used for piercing than slashing. She placed the tip of the xiphos against the back of the soldier in front of her.

The soldier twisted under her grip. They tried to turn and get a better look at her, but whenever they got their neck around too far, they felt a sharp jab in the small of their back. They were about to open their mouth to protest their disbelief before their mouth was opened for them. The small soldier that had been trailing Traya jumped onto the front of the soldier and dug its axe into their jaw. If the attack itself wasn't enough to kill the soldier, then the xiphos was.

Traya did not hesitate to pull back the xiphos and adjust it so that it would pierce through the soldier and into the invader. Her attack was critically effective. The death of her fellow soldier bought her just enough time to jab the xiphos into the tevnalish monster that clung to their chest. Traya was one of the two soldiers who would turn against her fellows, but her psychotic madness could only be shadowed. Her sins were soon put on pause.

Calm flicked his wrist, and everything slowed. Those unfamiliar with magic would be unaware of what was happening. It would take a powerful body and soul to detect the phantasm. The incoming bite of swords turned into a slow cut through air. The winds kick of the leaves turned into an icy freeze and died. The ashen flower petals floated slowly to the ground, almost invisible against the pitch-black sky. Slower than a feather, they did not ride the wind but instead sank downward like rain frozen in time.

Calm was unaffected by his own magic and walked onto the brutal battlefield. The soft dirt was carved by the nails of those dragged into the portal but it nary condensed against Calm's white slippers as the wizard walked nonchalantly toward Horror. He turned to solemnly see an Aerokitian family—a mother, father, and daughter—being dragged away by five different raiders. Their hands were frozen, reaching out to Calm, as if begging him to save them. But he did not reach back.

"You shall be safe in time. I shall not explain further," he smiled sadly.

The smile was not returned.

His soft white sandals indented the dark grass, coming upon Fredrick, the Captain of the Guard, who was cradling his face. Horror took relish in slowly walking up to his victim. Calm stopped a pace or two away from the scene and watched Horror come to a halt over the captain.

Again, Calm twisted his white hands. His nails blended with his skin. They were soft and well-trimmed, yet they were still aged and white. In response to his beckoning call, the grass around Frederick grew. Calm turned the decay into flowering plant life. Horror's neck snapped up to Calm, more teleporting with magic than moving quickly. Horror opened his mouth in a human roar, slowed by the magical field. Black spit flew from his gnarled moon-tinted teeth.

Calm clicked his tongue and set his face to be expressionless. He commanded the grass grow gargantuan, and so it did. The plants slithered up the air as vines climb a house. A few feet above the ground, the grass accelerated and shoved itself into the agape mouth of the skeletal figure. Horror's flesh ripped along the eyes. His skin was already stretched to an unhuman level. His surprise shock was too much for the thin flesh to handle. It was safe to say, Horror was very upset to have grass shoved so viciously in his mouth.

Calm lazily twisted the fingers of his outstretched right hand. The grass listened. It lifted the eight-foot-tall dark figure off of his feet. It looked for a moment like Horror would be crucified there eternally, but the grass instead hurled him back into the ocean. Before Horror could meet the current, the water turned to ice. Horror smashed against the frozen water. The ice cracked under the impact, but it did not break. The intimidating figure was reduced to a pile of bones spinning wildly forward on the frozen ocean. Shrapnel from the ice jutted itself into Horror's bony spine and guided the monster back into the portal. A wave of water pushed up against the ice and forced the ice to tilt him towards the marble mirror.

The dark sorcerer turned to face Calm. He scratched on the ice with all four of his arms, all twenty of his fingernails, leaving streaks of fluorescent blue in the wake of his floundering. As a final act of defiance, the horror bit into the ice. He sank his gnarled teeth into the frozen water before being sucked back into the Marble Mirror, leaving behind a single sharpened tooth.

With a heaving sigh, Calm released his hold on the area and let time flow normally. The battle around him ensued as if nothing had changed. When he looked back at the ocean and the mirror that rested on it, not even frost remained.

His cloak burst to life in the whistling night wind. The wind had picked up as soon as Calm removed the vacuum of time. The air scrambled to fill the vacuum. He turned to address the red-headed guardsman laying on the floor, now clutching a utility knife with both hands. His feet struggled to get up, not assisted by his hands. His scrambling legs left dark brown indents on the moist ground. His shining cuirass became covered in soil, as it lapped like water against his armor.

Calm fell to one knee beside Fredrick and the wind went down with him, now satisfied with its role in filling the vacuum. Frederick strained to let go of his knife and strained harder still to extend his hand to be taken. His face was blackened all the way to the nose, and some bone was visible underneath the peeling rotting skin.

"You fought bravely," Calm consoled the dying man.

The old man took the dying guard's decaying hands in his. He gently caressed the rotting flesh of the still living and still brave captain with his own white hands.

"You fought…" Fredrick thought for a moment, "Like a god…"

Calm's eyes wrinkled slightly looking down at him. He saw the question coming from years away. It could have been ten thousand years and still the question would have been younger than him. That truth did not make the lie any harder to bear. Tears almost stained the old man's eyes before Fredrick could ask.

"Are you a god?"

Chapter 5
You Must Die

All emotion flooded away from Calm's face. His mouth fell and his cheeks tried to follow. However, they were strained. There was a knowing tug trying ever so slightly to pull them up. His eyes turned downward on the man. He had only been looking *at* Fredrick before, but now he was looking *in* him.

His jaw was set, but his face was still slack when he said, "I am."

His tone was level and as unchanging as a mountainside. It was his burden to bear. The burden of godhood. Even if he was not a god, he was this man's god.

"Then save me... Save my people!"

Fredrick was not begging the god, he was commanding him. Calm squinted his eyes, and like a shadow, he was looming over the captain of the guard.

"You must die. Some of your people must die. Others must be imprisoned and tortured. Despair sees all. *We see all.* If you do not die, your brother will not take your place. If your brother does not take your place, your brigade **will fail**. If many of your guards do not die, your people will not be drafted. If your people are not drafted, your brigade **will fail**. If citizens are not captured, your conscripts will not march day and night. If your conscripts do not march day and night, your brigade **will fail**."

"No... That isn't right; there must be another way," Frederick begged now.

"There. Is. No. Other. Way." Calm spat, "Don't you see? I am a god; you are a mortal. I know. You do not. I save as many lives as possible, no matter the cost."

Frederick laid his head back in disappointment. He closed his eyes and pursed his lips.

His lips did not part again. His eyes did not open again. He was not buried.

***

Mayhem and Fear had been sent to eliminate any threat that would stop the people of Great Neighbor from seeking asylum at their keep. The old wizards moved on foot like unbearded young men running a sprint. Petals were their fanfare and black dust their procession. To look upon them would be to see a raging bull and a winged shadow hunting a fleeing deer.

"I say that we hit the dwarves with a burst of fear and rout them off the island," Fear suggested.

"Good idea!" Mayhem said sarcastically. "Let's do my plan; we drive them mad and make them tear each other apart!"

"I do not dislike that idea..." Fear answered. "But wouldn't it be fun watching them drown in the ocean while they flee?"

Mayhem's grin was like a child's. "Yeah... But how 'bout they get a taste of *this* first?"

Mayhem thrust the chain of his flail forward and dragged it across the petal inlaid road. Mourning Star forced up the stones that lined the street like a hoe would uproot weeds. The pristine black metal took on a rusted look when covered in dirt, but the surface was so smooth that when Mayhem took the black star in his hands again, the dirt fell like water.

"Sure, sure... whatever you want."

They arrived at a decently wide wooden bridge, maybe ten feet or three meters wide. The planks at the center of the bridge were starting to dilapidate but not to the point of danger. The bridge was made neatly out of cleanly shaven light brown wood, perhaps a shade darker than the average Great Neighbor house. Underneath the bridge, myrtle-colored moss formed at the touch of the water. At high tide, the ocean would lap gently against the discolored wood.

Humans were starting to file onto the bridge, followed by a procession of dwarves. The dwarves were chomping their teeth, ready to tackle any stragglers that were unlucky enough to be slower than their compatriots. The fearful, unarmored humans moved faster than the dwarves due to their long legs and unrestrained movements. However, these dwarves were trained raiders and fully capable of giving chase.

But no matter how well trained they were, none could effectively defend themselves when Mayhem rampaged before them. After the humans had crossed the bridge and none dared look behind, the black-haired wizard bound forward, crashing down like a lion in front of the bridge. He landed on all fours, sliding through the dirt, leaving a plume of black smoke in his wake. As the smoke cleared, he lifted his arms like he was lifting the sky itself, and in fear of his forceful heft, the dust in the air turned crimson red. The mist was the color and stench of dark human blood.

Something in the faces of the dwarves changed when they inhaled the mist. The crack of a spine, like the sound the spine makes after rising from a not-so-restful sleep, radiated from a handful of dwarves. Every vertebra straightened, clicking together like a puzzle. With this click, something in their personas changed. Perhaps it was how they held themselves or the way they looked at each other.

There was a stunned silence for a moment. Then, without moving, the dwarves slowly raised their axes above their heads. The iron reflected the setting sun, shining sanguine before the dwarves started chopping wildly in every direction. Black hair matted in blood started flying everywhere. It was as if the wind had suddenly stopped and the blood was only propelled by the motion of the axes. The dwarves didn't move even an inch from their starting point. The dwarves could only hit one thing, and that was each other. They hacked faster and faster, becoming maniacal in their agony.

Mayhem laughed heartily and joined the fray. He lazily swung the chain that connected the handle of Mourning Star to the black spiked head. His eyes flared red and fire burst out of his nostrils heating the metal on his nose. Mourning Star became more of a blur than anything, spinning faster and faster. Mayhem barely moved his wrist, but still the chain sought blood.

He casually positioned it above the dwarves so that the head of the flail would hit them at an angle such as to send them flying with every strike. The cries that rang through the cities were not that of fear, but anger. Mayhem danced a slow, almost romantic dance through the battlefield, flexing his muscles through his plate armor, growing and shrinking in size as need be. He relished the fruitlessness of the dwarves hacking at his ankles.

With his motion, the battlefield burst to life. The dwarves danced along to Mayhem's inner tune. As more dwarves joined in, the dance grew faster. Dwarves started ducking and diving over and under each other with their upper bodies, leaving scars from axes as parting gifts. Where Mayhem stepped, blood sloshed over his face, invigorating him like a child frolicking in a harmless puddle. Mayhem clumsily stomped his grieves against the ground, keeping an arrhythmic beat. After an eighth rest after his stomp, the dwarves mimicked the beat, and started mindlessly moving towards Mayhem. After a few seconds of crowd gathering, Mayhem sang at the top of his lunges, an ode to death.

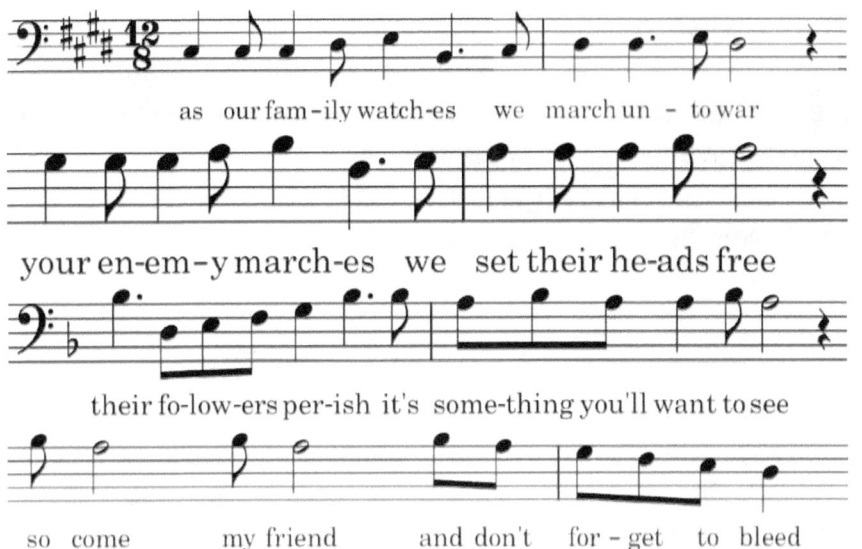

as our fam-ily watch-es we march un - to war

your en-em-y march-es we set their he-ads free

their fo-low-ers per-ish it's some-thing you'll want to see

so come my friend and don't for - get to bleed

The song was not in tune and not very good. Mayhem's voice was bass, but he sang relatively high. The first word of the first three lines was accented and swung into the next partial, finally finishing on a long flat note. Each line grew higher in octave but ended on the same note. The last line was completely different from the previous three in that it started with two long notes and ended with five quick beats. One would never find a folk song like it in the Northern Kingdoms, but it felt familiar to the dwarves. The familiarity was no comfort.

"HEY!" Mayhem shouted.

Mayhem's outburst was not due to the song, but instead to the sudden discontinuation of the dancing. He looked to his left and saw Fear still holding up his right hand in a dispel.

"How obvious do you want us to make it that we were here?" Fear asked. "Again, you leave it to me to clean your mess."

Fear twiddled his fingers like he was conducting a marionette and sent the dwarves back the way they came.

They walked one foot in front of the other like they were balancing on a tightrope. Their arms frantically tried to keep themselves upright while their bodies failed to adjust to the forced movement of their short legs.

"I am sending them to the mirror," Fear said. "Hopefully, others join them."

***

Hera and Aaron watched their home burn from the rooftops. They heard Viner's promise but largely ignored it. Instead, they started clambering across the roof, loose shingles sliding under their feet, clinking like bells. They scrambled to a stop, reaching the edge of the roof. The gray shingles threatened to carry them to the stone road below, but the threat was empty. Hera and Aaron looked over the edge of the building and saw several short warriors with axes in their mouths scaling the wall. The invaders were more dexterous than they looked, but not much, and their climb was slow going.

They did not hesitate. Hera and Aaron grasped each other's hands and, of one mind, they both leaped over the soldiers and onto the next building. They misjudged the length of the jump and ended up colliding at the chest with a hay roof. Their arms flailed, literally grasping at straws, frantically pulling themselves up before the soldiers had a chance to drag them down and away. Aaron climbed up slightly faster and tried to help Hera, but she was already far enough along that it didn't make a difference. They crawled to the top of the roof, the soft hay threatening to give way under their weight. The muffled creak of the wooden supports was far louder than the soft crunching of the straw.

A swoosh and crackle crawled up the building, followed by the blistering smell of burning wood and straw and a blunt wave of overbearing heat. The fire crept towards Hera and Aaron, melding into the red of the setting sun and soon consuming the horizon. Through the flames, Hera and Aaron saw, to their horror, that the building was surrounded by soldiers. The soldiers flickered in the firelight, like a hunting party setting camp at a bonfire. Their shadows were long and distorted, making tevnalish-demon figures in the red heat.

Hera and Aaron should have been afraid. But fear was second to what they felt. This feeling was hotter than the fire's lick and colder than the berserkers' attack. It was a feeling that they could not escape, and they did not try. It was dread, it was anger, but most of all, it was a lust for vengeance, biting and wrathful. Hera and Aaron did not have to look at each other to know that they agreed on what they must do. They must live. They must live to fight. To satiate the vengeance that filled them. Their hunger would not be content until they had ended their attackers' lineage. The invaders would hunt, but Hera and Aaron would not be prey. They would fight for their childhood. They would fight for their home.

They leaped again, back to the shingled roof. The jump was further this time and on an uphill incline. They might not have made it, but the wind howled them forward, suddenly kicking up as if to celebrate their anguished turn. The gust forced them onward and outward three paces more than it had any right to.

They scrambled to the peak of the A-frame roof. Halfway up, they could see a tall figure. Viner had a death grip on a raider's neck. The invader was kicking and squirming, trying desperately to remove the gauntlet from its neck. But Viner's fist was shaking with fury. The only time it had been more vehemently clutched around anything had been a few moments ago, when Viner was trying to pull Hera from the wall. Her ankle remembered.

The guard looked to be disarmed. He had discarded his shortsword and kite shield when he had scaled the terracotta wall. He wasted no time worrying about his sword and plunged the utility knife that had been in his boot into the panicking soldier's shoulder. He viciously crossed the knife down to the berserker's heart, killing the victim relatively quickly.

Viner bent to pick up the raider's axe and tossed the dull knife to Aaron. Aaron was unaware that Viner knew they were standing behind him, but Aaron had cultivated quick reflexes in his time as a thief and caught the knife. Even so, he fumbled with the tool.

Aaron felt a little of that bloodthirsty resolve leave him with the surprise. He stumbled backwards a step or two, and his eyes widened as he looked around at the situation. He spotted a pallid hand gripping the edge of the roof. A second later, another hand followed. The knuckles that curled over the roof turned from gray to white, straining to pull up the small rodent-like body of the raider. The raider was not alone in its struggles; another pair of hands followed suit. And another. And another.

Still crouched, Viner flipped his new axe in his hand to quickly assess the weight of the blade and then slashed at the nearest set of fingers. The axe chopped not only into the invader's hand but into the shingles of the roof too. Viner cursed himself. Even considering his limited axe skills, the cut was sloppy. Still, he pulled the axe from the wood and brought it whistling down again, this time on the arm of a raider that was almost atop the roof. It was too soon to already have berserkers getting that close.

Hera rushed to the nest of the A-frame roof. From her vantage point, she could see that raiders were moving from around the straw-roofed building to the one where they stood on now. They were following their target. The raiders climbing onto the roof were only a small handful in comparison to the ones that were on their way. She could tell that Viner would soon be overrun and the three of them had to be ready for the attack.

"Aaron, help Viner! Make sure we have at least one side open!" Hera commanded.

Even having one edge clear could be the wedge that split the log. Aaron followed the orders and went to assist Viner. He slashed with the utility knife frantically attacking any soldier that got too close and managed to dissuade the climb of several. The raiders were fighting an uphill battle and losing troops quickly, but they still did not need to bother regrouping. They would have the three citizens of Great Neighbor, whether it was by sheer numbers or by sheer force.

Tactical failure aside, the aggressors were relentless and soon overwhelmed the two blades that held them back. At three sides Viner, Hera, and Aaron were surrounded, Hera weaponless and Aaron with only a dull utility knife. Viner was well versed in most martial weapons, but an axe was not his first choice.

A clash of iron made the shackles of the roof shiver and threaten to fall again. Hera looked to see what had caused the rumbling. An enemy soldier had recklessly dug his axe into the rooftop. What the berserker was aiming for was unclear. All she knew is that the attack was too close for comfort. She couldn't dwell long on the reckless raider, because another soldier with better aim was already swinging its axe at her.

Hera ducked at the last possible moment, feeling the surprisingly strong blast of wind against the top of her head and neck. Aaron looked in the direction of the crash just in time to see Hera almost get decapitated. He reflexively pulled his knife back to throw it into the dwarf's head, but he thought better of it. Instead, he decided to throw Viner's knife to Hera.

Aaron may have been a thief, but the most he had done with a knife was skim an inconsequential amount of money from an inconsequential pocket. It looked for a moment like the knife would stab into Hera before she caught it. The wind was not on his side this time. But Hera wasn't about to let herself be so easily vanquished. She looked over her shoulder in time to see the knife rushing at her. She wasn't in a good position to move, so instead she attempted to catch it. Her arm curled just enough to close around the knife before it rotated to the blade.

Hera, knife in hand, gutted the soldier in front of her. She stabbed it into the attacker's stomach and tore down. It was difficult from the ducking position. Her legs collapsed under her, and she fell to one knee. The rest of the soldiers charged, the brunt of the Boulder Corps attacking Viner. One attacker got too close to Hera, and while still kneeling, she stabbed him in the stomach and forced him to the ground.

Aaron had raiders of his own to deal with and was now weaponless. Hera was still in danger, but she saw that Aaron was in need. With complete disregard for her own safety, she threw the knife to Aaron. A droplet of light colored blood accented the blade of the knife, moving down the edge as it flew through the air. If Hera had been aiming for the forehead of a raider standing behind Aaron, she would have been spot on.

Aaron's attention was captivated by the flying knife, and he turned to see it impale a raider between the eyes. Hera didn't spare any time to congratulate herself on the accidental fling and scattered to her feet. Aaron did the opposite and scrambled down to retrieve the weapon. He completely forgot the axe that the raider had dropped and went straight for the knife. Requiring more effort than he would have liked, he twisted it out of the raider's skull.

Aaron shuddered, but still remembered his manners. "Nice Throw!"

He pulled the knife out of the short creature's forehead and brandished it in his hands. He dodged the blow of another inaccurate attack and then another. He slashed wildly in all directions, trying to use the dagger as defensively as possible.

"The axe!" Hera shouted over the squeals of the hairy attackers.

Aaron showed no indication he heard her, so she closed the distance between them. She slid her way past an invader who was flourishing an axe. She ducked and dove between several more until she was only a few meters away from Aaron.

She commanded her friend again, "The axe!"

Still, Aaron did not hear her. "What?"

He slashed at the eyes of an invader that got too close causing the bridge of its nose to begin to bleed.

"The axe!" Hera repeated.

Unfortunately, the blinded dwarf howled in rage and combined with the other noises of battle, Aaron was still unable to hear her.

"You want the knife?" Aaron asked.

"Yes—" Hera began. "No," she corrected. "I want you to grab—"

Hera stopped talking abruptly and started to clamber to the ground. Her motions were over-exaggerated as she crawled across the floor and over Aaron's feet.

"Never mind; I'll get it," she spat.

The knife made an audible thunk in the shingle in front of Hera. She paused for a moment. It was official. Aaron was an idiot. She twisted the knife out of the roof, and rolled on her back, slashing above her. She was correct in guessing a soldier would be there. The attacker was rewarded with a new red mark on their lower stomach. They started to collapse, and the weight of the attacker's body flung aside the knife in Hera's hands.

The corpse fell on top of Hera, and the axe that the corpse had been wielding fell beside her head. First, she flinched at the thunk of the axe, and then she recoiled in disgust at the bleeding body on top of her. She panicked, wondering if she would be able to heave the soldier off of herself. She shivered with the blood dripping down the chest of the soldier. Her muscles tensed as she tried to shove the invader off. Her first push only moved the raider an inch, but it proved the raider could be moved. Luckily, the berserker was half the normal human size.

Hera pushed again, and the raider slid further to the left. Still, it was not off and still she pushed. She thought that the third time must be the charm, so she mustered all her strength to move the raider. The third time was not the charm. However, with a fourth push the raider was finally loose enough for her to start sliding out from under the hairy mess. She pressed herself against the ground and rolled to her right, freeing herself from her organic prison. She was still on the ground when she tightened her hand around the discarded axe. She noticed that this axe wasn't the only one on the ground, so she picked up another.

"I said," Hera got to her feet with the axes in her hands, "The axe! Stupid!"

She slammed the handle of the axe she held in her left hand into Aaron's chest. Aaron was red in the face and sweating. Apparently, he had been narrowly avoiding attacks while Hera was messing around on the floor.

"Oh..." he panted. "Yeah, sorry... cool! Axe. Yes."

He closed his hand around the axe handle at his chest and panted some more. As soon as Hera let go of the axe, it clattered to the floor.

"Oops..." Aaron sighed, breathing heavily.

He bent down to pick up the axe just as an enemy axe got ready to crash down on him. It was the axe of a raider whose sole purpose was brutal assault. Hera, quick as she could, slashed at the raider. She was untrained with an axe, but the raider was so focused on offense that she was able to hit him. Even with the wide-open target area, Hera failed to embed the axe completely into the antagonist. The axe head delivered a blunt impact to the invader, sending them back a few inches, before it slid off the raider's cuirass.

Aaron got to his feet. The axe seemed to weigh him down. His arms drooped in front of him limply while he held onto the heavy weapon. His fingers tried their hardest to clutch onto the leather handle, but they looked as if they would slip at any moment. He slashed at the nearest soldier only weakly scratching them up the face. Though the attack was sloppy, it was enough to send the invader reeling.

Hera used the momentum of her first strike and pushed another slash against the same target. She hacked into the bewildered soldier's neck, not quite cutting off their head, but still fatally wounding the creature.

"I think..." Aaron took a weak heave in. "We should get out of here."

Hera turned to Viner. More invaders lay dead around the guerrilla guard than Hera had fingers. Viner gritted his teeth, hacking away with his axe.

"We should run!" Hera shouted over to him.

"I..." Viner used all his strength to dismember the arm of an invader, "Could not agree... more!"

He swung around his axe. The blunt of the axe's head hit a raider, pushing the unwelcome guest off the roof, taking a couple of his comrades unlucky enough to be in his path with him. He motioned with his hands for Hera and Aaron to come over.

"Over here," he called. "Jump."

He pointed toward the next roof over—another hay roof but this one not on fire. Hera and Aaron complied and ran over to Viner. Viner forced them past him and to the edge of the roof.

Aaron looked over the edge fearfully. This jump was shorter than the last, but Aaron didn't know if he had the strength left in him. His heart was tired most of all, not in a cheesy romantic way—even though his heart was heavy with the sacking of his village—but more the way he would have felt if he had run ten-by-ten miles without stopping. He doubted the journey from Sunsoon to Layden had been as tiring, and those Witshore hotspots weren't even adjacent longcities.

Aaron wasn't unsure whether or not he could make the jump; he was certain he couldn't. Not only was his body not ready, but he didn't have the willpower to push himself further. If he was lucky, he would hit the ground and die. But the raiders wanted him to die. More importantly, Hera didn't. So, he had no choice. Everything told him he couldn't make the jump. His legs told him he couldn't make the jump. His emotions told him he couldn't make the jump. His psyche told him he couldn't make the jump. But he would. He had done it before, and he could do it now!

Aaron gritted his teeth and ran at the edge of the roof. It was a sight to see. A sight to see how painfully slow his full sprint was, that is. Even with the extra time given to him by his slow pace, he jumped too late and his push off the edge of the roof was imperfect. He glided through the air as gracefully as a turtle thrown by a particularly rambunctious child. His right foot barely collided with the edge of the parallel roof. His left foot was not so lucky. His arms waved around for a moment before he fell backward onto the stone-cold ground.

"I'll get him!" Viner was already jumping down after him with no heed for his own safety.

Hera looked to the edge of the unlit hay roof. She got ready to jump. Unlike Aaron, her adrenaline had not worn off. The thief took a quick look down at Aaron. His eyes were closed, and Viner was already hoisting him onto his shoulders. Hera looked back up to the roof, ready to jump. But could she leave Aaron? That's what he'd want, isn't it? For her to live on? What was it the guard said? No honor among thieves?

She made her choice. She discarded her axe and leaped to the other building. A loud thump accentuated her collision with the clay bricks. She slid down the side of the wall, not quite getting her grip on any real handholds, leaving her fingers raw and red and her shoes torn. It would be hard to pick a pocket when you could be caught literally red-handed. It didn't matter; Aaron was better at most of the sneaky stuff anyway, and if all went well, he would be alive. If there really is no honor among thieves, Hera wasn't a thief.

The wall did little to slow her descent, and she smashed against the ground. She landed on her feet and felt her ligaments compress. Shockwaves of kinetic energy made their way up her entire body. Her legs were too straight on impact, which didn't help the matter. Her knees buckled, and she stumbled to stay upright. Her vision turned white. She heard something clatter to the ground, and for a moment, she was convinced it was her. Then, her vision cleared, and she saw that Viner had dropped his axe to further hoist Aaron onto his shoulders.

"To the keep!" Viner commanded. "We don't have much time."

Raiders were already jumping down the building after them, their boots clanking loudly against the ground. Many of the raiders met the same fate as Aaron, and of the few that actually landed on their feet, most wore a similar expression to Hera's when she had unceremoniously collided with the ground.

Viner carried Aaron, opting to completely lift the young man off his feet, and run with him on his back. Aaron could do little to protest. The guard ran as fast as he could, carrying Aaron away from the blazing buildings and down the sloped stone streets. Hera followed in step, a new burst of adrenaline keeping her going. She was more swiftly footed than Viner; she wore no armor and carried no Aaron, but she didn't want to run in front of the guard.

That's not to say she didn't use her extra time. While they ran down the city streets, every moment she could, Hera knocked over the flowerpots that lined the houses. The puffs of dust that tailed their escape were less than consistent and didn't quite have the smoky effect Hera had hoped for. Dirt stung the invaders' eyes, but they were raiders and had been through worse.

Hera, Aaron, and Viner were on the northernmost coast of the central island. They were already a ways down the road to the east. Their destination was Great Neighbor Keep, and that was on the eastern island. They didn't have to go an immeasurable distance, perhaps half a mile. On a normal day it would have been a pleasant excursion but on this evening, it was a perilous journey. Raiders were already scattered on every corner of the residential island. They were efficient, that much was granted to them. The group chasing them contained no less than eight raiders and perhaps a few more. As the chase commenced, raiders would lose interest and other raiders would gain interest.

Hera ran away from the emissary manor down the east-facing road, not bothering to use any side passages in case she would be surrounded. Viner moved forward without any fear or hesitation, and Hera followed keeping pace. On her right, a door of a small hut kicked out with a bang. A raider was standing in the frame. They were clutching a young woman by the nape of the scalp. Hera screamed, and she wasn't the only one. The woman, too, was crying and screaming.

The raider swiped at Hera with its free hand, but they were too far away to latch onto the thief. It half-heartedly lunged out the door, but Hera was already down the street a ways. Hera turned to look at the woman being dragged off. She recognized her. She knew her name. She did nothing to stop the raider. Hera just watched. She watched the woman get dragged off by a raider, screaming the whole while, not knowing what would happen to her. She dared not think about it.

Once she was a safe distance, she turned her whole body to watch helplessly as the woman was kidnapped. Hera's eyes filled with tears. The woman's name was Solda, and she was the local apple vendor. She had once tricked the advisor to the King into buying an apple for five golden teeth. The nobleman was so rich from birth he didn't know he could get away with using just one. Solda sold more than just apples, but from then on, she was the apple vendor.

Hera took a step toward the woman now being kidnapped. Her foot was angled up against a rock on the stone-paved road. She hesitated. Then she took a step back. She turned around. She started running. She didn't look back.

Viner didn't notice Hera's sudden stop. She was able to catch up quickly, but the raiders were gaining on them now. Any head start they had gained from jumping off the building was now lost. The metal boots they wore clanked haphazardly against the stone and dirt, sometimes catching against the cobbles of the uneven road.

The petals that once adorned the street had gathered at the roadside, covered in dirt and muck. Though it was night, Great Neighbor was lit. Unfortunately, it was lit by the flames that the raiders had set to any and all buildings in their way. Viner knew the city well, but it was possible that if those houses were not ablaze, he would have gotten lost in the dark. He was not thankful.

An axe flew by Hera's head. It had a good spin but missed its mark and fell harmlessly to the ground, hitting a stone and bouncing gently. Hera went to pick it up, thanking fate that it had not landed headfirst in dirt or wood and gotten stuck there. She barely even considered the possibility that it could have hit her.

She had no intention of turning to face the raiders again, but it was all she could do to slow them down. She turned with the axe in hand and threw it limply at the raiders. It didn't make it more than a few feet. The axe fell weakly against the ground, with not even a bounce. But if she was lucky, a raider would stop chasing her so that they could laugh at her instead.

The keep of Great Neighbor had never looked so menacing on its stone shore, and Hera had never been so happy to see it. Its gnarled towers looked far less silly when placed next to the burning city. The glass castle cast down a dark shadow over the crimson sea.

Chapter 6
Orders Are Orders

Perhaps Hera and Aaron had been in Great Neighbor too long to realize the grand scale of the keep, for it brought the raiders to their knees at the sight of it. The castle loomed dark and tall over them. Twisted obsidian glamor gleamed down as if the rays of the moon had turned solid and deemed themselves fit to touch Malue, the world. Perhaps the people of Great Neighbor had never noticed the castle was so powerful in stature, or perhaps, just perhaps, something more phantastic was at work.

Either way, the red-headed woman with her hair in a bun who manned the gate to the keep did not think too hard about why the raiders didn't dare challenge her. Instead, she stood hunched over the chain that controlled the gate, ready to drop it if any invader stepped foot on the bridge. She noticed Viner carrying Aaron's limp body. His intense face crested the ridge of the bridge, forewarning the guard of his coming.

Viner and Hera, running as fast as ever, had not noticed that the attackers had stopped their pursuit. The bodies of several Great Neighbor citizens and one or two guards were strewn outside of the gate. The dwarves that seemed to have committed the act lay with them.

"Viner!" the gatekeeper shouted. "I'm glad you made it. Frederick- I'll tell you later. For now, get to the keep."

Her muscles tensed on the latch of the gate and her foot shifted away from the dead body of a guard. Evidently, something had gotten past the gate.

"What did you say about Fredrick?" Viner shouted back.

The one by her foot wasn't the only guard dead. Bodies with large slashes across their chests, necks, and stomachs lay deeper still in the keep.

"It's not important. Get inside," she insisted.

Viner turned to address Hera. "Girl, drag your boyfriend into the keep. You did well. Better than I have ever seen an untrained soldier fight. When he wakes up, tell him that he did the same."

Hera's face blushed red, almost hidden by the firelight that lit her face.

"He's—" She stopped herself. "I will."

Viner all but threw Aaron to the ground. Aaron groaned softly on impact. Hera scowled up at Viner, but his eyes were intent on the red-headed guard. Hera knelt to pick up Aaron's arm and started dragging him through the gate.

"Rose. My brother," Viner insisted.

"Get inside!" Rose begged.

"My brother, Rose. That is a command from your superior!" Viner shouted.

He had moved closer to her, and the shouting was unnecessary at this distance, but he did it anyway. Spit flew out of his mouth and Rose recoiled. She turned her head, but she didn't step back.

"You forget yourself, Viner. You are not my superior. I am Mouth of the King. But it is wartime, and I am obliged to lend my service to the military."

Rose took a long sideways glance at Viner. She waited for him to say something, but all he did was huff and puff out of his mammoth nose. Rose's placid face ticked for a moment, just below her left eye. Then, she returned to stone.

Without a frown, a grimace, or any sign of regret, Rose stated, "Your brother Fredrick, former Captain of the Guard, has unfortunately died in the line of duty. His time of death was about twenty minutes ago. The cause of death is still not understood. We speculate magic, sir. Dark magic, that which I am not allowed to disavow, less I go against the personal belief of the King."

"No... Frederick. He wouldn't have..." Viner shut his eyes hard and placed his bald head in his hand.

"I regret to inform you that you have been promoted on the field. With the death of the former Captain of the Guard, you are now the Captain of the Guard. This honor comes with much responsibility—"

"I know!" Viner's spit flew in Rose's direction again. "I know all of that! You don't need to tell me. I know!"

"Understood," Rose said, slowly wiping spit off her face, "Now if you will excuse me. I have a job to do."

"You disrespect a man who has just lost his brother?" Viner's voice shook in grief.

Rose frowned. "This is Great Neighbor, Viner. We are strong."

"Aye... we are." Viner turned to walk into the keep.

The attackers dared not enter the keep, and the guard of Great Neighbor likewise did not exit it. The cries of the invaders had dimmed shortly after Hera and Aaron entered the keep. Without the sounds of siege, the minds of the people were eased to some extent.

***

Many refugees had filed into the keep. You would have thought they were unwelcome, looking at the state in which they were left— without food, blankets, or any type of support from the King. But they didn't care about that. What they needed was something to blame. A lake could have been filled with their tears, but it would not wash away their blood. The people of Great Neighbor had never been so humiliated, covered in dirt and grime, cursing the black sky as they slammed their fists on the rocky ground of the keep's courtyard. Pillars of stone were the only thing holding together the Great Neighbor's keep. The people that hopelessly wove their sorrows in-and-out of the clumsily carved columns of ashen stone, had no-use for-structure.

Some wanted to be left alone while some wanted to talk to their friends and family about what happened. Most wanted to talk, but were alone nonetheless. A black-haired woman let her head hang against her shoulders as she crouched against a pillar of stone. Her skin was olive-tone, like those of Aerokite. Her hair covered her Aerokitian features. She looked at her hands as if they held an answer. Her family had told tales of Aerokitian palm readers, but they were myths, and the soot-filled creases in her flesh told her little more than that her nails were chipped, and her hands calloused.

After Aaron got his bearings, and discovered that it was exhaustion and not mortal wound that caused him to lose consciousness, he and Hera vacated into the cellar. Together they clomped down the stone stairs, their shoes loudly clicking and clacking against the stone. The antagonizing noise started to soften as the stairs were replaced with moon-tinted wood rooting in its isolation.

"What are we going to do?" Aaron stammered.

"I don't know. There's nothing left for us here. We can't stay in a burned-down little village where everyone hates us."

"We didn't do anything!" Aaron said.

"They caught us, Aaron. They caught us burglarizing a house while the city was attacked. I don't think they will be so forgiving under the new circumstances." Hera was almost crying. "I'm scared."

"I am too."

From the shadows, a third voice creaked. It creaked like a loose plank of wood being stepped on, only more drawn out. And more phantastic.

"We all are scared," it said.

A shocked pause followed the statement. The only noise that could be heard was the sound of the water dripping softly against the molding wooden floor.

Drip.

Dri-p.

Drip-drip.

Drip drip-thwip.

The water from the ceiling of the cellar dripped rhythmically. With each drip, the droplets synced to become more and more in time with one another. After only five drips all the leaks in the ceiling seemed to correlate into one strong drip all at the same time. They fell in a continuous pattern. *Drip, drip-drip, drip-drip-thwip.*

Aaron and Hera didn't know what to do. All they could really think to do was scream, so they did. They didn't know how to stop screaming, so they didn't try. The only thing Hera and Aaron could see through their screaming eyes was the cellar painted red. Out of the reddened shadow of a cellar emerged a tall, slender old man wearing a pointed hat and draped in what looked like several layers of robe.

"Calm down," said the old man.

His dark eyes squinted, bunching together the sickly flesh that loosely hung on his gaunt face. He lifted his hands showing his palms, and slowly motioned toward the ground in an effort to ease the two young adults.

Hera and Aaron continued screaming. A spherical vial of red liquid that could only be blood was at his hip, attached by several straps. He was dressed in multiple layers of cloth, the innermost layer being as red as the blood on his hip, and the outermost layers slowly fading into black. He looked akin to an old book with worn pages. But even with his menacing visage, Hera and Aaron had seen worse in the nightmare that was less than an hour behind them. But all the same, they continued to scream despite no longer feeling afraid.

"You should only fear me when you don't see me, you sniveling brats," the old man snapped.

His words had no effect on the sniveling of the perceived brats, and instead, they continued screaming in horror groping at their faces. Despite his irritated tone, a foul grin creased the corners of the old man's crusted lips. The grin disappeared with the soft pitter-patter of cloth and leather shoes against wood. The pitter-patter was followed by another set of drips coming from the profusely moist ceiling. The *drip-drip-thwip* of the synchronized orchestra now had a second quarter note overlaying the end of the first.

Drip, drip-drip, drip-drip-thwip.

Drip, drip-drip, drip-drip-thwip.

A much kinder, yet still old voice beckoned from behind Hera and Aaron, evidently coming down the stairs to the cellar.

"Ease your minds," it said. "He shall not hurt you as long as I am here."

When had Aaron and Hera stopped screaming? When had they gotten here? How long had they been down in this cellar? Hera and Aaron could have sworn they had been standing here talking to these two old men for an hour. Did they remember playing and winning a game of poker? Did they remember how to play poker?

They did not like the dark-clothed old man—not for an instant—but the man standing behind them, they liked just fine. He was kind and gentle. Yet they did not know what he looked like. They had not yet seen him.

They knew only his voice and only one phrase, "Ease your minds. He shall not hurt you as long as I am here." With those words, but not in that moment, he told stories of dreams long passed. Of love, of loss, of saddened kings. Of joy, of sea, of achievement. All stories ended the same way—with the world marching in melancholy.

"My children," the man behind them said gently, "I am Calm. You know me as the strategy of war, the tranquility of air, the light reflecting off the ocean as the sun begins to set."

By now, Hera and Aaron had turned to observe the old man standing behind them. They could place him as Sullivan the bookseller wearing his plain white robe. At least it looked plain at first glance, but when Hera squinted her eyes to look closer, she noticed two hands splayed in a fine engraving on the old shoulders. The threads blended in so well with the rest of the cloak that it looked as though they could have been woven there by random chance. She looked even closer and lost the thread altogether; she could only make out random lines and jumbles.

Calm noticed Hera looking at his coat, and his face tinged with a dull excitement. He smiled, showing pearly teeth that fit perfectly in his pale mouth. A wonder-filled and saintly glint glimmered in Calm's yellow-irised eyes for a moment. Then, the glint fled as if it had never been there. Even in its absence, the look of wonder remained mirrored on Hera and Aaron's faces.

The other man spoke maliciously, "Always with the air of greatness. 'You are safe as long as I am here' as if *I* was a threat? 'I am the tranquility of the air, the reflection of the ocean?' Oh, and what was that first one? Almost glossed over that. 'I am war!'"

"You will do anything to bring another down." Calm frowned. "Even take your own self with them. This is Fear—"

"I will introduce myself!" Fear insisted indignantly. "I am Fear. I am the conglomerate of the nightmare that holds this day together." With a sarcastic glance in Calm's direction, Fear threw his arms about as if he was conducting a rowdy orchestra. "The dark ooze at the corner of your eye," he exaggerated. "The eternal question!" He flapped his cape back in a satirical display of grandeur and struck a pose to accent his finish.

"That is a-a…" Aaron stammered. "Title."

"Yes," Fear nodded. "It is."

Fear looked so ridiculously foolish that it must have been a joke. Yet he didn't seem the type to play a joke. Hera didn't consider either factor and ignored thoughts of dark ooze in the corner of her eye.

"What's happening? Who are you? Why are you here?"

Calm warmly looked into Hera's eyes. Calm was only an inch or two taller than her, but she felt small compared to him, like she was still a child looking up to an adult.

"My child, why are you here?"

Hera was glad for the rhetorical nature of the question, because she had absolutely no clue how to answer it. She met his eyes, confusion covering her face.

"How many dwarves did you have to kill?" Calm looked pensively back at Hera's confused face.

Hera stopped to think for a moment. She looked to Aaron, who was already looking at her. They both shrugged at the same time. They would have laughed, had they the strength in them to laugh.

Aaron timidly asked, "Dwarves, sir?"

Calm looked down his nose at the boy, addressing him for the first time, "Yes, my boy, you have been fighting dwarves. Undead dwarves by the looks of it. Possibly liches or perhaps soul-captured corpses."

Aaron scrunched up his nose and placed his head in his hands. "What on Malue is a lich?"

Before Aaron had finished his question, Calm was already muttering something about vampirism under his breath. Then, after Aaron was done, Calm nodded to himself and looked into space, recognizing the boy's lack of knowledge. He turned to look at Hera and smiled warmly. He straightened his back and hid his hands behind the straightened spine.

"Hera, would you like to explain?" he asked.

Hera looked at the strange old man, puzzled by his question. How would she know what a lich is any more than Aaron?

Fear interjected, "Calm, they aren't supposed to know about any of this."

Calm closed his eyes and shook his head with a grin on his face. Suddenly his eyes snapped open, alert. He looked around at the two young adults in the room, and with a look of understanding, he frowned.

"Ah... Yes," he sighed. "I forgot about that..."

His voice trailed off.

"Thank you, Fear," he finally said.

Hera darted her eyes to the floor. She tugged on Aaron's sleeve and started to shift as silently and slowly as she could toward the door. Aaron looked to her, then looked to Calm, and back to her.

"I would like to..." he started, but he stopped when he noticed how on edge Hera was.

He was interested in understanding what these two strange old men were talking about, but he wasn't going to force Hera to stay when she obviously didn't want to. Calm made no reaction to the pair's movements and only tracked their faces with his eyes, darting curiously back and forth between them. His expression was blank, like he was thinking with cold, hard logic and nothing else.

"You have a purpose here," he spoke suddenly, swiftly, and to the point. "I asked you how many dwarves you killed. The answer is somewhere around fifteen between the two of you. You have never had any previous combat experience, and most of the kills were made with a knife you shared between you."

Calm looked meaningfully at the two. Realization started to dawn on Hera's and Aaron's faces. It really was remarkable what they had done. And one question raced through their minds.

"H-how?" Hera stopped moving for a moment and let her eyes explore a book lying on its side to the left of Calm.

"Through nothing but sheer willpower, you survived… mainly so that you could continue to share each other's company. Viner, in your defense, killed double the number of dwarves that you two did. Despite the enemy's lack of combat expertise, this is undoubtedly excessive and positively impossible."

Aaron spoke slowly, struggling to form words. At the same time, Hera also tried to speak but suffered the same dilemma.

"How did—" Aaron murmured.

"What are you—" Hera said at the same time.

They both stopped, hearing the other.

"That is where, I—*We* step in," Calm said.

Calm gestured around, linking himself and Fear especially. Aside from his gesture towards Fear, it looked like he was indicating the particles of dust that filled the cellar air.

"What did you do exactly?" Hera inquired.

The light bent and Calm's presence was magnified. "I cleared your mind, she guided your hand. Your life was decreed as of the utmost importance. You were an outlier, a wild card, that we intended to play. So we did. To perfection. The dwarves killed three hundred eighty-four people. Their motive was not to slaughter Great Neighbor, however. They wanted to capture it. The dwarves managed to ensnare three thousand two hundred seven men, women, and even children, before being driven back."

Calm placed his chin against his chest and cocked his head to the side, keeping that curious smile on his smooth face. "You will save them, and more importantly, you will kill the man that is capturing them."

"What!" Hera and Aaron yelled in unison.

Hera was on him like a rabid dog. "You come here into our home, use dark magic to fog our minds, tell us that all the fairy tales we've ever heard are nightmares coming to chase us, and now you expect us to somehow heroically save three thousand people!"

Calm's small smile turned sad and was followed by a wrinkling of the eyebrows that would have been better suited on a laughing face. The expression could only be described as bemused, yet the regret in the smile added something more. Pity? He waved his hand in front of Hera's face, calming her. Hera's eyes glazed over. All the panic and fear that had been ailing her mind dissipated like a rough tide returning to the sea, smoothing the sand in its wake.

"Three thousand two hundred seven people, my child."

"I see..."

Hera grasped for Aaron's arm. Once it was clutched in her scraped hands, she started to slide down it, using Aaron's arm like a rope as she descended into the dark cave that was the floor.

***

The King's eyes were red from stress. His Captain of the Guard, Viner's brother, had bravely died in the onslaught. And he was left with few men. The King had no clue what to do without the Captain of the Guard at his side and locked himself in his throne room, with Viner and Rose at his council.

Rose reported dutifully to the King, "My liege, we are not aware of our casualties... yet. But we know that most of our citizens were captured rather than killed. Eyewitnesses state that they were of... well... witness to several families being dragged off by groups of invaders."

"And the guard was unable to push back these invaders?" the King inquired, obviously upset.

The King's short stature made him look similar to a goblin. The appearance was completed by massive ears and a large nose, which further betrayed the King's already evident age. A lopsided crown constantly rested atop the old man's head, not successfully hiding the thinning wires of hair that the King clung to in lieu of a full and healthy head.

"No, sir, they were not. Of the nine to ten thousand people living in Great Neighbor, one in five is a guard. Despite this paranoia—"

"PARANOIA?" the King burst.

The King was clad in purple and red, matching his purple, bloodshot, eyes. His legs were skinny, slightly hairy, pale white, and exposed under his robe as he sat cross-legged on a small pillow beside his throne. His arms clumsily spun around each other as he crossed them, slapping his own biceps. His lips were dry, his teeth yellow, and his beard even more thin and wiry than the hair on his head.

The King clambered slowly to his feet. His crown clattered to the ground beside his bare left foot, threatening to tear off the toenails that loosely clung to his toes. The King had a habit of walking barefoot. He clumsily climbed atop his throne, using it as a pedestal. Once he was on it, he continued the clumsy arm motion, repeatedly slapping his biceps.

"Sir—" Rose started to say, but she was soon interrupted.

"Paranoia to prepare our Kingdom for this day!" he proclaimed.

"That is enough…" Viner tried to interject.

The King did not let him. "Even despite rigorous growth from the guard, which you supported," the King said pointing at Rose condemningly. "My guard still fails to protect my city!"

There was a long pause—perhaps fifteen or twenty seconds—before any of the three decided to speak again. During this time, the King clicked his head back and forth, looking from Viner to Rose with each rhythmic slap on his numb bicep hitting either flat or sharp. He looked like a clock with each motion of his head ticking like the second hand, and if the man was trying to be funny, some may have chortled or laughed.

Rose pontificated her report. "The guard has halved in number with troops MIA, or unfortunately, KIA. The attackers were relentless and fought more akin to organized animals than to humans. If the attackers valued their lives, we would have far more people here today. I estimate that each guard killed an average of five attackers before being overtaken. Unfortunately, it barely made a dent."

"What are we going to do about it?" Viner asked.

Viner had not changed or washed since the battle, but he was brandishing a new spear in his hands. It was similar in appearance to the one he had lost and would function almost the same. Viner was confident that this one would be put to better use.

"I have a suggestion," Rose said. "With our loss in numbers, both in guards and in civilians, the best course of action is the recovery of those lost. If a second invasion were to occur, we would most definitely be wiped out."

Rose spoke with certainty as if what she was saying could not be challenged in its logic, but Viner saw a glint in her eye that scared him more than the invaders themselves. A glint more red with fury than Rose's hair or the blood of their fallen comrades. Rose wasn't acting out of logic, but out of fear, panic, and most of all, revenge. Viner knew Rose was a harsh and intelligent strategist. He also knew that it would be worthwhile to hold his tongue to see what she had to say.

"So, I suggest a draft."

Viner's resolution to hold his tongue was immediately broken as he was hit harder with the information than he would be by an avalanche.

"A draft!" Viner shouted

The King was much more intrigued. "A draft?" he mused.

"Yes sir," she replied. "A draft."

"That is madness!" Viner bellowed. "It is immoral and dishonorable to send untrained civilians to fight against a nightmare like this where our casualty rate is fifty percent!"

"Actually, a majority of guards are MIA, not KIA," Rose interjected.

"To hell with that!" Viner raged.

"To hell indeed..." the King hummed to himself.

"We cannot sustain this island with so few people. If we continue with this draft, we will have no chance of having any home to come back to."

The King looked alarmed for a moment before Rose interjected, "Actually. We can. We have enough food to survive the rest of the season, and the farming district was completely untouched. A majority of our losses were in the market, where we lost mainly merchants, unemployed citizens, and, of course, guards. The estimated five thousand people remaining are more than enough to keep the island running. With a draft of one thousand soldiers—"

"Civilians, Rose!" Viner interjected.

"Soldiers," Rose insisted. "We should be able to remain fairly comfortable on the island."

"But there's still a risk," Viner was grasping at straws.

"So far, Rose has offered a solution, and you, Viner, have offered only more problems," the King pointed out.

"Wait!" Viner shouted.

"Rose seems to have the better option—" the King began.

Viner's face darkened. He hung his head in shame. He looked to his hands, wondering if he was going to go through with this. Trading lives is never a moral thing to do, and anguish filled every part of his body. Maybe they would die if he did; maybe they would die if he didn't. They were just kids, after all, but old enough for the draft, and the draft wouldn't be merciful.

"I witnessed something astounding on the battlefield. Two... kids, the thieves we have been trying to capture. They were able to..." His voice cracked in anguish as he continued, "To kill no less than a dozen soldiers between the two of them, wielding nothing but a knife... a single knife they shared."

Viner stopped talking. He took in a breath, not allowing the inhale to lift his head. For the first time in his adult life, he was unsure. He wanted to sink into the floor in shame.

The King already knew the answer to his next question, but he wanted to be sure. He could not believe what he was hearing. Perhaps another two thieves had suddenly come upon the island without his knowing. Strong, capable warriors?

"Who are they?"

Chapter 7
Composure

"State your case and make your plea before your royal highness," said the shrill voice of the King.

Hera and Aaron had been brought before the King and forced to their knees by two stone-faced guards. They had been apprehended easily in the cellar of the keep during a sweep.

Hera swallowed and spoke first, "Well, Your Highness, you should really be thanking us."

No shackles had been placed on either of their wrists. Instead, the two large powerful guards held them, keeping them on their knees, making sure that the thieves didn't try to hot foot.

"Thanking you?" spat the King, "Why should *I* be thanking *you*?"

Hera was red-faced with exhaustion. The polar opposite was true of Aaron; his face was ghastly pale and his entire body shook under the weight of the heavy guards. Hera looked nervously over to him and breathed out a stuttering and heavy breath.

"If not for us then the guard wouldn't exist; we are the only thieves on the island," Hera pleaded.

Hera and Aaron had been found so easily in the cellar due to very loud screaming. According to the guards, Hera and Aaron were screaming until they, the guards, arrived. After spotting them, Hera and Aaron supposedly stopped abruptly.

"Ah, well yes, I suppose. Thank you," the King said warmly.

Rose stood behind the King, her face stricken at her leader's stupidity.

"But not all is forgiven," the King continued. "No, no, punishment must still be handed out like lollipops to children."

Hera and Aaron looked around, confused. They scanned the faces of the guards but found no clues in their blank stares. They felt rather embarrassed that they had no clue what a lollipop was.

"And I think I have a good idea for that," the King sang. "A nice young woman told me that I need to draft people to go and attack our attackers. Hit them back and whatnot. You know the drill!"

There was a long, stunned silence. Even the guards holding down Hera and Aaron seemed surprised. An annoying chirping of a bird cracked its way through the mortar of the stone to bother the serious discussion.

"Draft us?!" Aaron and Hera cried.

True fear and disbelief carried in their voices. The question was more akin to the squeal of a pig than to a human plea.

"Yes, draft you! We need numbers to save our comrades and, let's face it, our guard is in a shabby state." The King was the only jovial one in the room.

"No!" Aaron whined, "You can't do this."

"Of course I can," the King mocked Aaron's voice. "You were caught committing a crime before the invasion started; this is your punishment."

"Death!" Hera let all her anger fill her voice, making her sound deeper, fuller, and much more intimidating.

The guards holding her down showed no sign of letting her up even after the outburst.

"Of course not!" the King snapped. "Chance of death. You will fight to reclaim our sovereignty."

"We can't fight," Aaron proclaimed.

"You lie!" the King spat.

Rose glanced at the hunched, short figure of the King out of the corner of her eye. After seeing that the King was not going to elaborate, she stepped forward.

"Our sources say, and I quote 'they,' being you, 'were able to kill no less than a dozen soldiers between the two of them.' Eh... you were 'wielding nothing but a knife. A single knife you shared.'"

Rose kept her eyes and face straight forward, outlining her rounded features. She made no attempt to look at Hera and Aaron while speaking and all but avoided eye contact.

The King nodded in satisfaction. "Thank you, Rose."

"Yes, sire." Rose quickly and rigidly saluted the King.

A Great Neighbor salute is identical to a Northern Kingdom salute due to their shared heritage. It involves making a fist with both hands and aligning the arms to form a ninety degree angle, knuckles touching.

"You are dismissed to the barracks," Rose ordered Hera and Aaron. "Do not attempt to leave; desertion is prohibited. Keep it in mind, Hera and Aaron, that if you try to run, we will find you."

Hera flared in rage and attempted to stand before being forced to her knees again. Rose's final threat was not meant as a power play. Rose had no intention of offending the two, but rather added the threat to make sure they did not escape.

After the proceeding, Rose exited the great hall and entered the courtyard. She took a look around; the faces of the people attacked by the hoard glowed in the light of bonfire. The bonfire was made of debris found in the city streets. The jagged shadows it cast were unnatural and would have been bone-chilling had they not been contrast to a much worse event.

The ominous faces all looked at Rose, staring at her, blaming her for all that had happened. They were lucky that the night was not too cold, but even so, the people of Great Neighbor huddled around the campfire draped in any cloth they could find. Their faces were blank with unspeakable horror.

Rose had lost many friends—her fellow guardsmen, her family, her little brother, and her husband. All the people of Great Neighbor looked to her now, furiously expecting for her to wake them up from the nightmare. Rose would not let a tear roll down her cheek.

So what if she had to sacrifice the few.

So what if she had to sacrifice the cowardly guards that would not have opened a gate while she faced down an army!

So what if she had to sacrifice herself!

Scar their hearts, sunder their flesh, she was going to kill every enemy warrior that crossed her path... like they had killed her husband.

***

Hera and Aaron slept restlessly the rest of the night. They had been forcefully guided to the barracks where they were given the beds farthest from the door. The barracks were made of smooth stone, and the building's ceiling was low to the ground. The taller members of the guard almost snagged their hair against it when walking. The beds were built into the floor and had hard mattresses placed on the slabs of stone. Each bed was four or five feet apart from the other. The stone building was long, spanning the entirety of the northern wall of the keep. Even with its immense size, the single barrack could not hold the entirety of the guard force and another slightly smaller variant of the building lined the southern courtyard.

Hera and Aaron tried their best to comfort each other while they went to sleep. They had few relations with the people on the island, but they still knew them and considered some of them friends, even if they were not as close to them as they were to each other. They did not know who had lived and who had died. Perhaps it was better that way. Perhaps they would rather not learn, just let the memory fade away. That's what they wanted for each other, for the memory to fade away. If Hera remembered, then Aaron could forget, and if Aaron remembered, then Hera could forget. Each held that thought in their minds.

Aaron's eyes darted open, quick as a bear trap would shut. A moment later, he heard Viner's voice holler down the barracks.

"GET UP!" The command was simple and well put.

A synchronized shuffling spread its way through the barracks like sap through a tree. One by one, each and every guard got out of bed. Many of them had not slept that night and were relieved to be aroused. Others wished to never wake up again.

The guards knew the drill better than Hera and Aaron. The army turned to the other wall to equip themselves in armor. They expertly equipped both weapon and sheath and were ready within moments. Most guards preferred a sword and a shield, but some would take greatswords or even axes and warhammers.

Hera and Aaron were unfamiliar with all of them. In fact, they were unsure if they were allowed to take a weapon at all. They waited until they had gotten a few odd looks before making a move toward the stands.

Hera would have been excited to be allowed to wear full guard armor on a day where she was not traumatized by a recent invasion. She often wore armor that looked similar to guards' armor, as to blend in with the abundance of guards that roamed Great Neighbor. She never dared wear true royal armor though. The guard would find any excuse to pin her to any crime, including impersonating a knight.

Now, she examined the armor in front of her and had no desire in the slightest to don it. Even so, she knew she needed protection and put on a set of half-plate. The only thing stopping her from putting on full-plate, besides not knowing how to strap it on, was that she wanted to have the option to run if the time came.

Aaron felt much the same way and followed her lead. He slipped into the chain gambeson that was curiously laid out for him at the foot of each bed. After strapping on the gambeson, he took a chest piece off the wall.

"Can you help me get this on, squire?" he jested.

Hera looked frowned at him, making absolutely sure she didn't need to state her disapproval. She stated it anyway.

"This isn't a good time to make jokes, Aaron."

"I'm nervous," Aaron sighed.

Hera complied and looped the cuirass over his shoulder from the left side. One side of the cuirass was already strapped together, forming a simple protection over the chest and upper back. Aaron took the honor of placing the chestplate over his head, but when he tried to get it through, it wouldn't fit. After a while of tussling and some minor arguing, they discovered that you were supposed to unstrap one full side and fit into it that way.

They unbuckled the right side, and Aaron slid his left arm through the cuirass. Hera fiddled with the buckle over the right shoulder for a while, but once she had it fastened, she was able to latch the two buckles under the arm and at the bottom of the chest with substantially less effort.

Aaron did the same for Hera, taking slightly longer to finish the job. Aaron noted his slow speed in his head, but Hera paid no mind to it. They were both able to strap on their shin guards by themselves. By the end of the whole ordeal, the two were uncomfortably familiar with buckles. But, even something as mundane as figuring out the complicated machinations of buckles provided a little glimmer of enjoyment into an otherwise desolate mood.

The small grins on their faces were immediately discarded as they raised their head to look around them. They had taken so long to adorn the half-plate armor that the other guards had already left the building. The only guard that remained was a guard that looked to be descended from Aerokite, attributed to her tanner skin, tighter eyes, and rounded features. She was standing near the door looking at them.

A greatsword hung over her back. It was sheathed in a scabbard particularly designed to help a weapon be drawn from the back. The scabbard had a large opening on the side perfect for easily sliding a greatsword into a draw while still keeping it firm on the back. A piece of leather adorned the opening, making sure the sheathing process was quick and easy. The back scabbard was of Ironforge design and allowed the greatsword to be hauled around easily without dragging against the ground or leaving a long tail. This was particularly helpful in Ironforge, where citizens would often carry around heavy weaponry for reasons few outside the province understood.

Her eyes were fixed on Hera and Aaron, nervously flicking between each of their faces. Her arms were crossed over the full uniform she wore. Her crossed arms covered the turtle shell insignia that embroidered her chestplate. The uniform itself was designed for action on a bulwark. Every part of her body was covered in silvery black steel. Besides her eyes, she stood unmoving. Her black hair fell around her shoulders, just the way she had woken up. To have long hair be loose was a danger, but perhaps she would tie it up later.

Hera started making her way across the room before awkwardly stopping at a weapon rack on her left. She had forgotten to take a sword. She reached out to grab a short blade while looking to the guard for confirmation. She made no movement. Slowly, Hera continued reaching for the sword. Her hand made contact with the hilt. The gladius had an inverted half circle guard with the open side facing toward the blade. The handle itself was tightly wrapped in linen.

With a quick screech of metal, she drew the sword, making sure that her face was as far away from the blade as she could manage. For a moment she just held the sword in front of her. She heard a similar screech come from behind her and turned to find Aaron grasping a sword in much the same way.

She looked around for a moment, realizing she was forgetting something. It dawned on her that she had failed to dawn a scabbard. She looked around a moment, holding the sword pointed up awkwardly. Her eyes scanned the floor and walls, locating a sheath on one of the unused armor racks. Hera moved to the armor rack, getting closer to the guard in the process.

Once Hera made it to the armor rack and started fidgeting with the scabbard, she heard a tight noise of defiance. She turned her head to look at the guard. The soldier was extending her hand out as if to place it on Hera's shoulder, though she was much too far away to do so. A look of blame was clearly painted on her face.

Hera let go of the scabbard and backed away slowly, red in the face. She thrust her hands in the air to show they were empty, before hitting her calf against the stone bed behind her. She was uninjured by the chink, but looked down anyway, to make sure that she had not knocked anything over.

When she looked back up, the guard was already rushing towards Hera. She had quite a ways to go but moved quickly. She was accustomed to her plate armor, a stark contrast to Hera and Aaron. The guard did not run, but her steps were long, and she was not short by any means. Her black hair crossed her shoulders and flowed behind her as she pushed forward through the barracks, passing two beds at a time. It was not long before the guard was upon them. But instead of stopping in front of Hera, she shoved past her to the other end of the room. Aaron scrambled to the side of one bed to get out of her way. The guard paid him no mind. With her back to them, she spoke.

Her voice was quiet but purposeful. "Your scabbard is over here." She pointed at Hera's bed, "Where you sleep."

She turned around and her gaze met Hera's. The soldier's eyes were red, but not quite watering. A frown struggled against the muscles of her jowls, trying its best not to form.

"That is Archibald's scabbard."

Hera followed the guard, keeping eye contact while she moved. The look on her face was that of distinguished mortification. She moved past Aaron, who looked as bewildered as she was.

While still looking at the guard, she picked up the sheath and strapped the scabbard around her waist and over her right shoulder. She clumsily felt for the belt clasp, and once she found it, she tightened the thin leather strap. Then, she backed away from the frowning guard, clumsily picked up her sword and tipped it into the sheath. She missed the first attempt and looked down to adjust accordingly. She fiddled the dangerous blade carefully into its place, twitching it up and down, trying to get it into the small sliver of an opening.

When she looked up, again the guard had started moving, this time to retake her post at the front door. Aaron followed behind Hera and took the sheath at the foot of his bed, making absolutely sure that it was the right one. He picked up a shield from an armor stand and nudged Hera on the arm.

"Here," he said.

Hera thanked him and strapped on the shield absentmindedly. If she was focused at the time, she would have been proud of how efficiently she put it on, but alas, she was not focused. With the shield on her arm and the guard up ahead, Hera walked to the door. The guard was already there, waiting. Hera awkwardly paused for her to go through the door before slipping through herself. Aaron followed behind into the courtyard.

The sun had risen to a cold day. The sky itself was tinted white in a way only the early hours of the morning could manage. The soft kiss of frost gently lingered on the tips of the finely cut grass that crawled its way against the stone flooring on the sides of the walls. Rays of light gleamed through white clouds. The rays were only visible because of the almost imperceivable fog that loomed over the island. Particles of dust caught the light before it fell gently on the grass.

Guards clad in armor stood in ranks before the recently appointed Guard Captain, Viner. They were formed in a tight grid, two steps apart from each other. Their armor faintly gleamed white in the cold morning air, polish betraying the scratches it was meant to cover. They were horrified to find that the King had failed to provide entrance into the keep to Great Neighbor's refugees. It seemed that the King's paranoia did not allow his own people into his castle.

Around the grid, the remaining citizens of Great Neighbor gathered, pressed to the walls of the keep. Those with blankets wore them as robes, having little better to do than watch the guards of Great Neighbor train. The crowd was eerily silent; only a hushed whisper could occasionally be heard but not distinguished.

Viner paced up and down the ranks of the troops, addressing their posture and stance, making meticulously sure that each and every militant was ready for duty. Hera could not distinguish which soldiers needed changing, but obviously Viner could.

Viner glanced from under his brow to the guard escorting Hera and Aaron. He looked down quickly and adjusted one last conscript before making his way toward her. He walked quickly across the field, keeping his eyes directly on the guard. Ten meters away, he addressed the woman.

"Calessa, well done keeping an eye on… these two," Viner hesitated mid-sentence before addressing either rouge.

"Yes, sir." Calessa saluted, placing her fists together.

"Aye… well, yes…" Viner scratched his neck awkwardly and cleared his throat. "Take your place, soldier. The King will address us soon. You two," he continued as he gestured weakly a little to the right of Hera and Aaron. He wouldn't make eye contact. "Stay where you are. Stay behind the group when we start moving. Got it?"

Aaron looked over to Hera, to watch her face look at his. They both looked confused, though they didn't know what they were confused about. The orders were clear, yet their response was caught in their throat.

Viner did not wait for the young adults to speak to him. In fact, he dreaded it. Quicker than he should have, he turned and started walking away. He had made an oath. What was that oath even worth if he was breaking it so quickly? He had promised that Hera and Aaron would live to be happy again. So far, his word didn't look like it meant much. Tears burned the giant man's eyes. He scrunched his eyes in an angry grimace of defiance. His veins bulged, he looked like and he felt like a snarling wolf, cornered with nothing else to lose. Viner was wrong. He had so much more to lose.

Rose took her position before the ranks of soldiers, eyeing them for weakness. She spread her stance, and placed her arms behind her back, daring any soldier to show sign of weakness while she watched over them. To anyone else, this would have been the most disciplined group of men and women they had ever seen, but to Rose, she saw only cowards that could not defend their home the first time.

The King walked out from behind her, swaying like a toddler just learning to move. The expression on his face matched the walk, like a combination of drunk and stupid. The purple cloak that went to the King's bare ankles drug the ground despite its shortness. Finally, after a tantalizing few moments of the King struggling to walk, he fell to the ground beside Rose's feet.

Rose looked down her nose at the King, pitying him and wondering if the royal bloodline was worth all the stock she put in it. Hopefully, the King's son in Goldenhill could live up to the wisdom of his father's earlier years, and not fall into his later habits. Rose nervously slid her foot away from the King, changing her stance to be taller.

"Soldiers!" she greeted the guards. "As you are aware, the esteemed Captain of the Guard Viner will be guiding your training today. Before that, however, I must inform you of the situation."

She looked around menacingly. It was impressive that she was able to look so angry without a snarl. Her eyes stayed wide despite the sun's rise and her mouth only curved downward at an almost imperceptible angle, something that could be chalked up to the shape of her face. When she moved her mouth to speak, it was deliberate and her lips closed fully after each sentence.

"Word is being spread, as we speak, of our movement to retake our citizens who were captured in the recent invasion. The King has deemed the name of the opposing army…"

Rose trailed off and sighed. Her posture dipped for a moment, as she shook her head in disappointment. The King scowled up at her and mouthed something to her in an angry tone that accentuated the letters k, i, n, and g in that order.

"Dwarfs," Rose said looking back up.

The soldiers in the line did little more than shift, but Hera and Aaron looked to each other uneasily, wondering how Rose or the King had found out what Calm had told them. That was one less bargaining chip.

Rose continued after a short pause, "I know you snicker."

Calessa second-guessed whether any soldiers had snickered without her noticing. To her, it looked like the most that happened was the adjusting of arms.

"But this menace is something that we all must train for," Rose finished.

Rose looked around meaningfully at all the guards making sure none defied her. The soldiers had not and did not intend to disrespect Rose in any way. If they were surprised that the King and Rose seemed to think that they were attacked by fairy-tale creatures, they did not show it.

"Along with our enemy's name, we are attempting to grow the ranks of our guard. Any able-bodied man or woman over the age of fifteen and under the age of sixty-six will be expected to volunteer. After careful consideration of the punishment for not volunteering, we have established that there is, in fact, none."

From the back of the army, Viner grumbled random gibberish in distaste. He did not like the way that Rose had phrased the news. Even though she was not directly drafting people, Viner still knew that Rose would sow as much social pressure into volunteering as she could.

"We already have two new volunteers." Rose actually smiled while saying these words. "Tython, age twenty-four, ambassador of Dimfir, has volunteered his support on behalf of Dimfir."

The ambassador for Dimfir nervously emerged from the sidelines of the courtyard. He had been standing in the shade of the wall, watching the procession like many of the residents of Great Neighbor. He took short strides, and on top of that, he was short. These two factors, combined with the long distance, made the time it took for him to file into rank drag on to awkwardness.

Rose's face fell from a smile into a slight frown while watching the short man take his time to get to her side. Tython did not notice the gesture and looked more preoccupied with examining the ground. Though the man was short, he was not nearly as short as the dwarves that had attacked Great Neighbor the night before. Tython was about five and a half feet from head to toe. To add to the dissimilarity, Tython was not nearly as hairy as the dwarves, for though he had shoulder-length black ringlets, his hair was quite kempt and his face clean-shaven.

He wore the clothing that Hera and Aaron had been intending to steal. A feathered hat sat tightly on top of his head, the plumage bouncing delicately with each step. The pants he wore sagged low to the ground and brushed lightly against his knees as he walked. The shoulders of his shirt puffed up like a pillow, making his arms look broader than they were. The palette of his clothing was primarily a well-dyed vibrant green and the light tan of a rabbit's hide. He looked silly in comparison to the normal clothing that the rest of Great Neighbor chose to wear. Tython had not noticed the absurdity of his clothing, and if he had, he chose not to care.

Once he got to Rose, Tython smiled nervously up at her. She was only an inch or two taller than him, but it felt like a mountain of difference. He had stopped a good three feet away. Rose beaconed for Tython to get closer. Tython inched forward a step. Rose's cheek spasmed for a nano second. She beckoned again. Tython glanced behind him, as if she was gesturing to someone that he had not noticed breathing down his neck. In his opinion, he was already close enough and to get any closer would be unusual, at least in Dimfir.

Rose frowned slightly, an expression that almost looked human on her otherwise stone-cold face. She took one large step toward Tython, making Tython jump just the slightest. She placed her hand on his shoulder, and her expression snapped back to the warm smile that she had been holding before Tython had irritated her.

"Tython is familiar with the bow, and his marksmanship can be easily applied to martial combat, at least if things get out of hand." She smiled proudly down at him as if she had known him for years and this was his moment to shine. Tython looked up and returned the smile half-heartedly. He had noticeable gaps between his teeth. "He killed more dwarfs than some guards…"

The nuance of her statement was clear. Rose was calling shame upon guards who had failed to defend the city as well as a hunter from Dimfir. The soldiers were starting to tire of the abusive mental tactics that she had been employing recently. In the past, Rose had refrained from over-decorating the achievements of her troops, but she had always stressed more on duty than on failure. By now, the veteran guardsman had picked up on her distaste towards the way they had handled the attack. Rose needed someone to blame; this time it was them.

Rose made an imperceptible motion to Viner who then walked up to greet Tython. Brief words were exchanged, and Viner placed his hand on Tython's back. He guided him to his spot in the training grid some few rows down. Tython was practically in place before Rose started speaking again.

"The second civilian who has already signed up to join our ranks is named Henry."

Viner's back straightened. All that anyone could see was the back of his head, just the same way it had been a moment ago. A slight tilt from his head signaled his beginning turn. He pivoted, taking several steps, lumbering like a moose. The spear on his back looked far more dangerous now.

Chapter 8
Cracks In Composure

"Soldier in training and son to former Captain of the Guard Fredrick…"

Viner looked dead in Rose's face, and Rose did all she could to not address him.

"Fairly far along in his trai—"

"No," Viner snarled.

Rose tried to continue, "Adequate—"

"NO!" Viner's snarl turned to a growl, audible from across the entire courtyard.

Rose looked around, a tone of defeat ringing in her eyes. She set her mouth and started swiftly jogging to Viner. Seeing her coming, Viner took long steps in her direction, moving just as quickly towards her. His jaw was set in an irritated clench.

Rose had already been hissing at him for a while before she was close enough for him to hear. "…Need this Viner. The boy is a fighter; he needs to avenge his father. If you can't see—"

"The boy is under my care and shall not go to war." Viner didn't bother whispering.

"He is not under your *care*. He is of an age to decide for himself. Legally speaking, you have no power over him."

Viner pointed to the sky as if that was his authority. "The boy is fifteen." He pointed back to the ground. "He cannot fight."

"He can fight—"

"NO! He—"

"Listen to me!"

Viner looked around and licked his teeth angrily. He fixed his neck which had been arched down to reach Rose's level.

Viner rested his gauntlets on the metal belt he wore and allowed Rose to speak.

"The boy has already signed up; I have already announced it," Rose stressed. "If we go back now, we will be seen as cowards. Some guards may even resign."

She stopped to look meaningfully at Viner. "But, if he joins now, we will have more volunteers, volunteers Viner! His bravery will give us the courage we need to save our people. We won't have to draft anyone. Hell, I bet we'll save some lives!"

Viner flailed around angrily, not buying what she said for a moment. "I have a responsibility to protect him, Rose. Trading lives... It never ends well."

At that moment, the boy in question approached. Henry was the son of Fredrick, former Captain of the Guard. He was fully aware of his father's death in battle and had grieved solemnly. He had lost his mother when he was born and was now under the care of Viner. He had not slept the previous night, nor had he spoken to Viner. He had stayed awake all night, thinking about the invasion. Thinking about how he wished he could have saved his father's life, if only he was strong and brave enough.

Now he stood before them, lines under his eyes, his sandy hair covered in salt for some unexplained reason. His small frame did not fit well with the armor he wore, the pieces clinking together awkwardly on the skinny boy. A shield strapped to his left arm and a rapier ready in its scabbard, Henry was armed, but perhaps not dangerous.

"Uncle," Henry said. "I have to do this."

Viner's expression softened, looking down at the sad boy. The armor-clad soldier did not hesitate to fall to one knee to greet his nephew. The gesture was unnecessary as the boy was taller than Tython, but Viner did it still. The

Captain of the Guard grasped desperately at the sleeves of the young soldier.

"No," Viner bellowed. "You can't, boy. You will die." His voice cracked on the word die, and his eyes started to fill with tears of sorrow.

"I have to," Henry insisted. "For my dad."

"Who put that in your head boy?" Viner insisted.

Henry looked offended. "No one did."

"Were you talking to Rose last night? I should have been with you, boy, I should have looked for you," Viner pleaded still on his knees.

"Rose didn't tell me anything about joining the guard, Viner."

Viner looked at Rose, "But you spoke to her?"

"We talked," Henry admitted.

Viner darted his hand to Rose's gauntlet. Rose pulled back her hand in surprise.

"You... you were my friend. How could you do this to me?" Viner was openly crying now, and his voice showed it.

He turned again to Henry and grasped at the young boy's face, scratching the bare flesh with his metal-covered fingers and palm.

"Don't do this... Henry." The captain chewed on the words in his mouth.

Henry closed his eyes in resolve. At that moment, Viner and Rose realized that Henry had been weeping silently, too. His blue tears rolled down Viner's gauntlet leaving a trail of silver across the dust.

"For my Father. It's what he would have done," Henry finally said.

***

Viner alone marched out of the castle, war paint scratched across his face. He had used his own gauntlets to bleed red streaks across his tear-stricken skin. A buckler shield grasped in the left hand and a long spear lazily clutched in the right, Viner ventured alone into the ruined Great Neighbor Square, leaving a lower-ranked trooper to teach the basics of being a soldier to the four volunteers.

They say that the enraged man found and slaughtered more than a dozen dwarves that had been left over from the invasion. They say that he did not hesitate, that as soon as he heard a sound, he would turn and quickly impale the creature that made it, be it rabbit or dwarf. The only thing he would not kill on sight were the men and women he rescued from the wreckage.

A bard named Dandilion and a scribe named Gentele were two of the rescued. The two grateful citizens wrote down the adventures of Viner. Thanks to their flowered words, the tale would go down in history as a brave action committed before an even braver quest. The story is incredibly well written, a marvel never before seen. When the story is performed on a stage as it is meant to be, it is filled with some of the best music that has ever graced the world, counting all three mortal paradoxes. The songs are laden with genius lyrics that any single person would kill to hear just once.

In truth, the bard and scribe cleaned their rust with acid. Viner's attack on the dwarves was nothing less than ruthless, bloody, and filled with rage. The tears he shed over the fear of losing his nephew mingled with the blood on his cheeks. He cried red and spit blood with every stab of his spear. If any dwarf had been lucky enough to escape his onslaught, they would have returned with news of a devil, more evil than any force in the world, even Horror itself.

They would have told how the tevnal-like man hunted down and killed any dwarf in his path with ruthless efficiency.

***

Hera and Aaron awkwardly tried to keep to the back of the group, following the orders laid out by the selected guard. The guard Viner had chosen to lead the training was tall and thin and didn't bother introducing himself. His hair was cut to be only an inch off his scalp and a thick scar ran through it. Despite the scar, the face of the guard was delicate and his expression confused.

"Alright," the guard started awkwardly.

He sighed, exasperated, and looked around with his arms up. He had been ushered in front of the entire guard force without really knowing what was happening.

"I don't know what the plan was..." he stuttered and flushed.

"We have a week," cried a shrill voice.

Most of the guards had forgotten they were in the presence of royalty. The King was small in stature with a forgettable demeanor, possessed with the curse of a beggar in that he was hardly noticeable.

"In that time, I will have figured out how to send us to the underworld," the King mused, mainly to himself.

Aaron's Adam's apple dropped to his stomach. Hera's mouth turned dry. Even Rose looked mildly surprised. This news was enough to cause uproar in the ranks of the guards who were not close enough to be silenced by Rose's death stare. A few guards stepped back, a few forward, and all of them stamped their feet in surprise. Gasps were followed by murmurs which were followed by shouts and proceeded by murmurs again.

"COWARDS!"

A woman's voice climbed shrill above the shouts.

"BLOODY COWARDS!" the voice cried again.

A shocked hush matted itself like fog on the soldiers. Suddenly Aaron's shoulders ached, and Hera was aware of just how hungry she was. Sheepishly, guards started to get back to their proper place in the square.

Rose had drawn her greatsword from the scabbard on her back. She hunched over, not unlike the dwarves that had attacked Great Neighbor. Saliva dripped from her teeth like a sneering dog. The greatsword almost touched the ground, but Rose's clenched fist grasped the large weapon strongly. This greatsword had two deadly sides, but the side now facing the ground was larger and shaped more like a cleaver, its purpose much the same.

It was evident that the outburst was hers. She closed her eyes and mouth and in one graceful motion was fully straight again, her legs together, her poise tall. She raised her sword outstretched forward to point at the guards in a threat. She opened her eyes and regained her composure, though her hair still tugged against the bun she had placed it in that morning. She reset her face, again taking on her default deadpan stare.

"Dwarfs live in caves. The underworld is a network of caves, i.e., the dwarfs... live... there!" She spoke audibly but with the tone of an enraged whisper, making certain that the guards felt stupid.

The guards snapped their heads straight, looking at the guard standing in front of them. None of them wanted to make eye contact with Rose. Hera and Aaron were late to the memo and still stared at Rose.

Rose took long strides in the direction of the guard placed in charge of training. She whispered something to him and pointed with her still-drawn sword. The guard flinched when she moved the cleaver and nodded when she gave orders. Rose looked surprisingly gentle handling the guard, even after her enraged outburst.

After several minutes of Rose talking to the short-haired man and him occasionally speaking up to ask questions, Rose made her way past the ranks of guards. The only ones who watched her move were Hera and Aaron. For a brief moment, Rose saw them. She showed no recognition on her face. Not in her stare. Not in the line of her mouth. But she saw them and she knew them. Naive champions.

"Alright," the lead guard repeated. "We are going to split into two groups. The first group will be guards with more than two years of experience. They will stay here. The second group will follow me. At this time, any volunteers should meet us."

The slender lead guard made a move to his left. He looked confident in his movement, which was a drastic change from his demeanor a moment before. He stopped mid-stride to turn his neck and address the crowd again.

"Oh, and group one, repeat yesterday's morning training three times, focus on strength. We aren't doing anything complicated until Viner gets back."

With that, he led group two a few meters over, leaving ample space between the quadrants but at a distance where the soldiers could still see each other clearly. The second group was much smaller, and it included Aaron, Hera, Tython, Henry, and a little fewer than one hundred extra citizens that had joined after hearing Rose's speech.

"Alright," the lead guard repeated. "This is group two. That means that while group one trains for strength, we will be building endurance, dexterity, and tactics. A sword and shield will be given to people that know how to use them, and a spear or longbow to people who don't. Tython will be using his shortbow and sharpshooting from the front of the ranger battalion, along with a few other soldiers. The rest of you will be safely positioned in the back, shooting volleys of arrows. You will be taught how to shoot long range so that it is safe for our soldiers in the front. After that, you will be taught how to use a shortsword in case of emergency."

The lead guard split them up into several groups, the smallest being Tython's group with no more than a dozen people, and the largest being the archers. Hera and Aaron made their way to join the archers, leaving behind the young men who had gotten it in their heads that they knew how to wield a sword and shield. Some of them, like Henry and his fellow trainees, were correct, but most looked like they didn't know what they were getting into. Aaron and Hera timidly walked to join the archers, only to be stopped by the lead guard.

"Excuse me," he said. "You will be joining the melee battalion." With his hands, he ushered toward Henry.

Hera opened her mouth aghast. "We don't know how to use a sword and shield."

The lead guard paused and made a hesitant noise from the back of his throat. "That's not for me to say, but I have different information straight from The Mouth of the King."

When referring to the mouth of the King, more often than not, the guards were actually talking about Rose. Rose was, in some respects, equal to the King and trusted to interpret his word. This differed from the Captain of the Guard who is trusted to carry out his word, in the best way they saw fit. The three worked in unison—The King, The Hand of the King, and The Mouth of the King. "And you're already holding a shield," he added.

Hera stamped her foot into the soft ground, indenting the grass slightly and brushing off the melting frost. She struggled to let loose the strap of the shield on her arm and almost blinded Aaron with the glint of the smooth metal.

"That is an outrage; we already don't want to be here!" She protested while trying to unlatch the shield from her arm.

She was finally able to unfasten the buckler and throw it to the ground in a childish act of protest. Aaron looked around exasperated as color drained from his pink face, turning his complexion as snowy as the frost that adorned the grass. The lead guard tried in vain to calm the two down. It was fruitless; Hera and Aaron were desperately afraid.

Rose watched on from the wall. Her dark brown eyes were glossed over black while gazing not just at an army, but at *her* army and *its* future. The windswept red strands of hair were becoming increasingly loose from her constricting bun. Her arms were crossed behind her back, and her lips were pursed just as tightly. She stood alone on the top of the wall, critiquing the army she intended to raise as her own.

She caught a glimpse of Hera and Aaron's startled expressions. She would not have noticed had Hera not stamped her foot and thrown down her shield and Aaron not looked up at the sky like the clouds would take pity on him.

An armored man placed his hand on her shoulder. He towered over her like a god. The bullish face contorted into an animal grin—one that you couldn't be sure was real or just the shape of the hair that one could interpret as a human face. Rose's frown was dominated by his grin. When she recalled the event, she struggled to remember if she grinned back.

***

The next day, Hera and Aaron were sore from their workout. Rose's orders were very clear to the lead guard.

The second legion that Hera and Aaron were assigned to would not be given strength training and instead focus on building balance, dexterity, cunning, and discipline. If they had instead focused on the harsh workout routine that was imposed on battalion one, then the army would be weakened before they could build up any real power.

Despite the softer and less physically taxing form of training, Hera and Aaron were still incredibly sore and mentally drained. The other soldiers had not hesitated to point out their mistakes, and the lead guard seemed to grow more of a backbone to yell at those placed under his command as the long day went on.

They had gorged on food to make certain they were getting enough energy, but the food they had eaten was less than gourmet. Henry wasn't too bad. He was a lot more intelligent than the average conscript. Though he said little to Hera and Aaron, the little he did say was kind. It was nice someone had gone out of their way to talk to them. Of course, Hera and Aaron had been difficult to split up. Just like they had lived their lives for the past few years, they trained as best of friends and stuck together whenever they could—much to the dislike of the lead guard.

Viner returned from his adventure to reclaim Great Neighbor a short while before sundown. With him were a handful of citizens, two of whom volunteered to enact their revenge on the dwarves and thus had blood on their hands that dimly reflected the blood that covered Viner. Despite their advanced keenness on the art of war, these blood thirsty civilians-turned-soldiers were placed in the volley battalion along with most of the less-trained army personnel.

With his return, Viner proceeded with the training, demoting the lead guard that had been taking his place the day before. Viner was much more comfortable with his teachings. He stood before the soldiers, arms crossed, barking orders and adjusting standing position, just as he had at the beginning of the previous day. And similar to the day before, the entire guard force was in line, experiencing the chill. The day was colder than the previous, and the gates of the keep had yet to open to bring warmth to its people.

Tython was a friendly type. As is often the case with friendly types, they can, in circumstances, be chatter birds. Tython was no different and sought to use his power of speech to try and lighten the mood. There was one issue— The Hand of the King. Viner didn't look kindly to anyone who chose to speak during his training. In fact, Viner had directly forbidden it. But, Tython considered his message important. What was more important than addressing the weather?

"Pretty cold out today."

Henry looked nervously in Tython's direction. It was unusual that someone dared speak audibly. Viner craned his head up and his eyes narrowed.

"There is an old saying in Dimfir," Tython said. "South of the Half-Thawed Mountain Range, it is winter, but north of the Half-Thawed Mountain, it is vetur. In Ike, vetur is just a word for winter, but in Icebreaker, winter is much worse than the rest of the Northern Kingdom."

Icebreaker is one of the five provinces of the Northern Kingdom. Similar to Great Neighbor, Icebreaker tries to separate itself from the capital. This is made easier by the Half-Thawed Mountain Range, a long mountain range spanning from the east coast of the Northern Kingdom to the west. The northern side is Icebreaker land, and it is a desolate lake-filled tundra inhabited by nomads who speak a language called Ike.

"Wanna say that louder, wood fairy?" Viner yelled from across the grounds.

"Eh-" Tython stuttered. "South of the Half-Thawed Mountain Range, it is winter, but north of the Half-Thawed Mountain, it is vetur!" Tython repeated, this time louder.

"I can't hear your puny elf voice, tree hugger!" Viner said.

"South of the half-thawed mountain range… is, is winter, but… north of the, north of the south thawed… mountain range is-is vetur!" Tython was so focused on yelling as loudly as he could, he forgot some of what he meant to say.

"South of the south of the south-what now!" Viner was relentless in his mockery.

Viner weaved through the masses of troops, intent on getting to Tython. He shoved aside any soldier he deemed in his way, paying no heed to whether they were supposed to be there or not. Grass was caught in his greaves and tugged from the ground like weeds. Once Viner reached Tython, he grabbed him by the ear and pulled the short man painfully up to his own mouth. Viner didn't completely pull Tython off the ground, but he stretched the emissary to a height he did not know he could reach.

Viner bent to whisper into his ear, "Thank you, the troops needed that."

The large man relinquished his hold on the much smaller Tython. The guard captain wiped himself down like he was covered in dust. Then, Viner straightened Tython's plume and, quickly as a hare, jabbed the soldier's chin to the sky, his feet together, his back straight, and his arms to the side.

A day passed under Viner's instruction, leaving Hera and Aaron more exhausted than they had been the previous day. In fact, Viner made the previous day look easy. His training method was so much more brutal and confident. Hera and Aaron wanted to throw up afterwards. After lunch, Hera did. They wouldn't have gone on, had they the choice. They hadn't the choice.

It was late evening; the sun would go down in an hour. The guards were eating dinner in the courtyard as they had done the previous day. Hera and Aaron were bright red from sunburn, and most of the drafted citizens were as well. Sweat salted their faces. They felt almost as dried up as the jerky they ate that day. Almost.

Hera and Aaron had taken a seat away from the crowd. Without chairs to sit in, they sat cross-legged in the grass getting themselves covered in silt. The walls of the castle made a sunset far less beautiful than it was on the ocean's horizon. They would have preferred there be no sundown at all. What everyone in Great Neighbor really wanted was to be let into the keep. Many of the citizens of Great Neighbor returned to their homes that night. It was safe now that Viner had dispatched the remaining dwarves. But still, many more individuals had lost their homes to fires and rampaging. And those that were being trained in the military didn't exactly have the option to go home.

"It's a shame, really. The sun sets on the sea, and we are here unable to see it," Aaron said.

Hera nodded her head, but she didn't have the strength to say anything at that moment. They sat in silence for a while. One could say they were enjoying each other's company, but enjoyment wasn't the word. It had been a while since they had been able to relax. Even longer since they had bothered thinking about twilight. But here they were, silent and wishing they could have their old lives back.

"You remember the first time we tried to get into the keep?" Aaron asked.

Hera nodded the same way she had a moment ago. Aaron knew what she meant.

"We were too scared to go through the front," he said. "So—"

"So we swam," Hera finished.

"My worst idea." Aaron chuckled.

Hera gave him a bemused look. "No, it was *my* worst idea."

"Are you going to argue about who has worse ideas?"

Hera grinned and broke eye contact. She looked away from Aaron, but not looking at anything in particular.

"You know," she said. "What's stopping us from climbing that wall?"

Aaron looked up the cracked wall. It wasn't the smoothest surface in Great Neighbor. He had climbed worse, that was sure. But every muscle of his was worn and weak, he doubted he could even if he wanted to.

"Everything."

Hera looked at Aaron's face again. She pursed her lips.

"I don't think everything matters."

"You just threw up a second ago. How do you expect to have enough energy to climb a wall now?"

Aaron looked over his shoulder and all around himself. "Also, there are people here. Looking at us."

"What will they do? What will they take? It's our foot against stone."

"You don't have the strength."

"I don't need strength," Hera puffed.

She got to her feet shakily. Her bones felt as if they were about to crack under her own weight. But there was something driving her forward, something she couldn't place. She didn't need strength.

"But I need to see the sun again."

Aaron grabbed her wrist with his hand. Hera looked back at him, and he realized that he was standing. She moved her arm forward and pushed his hand toward the wall. They were a few steps away, so Aaron could have stopped her if he wanted.

"You need to see the sun?"

"Before it's gone."

Hera planted her foot firmly on a good hold near the bottom of the wall. It didn't give her much leverage to move upward, but it saved energy. She lifted herself so that she was a few inches off the ground and used the stone as support. Aaron followed with a similar strategy. The next step Hera took was much higher so that she didn't have to rely on her tired arms to get up the wall. Her grip wasn't shot, but she wasn't particularly healthy.

A pair of citizens who were laying on the floor across the keep looked up and watched the two scale the wall. They were bundled up in a heap of blankets. Blankets had become abundant after some of the houses were repopulated and these citizens were evidently keen on making use of that oversupply. It was unusual to see two young members of the army climbing a random wall, but who were they to stop them?

"Who are you?" a voice asked.

Each citizen in the bundle of blankets almost believed they were hearing a voice from inside their head until the other reacted. But when they looked behind them they saw greasy black hair and yellowed teeth bearing down on them.

Aaron was halfway up the wall when his fingers slipped on a stone. The outer layers of his skin rubbed open, and a shy speck of blood started to peak out. Aaron cried out, and Hera looked down to see him lazily try to regain his balance. With the ache of his muscles, he was clumsy and couldn't react as fast as he usually would. But he hadn't been in a spot where he was prone to fall and was able to just barely get his hand back to another rock.

"Are you going alright?" Hera called down.

Aaron had to think for a second. This was stupid. It wasn't a long fall, but he could still die if he fell wrong. No responsible person would ever do this for something so trivial. But after all, was it so trivial? He looked up at Hera and the sky behind her. The light was retreating; he hadn't much time.

"It'll take more than that to get me to fall off this rock!"

He looked back down behind him and thought of why he was here and what had happened to his home. He looked at the disapproving face of one of the guards. They were his people, and they had been robbed of the world they lived in by some made up heresy. He looked back up to Hera.

"You're seeing that sunset, and I'm seeing it with you. It is our sun and our shore, and we are going to watch it go."

Hera smiled back at him, "Alright."

He daringly put his leg up as high as it could go. He moved his uninjured hand up and firmly grasped a handhold. He tested the hold and then heaved himself up with his leg and pushed forward. After a while of vigorous climbing, he was beside Hera. They reached the top at the same time and pulled themselves over.

As their faces looked across the sea, they saw the second half of the sun start to fall below the waves.

Aaron and Hera didn't dare take their eyes off the sun while it sank ever lower as if it was diving into the water. Only their heads peaked over the outer wall, but it was enough. Finally, the sun was consumed by the ocean's glitter.

"We need to get out of here," Aaron said.

"It might be fun," he added. "Just us and the sea!"

Chapter 9
A Hazy Recollection

A ferry is an unfit vessel in which to brave crashing waves, so it was always risky to send one out twenty miles to the mainland. Regardless, the waters in which this ferry were ordained to tread were Witshore's waters to the west of the once great Northern Kingdom. Because they were Witshore's waters, the crests of the waves were gentler. Witshore owed much to the sand shelf that spread for miles around the Layden peninsula. The famous reef provided the unique tropical biosphere that made Witshore's fish famous, and the shallow waters were good for smooth sailing. The only downside was that larger vessels struggled to avoid the seafloor abrading their hulls.

The sting of the recent invasion was starting to feel like a dream. Perhaps it was because Hera and Aaron dreamt of it that night. Torrents of dwarves leaking into the city like water crashing out of a broken dam. Every time Hera and Aaron conjured it in their heads, which they seldom did, they would be unable to remember all the atrocities of the day at any given time. It wasn't because they had forgotten them. No, it was because there were too many horrible catastrophes to count. Too many stories they had heard. And far more that they hadn't.

The nightmares that pestered the living nightmare battled for wakefulness while Aaron and Hera's enfeebled bodies battled for sleep. In the end, the bodily necessity of sleep won out over the fear of the mind, leading Hera and Aaron into the third day of their training.

Though they knew that Viner was not a bad man, they could not help but dislike him. He had viciously opposed them as thieves for the last four years they had been in

Great Neighbor, and now, under his command, he was a strict teacher. But, oddly enough, they rarely recognized his wrath first-hand. Viner seemed to avoid addressing them in any situation, even when unsteady during battalion two's balance exercises. During these balance exercises, Viner would try his best to unnerve the soldiers while they attempted to balance on one leg. The exercises were effective for teaching both humility and the virtue of being surefooted.

Troops were starting to notice the dissonance, and during lunch that evening, they planned to confront Hera and Aaron about it. Hera and Aaron were the subjects of much gossip, as they were the only soldiers not there by choice. Some soldiers even thought of them as cowardly for that.

Rose had the cruel tactic of creating a label of disloyal cowardice on any citizen who did not enroll in the military. The social pressure was effective in coercing more and more recruits into what Viner saw as a death march. Young and easily pressured men and women, mainly boys under the age of twenty-four, joined the ranks of the military rapidly. As a byproduct, those who did not join willingly, like Hera and Aaron, were scorned. Unfortunately for Hera and Aaron, there was no one else like them to scorn.

That day, the castle had finally opened to citizens, so they would no longer be forced to sleep outside or in storage rooms along the walls. As soon as the citizens stepped foot in the castle, it became evident why it had been closed for so long. All valuables that the King owned, including the books that usually scattered the creaky oaken floor, had been removed. Evidently, the paranoid little man was afraid of losing his valuables to his citizens.

The only citizens remaining in the walls were those whose houses were either destroyed or who had joined the military. Or both. The rest had returned to their homestead on the residential island and continued their lives. At least, they continued their lives as much as they could, circumstances being as dreary as they were.

The banquet hall was the first room inside the grand door that led into the keep, and beyond that was the throne room. The throne room was connected to the banquet hall and seemed almost like a small closet that had been added as an after-thought. The ceiling of the throne room was lower, and it spanned only half the width of the dining room. The two rooms did not transition well into each other. The walls of both were barren and void of any color other than brownish gray.

Inside the banquet hall were many grand tables pressed end-to-end to form four long rows. Some tables were slightly taller and some slightly wider. The tables were spotless and of the same general shape and color, but no amount of fuss could hide the fact that they were not meant to be put together. Alongside the tables were equally mis-matched benches and chairs.

The tables were naked of drapery, but overall devoid of stains. Each place was set with a very plain plate and fork made from either iron or copper. There were no knives or spoons in sight, and the more ornate fine silver had been swept away and hidden by the paranoid King.

Most of the guard was grateful to be let inside and saw it as a privilege. Much to the King's dislike, Viner had been pulling his teeth out trying to convince the King to let the troops into the castle. With the half-hearted help of Rose, Viner was finally able to secure his troops a small moment of comfort.

Hera and Aaron knew full well that they should have been let inside the castle sooner. What was the keep for if not to house its people in an emergency? Better late than never. Now they finally had shelter from the brutal sun. It was true that the barracks had the capability of providing that shelter, but the dining hall was much more comfortable.

One of the tables already had food lined on it—not a feast, but better than what they had been eating for the last three days. Among the food was a soup that consisted of what looked like potatoes and past ripe apples. The beef jerky and mysterious porridge they had eaten the two previous days still perched menacingly in their respective serving bowls.

The guards did not hesitate to make a move on the tables, attacking them with more vigor than they had with any of their wartime simulations. If the apples were practice dummies with buckets on their heads, Viner would have been proud and Rose may have stopped sulking for a moment. Despite their unified assault, the marching order was in disarray. The excited soldiers shoved past each other, taking handfuls of edibles to shove forcefully into their mouths.

Hera and Aaron were more timid than most, and let the torrent of people slide roughly past them. Tython was trying his best to be polite and apologized to anyone who rudely shoved him aside. Calessa stood completely still, seemingly shocked at the wave of people that rushed past her. Henry just let himself get carried by the crowd, and he was one of the first people to reach the food. Henry didn't have to sacrifice much dignity to quickly acquire a spot at the table, a great feat when put in the pugnacious context of the other top contenders.

Hera and Aaron looked around for an available plate to grab but found that almost every seat had been taken and every plate equally occupied. They approached the food table without a plate, just as some of the first people to enter the hall had done, but they had no intention of balancing a plate's portion of cabbage, apples, and bread in their hands.

The great hall proved to be incapable of housing the number of troops on hand. There were no less than double the amount of people than plates. If left to his own devices, the King may have made this mistake, but Rose was well acquainted with the number of troops she had under her and Viner's command.

"Excuse me," Hera said politely. "Where are we supposed to sit?"

The jolly-looking cook they had chosen to approach gave them a huge smile, crinkling the brow that already overarched her eyes.

"If you take the door behind me, dear, and cross the hallway six rooms down, you will find another cafeteria," she said smiling sweetly.

The cook hunched down to reach under the table and took out a large bundle of plates in her arms. Most people would be unable to carry the huge stack, but she made it look easy. The clinking of iron was more like a gentle lullaby than the creaking of a tower about to fall.

Rose had commissioned two other far more private dining rooms to be available. These rooms were far less grand and more suited to formal discussion than revelry, but the rooms would do well for the need that had arisen. Hera and Aaron, with plates full of food in their hands, took the liberty of leading the way to one of these rooms. A handful of guards and citizens-turned-soldiers followed behind, including Calessa.

The caravan walked down a hallway to the right of the banquet hall. It was dark and almost damp. The hallway was lit by three rickety chandeliers that hung from the tall ceiling. The floorboards creaked under the carpet that made the soggy wood look more appealing in comparison. The carpet was moth-eaten and faded from its long ago beautiful crimson hue.

"Why is it so dark here?" Aaron asked.

"Those chandeliers look expensive; maybe they were cutting costs," Hera guessed.

"On light? I'm not a big fan of the dark."

"You're a thief that's afraid of the dark," Hera teased.

Aaron was not flustered. "You don't really need the room to be all that dark if no one is in it. Besides, I'm not afraid of the dark; it's just ugly."

They took a sharp turn through the next door on the right. Aaron pressed Hera into the frame more than she would have liked.

This makeshift dining room was darker than the great hall and shared the same general feel and decor as the hallway. The tables, of which there were six, were circular and more similar to each other than those in the great hall. They were each made of dark wood, and smooth shapes were bent in and out of the general frame of the woodworking to create a far more natural and beautiful set of tables. Though they were beautiful in shape, they were stained in many places and scarred in others.

The roof was lined with cobwebs that strung from the rafters. It appeared that instead of creating two layers of wood—one for the ceiling and one for the floor above—the wise architects of Great Neighbor Keep decided that the floor and the ceiling could be one and the same. To avoid light from escaping either room, the ceiling boards were tightly spaced. Either the design mastermind's genius plan had worked like a charm or the room above them was unlit.

Aaron and Hera stopped just inside the door frame, deciding where to sit. The light rustling of troops following them convinced them to pick quickly. They moved to the end of the room—not quite in the corner, but fairly out of the way. An entourage of troops followed them, each carrying an iron plate, filled primarily with fruits and vegetables. Those carrying stews were left with little room for more in their hands. Some of those soldiers decided to dip a loaf of bread in their stew—both to carry more food and add a little flavor. Whether the stew or the bread was more flavorful was soon to be discovered.

Calessa was not the first troop to enter the room, but she was not the last either. Most of the guards that entered were either more disciplined or more shy than the troops that were driven by their stomachs. This was not to say that they were any less mean, however. Many of them suffered from being insufferable. Hera and Aaron did not know if Calessa was the same.

Hera and Aaron didn't care about whose bread was in whose stew and set their own plates down at the table. Whether to Hera and Aaron's chagrin or to their levity, Calessa chose to sit at the same table as them. Calessa had approached the table without looking at either of them. She kept her head down, fixated on the bench that was pushed up against the circular table. She placed her food on the table at the same time she sat down, making her look a little unbalanced. Her hair draped around her face, and the curtain of hair split down in the middle, revealing her lidded eyes looking down at the bowl of stew cupped in her hands.

Hera and Aaron were not sure what to think about Calessa choosing to sit with them. None of the other tables were full, but then again, none of them were empty either. They were not sure if they liked Calessa, but she was one of the few guards they actually knew.

Uncharacteristically, Calessa spoke without being addressed. "What are your names again?"

"Aaron," he blurted.

"Hera," she said much more hesitantly.

Calessa took a quick sip of her soup and nodded in acknowledgment. She made a noise that could have been attributed to enjoyment of the soup, but the soup was less than a delicacy, so that was unlikely.

"I am Calessa."

All three of the soldiers sat in silence, something that made Aaron uncomfortable. The silence stretched on for thirty heartbeats before someone spoke again.

"How did you two meet?" Calessa finally asked, breaking the silence.

Aaron couldn't help but grin. Hera rolled her eyes but didn't stop Aaron from doing his thing.

"How long do you have?" he said.

Chapter 9 and a half
The Thieves' Half

Calessa smiled shyly, hoping she hadn't hit a nerve. She knew that asking someone how they met a friend is usually a good starting question to get a friendly conversation going. But, she wasn't really used to friendly conversation.

"I didn't mean to intrude," she said quietly. "I was just trying to make conversation."

"That's alright," Aaron assured her, obviously the opposite of upset.

Hera was still a lot colder toward Calessa and crossed her arms while looking down at the table. It wasn't that there was anything wrong with the story—it was a good story—but Hera simply didn't want to talk to Calessa or any guard for that matter.

Aaron, on the other hand, was a natural storyteller and would make small talk with anyone he could telling them of his daring adventures as a thief. He embellished some details and often lied to make himself appear like the good guy, but most of his stories were mainly true. Including this one.

"We were on a ship to Great Neighbor from Witshore!" Once Aaron got going, he became excited and didn't notice Hera scowling at him and shaking her head.

"A ferry is an unfit vessel in which to brave crashing waves, so it was always risky to send one out twenty miles to the mainland. Regardless, the waters in which this ferry were ordained to tread were Witshore's waters to the west of the once great Northern Kingdom. Because they were Witshore's waters, the crests of the waves were gentler. Witshore owed much to the sand shelf that spread for miles around the Layden peninsula. The famous reef provided the unique tropical biosphere that made Witshore's fish famous, and the shallow waters were good for smooth sailing. The only downside was that larger vessels struggled to avoid the seafloor abrading their hulls. So you see, a ferry—though not the best ship by any means—is still the best option, especially if you are destined for the sovereign nation of Great Neighbor as Hera and I were.

"I had left the Northern Kingdom five years after King Richard the five hundred thirty-forty-something took control. Witshore had been suffering heavy taxation on all its fishing goods, and the once plentiful cities that lined the coast were now far less comfortable. All the rich losers vacated the city and moved to the capital.

"I was sixteen when I left my house to find a better place to live, and though the Northern Kingdom was my home, I knew that I could not stay in Witshore. And I loved the coast too much to leave it. Ironforge was a no-go because they have this weird military thing there. I hear they draft citizens to fight the Anarchy in the East. Can you believe that? A country drafting its own innocent citizens?

"I didn't know much about Great Neighbor, but I knew that it was once part of the Northern Kingdom, and the people they sent over on boats to Witshore were pretty good fishermen, and I was intimately familiar with their catches." Aaron laughed and rubbed his belly thinking of the delicious fish.

"It wasn't too hard to book a boat to Great Neighbor. More people came out of Great Neighbor than came in, so the ferry was less than full. All I had to do was wait, but I have never been a patient man and was not a patient boy back then. I knew that the ferry was currently up north visiting the cities that way. I didn't want to wait the months that it would take for the ferry to make its way down, so I made my way up the road to Layden.

"I started in Sunsoon, so the journey was only two days on foot. I hadn't packed much—an extra set of clothes, some jerky no better than the jerky we are eating now, and a knife, more for utility than defense—but what I wished I'd brought was a second pair of shoes. Within a day of walking, I had worn mine out.

"I wish I could have seen more wilderness, but the longcities of Witshore are so tightly packed that I might as well have been walking around in Goldenhill. I watched the sun rise and set. I would line my fingers up between the sun and the horizon to measure the time. I counted the steps from street to street, waved to as many children as I passed by. I was distracted, in a haze… I didn't steal a thing, not one… It felt good."

Aaron trailed off, lost in thought. His jovial manner had suddenly faltered. His eyes glazed over thinking about his walk from Sunsoon to Layden. Reflexively, he flexed his toes reliving the steps taken on the beach and almost expecting the waves to wash over his tired feet.

"Aaron," Hera scoffed. "I'm not even in the story yet."

Aaron snapped back to consciousness and regained half of the smile he'd had before. He looked at Hera who reflected a smile back at him.

"Oh right," he stuttered. "The boat. Yes… so we are on the boat, right? And I am thinking, 'I haven't stolen anything in a while.' I was really broke at this point, covered in days-old clothing and my shoes all but missing their soles. I had been robbed blind by the prices of the inns I had stayed at, so much so I had to learn how to set up a tent consisting of nothing but a cloth and a few sticks. That is when I spotted her… Hera.

"She was in a big crowd, and probably the second youngest on the ship, with the youngest being myself. She looked like she was *acting* like she knew what she was doing. She let the crowd rush around her moving out of their way, but the entire time she had this look of dominance that just didn't fit. All in all, the perfect target to pickpocket."

"Which wasn't true," Hera cooed.

By now, Hera was seemingly enjoying the story and had almost completely opened up. Only half of her food was eaten, but she put it down and placed her elbows on the table to lean in closer. A group of people had taken seats at the table, making it almost full at this point, but Hera wasn't bothered by it anymore. Calessa seemed to be the most uncomfortable with the new crowd.

Hera smiled tevnalishly. "This is where I come in. I suppose I had it easier than poor old Aaron, since I already lived in Layden. I had much the same reason for wanting out of the Northern Kingdom as soon as possible. I knew that other people had the same idea and were flocking into Dimfir. At this point, Dimfir would have more fishermen than trees.

"I thought that Great Neighbor would be a good place to go because fewer people would be migrating there. I didn't want to live in a place that was too populated, and I definitely didn't want to be considered a refugee. Aaron was wrong though when he said getting a spot on the ship was easy. By the time I got there, it was at full capacity. He might have been the last one they let on… But he had one major difference from me: he had a ticket.

"I wasn't able to buy one; the price was just too high, and I couldn't scrounge up enough money. Actually, that's not true; I could have afforded a ticket. But then I would look like Aaron, so I thought, 'Why not buy some nice clothes, save up enough money to actually live in Great Neighbor, and then just steal a ticket once I sneak on?'

"It wasn't hard getting onto the ship in the first place. Everyone knows it is easiest to get on a ship through the cargo hold, and luckily for me, the Great Neighbor farmers that went to market in Layden weren't used to people actually wanting to go home with them. All I had to do was blend in, get close enough to a container to use as cover, and sneak aboard the ship while their backs were turned. It was ridiculously easy, pretty sure anyone could have done it.

"The ship was light in color; its planks looked like they came from the tall marsh tree of Witshore, not the dark pines that make up Dimfir. The nail work was shoddy at best, but the sail was intricately beautiful. It was not one large sheet but instead several sheets sewn together. You could see the stitching threads making their way randomly through the sail. True, it was not the most elegant sail, but nonetheless, it was beautiful.

"Once I was on the ship, I decided to blend in with the crowd above deck. Most stowaways would hide in a container under deck for the hours that it took to make transit, but I thought I could get away with more comfortable living conditions. I doubted that the irresponsible people that manned the ship would notice an extra person.

"I wanted insurance, though—a ticket if the need arose. I watched the serene faces of the fishermen and farmers that had been sent from Great Neighbor to try to stimulate Witshore's economy, and I watched the far more nervous faces of those vacating Witshore. One face stood out: Aaron's. He was covered in ragged clothes and looked like he smelled. Despite that and the heavy sling on his shoulder, he had a foolish, fetching grin on his face.

"Aaron was the perfect type of person to steal a ticket from. If he was found without a ticket, no one would take his word against mine. I was delighted when he boarded the ship, with the planks bending under the weight of his tent, and made his way over to where I was standing."

Aaron interrupted at this point, "I am looking at Hera and I don't see her noticing me, and I was pretty sure she didn't notice me noticing her, so I show off a little trick I always like to pull. I knew that the sling over my back had to weigh at least sixty pounds. Both my shoulders ached from carrying it for two days. So, while I was making my way through the crowd, I gently forced the thing to the right and lost my balance."

"You came swinging right into me," Hera laughed. "The crowd was avoiding the boy; they had no intention of getting too close to a vagrant with a heavy sling. Which gave him enough room to lose his balance while he was walking by me. He comes tumbling into me and pushes me to the floor of the ship."

Aaron gave Hera a wide grin and said, "I apologized profusely, but really I had slipped my hand into your pocket and taken your purse. It was heavier than the one I had brought to pay for passage on the ship."

"I patted you down, too," Hera interjected excitedly. "But I wasn't quite able to get into your pocket, because I wasn't ready for you to charge me like that. After we got up, I was planning on going for another run and try to get the ticket the second time around."

"But I was already off!" Aaron announced.

"He was off," Hera confirmed. "The thought almost crossed my mind that he had stolen from me, but I was too anxious to focus on anything but getting that ticket. It had been so close; I had just barely missed the mark.

"I bent my head below the crowd and started weaving through them, keeping my eyes on the rucksack that popped over the tops of the fishermens' matted hair. Without the sling to deal with, I moved faster than Aaron just by a little bit and was able to get up behind him just after a quick second.

"I stretched out my arm between the crowd and gently pulled at Aaron's pocket. As soon as I opened it, I saw the ticket resting gently on the leather ready to fall to the floor. I let the crowd jostle him up a little bit, and I jostled him up a little more too, and after a few seconds of the ticket balancing on the edge, it finally came loose.

"I quickly let go of his pocket and the ticket fell toward the ground as gently as a feather. I caught it in my extended hand and straightened. But while I was—"

Aaron interrupted, "But I felt a slight tug and reflexively I—"

Hera interrupted right back into her part, "placing it in my pocket, I felt for my purse."

"Felt for my purse," Aaron continued. "But while I was checking, I noticed my ticket—"

"It was gone!" Hera exclaimed.

"It was gone," Aaron agreed.

"So, I stopped."

"So did I."

"And I turned."

"So did I."

"I felt like there were only two people on the ship," Hera marveled.

"So did I," Aaron beamed. "I had money but no ticket, and she had a ticket but no money. There was no way that I wouldn't need that ticket to prove that I was allowed on the ship, not with the way I looked. In a panic, I looked around and spotted Hera with a smirk on her face holding up my ticket.

"I rushed to her, my sling swinging side to side threatening to push me off balance. She slowly backed away from me. It was a marvel she didn't run into anyone. I got close enough so that she could hear me without me yelling, and said, 'Fine, if you want the money for the ticket, I'll take it.'"

Hera scrunched up her face. "I told him to stuff it."

Several people in the room laughed, most of them sitting at the table now, but some had gathered around just to listen. Finding a good story was hard in Great Neighbor given the times; few people were in the mood to tell a nice one. Calessa had been sitting back listening intently and now giggled slightly. Some guards had added their own commentary, but few of them had anything really interesting to say.

"So, I..." Aaron turned his head to laugh. "So, I made a grab for it, and she dodged to the left and made a run at me, going for the purse."

"I swiped down at the purse resting on his belt, and barely missed it," Hera sighed. "I still regret missing that slide. Next thing I knew, in order to dodge me, Aaron had used the weight of his sling, and now the full force of the tent was coming at me. I ducked as quickly as I could, my hand overhead shielding me from any blow. I felt the wind as the rucksack made its way well over my head. I got up in a blind rage."

"The look on her face was scary," Aaron nodded.

"And told him off for what he had just tried to do."

"'You just tried to hit me,'" Aaron said, mimicking Hera's voice.

"I did not sound like that!" Hera protested.

"It was surprisingly accurate," Calessa whispered.

Hera scowled at Calessa. Calessa shriveled at the glare. Hera saw Calessa cower, and her face softened. She smiled at the guard letting her know she was just joking. Calessa smiled back meekly.

"I told her that I didn't mean to hit her, which was totally true. I had been forced off balance trying to keep her money from her. She was already turning her back on me when the crowd started to close in front of her. I rushed as quickly as I could to get into the crowd before she disappeared into it.

"It wasn't long before I lost sight of her completely. In the hopes of finding her, I let the crowd carry me a ways forward. That is when I felt an elbow jam into my side. I fell to the floor and looked up to see Hera standing over me, flaunting the ticket. She made a grab for her purse, and I rolled to keep it out of her reach.

"I saw the ticket in her left hand and discarded my rucksack for a moment, so that I could get up and get it from her. I was up before she was given a moment to react, but when I looked from the floor to her hand, the ticket was gone. In a panic, I looked everywhere I could to see where it went. I spotted it floating in the sky like a feather. Hera had thrown it right into the air and was giving me a sly look. I was shocked and exhilarated all at the same time. There was no way she had just done that! I did what anyone would do and leaped for it."

Hera interrupted, "But that is what I wanted him to do. As he was distracted, I tackled him and went for a grab at the pouch on his hip. He was distracted and off balance and fell to the floor with a crash and a creak of wood. By now, faces were turning to watch what was happening. I'm sure it was probably the most exciting thing they had seen all day. They didn't do anything but stand back and watch, but some of them started muttering loudly.

"I reached to unlatch the purse from Aaron's hip, but he was already trying to vacate the area and rush after the ticket that had fallen to the floor. I had a full hand grasped on the coin pouch before Aaron accidentally caved in my elbow.

Don't worry, it bent the way it was supposed to. Even so, I lost my grasp of the coin purse and it tumbled to the ground. I tried to pick it up, but the crowd kicked it away. I'm still not sure if it was malicious or just an oblivious idiot doing his thing."

"Hey, you did the same thing with the ticket," Aaron interjected.

Hera ignored him. "The ticket had suddenly become far more important. I didn't quite fit in anymore. After rolling around on the floor with a vagrant, I would have a hard time convincing anyone I was an upper-class citizen. I wasn't in any better of a spot than Aaron. If either of us was caught without a ticket, we would be kicked off the ship one in the same."

"That's some pretty fast thinking," a guard noted.

Aaron rolled his eyes. "She does that."

Hera grinned.

"I hadn't even noticed the money had been removed from my possession," Aaron admitted. "My eyes were fixed on that ticket. I was crawling across the floor like some sort of insect. The feeling was exemplified when I touched people by accident and they recoiled in fear. The crowd was doing a lousy job of staying out of each other's way and were tripping all over one another. Consequently, the ticket danced between the feet of the people on the boat. As boots hit the deck, the ticket bounced upward with the wind. It was agonizing chasing the ticket while it slithered through the feet of the passengers like a snake. I heard a loud stomp to the left of my head and turned to look up at Hera. She had the excellent idea of actually getting up before chasing after the ticket.

"I grabbed her ankle and watched her crash to the ground. I felt bad if that makes it better, but I needed the ticket. Before Hera had a chance to recover, I scrambled to my feet. Luckily for us both, the ticket was kicked out of the crowd to the edge of the ship. Unluckily for us, it looked like it was about to fall into the water.

"The ticket flew up in front of the sun, and I shielded my eyes as I tried to follow its flow. I ran up as quickly as possible to the end of the deck and stretched my hand out over the lapping waves as far as I could. I was right—the ticket was about to fall into the water. I extended my hand as far as my fingers would reach, but it wasn't enough.

"With a final heave, I forced myself forward, not only stretching out my arm but also my back and legs. I just barely caught the slip of paper between my pointer finger and middle finger. I would have celebrated had I the deck space to do so, but alas, I did not. My knees hit the edge of the ship, and I started to tip over. Before I knew it, I was free-falling over the edge of the ship.

"But right before I passed the point of no return, something latched onto my left hand. I looked back quickly, surprised at being saved, and much more to my surprise, I saw Hera standing there, teeth gritted, pulling me from the edge."

Hera sat back, quite proud of herself. All eyes turned to her, in a mixture of confusion and surprise.

"So?" asked a guard. "Why'd you do that?"

"It's simple," Hera mused. "He had the ticket. I needed the ticket, and if he fell off the boat, I wouldn't be able to get it. It wasn't long after this scene, we were approached by the dock guard. He was a red-faced man, huffing under his walrus mustache. You know the type—some of you are the type actually—guards who are in it because they like being in a position of power."

The slight did not go unnoticed. Some of the guards shifted in their seats and grumbled at the disrespect. Others sat dumbfounded, surprised the young thief had the courage to accuse them of being power-hungry. The ones with large gray walrus mustaches turned even redder than they were and looked like they desired to give her an earful, though they decided better of it. The unaffected guards stifled laughter.

Hera continued as if she had taken no risk in her derogation, "Aaron and I now stood side by side, and the guard had gone straight to Aaron. I tried my best to walk away and leave him to deal with it, but before I could, I was stopped by the guard. 'Not so fast, missy,' the man said.

"I stopped where I stood, pretty much back-to-back with Aaron. I couldn't see him and didn't have the heart to look, but I heard the large man walk up to Aaron taking slow deliberate steps. I heard the shuffling of paper, which could only have been the man getting out a notebook of some kind.

"His breaths were labored when he spoke, 'Do you have a ticket to be on this fine vessel, young man?'

"He spoke like he was from Ironforge, gruff yet diplomatic. I felt, more than heard, Aaron's hand shift to reveal the ticket he had caught from the ocean. My heart sank much faster than the wet paper would have had it hit the gentle waves.

"The guard looked over the ticket, and I heard him adjust his weight. He confirmed that the ticket was valid, but still sounded suspicious of Aaron. I closed my eyes in defeat as his heavy footsteps made their way around Aaron to me. 'What right do you have to be here causing such a mess?' he asked.

"I had nothing and opened my eyes to look at the man. A frown was only suggested by the skin condensing around the giant mustache that covered his mouth. Sweat dripped down from under his helmet. I couldn't blame him; it must have been hot wearing that helmet outside all day. Despite that, I did not pity him.

"That is when I felt it. A piece of paper slipped into my hand from behind. I didn't feel or hear the hand that had given it to me. All I knew was that there was now a piece of paper in my hand, and it hadn't been there before. 'Right here,' I said, and held up the piece of paper."

"So Aaron gave it to you so you could stay on the ship?" Calessa asked.

"Yes," Hera said, smiling.

"Why?" Calessa frowned.

"She saved me from falling off the ship. I owed her," Aaron said.

"I guess," Calessa puzzled. "Though she really wasn't doing it for you."

Aaron shrugged, "I didn't think it through, I just did it."

"So that's how you got here," a guard observed.

"No," Hera grinned.

Aaron shook his head, "Not a chance."

"We got thrown off the ship," Hera shrugged.

"Yup," Aaron popped his lips in confirmation.

Chapter 10
Goodbye Grass

Hera and Aaron's story caused quite the stir. Not because it was abnormal, but because it was the most normal thing that had happened in the last three days. Any plans the soldiers had for confronting Hera and Aaron about Viner—or anything for that matter—were momentarily discarded. The thought had completely flown from their minds. Their jealousy of the treatment that the two thieves received from Viner had been similarly forgotten.

After finally being let into the castle, Hera and Aaron had come to the conclusion that it was time to make their move. They hadn't had much time to sit down and process everything that had happened in the previous three days, but now on the fourth day, they were finally able to put into perspective what needed to happen.

"So, we were the only two soldiers drafted, right?" Hera asked Aaron.

Yet again, they had chosen to hold their private meetings in a not-so-private area. The night after telling their story, just before the fires were put out, the two rogues were at the far end of the barracks. Only a few guards were present and they were out of earshot, at least out of earshot if the two whispered. Hera kneeled beside Aaron's bunk. This was preferable to conversing from the discomfort of her stone kip.

"I think so, yes," he said.

Aaron rubbed his eyes slightly, trying to stir away the blurred vision. He adjusted himself upward and sat straight in his bed, resting his head against the back wall. He let the blankets fall from his shoulders, leaving his bottom half warm under the covers and his upper half uncomfortably cold. It was safe to say he did not appreciate the new talking position.

"And why is that?" Hera prolonged Aaron's discomfort.

Aaron thought for a moment. "The King had a good reason to draft us. We were thieves, and this is our punishment."

Hera looked at him quizzically. "Is that all you remember? Why was the King so desperate to get two soldiers on his side?"

Aaron sighed impatiently. "We were good fighters, I guess..."

Aaron seemed puzzled at the words that left his mouth. He had never considered himself a fighter, and he was skeptical of inborn talent.

"Do you remember what I remember?" Hera asked seriously.

"Is it a memory?" Aaron asked back.

"I do not know," Hera sighed. "All I know is that there was something we don't understand happening. We were attacked by a fairy tale, but not all fairy tales are bad. We seem to have one on our side. Do you remember the names Calm and Fear?"

Aaron choked on a breath of air. His eyes went wide with a memory that he wasn't sure was actually there. He struggled to regain his composure.

"I do," Aaron nodded.

"Good, I was worried that I had dreamed them. They sent us here. They can protect us." Hera had earnest hope in her eyes. She shook Aaron's arm. "Tomorrow, we can go to the King, tell him about what they told us. Maybe then we can get out of this. Or at least get something out of this."

"Tell him that we are blessed by some old philosophers? Wouldn't that just make him want to send us more?" Aaron asked.

"If it makes him want to send us into the underworld more, there isn't anything extra he can do. We are already being sent there as part of the front lines," Hera said.

"Best case scenario, he sends us closer to the middle of the army," Aaron grimaced.

"Exactly! What do we have to lose?"

"I suppose you're right," Aaron finally agreed.

They both fell silent for a moment. Hera went back to her cot, and Aaron laid down to rest. But soon, their conversation shifted to lighter topics: "Training today was better than the last," "I think one of those guards liked your half of the story especially, Aaron," and " Did you hear about Victoria- or sorry, Vanessa? Traya is pretending not to know her."

But soon the pleasant conversation died down, much to the gratitude of those around the two young troopers. It was not long before their breathing became slow and calm, and their deepest, most tortured thoughts fell into a dreamscape, some of them never to return. They were unwelcome in their soul and blood now that it mended with sleep.

The next day, Hera and Aaron completed their morning routine, without anything of sizable note. They were sore, it was true, but they felt slightly stronger, and though they didn't exactly want to, they were physically capable of pushing themselves harder. Rose's training plan was effective in that regard—not destroying the muscles of the new recruits but instead nurturing them.

The whispers of the guards told Hera and Aaron that Viner was a new man. They hadn't known Viner personally before his supposed reform, but even they did not recognize the man that struck fear into the hearts of any wrongdoers. That was not to say the reform was negative. In fact, Viner's new measured and methodical way of thinking was respected, and Viner was starting to fill his brother's shoes nicely. Most of the people of Great Neighbor were born anew four nights prior, so Viner was not alone in his solemn mood, but even so, the burning passion that filled every aspect of the warrior's life was now an ember of coal. Though the light wasn't as bright, it burned just as hot and warmed a home just the same, with the added bonus of being unable to burn anything to the ground.

That day, Hera and Aaron resolved to speak to Viner and request an audience with the King. The Hand of the King was a busy position. It was his duty to make sure that every single guard in the army was obedient and ready for battle. It would take more than just confidence to get his attention, but the two rogues believed with every fiber of their bodies that Viner would have to listen to them.

The previous days had been getting progressively colder, and this day did not break the trend. It was, by several degrees, the coldest morning of their workouts. And if they squinted and really thought about it, the soldiers would notice that this day was the darkest day yet. The sun had not yet fully risen when Hera and Aaron woke, but the stars were not out. It was a dry day, so this time no frost clung to the dying grass. The grass in the courtyard was wilting and dead in spots. The castle looked several shades lighter and was far emptier than it had been. This was good because it meant that people had returned to their homes.

It was just over three hours after waking that Hera and Aaron tried first to talk to Viner, and they were still groggy from their restless sleep. Despite the discomfort and the inflamed soreness mainly concentrated in their calves, Hera and Aaron were set on confronting Viner about the King. On previous days, the grass would only condense and sag against the armored feet of the guards, but this day when

Aaron stepped onto the field a satisfying crunch sounded under his leather shoes.

"What are you smiling at?" Hera said, responding with a small smile of her own.

Aaron looked up with a foolish grin on his face. "The feeling of the grass crunching under my feet."

"I see." Hera's eyebrows rose with a hint of laughter. "Well, don't—" she started.

Hera wanted to warn Aaron against getting too attached to the grass. She knew that they would be leaving it behind soon. All they would see was the coarse dirt and stone that inlaid the underworld's floor. She stopped before finishing the sentence. She realized that maybe it would be better not to take that small comfort away from Aaron while he had it. After the thought crossed her mind, the thought of removing that silly smile from his face became impossible. Besides, maybe there was grass in the underworld, and maybe it was crunchy.

"Don't start preferring the grass's company over mine," Hera finished, with little more than a stutter on the word 'don't'.

It wasn't quite enough to get a chuckle out of Aaron, but among friends, often there is no worry about whether a joke gets an audible laugh or not. Aaron made it clear with a smirk and a faint hum of appreciation that he was amused. It is a thing hard to put into words, that which is shared between friends. A sense of belonging with one another. A trust.

Viner was never idle; he was always busy giving instructions to one soldier or another. When Hera and Aaron approached him, he seemed to be in a serious conversation with a soldier. Both men were nodding repeatedly at each other, as if in some riveting conversation where they were both learning much. Viner was making hand motions to better illustrate whatever point he was explaining to the soldier.

"—when you take a step," Viner said.

Hera and Aaron walked in on the tail end of Viner's lecture, giving them a perfect opportunity to interject.

"It should be a firm heel to the ground," Viner continued. "That way, you don't lose your footing and can keep up better."

"Sir," Hera said.

Viner patted the trooper on the shoulder and sent him on his way. Hera and Aaron had struck gold with Viner's ear. This was the perfect opportunity to speak to him.

Hera wasted no time with introductions and got straight to the point. "We need to request an audience with the King."

Viner did not look at Hera or Aaron, but he tilted his head as if he heard her. Everyone paused briefly, then with a quick inhale and a solid plant of the heel, Viner started walking past the pair. He moved quickly and with purpose, but not so fast to seem he was fleeing Hera and Aaron. Hera looked at Aaron, at a loss as to what to do. Aaron shrugged in response, as he often did. Hera set her face to remain calm and followed in Viner's footsteps.

"Sir?" she asked again.

Viner continued walking, the dark silvery iron on his armor gleaming like the moon. Sweat lined his face, as it did Hera's and Aaron's. The guard raised his gauntlet to his forehead and scraped off the sweat, leaving white streaks from where the metal had touched the flesh. It was obvious now that Viner was going to the lunch hall, but before he got there, he stopped to address another militant.

"You did good today, Anna," Viner told the guard.

"Thank you, sir," she replied.

That was not all Viner had to say. "But when wielding your weapon, I notice it often slips from your grip. Don't be lazy with the blade. I know you are familiar with it, but often we get hurt when we forget ourselves."

The guard began to respond, "Yes—"

"Sir," Hera interrupted.

Viner walked away again, patting this guard on the back the same way he had done to the other one. He moved slightly faster than Hera, so it didn't take him long to get ahead of her in pursuit of the castle, and more importantly, its dining hall. Hera grabbed Aaron by the hand and dragged him forward to catch up with Viner.

"Captain!" she commanded.

Nothing in Viner's movement changed. There was a large crowd of soldiers ahead of them, filing into the dining room. He patted some soldiers on the back as he neared the crowded dining room. He also threw in a few tips: "Your blades are getting dull," "Your balance was off today; lean back," "Your armor is on too lose; learn to wear it right," but he didn't stop to talk to any of these guards. Since it was hard to shove past heavily armored soldiers, Hera trailed behind, unable to get to his side.

Viner entered the eatery before Hera and Aaron got a moment to address him again. They positioned themselves to be next to him in line, so they could further press him. They were amid the entire army, all getting their food at once. The dining hall could not have looked more filled. The laughter common in a place of revelry was replaced with low murmurs and, at some points, just the shuffling of movement.

"Viner," Hera tried using his name to get his attention.

Viner grabbed a tray of food and continued to ignore Hera and Aaron. The server gave Viner an odd glance, noticing the captain's strange behavior. Aaron looked helplessly at the server. He wasn't sure if Viner was the one dragging him into this uncomfortable situation, or if it was Hera, who was literally dragging him into this uncomfortable situation.

The Captain of the Guard took a seat at the long table. The sawdust-colored chairs and tables were filling rapidly, but Viner's commanding presence guaranteed him a seat easily. Frederick would make it a habit to eat with his men. He would always say, "The Captain who eats with his men isn't eaten by his men" and would follow up the silly phrase with a hearty laugh, which was often, in turn, responded to with another hearty laugh—usually Viner's. Viner followed his brother's advice and knew that it was more important to gain trust with his men now than it would ever be again in his career. For a brief moment, he remembered that his career might be cut short soon anyway. But still, why should that stop him?

Hera and Aaron were less lucky in securing seats. As soon as Viner sat down, several guards followed him and loyally sat down next to him. One of them engaged in conversation immediately. Though the conscripts must have thought their own gripes were of utmost importance, Hera disagreed.

"Viner!" Hera all but shouted.

"I think that thief wants a word with you," a guard noted.

The soldier pronounced every "th" as a "t", giving him a strange accent that was more due to personality than nationality.

Viner looked down at the cup clutched in his hand. He tilted it to watch the liquid fall. He stopped all conversation, ignoring the world around him completely. Those around him trailed off, darting their eyes nervously from his face to the cup. Whether out of fear or rage, Hera's face froze. Aaron made no attempt to hide his discomfort and examined each and every eye that was looking at Viner. There were about a dozen total examining the scene.

Viner opened his hand and let the cup fall back onto the table. It pivoted on its edge and spilled some of the water contained in it. Then it rolled for a moment before finally settling. Viner's face darkened, and he forced himself away from the table. One plated foot stomped on the ground and then another. Viner rose from the bench, uncurling his knees and twisting his neck. Only now, as he towered over them, did it become evident how much taller he was than both Hera and Aaron. He tightened, bared his teeth, and grabbed both rogues by their arms.

Then the captain was off, marching stronger than any soldier on the field. If Hera and Aaron had not been dragged, they would not have been able to keep up with him. The room was commanded to attention without Viner having to utter a single word. The crowd desperately tried to clear a path and was mostly successful in avoiding Viner's wrath.

Aaron was used to being jerked around that day, and Hera was too frightened to struggle, so neither made any motion to escape. Instead, they were dragged into the throne room that connected to the dining hall. Even the rafters creaked with Viner's armored footsteps. The young adults were taken to the throne, and just when they expected to stop, they were taken past it.

Behind the throne was a low-ceilinged corridor that few guards had noticed when they first entered the great hall. Viner seemed to know where he was going and forced the thieves into the hallway before him. The hallway was made from moon-tinted wood, stranger than anything you could find in Dimfir. Not even a hint of brown dotted the oaken material.

Hera wasn't quite sure if she wanted to be shoved down a small hallway. On one hand, she desired to speak to Viner and the King and this cramped hallway looked like it might help, but on the other hand, who wants to be forced down a hallway that looks more like a mouse hole than a place where humans live?

Her mind was made up when she accidentally inhaled a cobweb that she had not seen. Even if torches were lining the hall, they themselves would pose an issue. The little crack that the three militia members were now awkwardly wedged in would not have been big enough to comfortably hold any light source. So, it didn't.

If the semi-secret tunnel had been lit, it would have been noticeably short. It took less than ten beats for Viner to shove the two thieves through it and to the other end. Hera and Aaron were forced forward by Viner's hand, right into the next room. They both tripped over each other's feet and almost fell face first into the disheveled wooden planks that made up the floor.

The small hallway had just been long enough to create a curtain of darkness. The room that stumbled into was small and filled with books. These books would have been blanketed by shadow had it not been for the assortment of dim wax candles that spread hazard across the floor. The candles had no tray, and the floor was covered in charred wax from candles that were long since deceased.

Instead of four walls, there were three, and instead of walls, there were books. Bookshelves covered every available inch of the wall, with many more books than shelves visible. The books were not in good condition— some were horribly torn, many were faded, and most were stacked multiple deep on the shelves to make more room. With the three new bodies entering the room, it became overcrowded, and its triangular shape was not helpful in making them feel less cramped.

The reason for Viner's kidnapping soon became apparent. On the floor was the small figure of a little man. His hair and skin looked like they were made of wax, and his purple cloak melded into a rug that poked through the mess of burnt candles. Clutched in his wax-statue-hands was a book, also covered in wax. The cover of the book was made from seaweed linen, and the pages looked equally oceanic. The King's crown was defiled by the messy wax of an additional candle that was assimilated into the spires of the circlet. The candle was dimly lit and provided an ugly shade on the King's already ugly face. Viner moved past Hera and Aaron, into the room.

"My King," he said.

"Saltwater!" the King mumbled loudly in response.

"They insisted on seeing you." Viner made no motion toward Hera and Aaron, but it was obvious he was talking about them.

"Interestking!" the King mused, chuckling to himself.

Viner shook his head in disgust. "You must wash, my King."

The King turned to look at the three. His eyes were red from sleepless nights. On the bright side, it looked like he had more teeth than last they saw him.

"My King," Hera started immediately. "We have something of utmost importance to tell you."

The King nodded to himself and went back to reading his book. Just then, a noise came from the hallway, like wood creaking. Aaron looked nervously into the darkness but saw nothing.

Hera paid no mind to the King's disinterest nor the noise down the hallway. "It is true that Aaron and I—without any training—killed fifteen soldiers."

"I know," the King hummed, still looking at his book.

Hera stuttered but pushed on, "But I am here to tell you that it was a fluke."

The King closed his book, irritated. For a moment, the madness seemed to melt away. He looked like a parent or a teacher, upset at a child for making a big deal out of nothing.

"A fluke? Do you have any evidence to prove that?" he croaked.

"I…" Hera swallowed. "I do."

Hera looked around a moment, fidgeting with her feet. She was more nervous about confronting the King than she expected to be. But once she thought about it, she realized that it made sense that she would be intimidated. This little man held absolute power over a country, even if he was small in stature and seemed dimmer than the room Hera stood in now. It did not help that her story was starting to sound ridiculous as it replayed in her head.

"After the battle…" Hera tried.

The King's eyes grew suddenly wide, as if he had just discovered something greatly shocking. He snapped the book closed and got to his feet. All the intellectual stability that had previously flooded his face was now replaced with a joyous, frantic, madness. Not a madness. A lust, a lust for answers. The confidence that the King had conveyed was replaced with curiosity.

"A man in white!" the King cheered.

"What—" Hera started.

They paused for a moment, then "Yes," the King and Hera said together. However, the King was much more confident in the answer than Hera, as if he was certain and she was not.

"And he was followed by a man in black and red?" the King pressed.

"Actually, the one in red came first—" Hera tried to interject.

"Of course he did. That guy is such a loser..." the King was dancing now, showing off his bare wax-covered legs. "They caught you alone, then the third one came in."

Aaron, by now, was thoroughly weirded out. How did the King know all this, and why was he so excited about it? A lump formed in Aaron's throat, wondering how much the King knew and how much Aaron didn't. But obviously the King didn't know everything, he had made a mistake.

Aaron shook his head. "There was no third."

"No third..." the King wondered aloud. "Rose, did you see the third?"

"I did not, sir," Rose replied.

No one had noticed Rose enter the room. Hera and Aaron hadn't first found anything odd about her introduction, but then they turned to look behind them. When they saw the woman behind them, the thieves jumped back a few feet into the King. Along with everyone else in the dining room, Rose had noticed Viner suddenly storm into the throne room's slightly-secret hallway. Unlike everyone else, it was within her jurisdiction to follow. The King looked sadly into his advisor's placid face. It wasn't clear which of them had fallen further. But they both had fallen. Some time ago.

"Rose... Did I ever tell you of the Queen?" the King asked.

"The Queen? Sir?" Rose said. "No, only the heir, never the queen."

"I didn't think I had but... it's foggy sometimes."

In this moment, where the King was indulging in his rambling thoughts, only then did he look like his mind was clear. Perhaps it was like fighting against the current of a river. A river can take you through all sorts of rabid pathways, but if you attempt to fight against it, you quickly find that you can't fight against much of anything anymore.

"She was a woman," the King continued nodding. "From Goldenhill. Her hair was long and black... and soft. Her skin was warm and dark, and her lips were full. When she looked at me, I thought I could rule an empire, a new world. I guess I could."

"She sounds like a wonderful woman. Why is it—"

"I already ruled an empire," the King interrupted. "She didn't want anything to do with that."

The King paused for a long moment. Hera was incredulous that they had gone down this awkward rabbit hole. Aaron and Hera had heard tell of the King's foreign son living in Goldenhill, but no one ever believed it. This seemed to be yet another of the King's web of lies.

"I left her in Goldenhill and returned to claim my birthright. One day my son will come to claim what is rightfully his, and when that day comes, I will finally have the right to give up my rule."

The statement was directed at Rose, but the reason was unclear. Rose seemed to disagree with the rest of the room and said nothing. She did, however, shift uncomfortably.

"If there is anything you have not told me, it would make things a lot faster if you did," the King said.

Rose looked down at him and furrowed her brow. "I am at your service, my lord."

The King looked at Rose for a long moment, and in quite the unnerving action, he hummed his thoughts in a rushed and incomprehensible tone. He looked down to waggle his finger in front of his face like he was having a well thought out conversation with the appendage. It was exactly what it looked like. The King was deep in thought.

"I have expected that The Order was involved for quite some time now," the King spoke aloud. "Thank you for telling me this. We will be leaving now."

"What?" Hera asked, "What do you mean 'leaving'?"

"Great Neighbor," the King sighed contently. "I have figured out all I need to get us into the underworld. Won't be anything too fancy, sadly, but it's the best I can do."

Viner's face turned to slate. He reached his hand out toward the King in a panic.

"My Liege," he said. "Wouldn't that be rash? I was told I had a full week. My soldiers are not where they need to be if we want to attack the underworld so soon."

"On the contrary," Rose interjected.

A smug smile tugged on the side of Rose's lips, and no matter how hard she tried to hide it, her lips would twitch into focus every other second. Something about the lids of her eyes... they were wider, more open. It was odd, especially combined with the left eyebrow that quivered in her otherwise completely calm face.

"My soldiers are completely ready," Rose said grinning. "They will serve their purpose."

"It's settled then," crooned the King. "We march now."

"You can't mean this moment!" Viner growled.

Rose sounded too happy to be normal. "The troops have just been fed and warmed up. This is a perfect time."

When Viner looked at her, her sickly smile was much colder than the soldiers' day of "warming up".

"I do mean this moment, and the soldiers are ready," the King commanded. "The soldiers need to finish eating quickly. Round them up!"

Chapter 11
Hello Marble

Hera and Aaron felt they made the biggest mistake of their life. Though there was some contemplation that the biggest mistake of their lives was saving up money in Sunsoon, so that they could escape a corrupt King just to fall into the hands of another tyrant. Rose personally escorted Hera and Aaron to the courtyard. She didn't look down on them with her usual expression of disappointment. Instead, she looked at them in a half-admiring way. But, when it came to Rose, all facial expressions were subjective.

Viner saw to it that his men, including both battalions one and two, were lined up in proper formation to stand before the King. The King was already waiting for the soldiers. He stood where Rose would usually take position—on the high wall, observing the troops. This time, Rose stood with the army but still made sure to distinguish her importance. While Viner stood in front of his army to lead the charge, Rose stood behind the army and made certain that no one would dare disobey.

The King preceded the procession with a proclamation, "Hello!"

A long, awkward silence ensued in which Aaron considered coughing for comedic effect. Knowing Rose was close behind him, he thought better of it.

The King cleared his throat. "Ok then... we are going to the underworld."

The soldiers erupted in an uproar. All the discipline that Viner had been working so hard to ensure, all the loyalty that Rose had tried her very best to implant into the army's mind—all of it was evaporating faster than an ice cube dropped in boiling water. In fact, from the things the soldiers were screaming, one could be convinced that they were being dropped into a pot of boiling water themselves. "This is an outrage," "We were told a week," "My family, I need to say goodbye."

The King looked frightened by the soldiers' outburst. With a jump, he started shuffling down the staircase inside the wall. The noon sun made certain no shadow prevailed over any stone, except to point harshly north. Its light touched all truth. It touched the dark stones and mortar of the castle; it touched the gleaming metal helmets of the soldiers; and it touched the whites of their eyes as they watched their King scramble down the wall.

Rose shook in anger, but this was exactly what she had expected to happen. This time, she did not unshackle her great cleaver from her back but instead took a different approach.

The King emerged from the wall's indented entrance at around the same time that Rose made her way beside him. Viner crossed his arms. He harbored the same feelings as the soldiers but knew not to disrupt Rose and the King. But, he was not going to help them either.

"Order," commanded Rose. "Order. Is this how you address your King?"

The crowd did not comply. They searched for words, a thousand mouths trying to form one sentence, but finally they stumbled upon the right phrase and one chant prevailed, "Not My King, Not My King, Not my King."

Rose's thoughts were racing, adrenaline pumping like it never had before. She had to keep composure, she was so close. For the thro... For the throne? The people were right. What had the King done? He hid behind his wall, hoarding treasure.

"Open the portal," Rose whispered to the King.

'He hasn't provided anything to Great Neighbor since she and Fredrick came to power,' she thought. Then it dawned on her.

The King waved his hands in front of him, and a wisp of white cut its way through the air. The King's mad gesture had no rhythm to it. On the outside, he looked a great fool. But inside, he was a glimmer of the once bright, once inspired heir to the throne. The man who once saw corruption and sought to escape it. A genius, driven mad by loneliness.

With all of that suppressed power, he conjured a portal, the strongest spell he had ever cast. A portal that broke the threads of the Inbetween, that reopened stitches, that both healed and sundered wounds, that could rival gods and destroy mortals, that could put out fire deep deep underground, that could chase the smoke high into the sky and catch it one final time. The King created a marble mirror.

Rose's thoughts were still racing. The King was not the righteous king of Great Neighbor she had known long ago. He was not suited for the job. He stole from his people, and they hated him. The King's spirit had died long ago, now he was nothing but an obstacle... an obstacle to be eliminated! The cries of the soldiers were drowned in shock. The only noise was the whistling of the wind against the astonished crowd's desperate gasps for air. Aaron was almost on the floor. Hera was on the floor.

Rose tilted her head to the right and found herself staring down the cast iron metal of her jagged cleaver. Crimson rivulets slowly dripped down the side of the perpendicular blade. She looked at the King and found him on the floor, his purple robe dyed red, small strands of his hair resting on his bloodied back. His head lay on the ground a few feet away. The cut was clean.

"You are not going to get away with this!" growled Viner.

Rose barely understood what she had just done. She had devoted her life to serving the King. She was the most loyal troop among her ranks. When detractors had jeered the king, she was by his side. Always loyal. Always loyal. Loyal. Loyal.

"No," she whispered.

And then, she stopped. She thought fast, faster than the brightest among the guards, faster than her sword had been unsheathed and struck down the King's head.

"—for what?" Rose cried, "For taking down a tyrant? He has done nothing for us."

The troops were still in shock. They didn't know what to think. Some of them wanted nothing more than for the King to be executed, to end the hardship they were put through. But they never thought it would happen. They did not cheer. No, that was out of the realm of possibility, but they did not charge either.

"He was too cowardly to come with us into the underworld, but fully willing to send his armies in his stead. He locked his own people out of the keep, leaving them to sleep in the cold that comes after harvest for nothing but his own paranoia," Rose rallied. "He hoards wealth and knowledge, and this was our last chance to make a difference!"

For Great Neighbor, Rose had just murdered their leader. Despite her reasoning, most people felt enraged more than impressed. Most people. But some. Some people felt exhilarated. They were liberated from the King's grasp of megalomania, the gray that had consumed the island. So they spoke, but more than spoke, they shifted. They straightened their knees together and placed their fists perpendicular in salute. When they spoke in affirmation, it was grating to the ears of Hera and Aaron.

"He was," Rose's voice faltered. "He was a tyrant, yes, a horrible leader, and a horrible man."

Rose turned her face. The noon sun's shadow was looming and dark over her. A moment ago, it may have looked like the crowd's shadow lurched towards her, but this must have been an illusion, for now it was not so. Rose and the wall were clearly overbearing on the army, casting them in a deep, controlling, miasma. Rose gently lowered her cleaver and let its sharp tip split the grass on the ground.

"You wanted a week?" Rose raised her head in determination. "You had a week. The first day, we were invaded. That was when you learned who the enemy was." Rose spit her words like acid, commanding everyone heel.

"The second," she said lifting her free hand, two fingers in the air. "Was your first day of training. You learned how to take charge for yourself and do your part to follow implied command."

She added another finger to signal the third day. "The third," she snarled. "Your second day of training, you learned to respect Viner and his command."

A fourth finger as she continued, "The fourth, you learned comradery, how to work together, how to get along. You learned who stood next to you."

Finally, Rose closed her fist and brought it close to herself. "The fifth, you learned how to attack, how to take charge, how to be a hero."

Rose opened her fist only to assist her other hand in sheathing her sword. For the first time, she glimpsed the portal that the King had opened before he died. Rose had commanded the King to open it before even realizing she was going to kill him. Some part of her must have already known.

As an afterthought, she added one final statement to her speech, "Congratulations, you get the weekend off. What better way to spend it than serving Great Neighbor and her queen? "

"Damn it, Rose, this is madness!"

Viner pulled Rose aside from the guard unit. It took some restraint of his own to not try to arrest her immediately.

"Tell me why I should not do the honorable thing and execute you now." Viner's tone was colder than usual, almost as cold as Rose herself.

Rose hissed at him, "The King needed to die. He only ever got in the way. We need to kill those dwarfish scum. And as to why you shouldn't execute me? I am Queen of Great Neighbor. I was next in line for the throne if something were to happen to the king. Unless you want to go to Goldenhill and find his son, who I am starting to question exists. You need a strong leader, one willing to risk her own life for justice."

"Next in line!" Viner raged. "You are a criminal. The only reason I'm talking to you is because I used to respect you, but this act was out of anger! And yes, we all know that the King has no son!"

It seemed that Rose was the only one who didn't know that the king didn't have a son. Perhaps it was because she wanted so desperately for it to be true.

"He was supposed to protect us," Rose said. "But he didn't. He closed the keep. I was alone at the gate. I opened it. People were already dead because the King ordered guards to keep the gate sealed."

"Rose..." Viner's tone was softer.

Rose turned her head up to him and loudly demanded, "Do you know who died outside the gate?"

Aaron was the first to approach the rift that the king had opened before them. Perhaps it was his disloyalty to the king that caused him to regain himself so quickly, or otherwise it was his innate curiosity. No matter what it was, he was first to know the knowable. All had heard stories of the horrors of the underworld. Everyone knew if you were immoral you were thrown to despair for the rest of eternity. Those myths now proved to be reality, though their accuracy was still up for question.

Aaron peered through the crack in the air and was surprised at what he found. Where myth had claimed there to be rugged and tight caves, a single continuous plate of smooth marble glistened on the floor. Where myths had claimed damp darkness, light showered down to the ground from fissures in the ceiling, also marble and paralleled to the floor. As far as the eye could see, only a flat ceiling and floor were visible, with no pillars to ensure the structural integrity of the interior design.

"What... is that?" Aaron's voice was filled with more wonder than fear.

His eyes grew wide as he stared at the immense size of the paradoxical door. He reached out his hand and let it slide through the rift. The guards around him shuddered, and Hera pushed past them to be near Aaron. She was ready to pull him back if something were to happen to him. Aaron took his hand out of the portal and clutched it with the other. He slowly turned to look at Hera.

He had an expression of absolute disbelief. "It's warmer in there. And look, you can't see where it ends; it's just white."

Hera stepped away, and shook her head, not as an answer to his question, but in pure shock. The King was dead, and the last thing he had left them was a portal to a white nothingness. Now they were expected to just go through?

"Henry, my boy," Viner hollered, "You wanted to avenge your father? Then stay close."

Viner came striding with wide steps across the field, cutting his way through the dazedly lumbering crowd. Rose stood behind him, looking directly forward with a completely blank expression on her face. She was obviously not seeing anything.

Hera and Aaron got their first good look at Henry. He was scrawny and no older than sixteen. Facial hair was just emerging on his face, but it was blonde and scarce. They doubted he ever had the need to shave. He was not taller than Aaron and stood with a minor slouch. Even so, he was skinny enough to look tall if there was nothing to compare him to.

Henry nodded, a certain tiredness seeping into his eyes. His blonde hair fell around his head like a torn curtain, amplifying his tired look. His armor did not fit him well, but the shield and the sword in his hand did, and Hera and Aaron knew that Henry was able to use them.

Viner gently pushed Aaron aside, the only way he had interacted with either of the thieves in a long time. He was the first guard to venture into the portal. He lifted his great armored boot. With it, he forced himself into the rift that had opened before him. And then, with the other, he gently placed himself on the floor of the underworld. He spread his arms, seemingly trying to keep balance. Then he took several great lumbering steps beyond the portal.

"My fellows," Viner announced. "Be prepared. There will be a winged man sitting in front of you when you enter the portal."

"What?" Henry asked.

Viner frowned. "When you enter the portal, there will be a winged man. Answer his questions. I made the decision to

188

answer with honor, so you will not reveal anything he does not already know."

Henry closed his eyes and shook his head. "I have no clue what you're talking about."

"Just enter the portal. His name is Mordecai. He's a nice chap," Viner replied with clipped words.

"What..." Henry started to protest.

"Enter the portal, my boy!" Viner commanded.

Henry shook his head and followed his uncle's orders. He took one step through the portal and then another. Suddenly, he slipped forward and fell hard on the ground. Viner shrank to his knees beside the boy, gracefully sliding into the position.

Viner placed his hands on the child's shoulder. "Be careful, Henry, the floor is slippery."

Henry shook the surprise out of his mind and cradled his head. "You didn't tell me Mordecai was going to look so creepy."

"That is a rude thing to say upon just meeting someone," Viner chided the boy.

Henry gave his uncle a confused look. "Uncle, he is part of the army that invaded us. He only let us in so we could die."

"But he was a friendly chap." Viner nodded.

"I'm still confused," Hera said.

"Enter the portal, and watch out; it is slippery," Henry told her.

Hera looked around at the other guards and saw that those within earshot were just as confused. Nonetheless, she did as commanded, and took Aaron by the arm while walking through the portal.

As soon as her second foot touched the ground, which was in fact slippery, she was in a different place. She had made contact with a slippery floor, but her feet now stood firmly on a rug. She took a frantic look around, reflexively shifting her weight and taking a step. She panicked for a moment, sensing she would fall, but the rug held firm.

She was in, without a doubt, the strangest environment she had ever seen. Everything around her was a pure void of white, including the floor. She stood atop a woolen rug that was a shade of brown with red threads accentuating it, forming a star-like pattern. If she was not standing on the rug, she would be worried she would fall into the void of white. She still wasn't sure if the rug was floating or if it was on solid white ground.

"Please, take a seat," a polite voice instructed her.

Hera all but jumped off the rug. She was so startled by the sudden voice that she started hyperventilating.

"Woah," the voice said jovially. "Please, calm down."

Hera's eyes darted to the speaker. She had to turn almost completely around to see where the quiet voice came from. What she saw baffled her more than Calm and Fear had. She saw a tabletop with four metal legs neatly sitting on the edge of the rug. The metal legs were gleaming steel and looked overly polished. The top of the table was made of a strange gray material that Hera did not recognize.

Behind the table stood a strangely shaped chair. The chair had one giant leg coming out of the bottom that sprawled into four legs. On the bottoms of the tips of these legs, there were metal balls that rolled around lightly on the floor. The chair's leg was made of the same unrecognizable material as the tabletop, but the upper part of the chair was predominantly leather.

Hera could not get a good look at the seat of the chair because someone, or rather something, was sitting in it. The creature was humanoid in shape, facial features and all, with several key differences. These differences were more than enough for Hera to characterize the creature as alien. The creature had wings curling around its body like a bat. The skin of the creature was not skin, but scales. The scales fit the monotone color scheme of the desk and the white void. Even sitting, the figure towered over Hera. She wagered it would be more than seven feet tall if it decided to stand. The creature was slender, almost stretched, and the neck alone comprised a good foot of its height.

Wraps of lightly colored cloth engulfed the mysterious being in a semblance of some archaic clothing. On the head of the creature, a golden crown lay, far more subtle than the former king's crown. It had no gems and relied instead on golden spikes jutting out every direction like a wreath of thorns.

Hera tried to regain her composure, but the gray scaled monster was not helping. The creature pulled its lips back and smiled gently at her. This did not help either, as it revealed menacingly sharp teeth.

"There we are..." the creature spoke softly, both in tone and volume.

Despite the reptile's assertion that Hera was calming down, she was not. Her vision was starting to go blurry. But then, she remembered. She remembered the horrors of the dwarves, dragging innocent citizens away. She remembered the attack out of the deep dark blue of the ocean right at sundown. This strange beast was nothing compared to that, and she steadied her breath.

"Would you like your friend here too?" the snake-like figure asked.

Hera didn't know how to react. Something clicked in her mind, and she started frantically looking around for Aaron. There were not many places for him to hide, she was standing in the middle of a white void, after all. Even so, she was convinced Aaron would emerge from some niche.

"I take that as a yes," noted the creature.

The wyrm made no move, but as Hera turned her head to look behind her, she saw Aaron.

"Where are we?" Aaron asked in a panic.

"I don't know," Hera said.

"So they speak!" cheered the lizard.

Aaron took a step back at the voice of the creature. His eyes slowly widened as he examined the figure who had spoken. He shuddered a little and froze in fear.

"Calm down; you have been through worse," Hera whispered to him.

Aaron nodded mutely, but he still did not move his arms or legs. Aaron was poised to run from the scaled man if the time came.

"I am Mordecai, the..." Mordecai, the something, trailed off. "I always forget what comes after that part. Any-who, I am Mordecai. What are your names?"

Hera and Aaron said nothing. Aaron just kept his eyes wide, and Hera kept hers narrowed.

"Ah..." Mordecai whimpered. "Well, I already know your names. I was just asking for conversation's sake. I see that your soul power spiked approximately five days ago. On top of that, you both have an impressive blood reservoir."

Mordecai drummed his finger on the side of his strange scaled head, as if he was trying to remember something. The only things that didn't look human about his face were his slitted green eyes, his bizarre skin, and his sharp teeth. Other than that, he had a humanoid nose and mouth. Even hair grew out of the scaled head. The hair was thick and white. It grew in more like a horse's mane than a human head of hair and clotted at the shoulder area. The hair was long thanks to the disproportionate neck.

"Who were your parents?" he hummed.

Aaron had been tilting forward so that he was standing more upright, but his posture began to slouch. Perhaps it was because being wound up like a spring was starting to tire him. However, Hera only grew more tense and reached for her sword. She rested her hand on the grip of the gladius, not trying to hide her intentions in the slightest.

Mordecai sighed again. "Welcome to my paradox. I do not exist, so you cannot kill me. For that same reason, I cannot kill you. But by all means, go ahead. Strike me with your weapon. I won't hurt, and I won't bleed."

"You don't exist?" Aaron questioned.

Mordecai was excited Aaron had spoken to him. "I am a memory. More of a humanity. A manifestation of soul... No blood... Only melonc—"

"That doesn't mean anything to me," Aaron said.

The snake trembled at the interruption, but his face grinned ever so slightly, and Aaron narrowly avoided going into a panic. It was a good thing Mordecai hadn't shown his teeth with that smile, or Hera would have had to continue the conversation alone.

"It will soon," Mordecai assured the rogue.

Hera chose to take a risk and asked a brazen question, "Can we leave?"

"Yes, of course," Mordecai said sadly. "I am an enchantment. You could say... I am the Marble Tower."

"The—" Aaron started to interject.

Mordecai waved his hand. "A heavily enchanted structure that your portal leads to." Mordecai twitched his head to the side and swallowed. A short pause followed and the opportunity to speak that Mordecai had granted Aaron passed. Then he continued, "As I was saying, I have to ask you some questions before letting you enter. Do not worry, after this is over, I will fade into memory, meaning no time will pass."

"Just because you are not currently living through something, doesn't mean no time has passed..." Aaron protested.

"Is that so?" Mordecai mused. "Interesting. Perhaps you are right. All that matters, though, is that your bodies will not age, and you will be left in the same place, at the same perceived time."

Mordecai looked around with a jolly smile on his face that did not match his gentle, soft-spoken voice. Hera could see why Henry was afraid of the monster, but she herself was only on edge, not quite afraid but not ready to trust. Aaron was starting to calm down. He could see why Viner liked this guy so much.

"But it will have happened?" Aaron asked.

"Maybe..." Mordecai smiled warmly. "Your names are Hera and Aaron; what brings you to the Marble Tower?"

Hera and Aaron had no desire whatsoever to tell Mordecai that they had come to the underworld to attack it, but Viner had told them that he answered all the questions honestly.

"We are here—" Hera started.

"To save our people," Aaron cut her off.

Aaron needed to make sure that Hera didn't make herself appear hostile. Viner had already spoken to Mordecai, and Aaron knew that Viner wasn't going to outright say that he desired the death of another people. Viner said he answered with honor, not with disrespect. Aaron didn't want to jeopardize anything that had already been set up.

"Ah... You are the ones. I knew from your names, but... I had to ask." Tears welled in Mordecai's eyes. "Are you champions?"

Aaron was processing many things at once. Why had the lizard man in front of them suddenly started crying? What was a champion? Was he referring to their state of mind?

"I don't think so," Aaron answered slowly.

"I guess..." Mordecai turned his face in mortification. "I guess that is all."

All three beings in the room paused awkwardly. Hera looked around, almost expecting to see a door in the white nothingness. When she looked back, Mordecai was holding back tears of mourning. She knew them well. She had seen more than her fair share of grief in the past five days alone.

"Would you like a cup of hot chocolate?" Mordecai almost sobbed.

Hera snapped to attention excitedly and exclaimed, "Like in Aerokite!"

"Why are you crying?" Aaron was far more sincere in his tone.

"I am remembering my friend Viner and his son Henry." Mordecai had gotten his weeping under control now but threatened to start up again at his own words.

Aaron debated informing him that Henry was not Viner's son but decided against it. Hera looked absolutely, fundamentally, institutionally, confused.

"You talked to Viner?" Aaron asked.

"We did more than talk." Mordecai gave Aaron a sad smile. "We talked a lot. He said eleven million, one hundred thousand, three hundred and eighty-four words. I said a few more. He was my best friend."

Chapter 12
Hospitable Hosts

"He must have told me his entire life, and I told him mine," Mordecai reminisced. "I had the pleasure of meeting Henry, but I scared the boy too much to keep him around."

Mordecai paused for a while before continuing. He flailed his hands, trying to grasp the strong emotions coursing through his soul. But the idea of a memory was a memory to him. He was old and tired. So very tired.

"Viner and I were going to stay here together forever. But we didn't. He had a duty to his people, and to Henry. And to you two."

"To us?" Hera asked.

Mordecai unfurled the wings that rested around his body, and with a great sigh, he spread them out. Hera flinched. It looked for a moment like he was about to attack them, but soon she realized that he was stretching.

The wings were fleshy skin and a gray just slightly lighter than his scales. Thin veins ran through them, but they looked like they didn't carry any blood. Some patches of the wings were pocked. Notably, there was a large bite mark on the left wing. Now that the rogues observed further, they noticed that his wings did not actually attach to his back but instead lay under his arms like a bat's.

The winged, scaled monster—no, he was a man, not a monster, that much was clear—the winged, scaled man reached his humanoid arms under the table and felt around for a moment. When he brought his hands back into view, he was grasping two cups of steaming brown liquid. Aaron darted his head under the table, looking for the cup's origin. But from his perspective, there was nothing underneath the table, not even a cabinet. When he turned his head up again to look at the table, all three of them were in a new place entirely, and three cups were steaming in front of them.

The white void had been replaced with a comfortable kitchen. The table in front of them turned into wood, and suddenly, to their surprise, they were sitting on wooden chairs. Mordecai grinned with a tinge of both sadness and dry mischief.

The room was warmly lit and homey. An apple pie rested on a countertop to their right. Something about this stead made them feel like they were in a place of rest, like they could walk into this house every day and eat a home-cooked meal. Light showered into the wooden-styled room and a door was visible leading outside into a plain green garden. A bed was tucked away in the corner, of a size that would not fit Mordecai. A hearth warmed the room, not that it needed warming.

Hera's suspicious nature got the better of her. "Is this some trick?"

"Of course," said Mordecai. "A magic trick!"

Hera eyed him suspiciously. She did not like being magically teleported from place to place in such quick succession. First, she was in Great Neighbor, then a white void, and now she was in a safe-looking kitchen. Two weeks ago, she had no clue that this would be a gripe of hers. Despite this, Hera was still too excited at the thought of drinking chocolate for the first time to pass it up.

Hera had never had chocolate before, but she knew from stories that it was a bitter candy in Aerokite. But with the addition of lots of cane sugar, also from Aerokite, it became a delicious treat. The opportunity to try it now could not be missed. Almost as soon as it hit her lips, she was bombarded with flavor.

"How does it taste?" Mordecai eagerly asked.

"It tastes fine," Hera grumbled.

She had never tasted anything as good as this. In Witshore, you ate the fish that you caught. You deboned it and grilled it yourself. Only the rich would waste valuable money on food, let alone sweets. If you wanted to spend your golden teeth on luxury, you bought a new blanket that was dry. Goldenhill was the capital of luxury, not Witshore. That is why Hera left for Great Neighbor.

Aaron did not even look at his mug before taking a sip. The sip was more of a gulp, hearty and full. Aaron wasn't too much of a brute, however, and he acted perfectly like it wasn't his first time. He placed the mug gently on the counter but kept his hand gripped around it so that he was ready to take another swig. Then, he grinned, spreading his chocolate-covered mouth wide, letting Mordecai know he enjoyed the drink without using words. His tempered attitude contrasted against Hera's less than relaxed demeanor. That's not to say that Aaron wasn't secretly just as tense.

Mordecai smiled back, showing his teeth. They weren't cuddly by any means, but they appeared now as if they wouldn't kill the rogues. His smile faltered and he leaned back in his chair. Only after a blue tinge left his face did either of the humans realize the pigment was present at all.

"Viner needs you to know that he considers his debt to you unpaid," Mordecai mumbled. "It isn't my place to tell you, but he wouldn't tell you himself. And... he needs you to know. So, I am both being a bad friend and a good one all at once... I suppose."

"His debt?" Aaron inquired.

"He swore you would be happy again. There is more to the story, much more, and that much more I cannot say," said the lizard.

"What are you?" Hera interjected.

The undefined creature shrugged. "Memory."

"Of what?" Hera insisted.

"What am I?" Mordecai mused.

***

He begged them to stay. Aaron had taken quite a liking to the man-lizard, but Hera never truly trusted him. It must have been less than an hour of small talk. Mordecai tried his best to convince them to stay in his paradox for at least a couple of days. He made certain they understood that they had literally all the time in the world. He gave them glimpses of all the wisdom he could offer, the wisdom of thousands of years. They refused. A decision they would regret until their deaths.

And at the end of a meeting that Hera and Aaron were sure never to forget, it was like it had never happened at all. Hera was back where she previously stood, as if waking from a dream. Not a dream in the night. A daydream. A memory. The sudden twist in motion made her almost lose her balance. Her stumbling was only aided by the slippery floor, but through some miracle and with the help of Aaron's hand, she was able to stay upright as if nothing had happened.

"I will warn you." She shook her head clear. "It gets real weird, real fast."

The guards seemed to be progressively becoming more uneasy than they already were. It was bad enough they had to step into a portal to the underworld, but with everyone in front of them warning them of something strange, it was becoming even more menacing. It was like a slab of iron was being pressed against their sleeping hearts as the force of gravity tried harder and harder to convince them to not venture into the portal.

"Please..." Viner sighed, his voice cracking ever so slightly. "Enter."

It was almost out of pity that the next soldier stepped into the portal. To Hera and Aaron, it looked like nothing had happened; even their expressions did not change until a few seconds later. Seeing realization spread over their faces was like watching the tide come in. Slowly, they fell into a deep sadness.

"That man... He wouldn't hurt a fly..." the guard stuttered sadly.

"Aye, how long did you stay?" Viner asked.

"Not long, only an hour or two," the guard answered.

Viner nodded, eyeing the conscript with a mutual understanding. He ushered the next soldier in with his hands. By now, curiosity was being sown into the soldiers along with fear. They were tired of being confused, and now they were filled with a slight lust for understanding. Even so, to say it did not take bravery to take the leap into the portal would be blasphemous to the self-preservation of the human mind.

Ten by hundreds of soldiers went to visit Mordecai. Every one of them had their own perspective on Mordecai. Some were afraid of him, others distrusted him, but the majority pitied him. To Hera and Aaron's knowledge, Viner was the one who stayed the longest with him. A blonde-haired guard with a sharp face claimed to have stayed for several days. She seemed to have an obsession with knowledge, but there was one key difference between her and Viner. While the guard, Vanessa, was driven by secrets of the unknown, Viner had something else altogether to learn: himself.

Only a handful of guards blatantly refused. After it was clear the guards would not enter the portal, Rose chose to reveal why she hadn't yet gone in herself. She calmly walked to the small group. They had naturally formed a tight circle of about fifty people.

"Care to explain what you are doing?" Rose sounded utterly disgusted.

"We aren't going in der," a simple guard cried in fear.

"You want to go back to your family so you can tell them how much of a coward you are?" Rose asked.

"I want to go back to my family at all! Who will stop me? You!" The guard was starting to panic. "You gonna kill me like you killed the King?"

"Yes."

The guard's heart could be heard beating out of their chest. A moment passed, thump-thump, thump-thump, and then their eyes fell to the floor. Figuratively fell to the floor. The silence was becoming tangible in the afternoon chill. It had been several hours since noon, and Rose did not want to stand around any longer.

"Well?" Rose prodded the guard.

"Kill me then!" The guard's voice was broken.

Then they started neighing like an animal, no human noise coming from their slobbering mouth. They attacked the air out of pure fear. The soldier's eyes were affixed directly to the sky as they cursed the heavens in the language of all those hunted and all those slain.

Rose wasted no time. She grappled them by the arm and tried her best to subdue the mad militant. Her heavy armor helped, but Rose was quite a few inches shorter than the rambling beast. Even so, she was an extraordinary fighter and had trained with much more composed foes. It would have been hard for even Viner to keep track of exactly what she did to subdue the guard, but somehow, Rose effortlessly overpowered the larger yet less-equipped soldier.

She dragged them across the field, their legs wildly kicking in every direction, and she took them to the foot of the rift. As soon as she let them go, the guard pushed away from her and backed themself into the portal. They ever so slightly lost their balance and almost fell involuntarily into the rift. After a second of panicked reorientation, they were back on two feet with the portal licking their back.

Rose took it upon herself to finish the job. She rammed her shoulder into the conscript's lower chest, knocking both the fightless fighter and the wind in from their lungs. The guard inhaled sharply before tumbling backward into the portal and crashing onto the marble floor.

"You tevnal, with your honeyed words!" the guard moaned to the ceiling. They drooled ever so slightly on the marble floor, and it looked like one of their teeth may have broken. They made no motion to stand. If their teeth weren't broken, their spirit surely was. To prove the point, blood was starting to mix with the spittle. The soldiers gave the conscript the respect of averting their eyes.

"I wish I could've killed you," the guard said.

It was unclear to Hera and Aaron whether they were referring to Rose or Mordecai. Either way, others soon joined in with the sentiment as Rose dragged guard after guard into the underworld. Most of them went willingly after the display of force; others tried and failed to run. In the end, only a few managed to evade Rose's wrath.

The entire ordeal was tedious. Sometimes it took upwards of fifteen minutes for Rose to come back with two or three soldiers at her heel, but Rose needed all the troops she could get. After almost the time it would have taken for a training round, every soldier that Rose could manage was on the other side of the portal. Viner and the rest had no choice but to scout out the blank area while waiting for the Mouth of the King.

Once the army was properly stationed in the marble plane, it was possible to assess the structure of the cave. The first thing Hera and Aaron noticed about the cave was that it was not a cave at all. When they entered the underworld, they expected what Rose had told them—a series of caves—but this place looked nearly identical to what Mordecai called his paradox. But, unlike Mordecai's Paradox, this white void didn't have a carpet and chair as a point of reference. Instead, they had each other and the rift to tell them where they stood. That was until they looked up.

Above them, cracks of light gleamed down. The light came from fissures in the ceiling that looked like they had come from gods smashing their great hands against the heavens. They could not tell how far away the fissures were, only that they were massive and that they cast down holy light. But even if they were identifiable as light sources, no shadow was cast beneath the two thieves' feet or any soldier's feet. It seemed that the ground itself was a light source and the rivets of power on the ceiling were only brighter. Luckily, the light wasn't too bright, but it wasn't easy on the eyes either.

The floor in the underworld was slippery, but not because it was like ice. It was slippery because it was perfectly smooth. The big, strong army men looked rather silly, falling over themselves whenever they took a step, hitting the floor with a loud crack, and then struggling to get up again. The shoes the guards wore had a piece of flat sheet metal on the bottom, and Venessa made the observation that the guards might have more traction if they took them off.

"Shoes make or break a soldier. Taking them off may be unwise," Viner warned her.

"It's rather hard to get off the ground in armor," Vanessa pointed out. "Besides, the flat surface should be gentle on our feet. I'm not sure about temperature though."

Vanessa took a quizzical look at Viner. After a moment of contemplation, Viner finally nodded at her and ordered the army to take off their shoes. Vanessa looked intently at the first guard to take off their shoes. They had recently fallen, so they were already sitting on the ground. Vanessa watched the soldier like a hawk and the militant seemed to shrink under her gaze. But after a little bit of coaxing from Vanessa, they took off their boot and tenderly placed their foot on the ground. They did not flinch when their foot hit the ground. They struggled for a moment to get the other shoe off and then rose to their feet. They still slipped slightly, but Vanessa was right— the soldier did have more traction without shoes.

Though most caves in Malue are cold and damp, the underworld is ripe with magma and pressure. For that reason, Dessees is known to be hot and dry. It would be logical for the floor to follow suit. However, the sheer size of the flat plain would indicate the floor be cold because it would be difficult to insulate such a large area. The marble floor displayed neither of these extreme characteristics. Instead, it mimicked perfectly the heat of the soldiers' feet.

Aaron and Hera took off their shoes without a second thought. They were more on edge and upset than ever, and their own anxiety was more than enough to keep them mentally occupied. They moved away from the crowd and spoke to each other for a while.

"Look at this place! I miss the sun already. Without it, we won't even know what time it is. We will have to search day and night," Aaron ranted.

He felt a hand gently touch his shoulder. Viner stood behind him, a sad smile on his face.

"Then day and night we shall search," he told the boy.

Viner turned to look at his army.

"Hour after hour," Viner said in a speaking tone.

Viner turned the corner of the group, where Hera and Aaron had stood, into a place where he could be heard.

"Rock after rock," he raised his voice.

The entirety of the army was now watching Viner, waiting to hear their captain's words. The conglomerate suddenly looked more organized, like a crowd ready for a speech.

"Leave no stone unturned!" was Viner's rallying call.

A roaring cheer echoed its way through the flat landscape. The cries bounced off the flat ceiling high above and vibrated the light fissures that affixed themselves to it. However, Hera and Aaron remained unimpressed.

"And what rocks are there to turn, may I ask?" Hera permitted herself to ask, not really caring for Viner's consensus. "It is flat here for leagues."

Viner still addressed the crowd. "It is a figure of speech!"

At this, the crowd cheered again, and Hera turned red with anger. Viner pointed away from the portal, taking a stance of great authority.

"Mordecai told me to go that way! For that reason, some of you will not trust my judgment, but as your commander, I command you to follow me. He is not our enemy. He is as much a victim as we are. I trust him, and you trust me, and I say we go that way!"

As quickly as that, the crowd was feeling the same way as Hera. Previously, the lack of shoes had been no concern, but all at once the guards' minds changed to be more pessimistic. Here they stood, in a white wasteland with no structure, natural or manmade, for miles. Here they stood with no shoes to cradle their tired feet. Here they stood with their heading set by an unknown enemy.

Viner's hand fell in disappointment at the disgruntled groans of the soldiers. He opened his mouth to try and rally them again and then closed it slowly. He crossed to the right and started walking. He left his army with no choice. They had already followed him to the end of the world. They had followed him after Rose assassinated their king. He and Rose were the closest thing they had to leaders. Hera and Aaron had to face it; if they had to choose between the Hand or the Mouth of the King, Viner was their best bet.

So they followed. First with their eyes, then with their feet. Viner didn't know whether he walked into the void alone until a hand grasped his arm. He looked down, and a tear rolled down his cheek, for he had already been weeping for his old friend whom he had just left behind and for what his old friend had gifted him. Henry looked up to him, and he looked down to Henry. In that moment, Viner knew that his army was soon to follow.

"My boy..." Viner choked, and he remembered what he had discussed with Mordecai, and it felt as if he had always known it. "We walk together now. To the end of the void. You were not born my son, but I have always loved you as my own. Now is my chance to prove it."

Henry wasn't as ready as Viner was. After all, Viner had a year to think it all over. So they walked, hand in hand, and an army marched behind them, and behind that army marched one woman with no child to hold her hand.

Chapter 13
Forests are a Luxury

Hera and Aaron spent the next few hours walking. They chatted between themselves but had little to talk about that could keep their minds off the gloom. It felt like days before Viner finally stopped to set up camp. Soldiers had wisely brought their own tents, but few knew how to set them up. The people of Great Neighbor rarely had a need for camping. Luckily, Aaron had learned how to set up a tent on his journey from Sunsoon to Layden when his pockets became too light and the prices of the inns too hefty.

Neither of the rogues felt inclined to help their fellow soldiers. In turn, no soldier was willing to ask for help not freely given. Aaron helped set up Hera's tent and then his own, and that was that. Hera was fully capable of making her own bed, so she did. Aaron left her to it so that he could win his own rest. The rogues were still ill-liked, so they set up near the edge of camp. They preferred to be on the edge anyway, as long as they didn't think too hard about it. Calessa felt much the same way and was only a few tents away.

"So, do you think the Aerokititan is really going to help us?" a rude guard grumbled to another. They were both within perfect hearing range of Calessa, and, in fact, it looked like they wanted her to hear.

The other shook their head in disgust. "You can't trust one of them foreigners, I'm telling ya'."

Calessa continued struggling to set up her tent. She refused to look at the aggressors. The rest of the guard was used to the distrust directed towards Calessa and didn't do anything to stop it. Much like the rogues, they didn't help set up her tent either. But something about her fellow guards' refusal felt more personal.

"Say, she's got a pretty face on her though," the first said meanly.

"Aye, she would be lucky to be the wife of a pure-blood like one of us," mused the other.

Calessa's brow furrowed, but she still refused to look at either of them.

The soldiers only paused for a moment before continuing their tirade, "You want to hear a poem, dear? Would that put a smile on your pretty face?"

"Are we singing songs over her?" A third voice added. It was much higher than the others. It took a long second for Calessa to place whose it was. A moment later, Tython, Dimfir's emissary, emerged from behind a tent. He walked with an arrogant swagger only replicable by those who had no clue what they had just gotten into.

"We've got another foreigner here," laughed one of the soldiers.

"Yeah, I suppose Dimfir songs would be foreign, wouldn't they?" Tython was either too kind or too dumb to be offended.

Tython had some sort of string instrument clutched in his hands. It was a beautiful instrument, but Calessa wasn't well versed in the names of such things. It was made of dark trimmed wood, surely from Tython's own home trees. Many strings ran up and down the back of the wood. But even bigger than the neck was the body. Combined with Tython's small stature, it looked as if he was holding a giant turtle shell.

As an emissary, it was Tython's job to present as charming and being able to play a sweet melody helped. Tython was naturally the jolly type anyway, so he already knew how to play before volunteering. He wasn't the greatest player in the world but whenever he needed the quick satisfaction of an instrument, he would play a small tune and sometimes even sing along.

"We have this little song—"

"We don't care!" a rude soldier yelled from a few spaces away.

Even the original two soldiers found the outburst a little too childish. The offender smiled at them, with pitiful allure. But still they couldn't pry a laugh from their friend's teeth. After that, the soldier turned rather red and darted their eyes to the white ground.

Tython appeared like he didn't even hear him, "It's called 'An Ode to Home'."

The guards didn't have time to grumble before the delicate strings were already being plucked by Tython's nimble fingers. Much like him, his fingers were short, but he compensated by dancing them quickly across the strings. After years of practice his physical disadvantages abated. He did live up to the elf insult Viner had flung at him. And so, after a brief few measures of finding his beat, he started to sing in a comfortable octave.

"Even if—" Tython prepared to start the next verse, but just then his fingers faltered. If he had dwelled on the mistake any longer, it might have ruined the performance. But he was too quick for that. With a hidden stutter and an ad-lib recovery, he was back on track.

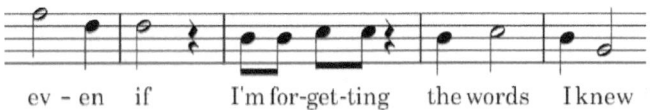

ev - en   if   I'm for-get-ting   the words   I knew

This reaped a hearty laugh from the growing crowd. Though he intended the line as a joke, the laughter put him on edge. He grasped in the air for the missing words but resorted to freestyle and looked rapidly around for something to sing about. He was considering repeating the first verse when he rested his brown eyes on Calessa. She was watching him with some semblance of gratitude. After seeing her there, he knew what to sing about. His pace quickened rapidly and he crescendoed to a forte. Despite Tython's newfound shakiness, his voice grew in confidence.

you say that she's for-eign but she does   a north-ern   sa-lute

The offending conscripts knew what this was about. They turned hot in rage and embarrassment. Calessa herself also turned red. Being in the spotlight wasn't usually something she liked. But no one looked at her now; their eyes were glued to the nervous bard. Both parties had to hand it to him; Tython was a masterful performer. His next line proved that.

if that's true let's back up   I'll pack up   my lute

Suddenly Tython's strumming stopped. It took seven beats before the crowd realized what had happened. They all jeered but not in a mean-spirited way. They called out words and phrases like "No", "Come on", and "Encore". Tython quite liked that last one. With a great sigh, he returned to his song. He started from the beginning, returning to his soft tone and slow pace.

though days a-part know that my heart be-longs to you

though it's a start my jour - ney home is true

Slowly he began to hasten, excited for the next few lines he had dreamt up. With a heavy major chord, he accented every white note as he delivered the finale to his opener.

though hope is sparse it's not a farce it's true

Tython followed his lips with his strings leaving plenty of space between each phrase. His voice cracked as he said the word 'true'. But as any good musician knows, a voice crack emboldened by passion can be a beautiful thing.

to-geth-er we wea-ther we walk we see it through

we faced the new what did we do we grew - we - grew

It wasn't the most thought-through ending in Tython's career, but it would do. It didn't matter to the onlookers what Tython thought. It was just what they needed to hear. The crowd cheered loudly. If they had had cups in their hands, they would have toasted, but the best they could do was raise their arms above their heads. For a moment, and a solitary moment at that, they forgot their worries.

Hera and Aaron got to their feet and, following suit with the majority of the company, gathered around Tython. Tython took a long sweeping look around the crowd. He made eye contact for a moment with Calessa, and Calessa quickly turned away. He paid her no further mind and instead focused on his fingers. They ached in anticipation of the battle of ballads he was going to have to play. Rose was mid-conversation with Viner when Tython started on his second Dimfir classic.

"They should sleep. This is a waste of time," Rose muttered.

"They need this," Viner nodded. "You're lucky they are taking out their anger in a healthy way. I've had a year to forgive you, to understand why you killed my king. I understand. But that does not make it right."

"Always about business, even when your people dance," Rose mocked.

Viner shook his head like he was talking to a bratty child. "Rose. One day, you will run out of venom to line your words. Best stop now before you grind out your tongue's poisonous lining."

Rose looked forward to the horizon. "Petty insults will get you nowhere," she quipped.

She kept a blank stare at the ceiling. If she thought hard enough, or maybe if she thought not at all, the white roof could almost be mistaken for a clouded sky. She closed her eyes for a moment. They made more movements observing the darkness of her eyelids than when she was seeing the light. She snapped them open, and the fire that had been burning behind the lids panicked and dwindled.

Rose smiled sadly. "You should join them, General. The captain who eats with his men isn't eaten by his men."

Viner could have been insulted. It was his first reaction. She dared bring up memories of his late brother now? But Viner chose not to. He *chose* not to. A year, or maybe it was a day ago, he would never have let that stand. But now, for better or for worse, he was a calm man. When his head was clear, he agreed with Rose; he should revel with his men.

"Henry!" Viner greeted his nephew with as much happiness as he could muster.

Viner was a saddened man. A broken man. But Henry was his boy, and, for Viner, happiness was not difficult to conjure when looking at his face.

"Hey, Uncle." Henry was as much in the crowd as anyone else, though he was alone as ever without his father by his side. How much he was grieving must have been almost impossible to tell for anyone in the crowd but Viner. Viner knew too well.

"Any girls your age?" Viner smirked.

"Uncle!" Henry protested and turned red.

"Let's see..." Viner knelt down to the boy conspiratorially. "I'm sure you can find someone to talk to. A few soldiers out of a thousand are most definitely under seventeen."

Henry turned away a little sheepishly, desperately wanting to get out of this conversation.

"I wasn't talking about girls that time." Viner nodded seriously. "You have to make a friend, even if it's not a girlfriend. If you don't, you'll be lonely." He looked seriously at Henry for a moment, but then his face broke into a grin. "It's a celebration after all!" The large man laughed.

"Of what?" Henry asked sarcastically.

"Tython being a good player," Viner said. "In more ways than one."

Viner was of course referring to Tython's defense of Calessa. A large number of the guard had observed what happened. The only person on whom the relevance was lost was Tython himself. Henry shook his head but couldn't help but grin to himself.

"Stop, stop, stop. I understand," he said.

Hera and Aaron danced a little together. Mainly, Aaron danced while Hera watched him. Every once in a while, a soldier would come and join them. A large crowd formed in a lumpy circle around Tython, and several smaller assemblies stretched out around the large gathering. Tython had to play as loud as he could to be heard by the more distant groups. He sacrificed both his fingers and some dynamics to make sure it was possible to be heard clearly.

After a while, the crowd entertained itself and no longer required Tython's assistance for the lively atmosphere. With much cheering and applause, Tython unceremoniously exited. He stumbled toward the tents and was promptly forgotten about.

"You could always talk to Hera and Aaron. They are fairly young. How much can really happen in four years?" Viner continued with Henry.

"Yeah, I guess," Henry said halfheartedly.

"But she is too old for you!" Viner said.

"Come on! Are we still talking about this!" Henry squirmed.

"I am just teasing," Viner giggled. "No-I'm-not," He added under his breath all in one quick word.

Tython waddled past the crowd and into a far tent. He was about sixty percent sure it was his. He laid down on his flat mattress, which the guards called a bed, and wondered how he had gone from feather pillows to this. One day, he sailed the sea to a curious new land, the next that land reaped nothing but horror. Was Tython crazy for looking into that abyss of gloom and seeing nothing but opportunity? A chance to finally prove he wasn't some weakling. Tython turned on his mattress and tried his best to add any fluff to the completely flat, hard ground. 'That settles it,' he thought. 'I am raving mad.' He was only half-joking with himself.

A rustle shook through his tent, and a timid footstep followed it. Tython sat up to the noise. His movements were astoundingly slow for someone who was currently in the underworld. He blinked his eyes to alertness after realizing that he probably should be panicking. But to his pleasant surprise, he turned to see Calessa kneeling down to open the door of the tent.

"Oh..." Tython said awkwardly. "Hi."

Calessa was already flushing, "Um. Hello there."

Tython waited for her to say something. He relaxed a little in his bed and didn't bother to stand up or further greet her. After a moment of twiddling his thumbs, he decided Calessa wasn't going to be the one to speak first.

"What's up?" he asked cheerily.

"I just wanted to..." Calessa stopped herself and almost decided to leave. "Thank you for that song."

"Oh," Tython nodded.

He went back to twiddling his thumbs for a while. Tython's feet started to dance under the covers to the imaginary tune of his favorite song, "*Where the Pines Grow.*" He waited for Calessa to add anything. She didn't.

"Which one?" Tython was genuinely clueless.

Calessa stuttered for a moment, taken aback by the question. "The one about me..." she said with a sad uncertainty.

"Ah," Tython nodded. "I made most of that up."

Calessa nodded slowly, "I know."

Calessa didn't quite want to admit to the idea that this boy who had swooped her off her feet was painfully stupid, but that fear was starting to dawn on her.

"I thought that was very nice," Calessa started in her meek tone. "Even if it was a little embarrassing," she chuckled.

"Oh," Tython laughed along. "Yeah... Sorry."

"I was just thanking you, wasn't I?" Calessa teased.

"Yeah... I guess," Tython replied sheepishly.

"Well if..." Calessa mumbled sadly.

Calessa started to turn away from the tent. Tython couldn't tell if she was moving too slowly or too quickly, but either way, it was a defeated turn.

"Wait," Tython surprised himself by calling after her.

Calessa stopped immediately. She turned to look at him again. Tython was certain this motion was faster than it was slow.

"Those guards are pretty lousy," Tython pointed out.

Calessa was touched by Tython's obvious desire to continue a conversation. If Tython had said anything even remotely more intelligent, she might have thought he cared about the answer. But the fact was, he just wanted to talk to her. Calessa desperately tried to not get flustered.

"They were," she laughed.

"You know, they remind me of some people back home." Tython grinned. "Want me to tell you about them?"

Chapter 14
Rose's Marching Order

Once Rose had decided the troops were sufficiently rested, she gave the order to awaken them. Rose's idea of a good rest was six hours at best, but Viner didn't have the energy to fight her yet again. Aaron was correct when he said they had no basis for time in the underworld. Without a sun to cast shadow and with clocks being a rare thing even in Anarchy, the army was ill-prepared to track the hour.

Rose organized the groups into a pattern of proficiency. She ditched Viner's battalion one and battalion two hierarchy and reassigned the army into five battalions. The first battalion was the ranger battalion and consisted of shortbow archers, leading the charge. Tython was part of this group. With him were no more than one hundred others, making it by far the smallest group. If trouble were to arise, the battalion was instructed to stop moving once the enemy was in range and let those behind them overtake the frontal position. This ensured that they had as few casualties as possible.

The ranger battalion was followed by the wall shield battalion. Viner led this battalion personally. Taking full wall shields on their journey would have been too taxing on all but the strongest soldiers, so instead they brought with them slightly smaller kite shields. True to their name, the kite shields were a large slightly curved triangular sheet of thin gleaming metal. A single hexagon was embossed on every shield and when put together into a shield wall, they vaguely resembled the turtle shell insignia embroidering the guards. The wall shield battalion was equipped with spears. Their job was to protect the rangers once they fell back.

Behind them marched the light infantry, consisting of those like Henry, Aaron, and Hera. They were the second-largest force and the ones that would be pulling the most weight if all else failed. They were equipped with a light buckler shield, more helpful for quick defense than for anything else. Blades ranging from rapiers to gladii to broadswords were sheathed at their waists. The straight weapons of each soldier varied according to personal preference.

The final line of defense that could prevent the army from being overtaken was the heavy infantry, which Rose led from behind. They would focus on disposing of large groups of enemies as quickly as possible. For that purpose, the soldiers were equipped with greatswords almost exclusively. Calessa fought with this group. In the past, she had fought with the wall shield battalion, but something made her feel more inclined to take a more offensive approach.

Bringing up the rear marched the long-range artillery. Some of the higher-ranked soldiers were given crossbows, but most of this large group was composed of longbow-wielding conscripts. The artillery was by far the largest of all five battalions. If all went well, it was also the safest position. However, it was not without its downfall. If the army were to be flanked, the artillery would be targeted first. It was the heavy infantry's job to make sure that didn't happen.

Henry was positioned on Hera's left and Aaron on her right. The troops had fallen into order in the location they wished, so naturally, Hera and Aaron were next to each other. What they did not expect was for Henry to eagerly stand next to them. A strange glow shown in his eyes—that of a fairy-tale adventure. Despite being in a literal fairy tale, no other soldier shared that glow, except, perhaps Tython. The army had been marching for no less than thirty minutes when Henry decided to say something.

"Hello," Henry excitedly whispered.

Hera looked at him for a moment and then set her face forward again. She stayed that way for a moment, but out of the corner of her eye she could see Henry fidgeting.

"I don't think we are supposed to be talking," she hissed.

Henry sighed, but if Hera didn't know better, she would have thought the boy was grinning.

"It's fine," he said.

They continued marching for a moment more before Henry's nature got the better of him. Previously, Hera had thought the boy was rather mature, but she was rapidly discovering how mistaken she was.

"I'm bored," he whined.

"So am I," Aaron echoed.

Hera snapped her head over to Aaron. He was already looking at her. An annoying grin creased the side of his mouth, telling Hera that he and Henry weren't so different.

Henry lunged forward to start speaking to Aaron around Hera. "Do you want to hear a story?" he asked with more delight than the underworld had ever seen.

Hera tried to shut them down. "Wait—" she said.

But it was too late. Aaron was already nodding enthusiastically. "You bet!"

"Great!" Henry said.

Despite his whispering, it was quite easy to hear the boy across the crowd. The only thing that could muffle his voice was the sound of bare feet softly hitting the marble ground. But that soft noise was only a piano-pitter-patter. With no one else saying a word and the hard ground refusing to make more sound than a stealthy cat, Henry was the center of attention. He didn't even know it.

***

"This one comes from Witshore," Henry began.

Aaron nodded in appreciation of a story from his birthplace.

Great Neighbor had historical ethnic roots in Witshore. For that reason, they shared a similar culture except that Witshore was a little more focused on fish. A little *too* focused on fish.

"Deep in the bogs of Witshore, an even deeper fog sleeps somber," recited Henry. "A fog so dense that a fisherman could lose his own lure. In these mists, few decide to venture. You could go days without seeing any huts inhabited by normal folk. But how the mists came to be is a story as old as the royal lineage. It starts with the first of the royal bloodlines... long, long ago, when King Charles the first ruled Witshore and, with it, all the Northern Kingdom.

"His daughter was remembered as the Mistress but born then as Jezebel. She was notorious for her extreme intelligence and desire for knowledge. She was fascinated with the stories of the past, so ancient that they were already long forgotten many years prior. Even more, she was enthralled by the swamps that barricaded her land from invasion. Even then, she did not trust Goldenhill and, even then, Ironforge was Goldenhill's puppet. She soon expected a civil war and feared it above all else.

"To the rest of the kingdom, Jezebel was mysterious. She spent almost no time with her people and instead focused on bolstering her country's defense and reading all she could about anything that could defend her land. She was born into power. It was her responsibility not to lose it.

"It took her years, but soon she had read every book in the library, heard every tale from every tavern. For a time, it looked like she would be satisfied. But she was clever, far more clever than she had any right to be, and she noticed something that only clever people notice—a pattern.

"Behind every war, one entity. Behind every eye, one guiding light. Behind every sword, one arm. So it was that this knowledge, this realization, freed her from her own paradox. 'Should you not be the rightful ruler of all land?' the knowledge told her. 'And if land, why not sea as well,' it cooed.

"She agreed. What purpose had land if not to teach her its secrets? What purpose had sea if not to whisper in her ear with its shores? What soldier would not die to know the truth?"

For a moment Henry's voice became soft and rubbery, like he was speaking underwater. The next few words he said felt like the details of a dream. They were forgotten before they were heard as if they were never supposed to be said at all.

"'I am a god,' it told her at last. But to this, she did not celebrate. Her god did not sound like that. It did not speak to her so directly. How dare the voice presume it was a god. She had conjured it, and it worked under her power. She told it so, and it did not grace her ear again."

Hera's, Aaron's, and Henry's ears popped as if they had breifly been fillied with air. A sense of foreboding filled the air, as if somehow this was a story that should not be told. In truth, none could place their finger on what was wrong. But something about the concept of a god made Hera and Aaron uncomfortable. However, it was not enough though to interrupt what was turning out to be a surprisingly sophisticated story, if not too pretentious, and the story continued with barely a pause.

"So, to the top of her tower, she climbed, her chilling robe flowing behind her—a better entourage than any followers. With each step, the stone froze and turned to ice so that none could follow her. To the top of the tower she climbed, until she could see her thin city stretch across the coast. To the ocean, she commanded. 'Bring me not only their souls but their blood as well. Let me use it for its divine purpose. May I ascend in the name of my people as it's one true ruler.'

"The ocean turned red and the souls of her people were sundered from their mortal minds. Her father turned to his death bed and laid in it, so that he may fall unto pale illness. She saw what she had done, and in a panic, she summoned the mist of fog to cover her city and in doing so, her dark deed.

"She took control in blood. In absence of her father, she was the heir. Anyone who opposed her would be swallowed by the mist. She soon learned that there was blood and power in her people. She took to regaining control of the rest of the Northern Kingdom. Her citizens would be her sacrifice in her ascension.

"The forests of Dimfir would not bow to her, so she cursed the woodland to be filled with vile monsters. The hills of Goldenhill would not prostrate, so she cursed their soil to become infertile. Icebreaker would not kneel, so she erected the Half-Thawed Mountain range and called forth ice to cover their land, even in summer. To Ironforge, she decreed that they become her army, and seeing what else had been done, iron bent.

"In only three years, which shall be known as the darkest years, she had taken the Northern Kingdom into her clutches. She bore an heir, and to prove that her power flowed through the boy's blood, she named him Charles after her own father. She decreed that only the strongest bloodline may rule the Kingdom, for no other could have the will of magic on their side. To prove they were truly strong in blood, all royal children from Witshore would be renamed after the Mistress's father or herself.

"On her explicit request, the dukedoms did the same. So Richard would be the name of Goldenhill, Alexandria be the name of Dimfir, Diane be the name of Icebreaker, and Arthur be the name of Ironforge. After only three years of her new system, with her son one year of age, she had fully gained control over her kingdom. No one dared question her authority or strength, lest the fog consume them.

"Her troubles were not behind her, however, for the noble people who lived to the east did not approve of her evils. The people of the Republic in the East had come together to support their neighbors as the North had done for them so long ago. The Republic was growing in prosperity with the warm sun helping bear good crops from their knolls.

"They sent word for scholars across all their land and created the greatest weapons known to man. The Republic of the East united to face off against the Mistress. They had many sorcerers in their midst who knew best how to ride horses. With swords made of pure light, they left their beautiful rolling hills and galloped to Ironforge.

"The meeting of Ironforge was an unconventional conquest not soon forgotten. It is said that before the invasion, a wise wizard marched alone a day ahead of his army to the walls of the iron-rich mountains of Ironforge. It is also said that he preached his wisdom to the people of the gate, bidding they let him enter their grand kingdoms and speak to the noble Duke Arthur. Ironforge found their courage and the wizard was brought before the Duke inside the wall.

"The old man was escorted with blade, but the wizard raised no finger in his defense. It was true that his forces were more than a full day behind him, and it was true also that the wizard would not hurt the duke. However, one could not blame Ironforge for being cautious of these claims. When he met Arthur, he discovered that the once-noble duke had fallen into a deep depression, ashamed of himself for kneeling to terror.

"The wizard did the unthinkable and placed his hand on the chin of the duke. He raised the duke's face to meet his, and in the duke's sad eyes, a spark of fire sputtered to existence. Arthur snapped to attention and with little more than a word. He began rallying his troops to make a stand for righteous good.

"A day they waited and a day it took for the people of the Republic to arrive at the gates of Ironforge's wall. When the army arrived at the gates, their swords of light were sheathed and they were ready to greet Ironforge as friends. Ironforge's king gave a tearful apology to his people for disgracing the name of Ironforge and bowing to an unjust ruler without a fight. His people were filled with shame, but the Republic pardoned them and promised that they would see glory again.

"Once past the gates of Ironforge, reaching Witshore was less difficult. Ironforge controlled most of the Northern Kingdom's military, and most of the space in between Ironforge and Witshore was empty. The army traveled to the south, around Goldenhill and approached Witshore from its southwest.

"It is said they were surrounded by mist before they knew it. The swamp itself rose and fell with the sweet, sickly dance of the fog. The smell of the vapor was disgustingly fecal and made the soldiers' eyes water. Yet still, the mist did little more than mask the few feet ahead of the soldiers, and they trudged on.

"In the bog, they met monsters such as tranodiles, crocodiles the size and shape of bears. They met the valtor, a folk of vulture-like people that were barely sentient but able to make tools. They even met the deathly greg, a blind serpent with millions of legs."

To this, Hera and Aaron laughed, and Henry looked at them, confused.

"They avoided what they could, but occasionally they were forced to fight off monsters that attacked them. The only reason they were not slain in the swamps was the swords of light that drove away the fog.

"It took them several weeks, but they finally reached the foot of Ocentia, the greatest of all the long-cities in Witshore. Jezebel the Mist Mistress stood perched atop her tower, watching the attackers approach.

"'I have seen your future, oh great Republic, and it is not I who am your adversary,' she said. 'Don't you see... they sent us to destroy each other. Your science is unnatural, and the greater forces want it reset.'

"Her lies fell on deaf ears, resolved in their stance against her. They summoned their swords of light and readied their great weapon—a weapon so powerful it deserved its own name, even if it would never be seen again. Atom, the king of weapons, the deadliest force that could ever exist, penultimated by none, was levitated above the ground by a wizard of light. 'If you do this, you will be turned to desert, and your justice will be transformed into lawless chaos,' she warned.

"They would not listen. They needed to stop the Mistress. And because of this, the Mistress needed to stop them. A beam of smoke formulated into solid matter and slammed itself against the army, taking dozens of lives at a time. With a swish of his staff, the grand wizard dispelled the attack.

"The Mistress was not out of tricks and called forth her armies, the behemoth of man. Of her armies, there were three. And each of them multiple souls trapped in one body.

Endoshale-Army, the conglomerate of human suffering, seeped from the walls of Ocentia. Endoshale-Army resembled a man wearing the skin of a dark bug. The army wielded two curved swords. It was several meters tall and in place of its face was a dastardly helmet that resembled a beetle.

"After Endoshale came Gildonan-Army, the brutality of humanity, with plates of iron clumsily adorning stitched together flesh. Gildonan-Army gently strummed on the string of a bow with arrows that would have been better used for a ballista.

"And finally was Hlijankini-Army, the dreams and ambitions of every soul sacrificed to create such a monster. Hlijankini held in its grip an orb of souls and blood, ready to be used to vanquish any soldier in its path. It looked like a giant reflection of Jezebel, but instead of a face, a dark shadow loomed.

"These armies were the fruits of the Mist Mistress's labor. The Republic realized in despair that they were too late and that the soldiers of Ocentia had already been turned into these three monsters. Not only was it too late for the people on Witshore, but nothing the wizards could conjure would defeat these armies. It was too late for The Republic.

"So, they dropped Atom.

"The Mistress laughed a wicked laugh, 'Your weapon means nothing.'

"Atom did fall, but he did not fall on Ocentia. The lives of the soldiers were spared, if only for a moment. The war drums stopped, Endoshale-Army knelt, Gildonan-Army relaxed its string, and Hlijankini-Army admired its orb. The warriors of light breathed a sigh of relief, even if their onslaught had failed. Do not blame them for that sigh as they blamed themselves. They knew they had failed, but it was only natural that the burden of death be lifted off their chests.

"The burden was replaced with burn. A bright light, that light which is given off by a raging forest fire, a light grim in its immense power, blazed behind their backs. They turned east to see a bloom of smoke like a great oak reaching for the sky. So complete was the fog of war that it looked to be a structure more than a residue.

"Though the eruption was minuscule on the horizon, it lit the sky like the rising sun. But unlike the rising sun, it did not breed prosperity. Let us take a moment to bow our heads, as the soldiers did when watching their homeland go up in flames. Let us remember the sweet springs that trickled across the landscape of the old Republic. Let us remember the happy people who bathed in those springs. In paradise.

"From the ashes after flames rose an evil. Jezebel directed her three armies to slaughter all Republic members while preserving any Ironforge citizens they could. Her armies did as she commanded. They slew them on the spot and the armies of light did not raise a finger in defense.

"To say that Jezebel took pleasure in the extinction of the country would have been inflammatory and false. 'I can make this right. You... you don't need your bodies!' The madwoman ranted in fear of herself. 'Yes, of course, I'll make you new ones. After I have become a god. Yes... I'm sorry. I'm so sorry.'

"In the face of her greatest evil, Jezebel felt remorse. It was as if the evil that had set her heart in stone had suddenly lifted, so that she could feel the true sting of what she had done. What had she done? Why had she done it? Only her final words can hope to even try to explain her maddened mind. 'After all this is done, it'll be... oh... no... I've lost... it's not my fault! They made me do it. Don't leave me! I can't bear it,' she cursed to the sky.

"Historians claim that she looked like a different person

altogether. When Duke Arthur marched to her, she was strewn on the ground, weeping maniacally. She let him detain her and take her to her own palace so that she could be tried.

"His lieutenants reported to him that the three armies had dissipated, leaving behind the corpses of the people used in the ritual to create them. The bodies were lifeless. Arthur was saddened by their deaths, but he couldn't help but be relieved by this revelation. He ordered that the few remaining citizens of Ocentia be brought to the royal hall. He explicitly stated they not be punished, for they were victims most of all.

"In honor of the fallen Republic, they hosted a republic-style trial for Jezebel, Mistress of Mist. In that trial, Jezebel pleaded not guilty by reason of insanity. The plea was ruled correct by the judge—an unpopular opinion. She was thrown into the swamp, to be exiled there for all of eternity. She did not attempt to return. On a foggy night, it is not the tranodlies, nor the valtor, not even the greg to fear. What is feared most of all, is the mist."

***

As usual, Hera had taken a moment to submerge into the story. Even after she was enthralled with the legend, she refused to show it on her face for quite some time. Aaron, of course, was supportive throughout and made appreciative noises at all the right intervals. Henry's face twisted into a self-satisfied smile with Aaron's affirmation. He had told the story almost as well as any muse. Hera found his goofy grin quite endearing, as she had seen it many times on Aaron.

"So, you guys have anything interesting to add?" Henry joked.

"That's one of the best stories I've heard," Aaron said, astonished.

"Come on!" Henry all but shouted, aghast. "Really?"

"It was pretty cool," Hera admitted begrudgingly.

Other guards too had heard the story, and though a few of them didn't find it to their liking, it was of little annoyance in the end. But Henry hardly noticed them, he was happier than he could put into words that Hera and Aaron were impressed with his story. The two seemed special in a way, and all the guards knew it. They were the only ones forcibly drafted for reasons no one knew. It felt like they had gone from thieves to respected soldiers overnight. It was no wonder the other guards were suspicious. It was Henry's curious nature that made him want to know them. He, being naive as he was, never considered the possibility that they were bad people. If others weren't so worried about the thieving past of Hera and Aaron, perhaps they would have shared Henry's curiosity.

"Why do you steal stuff?" Henry asked.

"I think you mean, how do you steal stuff?" Aaron grinned.

Henry shook his head. "No, I mean why."

Aaron's grin faltered for a second, "Well... it's fun; it makes for a good story... I can tell you about it if you want."

"No," Henry said, "That sounds like a sad story. I would feel bad for the people you stole from."

Hera went on the defense. "We don't steal anything they need."

"You don't know what they need," Henry said, cheerfully enough.

Henry had no clue that he was picking a fight. He didn't realize the taboo nature of the subject. Hera and Aaron usually wouldn't have noticed either, but they were in a bit of a different situation than usual, being in the underworld and surrounded by soldiers. Neither of the rogues spoke, and they waited instead for Henry to change the subject. He never did. Hera and Henry were completely content with the conversation being over, but Aaron felt rather awkward about ending it on a sharp note.

Aaron tried several times to keep up a good conversation, but his starters always fell flat. Aaron thought flat was even worse than sharp. The awkwardness that Aaron felt was much like the ground. It was completely flat and boring, but with each step, the hard surface would send a sharp jolt of energy through your muscles. All in all, the jolt was not painful, but it was noticeable and irritating, especially with bare feet.

From the back of the line, Rose mentally critiqued the march. Every electrical step, another soldier was out of line. Viner had no problem with his soldiers not keeping a rigid formation. It was speed they were after, not intimidation. But Rose knew better. She had never seen war, but something in her head told her all she needed to know. If an army could not march, how could they fight?

Chapter 15
Rule

The next rest did not bring about a replication of the lively celebration of the rest before. When Tython took his spot to play, he read the mood, and instead of choosing an upbeat ballad, he decided to stick with some sweet lullaby tunes with little to no singing involved. Though it was fun to drink in celebration, it was not the best choice to do so every day. Besides, Rose had taught them to soak up all the rest while they could, because she certainly wouldn't be letting them have any extra.

Calessa did feel quite lonely, however. Grief still consumed her, and all she could do was try to forget. In the raid, she lost her sister and her closest friend. They were one and the same. For some people, grieving means taking their minds off it, even just for a moment, and that was the case for Calessa.

There was only one person Calessa really wanted to talk to, and it was the boy from the woodlands, Tython. Tython liked Calessa well enough, but he had no clue how highly Calessa held him. If he had known, he might have been worried about disappointing her, but without that worry in mind, he found her easy to talk to.

"Hello again," Tython greeted her as she entered his tent for the second night. "This is my tent, you know," Tython said.

Putting a smile on her face even before entering the tent was a feat for Calessa, but she managed it with Tython's help.

"I know," she laughed. "I just wanted to…"

She stopped awkwardly and tried her best to hide her nervousness.

"See how you were doing," she finished after a while.

"Yeah, I'm doing great," Tython said honestly.

If he had noticed Calessa's awkward hesitation, he was polite enough to not point it out. But his wide glassy eyes suggested he had not really considered it strange at all. Calessa just looked at him for a moment, wondering what he was thinking. The fear that Tython was dull crept into the corners of her mind again. But the last night—assuming it was indeed night—that she had spoken to Tython, he had started much the same. Once he warmed up, he was a masterful storyteller.

"This is familiar," Tython said cheerfully.

"It is," she slowly agreed.

"You should grab your bed. It would be more comfortable to sit on," Tython suggested.

To this, Calessa's nose burned as well as her cheeks. The blood in her face must have been tired of returning so often just to be dismissed later. Calessa waited a moment and nodded in response. Then she got up and turned to start walking. Her feet stumbled, not quite able to decide which direction to go. The movement didn't really make any sense; it was just a reflex. She stalled for a moment, panicking about her body's refusal to follow her commands. After a second that seemed too long, she started walking away again.

Hera and Aaron, on the other hand, were not so eager to carry on a conversation. In fact, Calessa and Tython were somewhat of an anomaly in the army. Most went to sleep rather quickly after Tython retired. With a toast to comradery and a jovial "All in a day's work," the rogues and the army fell to bed.

Calessa awoke to find her sleeping bag far from any tent. She and Tython had decided that the tent was useless when they were indoors, and they would both much rather be less closed in. They were gazing at the ceiling of the underworld when Calessa had fallen asleep. She remembered looking up at the cracks in the mock sky and pretending they were stars. She wasn't sure what was a dream and what wasn't. But, some of it must have been real, because Tython rested a few feet from her. He was snoring loudly and still asleep. Calessa was grateful that he hadn't awakened quite yet. She got up as quietly as she could and returned to the larger group.

The morning left little room for the telling of sweet stories about the beauty of the bygone sky. For the soldiers, it was dreary and aggravatingly gray. Rose herself had not slept at all, neither this rest nor the rest before. Rose's willpower was extreme, but not sleeping for more than forty hours in a row is damaging to any mental fortress. Many soldiers wouldn't be able to keep themselves awake for so long, but Rose was held by hatred.

The day of walking included what one would expect from a group of not-so-well-trained soldiers. Though the number of real guards outnumbered the number of citizens, the army was treated more as a militia than as a legion. This had its benefits and its drawbacks. The army's morale was actually being boosted as they walked forward. Talking through a mutual problem with a comrade was a popular form of therapy among the soldiers. Hatred was often an interesting discussion point. Viner knew that, in the future, this lack of discipline would be akin to a cancer for the army, but as of that moment, the short-term benefits outweighed the long-term consequences. Rose was not so lenient. For now, she broiled in her own spite, but sooner or later, she knew it would be for the good of her people that she ended the blight of disorder.

This day, Henry told a slightly shorter story called "The Genie of the Woods," which Hera and Aaron found interesting but not quite as impressive as his first story. Some other troops joined in on the banter and talked of their days at home and what they had done "before all this began". They never named what had begun. They never said "before the war" or "before the attack". They would always say "before all this began". But late in the supposed night when all were meant to be asleep, there was one other term thrown around. It was uttered in dreams, or perhaps not dreams but nightmares. It was only then that they said "before this nightmare".

When the soldiers awoke from their dreams of better times turned to ash, they were in a foul mood. Most of them were getting tired of being able to count their hours of sleep on a single hand. They were not only tired physically, but also mentally tired of being pushed so hard to achieve a goal they could not visualize.

The day started as usual, the soldiers' morale like an hourglass filled with grains of sand. The soldiers rose to their feet and packed up their tents. A nicely sized pile was left in the top of the hourglass. Soon, they began marching, and for an hour or so, the hourglass remained half full. But things became dire when the soldiers began to suspect that their rations were soon to run out. Paranoia became rampant. Soldiers began to wonder if perhaps a neighbor had stolen their rations. The hourglass of morale dwindled to nothing but a small pile of hope on top with a heap of problems below. For a moment, it would look like the hole had been plugged and four grains were stuck together in the upper chamber. Daintily, they kept themselves upright, holding against each other. But a mere slip and they would all fall down.

"Son of a—" cried a soldier.

The next thing Rose knew, she was standing over the body of a soldier on the ground. The clumsy man had been in a conversation and evidently whatever topic they were discussing distracted him enough that he lost his footing on the slippery ground. He had rolled his ankle and collapsed under the weight of his full plate armor. Luckily for him, he was near the back row in the archery battalion, so he wasn't trampled when he fell. However, he did receive a soft accidental kick from the soldier behind him. Now Rose stood over him. She extended her hand down to the soldier, a friendly enough gesture, but the soldier scowled at her. He shakily got to his feet. He made a point of not taking her hand while doing so.

"Don't try to touch me, kingslayer," the soldier spat. "Give us a little more rest, then maybe your precious army won't fall."

Rose snarled ever so slightly, just enough to make a face of disgust. "What makes you think you are precious?"

The soldier turned red in outrage.

"I have got more to say," he started. "What are we doing here? Hmm? They're dead. We are dead. We have been sent here because we are dead. That is the only option."

"Ridiculous," Rose said slowly.

"No," the soldier retorted. "What's ridiculous is only giving us one meal a day, only letting us sleep for maybe five hours, and marching us the rest of the time!"

"What's ridiculous is how lazy you are!" Rose growled.

"I am not—" the soldier began.

Rose grabbed him by the shoulders pushing him back a step. She made sure to send extra weight to his previously injured ankle. For a moment, it looked like he would stay standing, but Rose was holding back. With one final twist of her wrists, he clattered to the floor with a loud thump.

Most of the army turned to see the commotion. They saw Rose standing above the fallen soldier. Hera, the curious type, rushed back to get a better view of what had happened. Aaron hesitantly followed her, not quite as interested as she. They saw Rose looking down at the soldier. He was a conscript, no doubt about it, with a simple bow strung across his back and a large tent holding it in place.

Rose picked him up by the breastplate, almost tearing it off. She pressed her face close to the soldier's. There was no doubt about what darkened her expression. It was madness. She made her hand into a fist, and it looked like she would punch him.

"You are a soldier. If you believe your family is dead, you will avenge them." Everything about her tone was a shout. The only thing that wasn't was her volume.

The soldier was still indignant and not ready to succumb to the bullying.

"Let us go home!" he yelled back.

Rose readied her fist for a punch. "Coward!"

The militiaman flinched in anticipation of the punch. Not only did he close his eyes, but he pulled his head back. After a long moment, Rose, her stance unchanged, left her fist hanging in the air.

"Speak." She spoke in a commanding tone, not a cry or a yell, but a controlled cadence.

The militiaman flinched at her words as much as he flinched at her fist. Several soldiers almost rushed to help the man, but they were stopped in their tracks by the look on Rose's face. None had the courage to intervene. Viner frantically pushed his way from the front of the crowd to the back attempting to see what he could do.

"I—" the soldier stuttered. "You killed the King."

She lifted him to his feet. "I did what needed to be done, something you are not strong enough to do."

The soldier's legs uselessly scrambled against the ground while Rose did all the heavy lifting to bring him to his feet. A little more bravery returned to his face and the soldier dared look into Rose's eyes. Rose again pulled back a fist and again the soldier flinched.

"Coward."

She let the punch fly and the soldier scrambled under Rose's grip. It would have made contact had Rose not purposefully stopped her hand before hitting his eye.

"Coward."

She pulled back her fist again and again the soldier turned his face away.

"Coward!"

She followed through with the punch, sending her fist tearing through the air. Not a single person in the onlooking army did not flinch; not even Viner was free from the knee-jerk reaction. The soldier in question almost fainted in fear. To the onlookers, it looked like his neck had already been twisted so far back that it had snapped on impact. In reality, she had merely brushed him against the cheek. It was a soft caress of a punch and with it, all color drained from the soldier's face. She dropped him, and he fell to the floor only semi-conscious.

"The next soldier who falls shall get the same treatment," she announced to the crowd.

Viner finally broke through the crowd. He slipped to a halt a few feet in front of his trainees. His face filled with anger and fear all mixed into one. His eyes went wide while his brow furrowed. He stood there looking at Rose in complete disdain. Then, he slowly shook his head. Rose did what Viner had done several days before and started marching in the correct direction. There was one key difference between her and Viner. Viner had Henry; Rose had her sword.

"Place thine hand on his chin as I hath done twenty thousand years ago," a voice commanded.

Hera looked around to see what soft-spoken man had whispered the command. She found that no one seemed to be responsible for it, and she returned her gaze to the man on the floor.

"My champion, I beckon thee, place thine hand on the soldier's chin and raise his eyes to meet yours," the voice continued.

Hera mulled over the words "my champion". It would be illogical to assume the voice was referring to her, but the term "champion" had been thrown around a lot lately.

"Hera, I speaketh to thee. Listen to me, and do as I command," the calm voice said.

Hera was in no position to argue. She was desperately curious about what this voice was. Was she going mad? Was this going to be a problem in the future? Her steps faltered as her curiosity turned to fear.

"It is I," explained the voice.

All the fear washed away from Hera's body. The night sky was lit above her head. She looked up in wonder marveling at the moon and stars. She was ankle deep in a cosmos of water. It reflected all the light of the night sky as if it would teach her the wonders of the stars. Standing across from her was a familiar man. Even in the dark, his white cloak shone against the hue.

"I must admit," Calm laughed. "I have a deep love for the romantic."

"Don't do that," Hera said, but a smile tugged her lips. She hadn't seen the night sky in so long.

Calm stifled his laugh to a simple grin and outstretched his hands in welcome, mirroring the hands engraved on his cloak. The moon shone upon him, knighting him as the ruler of all that was starlight.

"Hera, welcome to the Paradox of Enlightenment. It is here that you may finally understand what it is for me to grace my will on the human race."

Hera was far too caught up in the majesty of it all to question the bravado in which Calm chose his words. That trace of a smile still glimmered on her mouth as she looked around. She found that there was little of note to see. The water stretched on until it touched the night's horizon. In its simplicity, it was gorgeous. She looked back to Calm with curiosity in her heart.

"What is it you said just now? You want me to place my hand on that man's chin?"

Calm nodded. "Yes, in each person is power. That power has been taken from him and it must be restored. Look across the water."

She looked again across the water, past Calm until the stars were all she could see.

"The water does not flow. It stays here, a perfect basin to reflect the stars. And there is power in the stars. They are akin to magic, Hera, for they tell the will of the universe. All time passes while you and I confer here on Liax—sorry—on Malue and those outside are completely unaware. But the stars, they know."

Hera nodded. If she squinted and imagined, she could almost visualize the movement of the stars across the night sky. It was easier when all else was still.

"But imagine if a hole were to be torn through the ground and this basin became a maelstrom. Then all the stars would blur, and all time would be lost. Even the water would fail to know the true will of time."

Hera looked again to Calm. The golden irises of his soft eyes were gentle and wise.

"The basin is the people," Hera said.

"Clever," Calm smiled. "Clever, indeed. But Rose has torn a hole through this man's heart. Do you understand Hera? Why I chose now to speak to you? Why this is one of the most pivotal moments in the life and death of Great Neighbor? Because this one soul needs to be strengthened."

"I—" Hera tried to say. But she struggled to get the words out. It was all so surreal. She waited a moment before continuing, "I'm sorry," she said, "I do not."

And Calm smiled widely. A relieved and proud expression shone on his face.

"Good," he said. "You shouldn't."

He outstretched his arms in that same motion of greeting, but this time it was obvious that it meant goodbye. The water under Hera's legs started to swirl and dance with the stars. It all surged away from Calm, slowly taking Hera with it like the tide of the sea carrying a piece of driftwood to the shore. She slid into a vastness that she could not fully comprehend. She stepped forward with her hand outstretched to Calm. Then, after that one step she ran.

"Wait!"

Her legs carried her forward through the water, but they were not fast enough. Calm was becoming further away.

"You said I would understand your grace!" she cried.

"And you will," Calm called back.

"Then tell me, why is Aaron not here?"

Calm gave her a questioning look. He licked his lips and placed his hands together.

"Because Aaron is not my Champion. You are."

Hera knew then that she had been thrown back into the nightmare. She looked around to see endless white where there once was night sky. Her grief hit her then, but not for long. She had a job to do. She knelt in front of the soldier with her hand outstretched toward him. The soldier looked up at her in distaste. Hera saw herself reflected in his armor and noted that she shared some key facial features with Rose. This similarity horrified her vanity, but it was of no true consequence.

"I don't want your hand," the soldier said.

"I didn't want you to take it," Hera replied.

She gently placed her hand on his chin and lifted his neck and jaw. Even when sitting on the floor, her adjustment made the poor soldier look proud. He looked up at her questioningly.

"Raise your head high, for you are brave." She spoke in a soft tone, only just loud enough for him to hear. It was the complete opposite of Rose. "If you must return home, we do not fault you because even returning home is brave. Rise to your feet."

A sad smile creased the conscript's lips. The soldier kept eye contact with Hera while getting up. Hera offered him no hand and allowed him to find his own footing. With little more than a stumble, the man was level again. He was slightly taller than Hera and looked down at her when she spoke.

"Our people might be dead," she said. "But they may very well be alive."

"Do not lose faith," Calm whispered in her ear.

"Do not lose faith," she repeated aloud.

"Will you save your daughter?" Calm whispered.

"Will you save your daughter," Hera said flatly.

The soldier looked at her, and what resonated in the turn of his cheek was ever so slightly different from shock. To have someone know your motivation, especially such a personal motivation, would be stunning to anyone. But this man was far too dazed already and his train of thought followed a different path. A path of fear. Yet, this path turned again. He could easily have been afraid of Hera, or perhaps Rose, but this too was not true.

The militiaman remembered the days before he even dreamed of using a bow to kill a foe. The days when the sun baked his face into a smooth tan while he watched his daughter play with her mother in the salty ocean. He remembered not the times of turmoil, nor the boring nights of cleaning an old, dreary library. He remembered going home and finding his daughter still awake. He remembered his daughter's brazen insistence that he read her a bedtime story before she fell asleep. He remembered his wife's helpless look.

A smile tugged at his lips as he remembered bringing out the book he had checked out just for the occasion. He had promised he would read a book to her, after all, so he had chosen this one from the library special for her. He almost felt for it in the place where his old coat pocket used to be.

The man was not afraid of Hera. He was not afraid of Rose. He was not afraid of the underworld.

He was afraid of failing his family.

He was suspended in a moment of turmoil. To turn back from what he feared would mean giving into it. To move forward would risk that the sweet hope he clung to would crash to the floor and shatter.

His voice broke, "My daughter is dead."

"Not if you save her," Calm assured him through Hera.

"She will be dead before I get there," he replied with a sob.

"Will she? Do not listen to your pessimistic self. You have spent enough of your life being a realist. You can't hope to prepare for success if you only prepare for failure," Hera told him.

These wise words were news to Hera as much as they were to the conscript, but Hera elected to mull them over later and focus on the present now.

"I- I can't," he pleaded.

"Do you want to?" Hera asked.

His head looked to the floor. "More than anything."

"Then you will." The will of Calm rang strong through Hera's mouth.

The soldier finally broke into tears. Not tears of fear, but tears of joy and hope. He laughed in his sobs, and other soldiers watched on. At this point, he didn't care if they saw him. He returned to the marching order and got ready to start moving.

Hera returned with him, and every single set of eyes followed her, Aaron's most of all. This way of speaking was so unlike her. The whole thing had come out of nowhere. Since when was Hera telling others they should fight this war? Haven't they been trying to get out of it this whole time?

"What was that about?" Aaron asked her.

"Aaron," Hera replied. "I have done two things right in my life. One was choosing to steal from a poor sod like you and the other was that."

"Thanks," Aaron said awkwardly. "I think."

By now, the troops had started awkwardly following Rose. Viner and Rose had switched spots in the line, Rose now marched in front of all the troops forcing them forward uncomfortably fast, while Viner grudgingly watched them from the back.

"Maybe these people are worth fighting for," Hera mused.

"Have you lost it?" Aaron started to raise his voice. "Remember how horrible it is to fight? Tell me that again when you see one of those short tevnals!"

"Aaron," Hera told him. "You know I don't play fair. I have an ace up my sleeve."

"You're going to kick one of them in the crotch?" Aaron said sarcastically.

"You'll see," Hera laughed.

That day, the army marched harder than it ever had before. Perhaps it was a form of punishment from Rose, or perhaps Rose was just so driven to move forward she completely forgot about her army. Either way, the army did not even consider complaining, but not because they were afraid. Never before had the army united for a purpose so strong. Every soldier now understood what they fought for and what they wanted. With that passion, the day went by faster than ever before.

A squad of four soldiers almost forgot their plan to assassinate Rose while she slept. Almost.

Chapter 16
Righteous Right

Camp was set up as normal with tents spread apart fairly evenly. Some of the soldiers had given up on erecting tents altogether after realizing that it didn't make any difference. The only thing the gray linens provided was privacy and for that reason, they were really only useful as toilets.

The army was upset with the Mouth of the King, understandably so. Rose was a tyrant. But none were more upset than four of the shield wall soldiers—Traya, Winston, Mikile, and Josephine. The four made better use of the tents than most soldiers. What they were doing was a matter much more private than others. They had gathered together to plot the assassination of their hated leader-by-assasination. These soldiers were upset by the death of the king and disappointed that Viner, whom they respected greatly, had not done anything to stop Rose's rise to power.

"He must be worried about losing control," a man named Mikile raved. "He would want us to do this!"

"I agree wholeheartedly," said his friend Josephine.

A third added, "We need to get her secluded and make sure that if anyone notices the mark on the horizon, they don't investigate."

Although physically she looked frail, the third was by far the most sinister. Her name was Traya, and she was a hunched-over elder. Cataracts were forming in her eyes, surely making it harder for her to see. But even with the pale cloud over her eyes, they had a sort of somber knowing gleam to them. Her hair was long, black, braided, and hung loosely on her scalp. Her armor fitted the same way, the metal plates grating each other when she moved. She had retired as a guard several years ago but when the invasion came, she was a little too eager to spill some blood.

The four knew each other the same way Henry knew Hera and Aaron—they had been positioned together in the second battalion. Once they got to talking, they discovered that they each harbored the popular hatred of Rose. In their ramblings, their hatred grew more and more and they became obsessed with stopping her. First, they fantasized about confronting her, then they considered jailing her, but after the events of the earlier day, they saw only one option. Murder.

Winston was the fourth, and he was just as interested in giving Rose a piece of his mind. He was built like Viner, but quite a bit more overweight. An auburn walrus mustache, the type that Hera had insulted, rested on his upper lip. He was naturally red in the face, but his complexion became more crimson when Hera had insulted "guards like him". Come to think of it, Winston wanted to give Hera a piece of his mind, too. None of them were academically or physically prodigious, but out of the four, Winston was the strongest.

What Mikile and Josephine lacked in craftiness and size, they made up for in dogmatic ambition. Their ideas about Rose were ravenous, and Josephine was the first to reveal her desire for Rose's death. Mentally unstable or not, Mikile's and Josephine's ideas were not completely unsound. Rose was a horribly abusive leader, and it was a marvel that no one had tried to stop her sooner.

Mikile had a greasy look to him. His blond hair was slicked back and an insane smile stretched across his face. That alone would not have made him appear bizarre, but closer inspection revealed that his left eyebrow was missing. The lack of eyebrow would have been more noticeable had his hair not been so fair.

Josephine was an exception to the four. She was traditionally pretty. She had tanned skin and brown hair. Her lips would have been pretty, too, had they not betrayed the rest of her face. She held a smile that, in comparison, made Mikile look completely normal. It stretched across her entire face from jawbone to jawbone showing eerily white teeth.

Each of them held a large shield in front of them, ready to be on the front lines of defense. They balanced their dangerous position with the relative safety that a shield could provide. But Rose had made it clear that she considered soldiers who hid behind shields to be cowards. The commander acknowledged their usefulness to the army but knew that their first and foremost motivation was to protect themselves.

That day, the four were already fatigued with Rose's constant belittling, but her attack on the fallen soldier was the last straw. Traya led the charge while Winston and Josephine stood on either side of her. Mikile tried desperately to walk with them, but for whatever reason he always trailed behind like a mangy hyena hound. Only a few heads turned to look at the four. It was late at night according to their sleeping schedules, so most were not awake. Those who were awake were largely uninterested in watching four soldiers walk by.

It was not long before they had crossed the entirety of the camp. They were easily able to distinguish their target thanks to her bright red hair. She sat on her knees in an almost meditative stance. Her eyes were half-lidded yet simultaneously alert. She sat directly underneath one of the vents of orange light that lit the underworld like small suns. However, she was not any more outlined than any other soldier.

"I've come to a conclusion," Rose spoke suddenly.

It was not unreasonable to assume that she had heard the footsteps of her traitorous soldiers, but still, it was a surprise that she had known of their presence. In fact, it was so surprising that Traya almost believed that Rose was talking to herself. The question remained unanswered when Rose continued to stare solemnly at the ground, her eyes barely showing awareness.

A stunned minute passed before Rose formed words again, "We are not in the underworld."

Traya smirked to herself. Rose was every bit the lunatic she thought she was. Why was she bringing this up now? She really was dense.

"The lizard monstrosity was able to bend a similar world to his control. In fact, it may have been the same world had these cracks not existed in the ceiling to provide light," Rose told them. "But that's when I realized the cracks aren't actually providing light. They are too high up to cast light at that brightness with their limited luminosity. Also, have you noticed that all the shadows are vertical? That doesn't make sense. When several lights in multiple locations are shone on one object, faint shadows are created on multiple sides, not one dark shadow vertically down."

"What is the meaning of this?" hissed Josephine.

"I am not finished," Rose continued. "I have noticed one more vital thing. For the last few days, the cracks in the sky have been bothering me. Only today did I realize I have seen the same one several times."

"Are you telling me we are going in a circle?" Winston growled.

"That is what I thought, too… at first. But then, I created constellations out of the cracks," Rose said. "I realized that though the cracks are repeating in structure, they are placed sporadically. I have counted seventeen unique designs. This leads me to believe that this cave is man-made. Or rather… magic-made."

"What does that have to do with anything?" Mikile asked.

"Nothing. All it means is that I know how to get back to this location," Rose moved her eyes so that the slightest hint of her irises were visible to the assassins. "So, the question is, will you follow me? You do want to kill me, don't you? An isolated location would be preferred. And now I have just told you how to navigate back once you have dragged my corpse away."

Josephine started laughing maniacally for an uncomfortably long amount of time. Her comrades looked incredulously at her, but Rose didn't even bother to turn around. Her fit of laughter was so high-pitched that Traya was worried that other soldiers would come to make sure no one was in trouble.

Traya lost patience and readied her spear. Rose sprang into battle position, her stance wide enough to allow her good balance, but tight enough to give her the ability to dodge. She pivoted to face Traya and immediately started moving to the left. Once she had gotten out from underneath the vent of light, she started to dance backward. Her cleaver rested comfortably on her back while she moved. Josephine stopped laughing so that her vision wouldn't be so foggy. Once she regained her composure, she saw that Rose was scuttling away. Rose's strange movement patterns combined with the way she crab-walked across the floor was so ridiculous that Josephine started laughing again. The other three followed Rose, careful to keep out of striking distance, making sure their shields were raised above the ground.

By the time Winston even thought about making a stab at Rose, she had already dodged it. Traya took that moment to send her spear into Rose's shoulder, but that, too, was predicted by the commander. Rose launched a counter faint, unsheathing her cleaver with a slash. The cleaver grazed the edge of Winston's kite shield and glanced to the ground. Rose used the momentum of the missed attack to spin backwards several feet.

Mikile took the opportunity to make a daring assault, something unusual for a shield wall specialist. Mikile was unusual, however, and attempted to pike Rose in the neck with the side of his spear. Rose deflected the blow with the flat of her blade, then let the weight of the heavy instrument carry itself and the spear to the ground.

Rose was still on the defensive and rapidly moving backward. A bead of sweat crept down her brow as she strained to pick up the gigantic cleaver. She was able to force it into the sky just in time to deflect a spear blow from Winston. She almost popped her shoulder from its socket, sending her back toward the ground behind her. The ground did not crack, but instead made the cleaver bounce. Rose was taken off guard by the strange physics of this bizarre place. Traya took that moment to go for a stab at the Mouth of the King. However, her diminished vision made her strikes much less accurate.

But even with the impaired accuracy, the stab collided with Rose's pauldron. Under normal conditions, the strike would have pierced Rose through the shoulder, but instead Rose was pushed back several feet. The ground's lack of traction seemed to have worked in Rose's favor. The blow nearly knocked her to the ground, but her cleaver propped up behind her and kept her standing like a third leg. The attack did not maim Rose, but it did compromise her shoulder plate. She shrugged it to the floor, where it clattered with a spark.

Rose glanced down at the spark, and a smile tugged at her lips. The smile was imperceptible to the four guards. But they could see one thing—a crazed glint in her eyes. Josephine's eyes matched the glint. She had finally regained her composure and clumsily sprinted to follow behind her comrades. When she got close enough, she jumped forward like some sort of rabid animal. Her feet made a grotesque noise upon reuniting with the ground. Bits of skin and blood were left behind as she slid across the floor, spear and shield pointed forward like a hornet.

Rose turned her arm guard to parry the spear, and miraculously, it worked. The spear slid down her arm, leaving a large white scratch across her dark iron armor. Rose could not avoid the blow from the shield, however, and it came smashing into her, forcing her to the floor. She clattered against the ground, sparks blazing upward as she slid. Rose pushed her weight down on the ground and made sure her cleaver's blade scraped the hardest. Josephine ravenously pursued Rose, running after her with that huge grin on her face.

Josephine's crazed triumph at knocking down her commander soon turned to sheer panic when she felt the metal around her arm begin to heat up rapidly. The sparks from Rose's cleaver had caused flame to ignite on her wooden shield. Josephine lost balance and fell face first onto her shield, suffocating most of the flames but burning herself in the process. Rose used that time to get to her feet again just before Winston came charging at her.

The Mouth of the King saw him coming well before he arrived. She spun out of his way, making sure to send up sparks with the end of her cleaver. Her graceful acrobatics narrowly dodged Winston's reckless charge. She brought her cleaver down again just in time to slice him from neck to hip. Winston screamed in agony like a great elk. He took five steps forward before falling to the floor and sliding, his armor leaving a trail of sparks in his wake.

"Hopefully no one heard that," Rose said aloud.

All this time, Rose had been leading the four away with her skirmish fighting style. It seemed like they had a good chance of being out of earshot of the camp. Mikile looked back to see the camp far away. When this attack had started, he would have been overjoyed, but now he was horrified. There were four of them. Surely, they could take her. He looked down at Winston, fully expecting him to get up and start fighting again. He didn't. A sense of panic started to set in on Mikile. Had she really just killed one of them? Not only one of them, but Winston. Mikile shook his head but instead of seeing clarity, he saw red blood. He looked up to Rose and charged her in a mad rage.

Rose slid to the left before Mikile's spear could strike her the same way Traya's had. The Mouth of the King flourished her blade into the air and brought it crashing down on Mikile's unshielded weapon the same way she had killed Winston. The force of the cleaver slammed the spear to the ground, leaving Mikile stunned and his spear split in two. He hadn't telegraphed his charge; there was no way Rose could react that fast. Mikile was stunned that she was able to leave his spear splintered on the ground.

Rose could not see his dumbfounded face behind the shield, but the moment of hesitation was enough for her to know what Mikile was thinking. She drew back her sword the same way she had readied that punch against the fallen militiaman. Then, she plunged her cleaver all the way to its hilt into the shield. The flawless strike pierced the thin metal of the kite shield and skewered Mikile through the arm and chest. If anything, Mikile should have been thankful for one of the most elegant kills obtainable. As for those who witnessed it, they were starting to doubt whether they would live to tell the tale.

Traya tried to gore Rose while her blade was stuck in the shield. Before she could, Rose used her cleaver as a lever and unstuck the blade from the body. The shield was still firmly in the cleaver and Rose heaved it up to defend herself from the attack. Traya's spear stuck limply against the backside of the shield, almost breaking through, but not quite. Rose retreated to the floor. She put both of her feet against the thin metal shield and started trying to pull her sword out.

Josephine peered down at Rose with only a spear in hand to defend herself. Her left gauntlet was discarded, and burn marks were visible on her bare hand. Her pretty face had also been burnt, leaving a fresh slash across her giant mouth. Her eyes stung with tears of pain, and it looked as if she couldn't put up much more of a fight.

Rose identified the weakness and unsheathed her sword from the shield just in time to slash at her. She slid from a prone position into a heavy attack. The great slash helped to dissuade Josephine from getting any closer. Josephine backed away skittishly and gave Rose enough time to get to her feet. For most warriors, a weapon that size would be an obstacle, but Rose was a master of using the weight.

Traya again tried to utilize the opening and attempted to skewer Rose. Rose rapidly shifted her momentum to the left, barely dodging the strike. Rose swung her weapon to return the counterattack, but her bloodied cleaver only scraped against Traya's shield. Rose tried desperately to keep the momentum of the battle in her favor despite the shield's best efforts and shifted focus to attack Josephine. Josephine was behind her, still too afraid to move forward. She was surprised when the cleaver came cascading upon her,

Rose's full weight behind it. The strike looked flashy, but it was hardly effective and only impacted Josephine's one remaining armband.

Rose bounced her large blade off the armband and went for a flat sword strike aimed at Traya's shield. Traya had not expected the attack and was not ready for such a blow. The sword knocked her shield aside. Rose didn't have time to attack again so she dropped her cleaver onto the floor and lunged at Traya.

"King killing sc—" Traya tried to say.

Before she could finish the sentence both of the king killer's hands were around her neck. She pushed her to the ground and pinned her down. The spear Traya held was too long to properly stab into Rose while on the ground. But she didn't have many options, she tried frantically to hit Rose with the spear shaft with little effect. It became quickly obvious that the method wouldn't work. Rose wasn't even flinching. Traya was running out of time. She remembered the knife that all guards carried in their boots. She reached down... if she could just reach it. But her vision was already turning black.

Josephine shook her head in horror. Her face was still burning and she couldn't see out of her left eye. Sky above, would she never be able to see out of that eye again? And her nose, if she wasn't wrong, was sealed shut. How horrible—Traya was being choked to death right in front of her, but all she could do was turn around and run. Run back to camp, tell them what Rose had done. Then they would listen, then they would stop her.

Traya looked up at her despised enemy. The worst part was her expression. Her teeth were borne, yes, but other than that, it was completely blank. Traya knew she could reach the knife... just a little further. Her hand worked its way down the armor strapped to her leg, but it was too hard.

Perhaps, just this once, she could give in. It hurt. Her old eyes flickered and became dark for the last time.

Rose pulled herself from the body and listened to Josephine's scrambling footsteps. Rose couldn't let her escape. She slid herself forward across the ground. Like a lizard she crawled until she could regain her bipedal position. Once upright, Rose recklessly charged the armed soldier with nothing but her fists. She was gaining on Josephine. It was obvious that Rose was smarter, stronger, and faster than her prey.

Josephine heard Rose rapidly approaching behind her. A crazed smile crossed her face as she shattered the threshold between fear and hysteria. Rose pounced on her former subject like a mountain lion. Josephine would die for her beliefs, and in a final sacrifice, the madwoman pointed her own spear into her chest. If Rose was going to tackle her, she wanted the spear to pierce her own body and run Rose through. Rose pounced on Josephine, landing on her back and pushing her to the floor. The spear wrenched through Josephine's heart as both soldiers went plummeting to the blood-stained opal ground.

***

"Open the gate, soldier!"

"I cannot, ma'am. The King has prohibited it."

"I said, open the gate. There are people on the other side. They are about to die!" Rose insisted.

"Ma'am, I cannot go against the King. You know as well as I—"

"Rose!" a third voice shouted somewhere to her left.

Rose turned to see a panicked face reaching through the gate. In the horde of people who had come together around the gate, Rose had been unable to pick out this one face. Until now.

"Open the gate!" Rose screamed.

The guard manning the gate simply shook his head. It was the last mistake he would make before he was sliced up the back. Rose unsheathed her cleaver and with a single fluid motion cut him down the spine. The guard was not alone in guarding the gate. Another soldier was dumbfounded that the Mouth of the King had just killed one of her own. He took a moment to regain his composure before charging at her faster than a bear. Tears ran freely down his face. Rose positioned her greatsword to use the charge against him and the sword slid almost effortlessly through the wooden planks of the shield.

A sharp, blunt pain made its way down Rose's shoulder, smashing away her shoulder guard. Rose was quick as ever to retaliate, and she slashed aside the mace. She did not hesitate to go for the kill by stabbing the insolent guard in the chest. She immediately pivoted to the gate. With all her might, she pulled against the wheel of the evil contraption. Something glinted in her eye, not coming from her, but from the setting sun.

She turned to look at the gate and saw blood spewing in every direction. Limbs and fingers flew as axes glinted in the crimson sun. The raiders had gone mad and were killing everything in sight. Tears streaked down Rose's face. It took all her might to not let go of that gate. She would face down the crazed hoard if she had to; she wouldn't lose him. But she feared it was too late. For a moment, she was filled with hope. Could it be true that the dwarves were retreating? She waited a moment more, and yes, they were walking into the ocean! It was just then that a piercing pain split her armor and flesh. She looked down at her stomach, and to her shock, a spear was poking two feet out of her. She would have died. She should have died. But she was held by hatred.

***

Rose was able to construct a set of armor fairly well out of the equipment left behind by her assailants. She could do little more to hide the bodies than drag them away, so she hoped that the dark specks on the horizon would go unnoticed. That hope was small when she looked at her own horizon and could clearly see the campsite where the troops had been sleeping. She started her walk back to the campsite. She wished the walk would have taken longer. But finally, after a hard-fought battle, she resumed her meditation.

On the morning of awakening, the army was better rested than they had been for the last three days. Arising on the fourth day, they had no clue that the extra few hours that they had gained were thanks to the death of four crazed yet righteous soldiers. It was the first sleep on their journey where they awoke feeling reasonably restful. The army donned their armor at a record pace and got ready to march the rest of that day. Rose resumed her preferred position behind the army, and Viner took his queue to lead it once more. It felt like it would be a good day. Sure, those ranked near the four missing guards noticed their absence, but who were they to judge a deserter? No one can hide in the marble plain for long.

Chapter 17
In Earnest

Henry was in the middle of an interesting story about Anarchy pirates, back when they sailed the seas, when a shout echoed through the ranks of the formation.

"A shape in the distance, a shape in the distance," the soldiers cried.

It was true, a darker shape now showed in contrast to the white void. It was minuscule but there nonetheless. Rose frowned for a moment, worried that her kills had been spotted, but that would be impossible. She had hidden the bodies in a place no one except her knew even existed. Besides, they had been walking for quite some time with no mention of that particular site. Rose shook her head and almost laughed at herself. Her breath steadied and she forced herself into sharing the same wonder as the other soldiers.

Hera peaked her head around Aaron to look. Aaron stumbled backward almost causing the soldier behind him to trip and fall. The soldier glared at him, irritated. Though the fall wouldn't have been lethal, Rose might have been. Neither rogue paid the perturbed conscript any mind, and instead crawled over each other to get a glance at what had been spotted. Sure enough, they were rapidly approaching a light gray shape that looked almost black in contrast to the nothingness that surrounded it.

The pace of the army quickened all at once. People were tripping over each other in excitement. Viner was not as quick to celebrate as the others, but he didn't try to stop the army. He let them go slightly ahead of him while he jogged beside. Rose kept her spot at the back of the line, keeping perfect pace with the excited army.

The shape refused to get any bigger. It made sense once Hera thought about it. It was probably many miles away. The flat plane they stood on distorted every aspect of marching, including vision. Though they moved faster than usual because of the flat floor, they also had no idea how far they had really moved. None of them but Rose.

Rose had not revealed all her navigational secrets to the four assassins. Maybe it was out of spite that she didn't tell them her crowning achievement. She had learned through careful observation that the cracks in the ceiling formed a pattern and were placed in massive arcs. These arcs grew wider and wider the further they marched. The arcs were each placed about twenty feet apart, and despite sharing a general shape, they seemed to be more imperfect the further away from the source they were. Now they were becoming almost nonsensical.

"It can't be more than three miles away," Aaron panted.

Hera turned to him, "Why- is- that-" she said through panting breaths.

"Aero- kite. The sailors can see about th-ree miles away," Aaron said.

Hera turned back and nodded. He was right, Aerokite was good at navigation, and they knew full well that flat surfaces, like the ocean, curved enough where objects are hidden under the horizon after a little over three miles. The fact that Aaron knew this off the top of his head surprised Hera, and she let him know with a look. Aaron grinned tiredly and shrugged.

The excited pace of the soldiers died down less than three-quarters of a mile after their charge. Tython's battalion was lightly armored and could have jogged for a while more, but when Tython looked back and saw the tired shield battalion behind them, he remembered himself. He was one of the first to slow down to a more reasonable pace. The heavy infantry was grateful. They may have been the strongest, but muscle could only do so much when adorned in full steel armor.

They slowed down for the next while. It was only a minute or two after Tython caught his breath that his empathetic nature got the best of him. He peered closely at the shape, and he could have sworn it was ever so slightly closer. He leaned towards the ear of the shortbow soldier next to him, a taller man with black hair and a clean-shaven face.

"I think the shape is getting closer," Tython whispered.

The man squinted forward, and a small smile creased his lips. He did a quick double-take before calling out, "Oi, it's getting closer!"

His call was echoed by the soldier behind him, "Aye, it's getting closer!" and a fainter repeated cry, "It's getting closer."

Tython's smile turned to a panicked frown, "No, that's not—"

But he was too late. The army was already off again, running faster than they had before. Viner rolled his eyes and moved aside, letting the army shove past him. Tython was practically dragged forward. With a heave of their great shields, the infantry reluctantly started running harder than they had before their short-lived break.

The shape's distortion was rather odd over the horizon. Though it was growing wider as they got closer, it was also growing exponentially taller too. This surprised Rose, leading her to question the validity of her guess on its distance. She had forgotten to take into account how tall the shape was. It could be anywhere from three miles away to one hundred, and Rose would not be able to tell without knowing its height. Rose turned hot for a moment, disappointed in her foolish optimism.

The soft hum of two thousand feet rang its way less than rhythmically across the pure marble floor. Rose did not have to force herself to move faster; she was as excited as any of the soldiers, even if she did not show it. But hidden behind that excitement was a less wholesome motivation than most of the soldiers' own. The only militant that was not anxious to meet the end of the white void was Viner. He would rather conserve energy in case what they met next was less than friendly.

"The shape isn't going anywhere," he announced. "But our wind is. Let us slow down for just a moment."

The army started to slow down at their Viner's command. Hera's left foot hit the floor, then her right, then left, then right, left, right, and she sped to a slow. The troops were even more exhausted than the last time they started to jog. Some of them purposefully raced ahead so that they could stop and rest for a moment, but even then, the conglomerate did not stop moving forward.

They walked slowly for a while, taking time to catch their breath. Hera and Aaron were young and strong, but other soldiers, Henry included, were heaving out great sighs of exhaustion. Viner was truly exhausted, but he would never show that to his soldiers. He stood straight though his back ached. With narrowed eyes he stared down the ranks of his tired soldiers, questioning if these undisciplined warriors could really save their families.

Just as Viner was wondering this, he heard a cry, "We are so close!"

The soldiers rumbled like a volcano. They did not know who had spoken, but some of them nodded. A hum of agreement rang through the army setting them to action faster than the command could alone.

"We are close!" they agreed.

One second, two second, three, they ran again faster than a ravenous pack of wolves. Determination sweat from their bodies, their limbs forced to exert themselves more than they had during training. Hera set her teeth, gritted her eyes, and forced herself to run through the exhaustion.

"This is unwise," Viner weakly warned.

The soldiers did not listen. They continued their double-time march forward without heed to their commander. Viner took one step towards the army. His gauntlet was extended as if to grasp them on the shoulder, but the army had already started running faster than ever before. All it took was one voice, and the entire army, Hera and Aaron included, had readied their legs and put their heads down. Rose ran after them, a little less graceful than usual. She made exasperated eye contact with Viner. Without a word, she told him that she was oddly proud. For once, Viner agreed with her.

The soldiers ran a quarter-mile more before coming to a complete stop. Viner slowed down to address the crowd, ready to strike them with a little wisdom about discipline. He caught his breath after a moment. With each exhalation, his whole body heaved. If the floor were not so firm, it may have rumbled from the giant man's great breath. He opened his mouth to breathe out an address to his insubordinate subordinates.

"Almost there!" came the command.

But it was not Viner who shouted it.

The captain's words were caught in his throat. The moment before he was able to bid his troops to save their energy, they were barreling down the marble floor at a full sprint. Hera almost laughed, and Aaron did. Many soldiers shared in laughter, and it would have been hearty had they not already been gasping for breath. Their sprint was ridiculous, and the soldiers knew it, but without a doubt in their mind, they were moving forward faster than ever.

It didn't take long for a younger, slower soldier to trip and fall. Viner slowed his pace before the soldier. Viner looked down at them and decelerated to a stop in front of the soldier. The Hand of the King shook his head slowly, disappointed with his army's recklessness. Viner was worried that it had gone on too long. He would surely look up from under his brow and see the army a hundred feet away. But when he looked up, his sharp gaze softened. What met his scrutiny were the whites of a pair of eyes. Thousands of eyes. His soft glance turned to amazement as he realized that the entire army had stopped. He looked down again at the fallen militia member and noticed that they were already being helped to their feet. Viner followed the soldier's rise, and his disbelief turned to astonishment, which then turned to delight. The army too turned, all as one unit. They kept eye contact with the general until their necks would permit them no longer. Then, all together, they started sprinting again toward the gray shape in the distance.

Viner was humbled. He walked slowly forward and watched the army run away from him. Rose came up behind him and passed the captain without looking back. Viner followed her with his eyes. He lifted his gauntlet to his heart. His eyes fell on the metal glove. He frowned with an open mouth, letting the army run as fast as they could away from where he stood. The commander took off his gauntlet and placed his bare hand against his armor. He felt that it was warm with body heat. With widened eyes, he stared at his tired soldiers, now shapes in the distance. He again questioned if these undisciplined people could really save their families. He had never been more certain of anything in his life.

Viner leaned forward and started to run with great leaps and bounds. He didn't look like a leader, but like a man, no a child, trying desperately to keep up with a sprinting crowd. Every step he took, he almost fell, tumbling forward until he reached the people that he trusted with his life.

"You're so close!" he shouted.

He had run up behind the army quicker than he looked like he could. His bare feet slid against the smooth marble, but it was nothing the giant man couldn't handle. He waved his arms around, wild exuberance in every flex of his muscles.

"Keep going!" he rallied.

The soldiers had no breath in them, and with that absence of breath, they cheered.

"You're—almost-to—"

With every step, he said a syllable. He was struggling for air, but something in Viner told him that the words were more important than his tired feet.

"Your—fam—il—ies!"

Rapidly, the gray shape started to grow. It looked like it was trying and failing to run away. One moment they could almost touch it, the next it slipped through their fingers. But to say the army was not gaining on it would be more foolish than attacking Great Neighbor! That was the rally of the soldiers, and they could not be filled with more triumph.

It took hours after the shape was initially spotted, but after those long hours, the gray shape was actually close enough to grasp. Some soldiers took the opportunity to feel the fruits of their labor, almost crawling to the object they had worked so hard to get to. They gently rubbed their metal hands against the gray stone before them. The light gray slab was out of place in the underworld, but as one would expect, it served a purpose. It was evident that what lay before them was a staircase. It looked like it was naturally carved from stone. Each grand step was six meters deep, six meters wide, and six inches thick. They grew in an angular spiral with no guard rails. The staircase was akin to a stone pillar with steps carved into it. It was sturdier than a mountain but made the soldier's quake more than a hill during a landslide.

Hera tried to get a look at it from the other angle. She walked further into the white void, but when she was perpendicular to the staircase, Aaron heard a loud thump and watched Hera bounce off of thin air. Hera grasped her head in her hands and tightened her eyes in pain.

"What the..." she startled.

Gently, she inched towards where she had hurt herself and reached out her hand to feel for the invisible force that had so rudely attacked her. Her hand made contact with a flat surface, like a wall. Yet, before them the wide void still stretched.

"What is this?" Hera pondered.

A shuffling footstep approached from behind her.

"It's called a wall soldier," Rose said sarcastically.

"What do you mean, a wall?" Hera asked.

"I mean, you are touching a wall," Rose told her. "The wall is made out of the same material as the floor, and because the material that makes up the floor is flawless, so is the wall."

"But how do you know it is a wall and not just an invisible barrier?"

"Why would it be an invisible barrier? Do you just immediately assume invisible barriers are all over the place?" Rose said.

Hera turned to her, surprisingly unthreatened by her mocking tone. She shook her head calmly at the insult and continued marveling at the wall as if she had never seen anything like it. Something about the wall was far more impressive to her than the floor, but she couldn't place why.

"It could be an invisible barrier," Aaron interjected.

Rose shook her head with a completely straight face. Somehow, it was more condescending than shaking her head with a frown or smile.

"Exciting isn't it?" Viner asked the three.

He had been instructing his soldiers with a smile on his face. Some of the soldiers he hadn't talked to were also discovering the barrier. They had each come to their own conclusion about what was happening, but most agreed with Rose. Viner did not care for such things; he only cared about making certain his troops felt as good as he did.

"This has to be the right way! Fate is on our side!" Viner grinned.

Rose turned to him with a quizzical look, "You're in a -er happy mood. Are you so sure, Viner?"

"My friend told me everything," Viner gazed contentedly at his people.

Rose scoffed at the remark. Viner furrowed his brow at her and refitted his gauntlet over his clenched fist. Something about Viner's body language took control of the situation and commanded the three people in front of him to fall silent. Rose kept eye contact with him while she walked to the stone dais, glaring all the while. She found the enormous spiral staircase far more worthy of inspection than a blank wall. But even Rose had to admit that the army was tired, so after a long rest Rose wasn't the first soldier nor the last to start ascending the steps. She didn't want to admit it, but being in the center of the army provided her with some comfort when it came to the long climb.

Hera and Aaron waited a moment before following. Rose was unpopular for obvious reasons, and they would much rather be near Viner or Henry. All marching order was disregarded, but the army kept mostly in shape while escalating up the massive staircase. They made sure not to pack themselves in too tight or risk falling from the edge of the stone step onto the floor where they would certainly die. Sweat ran down many of the soldiers' faces as they tried their best not to think about their precarious situation.

Most soldiers were comrades with the people they marched next to and tried to keep by their side. Calessa noticed that Traya was missing. When she fished in her memory, she recalled that Traya had not been running beside her during their sprint to the staircase. A crease of worry crossed her brow, but she couldn't imagine what had happened to her, so she continued forward, assuming that she had just missed her.

She came to the conclusion that she really didn't like most of the guards, but she didn't necessarily feel like meeting anyone new or being bored while walking up the steps. Before commencing with her climb, she wormed her way through the crowd to find Tython. It was simultaneously hard and easy to find Tython. It was hard to find him because she had to look over the heads of a hundred shortbow men to find the only one who was actually a short bowman. On the other hand, Tython was distinguishable even apart from his height. He still wore his strange clothing under his light armor.

It took Calessa a while to find the Dimfir emissary. She was worried that he had already started the hike. But eventually, she spotted a little man wearing exotically fancy clothes that looked a little worse for wear. Tython looked like he was walking through a pleasant dream. A silly grin etched on his face, and he leaned forward ever so slightly more than the average person would.

Oddly enough, his grin was not inappropriate. Despite being in the literal underworld and having sprinted the last two miles, many guards felt exhilarated. They were so close to their goal, and most soldiers expected to turn the corner and see their families at any moment. Tython was riding the emotions of the army, and though he didn't have a family he was trying to save, he still felt exuberant about this dark adventure's end.

"Tython," Calessa called to him.

Tython tripped out of his trance and turned his upper body to see who had called out to him. A smile of recognition crossed his face as he saw Calessa.

"Calessa!" Tython exclaimed, happily.

Calessa noticed Tython's dreamy look and inquired about it, "What's on your mind?"

Tython dove into his questions quicker than a flash flood. "I was just thinking… where are we? Why is a random spiral staircase just placed in the middle of a void? I thought that Dessees was a cave."

Calessa stopped to think for a moment, though she kept on moving with the flow up the stairs. Though the staircase's slabs were wide, no guard wanted to be near the edge. Few wanted to walk with more than two abreast, and most organized themselves into a single file. Those that dared walk close to the edge used their training to keep their footing firm. Though they could easily have walked with more in a single line, none particularly wanted to be anywhere near the unrestrained edge of a staircase that stretched far past lethal falling distance.

"Are we even in Dessees?" Calessa wondered aloud.

"I don't know..." A smile spread across his face. "But you know what? I bet Viner knows! He talked to Mordecai for ages."

"You mean the magical lizard?" Calessa asked with a grin.

Tython turned in mock hurt, "Yes! I do mean the magical lizard!"

"Do you want to find Viner?"

For what seemed to be the first time, Tython looked around him. He took an awkward glance in front of and behind himself. He was significantly far ahead in the line of people walking up the staircase, but he didn't see Viner ahead or behind him. As far as it looked to him, guards were appearing around one turn and disappearing around the next. He couldn't see anything else. It was like he was in some strange painting with a white background.

The staircase they were on was not only massive in width and length, but also in height. It stretched to the distant ceiling. As the soldiers got higher and higher, the cracks started to disappear into themselves. Evidently, the marble matter was blending together with perspective. To Tython's horror and shock, when he looked down, he saw a sea of cracks dotting the floor as well. Without any visual perspective, they had been unable to see the divots in the marble floor. It was a wonder no one had fallen in.

The thought struck Calessa—what if someone had fallen in? Is that where Traya could be? Calessa already knew that what she thought was true. A sinking feeling filled her heart faster than she believed Traya to have sunk into one of the light fissures. Calessa turned slightly sick before returning to Tython to continue her conversation.

"Not right now; it looks like he would be hard to find," Tython noted, sharing some of Calessa's complexion.

Relief flooded over Calessa. She didn't want to weave her way through the crowd now that they were so high up. They chatted a while longer about their findings in the underworld and talked about how beautiful it was coming together to chase down the shape in the distance. There was one thing that they talked about that they had never before discussed. Hope.

"It was nice to be running towards something, not away from it," Calessa told Tython.

He nodded without a word, indicating that she should go on.

Calessa searched for words with her hands. "I don't know. Before, it was fear that drove us, but when we saw that shape in the distance... It was exuberance. It all came in a sudden burst, the realization that... we might do this."

Tython smiled. "We can do this, Calessa."

Cliche, no doubt, but despite that, the words put a smile on her face—a smile that lifted her higher than any staircase. She might have already come to the conclusion herself. She might have desperately held onto the idea. But to have Tython confirm it so genuinely... something about that confirmation struck a chord in her that all peoples possess— a desire to be affirmed. It was a good thing Tython had said it, too. He did not realize how important it was for her to hear. Sometimes people think such basic confirmations need no affirmation, but more often than not, people want to hear them anyway.

The rising spirit that lifted her up the staircase was reflected in the hearts of most of the soldiers. They floated like smoke up the stairs, and in no time at all, they were at what looked to be the top. A deep rumble moved through the throats of the crowd. Or at least, that is what Hera and Aaron thought. In reality, as the army had emerged into a dark hole in the ceiling that the staircase led to, some strange guttural noise began that they could not explain.

The marble tunnel turned from white matter to real stone. Hera and Aaron's eyes sighed a breath of relief when some texture was finally introduced to their surroundings. Aaron rolled his head around, stretching his neck muscles just to realize how tired he was. He had been running or climbing stairs for the last several hours. He looked at Hera to see if she felt the same as he did. She was refusing to show it, but he could tell she was tired.

"What's that sound?" Hera asked tentatively.

As they entered deeper into the dimly lit cave opening, the low rumbling that Hera and Aaron had assumed was the guards got louder and louder. Hera's heart started beating ever so slightly faster as the realization that the noise was not the guards crept down her throat. So one question was left.

What was the noise?

The noise personified fear, and the hope that lifted the soldiers began to waver with its cutting chill. The cave entrance was much shorter than the stairway had been, and they were not forced to endure it for long before they discovered what was at its end. Gradually, the staircase ended, and the soldiers emerged into a glistening cave. The cave contained the usual disgusting stone formations shaped by water, but on top of the stone was a blackened film akin to glass. It glistened like crystals covered in dew and filled the soldiers with wonder.

The cave was large and expansive, longer than it was wide. The main structure of the cave was deliberately pointed away from the stairs. Different types of stone colored the walls, ranging from dirty white and basalt gray to night black, and divots of dirt created a pocked complexion across the cave wall. The floor was not perfectly flat, and when the soldiers stepped on the gravel with bare feet, the sharp rocks were uncomfortable, but not quite unbearable. The soldiers took their boots from their backpacks and strapped them on without waiting for Viner's command. With the cave dimmer than the marble wasteland, the soldiers were struggling to keep their eyes open. Their tired eyes wanted a rest from the white marble, and now that they had it, sleep was of ultimate importance.

"This is a dangerous place to make camp," Rose noted flatly.

Viner shook his head sadly. "We will have to, won't we?"

They stood observing the land slightly apart from the army. Both of them had their arms crossed, and despite their completely different appearances, they mirrored each other's stance.

"Perhaps we should not have let them run so far," Rose's tone was not accusing, but coldly and assessing.

"Perhaps, but they had a type of energy that they will not have tomorrow. We needed to use it. Besides, how do we know that sleeping another day down there would have been any safer than sleeping here?"

"Hey!" The words rang down the cave. "Hey! What are you doing?"

The voice was quick, panicked, and weak. Viner and Rose were furthest away from the voice, as it came from down the cave hall. Hera and Aaron were much closer. They had been in a deep conversation about how irritating putting on armor was when they heard the call. They heard the noise immediately and, thanks to their days as thieves, their first instinct was to run. Somehow, the two former vagrants were able to quell their instinct and keep level heads. Hera looked up to see Viner and Rose already heading her way. She bumped Aaron on the shoulder to get his attention.

"We should go investigate," Hera whispered.

"Why?" Aaron hissed back.

"Because," Hera said shortly. "If we take initiative, Viner and Rose will like us more, and maybe we can stay alive a little longer when push comes to shove."

"Or we could stay away from the scary voice."

Hera frowned. He had a good point. However, she was too indignant to agree with him and would much rather plunge herself into the midst of a dwarven army than admit her curiosity was unfounded. She started walking forward, and Aaron decided that he no longer wanted to be friends with Hera. He followed anyway.

Viner saw them and shook his head in disapproval. In contrast, a small, proud smile tugged on Rose's lips while they watched the two recklessly charge forward.

"Self-righteous, spoiled, entitled, good-for-nothing thieves! They are going to get themselves killed!" Viner cursed.

"I like the initiative." Rose's tone was the polar opposite of his, and she was completely calm.

Viner darted his eyes at her in disapproval. It may have been a long time ago, but his resolve to protect those kids still flowed through his heart as if part of his blood. He stomped around the soldiers as quickly as he could, attempting to catch up with the thieves.

"What's that?" the voice asked.

Hera and Aaron tightened their lips and quited their breathing. They placed their recently armored feet against the gravel as quietly as they could, but even with their skill, it was too loud for their liking. The cave didn't care how loudly they walked. It kept calling out, sometimes saying words, but more often than not moaning. It was only a few meters further before Hera and Aaron saw what was making the noise. They could not have been happier.

What they saw was not a dwarf, but a man, lit only by blue-light torches haphazardly attached to the walls at random intervals. A grimy, short man wearing a long coat and a strange hat stood before them. But of more interest to them—for they couldn't care less about a grubby little man—was the fact that he was in a cell. Though they had no desire for the little man to be in the cell, once they saw him, it became evident that there must also be other people in other cells.

The cave curled and curved like a worm through the soil, and in its bends, it became evident that this disgusting structure was the prison that they had been searching for. The residents of Great Neighbor were alive. Aaron did not know when the army had followed them, but they were on Hera and his heels in a moment. At the new sight, the sleep-deprived soldiers could have stayed awake for another hundred days without feeling a moment of fatigue.

Chapter 18
The Complex

Caution was thrown to the wind. Even Rose did not care whether they were heard. It was as if Great Neighbor was in the throes of a massive wedding ceremony with waves of cheer spreading through the guards. All the turmoil of the last few days had led up to this moment. It felt glorious. With an emotional cry or a jubilant shout, the hands of over a thousand citizens pushed through the bars of locked doors. They paid no mind to the rough iron that held them back, nor to the tight squeeze of their elbows. They knew only Euphoria, her embrace, and most of all, the sight of their first friendly face.

The fact that no dwarven guard was stationed on the prison floor displayed the mind-boggling pride and tactical ignorance of the enemy. It was their belief that the marble wasteland would protect the prison that allowed for such an oversight. The dwarves conquered all they touched. They cared not for their own defense. Should it not also follow suit that their homeland be the same?

The gravel under Rose's feet did not dare to shift, lest it face the wrath of Rose's steel boot. She moved with purpose down the hallway, but the man who had alerted Hera and Aaron was not so ready to be ignored. The small man reached his hand through the cell and clasped it around Rose's armored arm. The grime on his hairy fingers left its residue on the end of Rose's slightly bloodied armor. If it were not for her clear-headed tactical mind, Rose would have recoiled in disgust. Instead, she made eye contact with him, somehow conveying more disgust than if she had recoiled.

She sized him up and was instantly able to tell he was not a physical threat. The overcoat he wore was durable, but even so, its expensive silk was tarnished. Tufts of short brown hair poked from beneath his round hat but only fairly far back on his head, implying he was going bald rapidly. His toes poked out of his leather shoes. To Rose, the shoes looked like some lazy attempt at a platform shoe in which only the back was raised. They were similar to high heels but not quite as elevated. The shoes worked their way up to the knee and stopped without a strap.

"What is your name, prisoner?" Rose asked.

The little man grinned his golden teeth up at Rose, a hysterical glee in his eyes. "I am Richard the eight hundred... something-or-other."

Rose looked at him skeptically. Did this man intend to convince her that he was the rightful heir to the throne? It couldn't be. The long coat, rounded hat, and knee-high boots indicated that this man had to be Anarchist. But Rose had no way of knowing for sure.

"Are you trying to tell me you are the rightful King of the Northern Kingdom, King Richard the 800th?" Rose asked skeptically.

"King? Oh please, my friends call me *Rich*," he responded.

He smiled an evil grin when he said his name. Rose stared skeptically at him. The grin could only stand solid for a second or so before it faltered. He bit his lip, waiting for just a moment more before trying again.

"*Dick*?" he said half-heartedly.

When, again, Rose did not respond except to remove his grimy hand from her arm, Dick looked offended and full-on frowned.

"Usually people recognize my name," he muttered.

Rose called the bluff. "No they don't."

He looked up at her and though he was the same height as she, he crawled away from the bars and made himself small in her presence. He cradled his coat like a favorite blanket and a defeated look crossed the poor man's face.

Rose remained deadpan. "Are you a pirate?"

His head turned from his coddle of cloth and a sly smile crept across his face. The smile revealed the golden teeth that were a staple for Anarchy's most wealthy.

Aaron and Hera were excited to have succeeded after so much hardship, but the sweet embrace of family was not something they had the pleasure of partaking in. Aaron took a quick look around the prison complex to see if anything caught his interest, and a glint of a silver ring attracted his eye like a torch in the dark.

The ring belonged to a tall, slender man, one not native to Great Neighbor. At least Aaron hoped he was not from Great Neighbor, for if he was, he was worse for wear and unrecognizable. Massive bags hung under his eyes and his lips looked shattered. They were pulled back in a snarl, revealing misshapen pearl teeth. The man was skinny and weak. He looked malnourished and crooked. A black curtain of hair greased over his face, letting only a purple glint shine through. Aaron was intrigued by the cryptic question, perpetually pertinent, prominently pondered by the woven together man, and he crept forward to interrogate the strange sight.

"Who are you?" he asked.

As Aaron took a closer look at the man, he realized just how dire the man looked. His pace quickened. This man was as thin as bone; he looked like he would starve at any moment. Aaron completely lost interest in the ring and rushed to the cell door. The man was slumped down in a crippled sitting position. When Aaron approached, instead of straightening his back, he craned his neck to look up at Aaron. Aaron waited for a response, but none came.

"Are you from Great Neighbor?" Aaron said.

"Where I'm from doesn't matter..." the man responded in a drone. Under his breath, he whispered something Aaron could barely hear, "Make my martyrdom merciful, oh mirror of marble."

Aaron stood awkwardly, not sure how to respond. He decided to slide his pack onto his arm and start rummaging for food. The man lifted his hand and gently told Aaron to stop.

"I am fasting. I have not eaten in several sacred months. My solitude is solely sustained by the magic that flows through the somber sounding strings of reality."

Aaron, sensing something wrong in the fringes of his perception, suddenly felt far more uncomfortable than he had a moment before. It was true that Aaron was looking for food, but that was a hasty assumption for the figure to make.

"Who did you say you are again?"

"I didn't," the man snapped. "I am Filius. I am from Mercery of Goldenhill. I was reclaimed after my attempted pilgrimage to Drasil."

Drasil was a country south of the Northern Kingdom that bordered Ironforge and Witshore. The territory splits the Northern Kingdom from the southern countries. Drasil is a place of many mysteries. It is said a single tree roots under all the country's land. Some of its roots even extend as far as Goldenhill. For that reason, the tree is considered holy and protected by the people that live under its canopy. Mercery, on the other hand, was a much less pleasant place that Aaron knew decidedly little about.

"Alone?" Aaron asked.

"Besides the nine-foot-tall dark sorcerer and his entourage of a dozen dwarves, yes, I was alone," Filius said.

Aaron left in a nervous hurry, but Filius made no fuss to try to stop him. The strange man seemed to have little to no interest in leaving the cell and preferred to sit and meditate with his eyes closed. Aaron spent the next while questioning those who were not from Great Neighbor. He found that most had a similar story, but lived in a different part of the world. Plenty of people were from Aerokite, mostly small islands off the coast. They spoke Northern with a heavy accent which made communication hard, but Aaron felt it was more his fault for not knowing a word of Aerokitian.

Very few people had been alone when captured, but Filius was not the only one. An old woman who looked to be blind also had a similar story. One thing remained consistent, though—the imprisoned people were always isolated from the powers that be.

Viner took Henry into his arms, and the surprised boy embraced him back. The Captain of the Guard closed his eyes in his first moment of rest for a year of living with a lock on his heart. For others it had been a shorter time since the people of Great Neighbor had been captured. But for Viner it had been a sorrowful reality for far too long. Henry welcomed the embrace, needing it now more than ever. He knew that his father was not in this complex. That thought left a taste in his mouth so bitter that it almost drowned out any hint of achievement. After a solemn moment, Viner let go of Henry.

He walked to the nearest guard in a cell. Viner looked into their wide, hopeful eyes, and his gaze darkened and his breath became labored. His great chest heaved in and out and he bared his teeth like a gorilla. He exhaled slowly at first, then faster and faster. His snarl turned to a growl and his growl to a roar. The guard in the cell stepped back in fearful surprise. Viner unstrapped his kite shield and took it in his hands, holding it with the sharp end pointed down.

Through his reddened eyes, he could see the rusted iron padlock that held the door in place. With a roar of strength, one that would scare a raging bull, he brought the sharp end of his mighty shield down against the padlock. The clumsy locking mechanism was no match for the full strength of the shield and of Viner. It shattered open in three pieces without so much as leaving a dent in the thin metal of the kite shield.

Opinionated historians may call him dramatic, but that thought didn't cross the minds of any soldier present when Viner fell to the ground with his blow. The Hand of the King wept. He wept for the interrupted childhood of his nephew and the loss of his nephew's father. He wept for the hardships of traversing this white hell. He wept for those he could not see at that moment, those who had died rather than been captured.

The guard Viner released did not know what to do, so they stood there not doing a thing. They looked down at the man, but the guard felt as if Viner could not be greater. When Viner rose to his feet, his back hunched under the weight of his armor. Looking at their commander, the recently released guard was finally given a purpose. They placed their fists together in a Great Neighbor salute.

Viner turned his head up to see what had made the shuffling noise and to his amused surprise, he saw the guard saluting him. Shortly after, he heard another shuffling sound in his left ear, and he turned to see what was afoot. He shifted his gaze upwards again to see another fist on fist greeting him. This time, there was an even greater bending of leather and shifting of metal. The noise persisted through the air for several seconds before coming to a standstill.

Viner took a step back in wonder, taking in the scene of the people of Great Neighbor coming together to salute him.

His jaw would have hit the floor, had his defined jowls not kept it in place. Not only did the guard salute, but so did the civilians, both those in and out of cells. Even Hera and Aaron gave reverence to the Captain of the Guard, a grin on their faces as they did so.

The tears gently lapping down his face did not stop. The Captain of the Guard raised his arms to impose his own mighty salute on the surrounding area. He was proud of his guard. They had ventured into the underworld to save their people, but something nagged at the back of his mind. It wasn't hard enough. Each step had taken the strength of a thousand oxen, but still, they had faced no army. Was it really over?

He paused for a moment, his arms still suspended, and then he called, "My friends. Are these locks really going to stand in our way?"

"No!" the army uproared.

"We have faced an army ten thousand fold and sprinted across desolate wastes. Can these puny padlocks stand in our way?" Viner rallied.

"No!" the soldiers cried again.

They finished their salutes and each started moving toward the cell nearest them. With kicks, slashes, bashes, and bangs, the army attacked the doors with all their might. Hammers pierced contraptions, and spears bashed them in. The metal boots of several guards made contact with the padlocks, and after several hardy kicks, they came undone.

Hera and Aaron had what they considered a far more civilized approach. Hera and Aaron each turned on their heels and calmly walked away from the destruction. They looked at each other. Hera rolled her eyes, and Aaron shrugged. Prisoners reached out their hands to try and grab Hera and Aaron and demand to know what they were doing.

To the prisoners, it appeared as if Hera and Aaron were just walking past them.

Once they were a sizable distance from the uncomfortably cramped crowd, Hera made a ninety-degree turn to the left and Aaron made a ninety-degree turn to the right, both at the same time. Hera searched in her backpack and found a piece of cloth wrapping. She unbundled the bundle, making sure its contents did not spill out. Very gently, she placed several straws of iron into her hand and took her utility knife from her boot.

"Glad I'm lucky enough to be chosen by the master locksmith," the prisoner said sarcastically.

Hera had to admit that it was either brave or stupid to mock someone intending to release you from a cell. She decided against taking it personal and went to work with her lockpick. She tried to jam the knife into the padlock, but it was too big to properly fit, so after a few seconds of twisting and turning, she was forced to give up on it. She decided instead to use the flat side of a separate lockpick to apply pressure to the lock. The picks were designed with a slightly stronger piece of metal on what would be the handle that could also be used to apply pressure in a pinch.

She started work on the lock, feeling for the pin that had just that little bit of extra tension on it. There it was, the third pin down. Now, all it needed was a little-

"Hera."

Too much, the lock pick snapped. Hera turned quickly toward Aaron, upset that he had broken her concentration and her pick. Aaron looked back at her sheepishly, kneeling and rummaging through his bag.

"I can't find my lockpicks." He was clearly upset.

Hera sighed and walked over to Aaron. She was in a lockpicking mindset, so she made sure that she made little noise and whispered when she spoke.

"Let me see," she hissed.

She too started rummaging through Aaron's bag, moving aside his tent and rations to find the cloth pouch. In less than a minute, she pulled out the pouch tucked away in a corner of the backpack. She darted her eyes at him and forced it into his hand. After a moment or two, her face softened, and she let a small laugh escape her lips before returning to the lock she had been working on.

Aaron was trying his best not to make eye contact after so foolishly being unable to find his lockpicks. The prisoner whose cell Aaron began working on was not amused. Aaron looked up at the frowning guard apologetically. He took his lockpick bundle and let it come undone all over the floor. The lockpicks clattered to the ground, and Aaron picked two up with his right hand. He nimbly switched one to the left and jammed that one into the lock so it could provide the tension he required for the real pick to do the work.

He felt around in the lock for only a moment before finding the first tense spring. Cling, the second spring went up. Cling, the first followed suit. Cling, cling, went the third and fourth. Aaron was surprised to feel the lock mechanism release after the fourth pin. He huffed out a little breath, wishing the lock was a little more complex, but alas, he pulled open the cell door.

The guard on the other side went from frowning while shaking their head to frowning while nodding. A different expression altogether.

"Aaron."

Aaron pivoted on his heel to see Hera still working on her own pick.

"Can I have a little help with this?" she asked.

Aaron nodded. He got to his feet, still crouching, and slinked over to Hera's side. She was struggling with her lock.

She had the third and second pins up, but she couldn't quite get the fourth or first. She had concluded that the fourth pin had to go up first, but it wasn't sticking.

"Let me take a look at it," Aaron told her.

Hera moved aside, gently passing the tension pick over to Aaron's left hand. He held his breath while tenderly taking the pick. Hera made sure he had it strong before letting go. Aaron felt around the fourth pin and gave it a few test pushes. It was pretty firm but had a slight spring. He moved his lock to the first pin, just to be sure. For a moment, he thought the first pin was just barely easier to move, but after a little wriggling, he came to the same conclusion as Hera. With a puzzled look on his face, he took the lockpick out and twirled it slightly in his hand.

"Looks like it's jammed," Aaron mulled.

Hera face fell into a frown. "What are we going to do?"

The person that looked most upset was the sarcastic citizen who was stuck in the cell. They backed into the wall, and their face darkened from the shade of their slanted brow. They seemed to be more upset at how long it would take to be saved, rather than being worried they would be left alone.

Aaron fiddled with the lock a moment more before asking Hera to go and start working on some other locks. She agreed and took her picks to an unopened cell. Aaron wiped dry sweat off his brow and let the pin pick fall to the floor. He picked it up again and flipped it, so it was facing backward. He jammed the hard side of the lockpick into the lock. He applied as much pressure as he could to the lock without letting it break. Slowly, his pointer and middle finger of the other thumb started to curl around it, but before he could get a good grip, the lockpick snapped.

Aaron took in a sharp breath. As nimbly as he could, he fished out the broken half of the lockpick. He wasn't going to let his tension pick release those two pins and kept it in his grasp as strongly as ever. He fished another lockpick from the floor and again used the strong metal end as the lockpick. He jammed the reinforced metal wire against the pin, pushing it up with as much strength as the lockpick could hold. The lock would have been picked just then had the reinforced end of the lockpick not been too thick to fit into the pinhole.

Again, Aaron attempted to switch hands, this time even more carefully, to make sure the lockpick didn't break in his grasp. Once his left hand was free, he was able to conjure another pick from the floor. He shoved the second pick into the same lock, past the reinforced end of its older brother. With a twist of the lockpick and a trepidatious breath, the fourth pin finally clicked into place. Aaron let out a sigh that he had been holding for longer than he meant to. He almost expected cheers.

To Aaron's disappointment, the soldier in the cell did not notice the click and kept on examining the floor. Aaron considered halting his dexterous exercise then and there if the soldier wasn't going to pay attention, but he decided he might as well finish what he started. He gently removed the backward lockpick and used the other one to push the first pin up. The pin was much easier to undo now that the fourth pin had been released. With a delicate twist, the padlock came undone and fell to the floor.

With a creak of metal, the iron cell door swung open, and the prisoner inside was released from the cave. The prisoner thanked Aaron for the rescue and then, wasting no time, reconvened with the larger group. Aaron looked over to Hera and saw that she had released three prisoners already. He would have to step it up. The clattering noises of the barbaric guards annihilating the padlocks grew louder as Aaron worked. Soon they would catch up with him. But he knew this was what he was good at. Maybe this was his purpose here.

Chapter 19
The Real Enemy

Tython didn't have anyone's arms to rush into or anyone to rush into his, but nonetheless, he looked to the crowd with a satisfied smile. He was not strong enough to break a padlock, nor did he have the proper weapon to do so, but he was perfectly content watching Calessa reunite with her family with a goofy grin on his face.

Calessa had been one of the first to identify her family and speed into their embrace. The three were locked in the same cell, as were many of the people who had been captured together. Calessa and her family were not the only Aerokitian people in the complex, but they were the only ones that did a northern salute. Tython's smile grew from gentle to almost tearful watching Calessa rush to her father's extended hands. Her father cupped her face in his hands through the bars of the cell and just looked at her for a minute.

Calessa turned to look at Tython and blushed ever so slightly. Her mouth moved rapidly, while her mother's and father's moved little. After a while, she seemed to remember herself and took her kite shield into her grasp. One smash turned to two, and the lock was split just enough for her to wriggle it off. The embrace and reunion were tearful.

Calessa's sister was about her height, and it was unclear if she was younger or older. They chatted rapidly, taking turns. They talked mainly of how good it was to see each other again and how much the trapped sister missed the sky. They talked about Calessa's harrowing conquest that brought her here, and how she too missed the sky. And they talked about light and how superior Malue was to this world called Dessees.

Calessa looked again over to Tython and again she blushed. Tython looked past her but caught Calessa's sister sneakily gesturing him over. He took one step and then stopped. He took a step forward again and immediately retracted it, taking a hesitant, nervous step backward. Finally, he made up his mind and walked forward to Calessa. He ran into several guards and common folk while doing so. It was painfully awkward.

"So, it's over," Viner grinned.

He had finally finished releasing the last prisoner, and the soldiers were becoming organized. Rose, to his right, burst out in inappropriate laughter at his statement. Rose, being Rose, did not double over, or laugh any louder than a speaking voice, but even so, the idea was transmitted.

"So we can be attacked again?" Rose said.

"We can be ready!" Viner rounded on her, already burning with the bright passion of a forest fire.

"How are you going to get home?" Rose asked calmly.

"With the..." Viner stifled his words.

Viner's mind was racing with possibilities, none of them good. How were they supposed to get home? He cursed himself for not leaving a trail. How foolish could he be? He had thought they could just walk back, but what if they didn't notice the portal. No, the land was so flat, it would be impossible to miss the portal, impossible!

"No. The portal would be impossible to see. It is two-dimensional Viner," Rose's inflection gave no inclination to her feelings.

Viner looked at her with a resentment he had not felt for anyone in a long time. Was this her plan? Why was she so calm?

"Why are you so calm?" Viner demanded.

"Because..." she said, a second, bemused, laugh forming in her throat. "It doesn't make a difference. I wasn't going to let you leave these fairy-tale monsters alive."

"What?" Viner spat. "That is madness!"

A spirit flickered to life in Rose's face. An oxen-rage in the gleam of her eye. She opened her mouth and spit came flying from the oxen's horn.

"Then I am mad!" she laughed. "Because we will march. We will fight. They will die. And I will die to kill them. Kill them all."

"Calm yourself," Viner ushered in a panic.

He had never seen Rose like this before. He looked around defensively, trying his best to shield her from view. His attempts were in vain; most of the guard force were witness to Rose's outburst. It was as if a tevnal possessed her. She raised her hand in the air to address what she considered to be her subjects.

"Do not hear me with your ears, listen with your heart!" she said. "Do you not see the monster on that flat horizon? These dwarfs cannot be let live."

This was the most animated Rose had ever been. Again she was stuttering over her words like she always had, but now it felt almost poetic. Even after killing the King she had not been so vivid in movement. Her emotion caused little more than frozen panic in the crowd. They were caught again in the same way they had been immobilized when Rose had slain their leader, unable to do anything more than watch the fire burn.

"We must end them. You have fought and died for this!" She grew frustrated at the crowd's lack of agreement. "Aren't we going to finish what we started!"

Hera walked closer to the center of the crowd. She had peer over a tall guard's shoulder to see the rather short

Rose. In this, she failed. Without as much as a gesture towards Aaron, she started slipping her way through the forest of limbs. Aaron noticed her leave and began to follow, slightly offended that she had left him behind so readily.

Before she knew it, Hera was at the forefront of the crowd. Her complexion paled while watching Rose's mad tirade. She took a moment to look around and saw the stunned fear on the faces of all the other guards. She looked back at Rose and used her eyes to fire arrows in her direction. Were these big, brave guards going to cower in fear of this bully? While thinking of Rose, only one word ran through Hera's mind: Punk.

"Not our queen," Hera said.

No one realized that all had been quiet in the wake of Rose's speech until now, including both Rose and Hera. Both were surprised to hear Hera's cold words. Even Viner hadn't dared stand up to Rose, but now this random thief thought it was her place? All the guards stared at her, not sure what to think.

"Not our queen," Hera said again, as if that answered any questions.

Rose's nostrils flared at the insult. Hera was nothing but a young rogue. A god-touched rogue, but what was a single god to her? She was strong; she was blessed with holy righteousness.

"You are naive and young," Rose told her in her most condescending tone. "The world is hard. You need to be hard back."

"None of us want to risk what we have," Hera told her.

Aaron put his hand on her shoulder, "Hera…"

Hera turned around to face him, "We have to be brave, Aaron. We can't let this happen. We messed up. *We* messed up. Our whole lives. Now we have to stand up for ourselves."

"Hera," Aaron said.

"No, Aaron, I don't have—" Hera started again.

"I'm with you."

Hera looked back at him, and with a soft smile, she put a hand of gratitude on his shoulder. She turned again to look at Rose, who had returned to an emotionless husk.

"Like me or not, you have no choice," Rose spelled it out. "We. Cannot. Get. Back."

"So what?" Aaron said.

"Are you just going to die instead of trying?" Hera finished the thought.

"I have a plan," Rose said. "If the dwarfs can create a portal, so can we."

Viner interrupted, "You just want to kill them."

"True," Rose nodded. "But I make a good point nonetheless."

She made a good point nonetheless. No guard fully understood magic; not one in the whole company of people could possibly comprehend—

"It's more complicated than that," a voice said.

Hera, Aaron, and Viner looked to see who had spoken. They couldn't quite distinguish anyone in particular from the crowd, but they knew where the voice came from.

"You see, the magic required to move an entire army cannot be done by a simple teleportation altar." The voice jumped from one point of the room to the next, as if it too had teleported like the army it spoke of.

The voice spoke again, "Not to mention bridge the Inbetween."

This time the rusty voice was closer still to the crowd, as if it had been moving through the guards.

"Things are going to get..." the voice croaked.

And then it stopped. It faltered, it gave up. And it changed. It laughed. A noise of sadistic glee, boundless ambition satiated at long last. A laugh that displayed an understanding that could not be stated in any other way. It was a laugh of love, of mad love, that goes by a different name. Obsession.

Then the laughter stifled. "Phantastic" it said, and then, there he stood, before Rose, before Hera, Aaron, before Viner. He looked like he had grown from the fabrics of reality. He had woven through the crowd and now stood, a tapestry before them, blackened hair greased over his purple threaded eyes. He held in his hands a slightly curved knife with a purple gem on the end. He was admiring it like a piece of art, the playful tug of mania still playing at his lips.

"Filius?" Aaron asked.

Filius made no response and continued his explanation, "When I say no simple teleportation altar can move an army across Dessees into Malue, I do not mean no teleportation altar can. I mean, no *simple* altar. The Restless Sleeper. The soul entrapped in the altar."

"Mordecai," Viner said.

"Perhaps," Filius nodded. "Depending on when Mordecai ends and his mountains of memory multiply."

No one knew what the malnourished man was trying to tell them. But then again, who was going to ask? Hera and Aaron certainly weren't.

"What you stand in now is the altar. Of course, it is not really an altar. It is a tower. A marble tower," Filius told them.

"You're telling us this isn't the underworld?" Aaron asked.

"No," Filius snapped. "I never said that, boy. I said, we are in a terrible and tainted tower within the underworld. We are inside a building right now. One magnified in size by magic. Such a powerful spell requires a fuel source. Someone gave up a humanity."

"A humanity?" Viner inquired.

"The most powerful enchantment one can give. A living soul. Give up all of it and you become a husk, not capable of doing more than breathe. But give up some of it, and you will lose only that which you choose. Your sense of smell, perhaps. Or maybe your ability to love," Filius told them.

"What does this have to do with escape?" Rose asked.

"We must find the philosopher's focus. You will be pleased to learn that it is likely deeper in the marble tower," Filius told her.

Hera's heart sank. Deeper into the tower? The way out was deeper in the tower? The last thing Hera wanted to do was go deeper into the tower, and now she was learning that she must. What an abysmal world.

"Let's strike a compromise," Viner said through gritted teeth. "We go deeper into the tower, we avoid as much danger as possible, and once we find this 'focus', we leave."

With the plan set in stone, and Rose thoroughly humiliated, many of the prisoners who were released from their cells desired to join the ranks of the marble tower invaders. Alas, most were citizens, and though some of them were locked away with weapons that the dwarves didn't bother confiscating, such as Filius, even more were unarmed. That left Viner with a difficult decision to make. What to do with the unarmed former prisoners? He could leave them here, but what if a regiment of dwarves came upon them? He could take them with them, but wouldn't that also put them in danger? A crowd of such immense size would be impossible to move effectively.

After some deliberation, he decided. They would all go together or not at all. They could not risk leaving citizens defenseless, and they would have no chance of winning a single battle without the full strength of their army. Would they have a chance with even that? Many guards had already died in the initial invasion. Fewer were found alive than he had hoped.

With unease in their chests, the army was forced to move deeper into the cave than they wanted. They reached the end of the prison cells, but still, the cave went on. The cave only felt deeper and darker, but in reality, as it went forward, it became more uniform, and the blue flame torches turned brighter and redder. The floor became stone slab and the gravel at the guards' feet became scarce.

Eventually, the hall straightened, as if the people who had chiseled it had finally figured out how to tame the cave from which they carved it. The blue flame torches now blazed a bright red and were set equidistantly throughout the hallway. Though it was still dim, it appeared significantly less so under the warm firelight of the torches. Hera mused that if the torches burn, there must be someone who replaces them.

Once the hallway straightened, it was evident that it ended in a staircase. No door separated the chiseled hallway from the staircase. Instead, the staircase disappeared into the ceiling as it ascended upwards. Viner's steps did not falter, and if anything, Rose's pace quickened. The same effect was not present in Hera or Aaron. The young thieves wanted nothing more than to fall asleep in a pile of hay.

The hallway was becoming uncomfortably narrow for the large number of soldiers that had to cram their way into it. It appeared that soon the army would be unable to move at all. Viner went to reconcile the error before it was too late, and he adjusted his ranks accordingly. The heavy infantry was now in front, with the shortbows and the longbows combined, following. Holding the rear was the regular infantry combined with the greatsword infantry. This made sure that they would not have to adjust ranks mid-combat.

They ascended the steps, each with their own jolting feeling. By now, they were used to marching. Were they ever not soldiers? Did they ever not move forward? Why must they be dragged along by a tevnal with a temper as red as her hair? Why did they have to stand for her? Did they not already have what they wanted? First, they lost their families, but now that they had them, they lost their home. They would die here. They knew it.

"I can't take this anymore!" they wanted to shout. "I want to go home." And it was true, but what would giving up accomplish? So, they kept their complaints to a small grumble that waved through the crowd like an unwelcome wind that messed up your hair. How they wished there was a wind that messed up their hair, for all they felt was a cold chill that shivered down the steps, forever pushing them back.

The staircase was not all that long, but it grew narrower and narrower. It was all Viner could do to stay in the front. Rose was always by his side, whether he liked it or not. Viner was emotional enough to let Henry break the line and stand next to him. And that is why Henry was the first to lay eyes upon the next room in the tower. A ghastly sight.

The next room was a catacomb. No other word could do it justice. It was not a mortuary, nor a morgue, nor a tomb; it was a catacomb. The smell of charnel flesh was fainter than one would expect, yet oddly present nonetheless. Most rancid of all was not the flesh, but the twists and turns that the catacomb took. The angles were sharp but not perfect. Rarely was an angle at ninety degrees. More commonly, the passageway turned ten or fifteen degrees to split, ever so slightly, into an unnatural path.

If looked at as a whole, the catacomb often folded in on itself without the walls meeting. Meaning that it was larger than physically possible. The volume was somehow greater than the wall areas indicated, and even with the guards' lack of geometric skills, they could tell it was unnatural. The red lights that filled the previous room were now absent, replaced instead with nothing. Yet in this nothing, the room was not pitch black. It was filled with dim light, like that given off by a full moon on a beach shore. If only the catacombs were as picturesque as the aforementioned scene. The room was made of grayish stone, and though the carvings scored in the wall were complex, the lack of contrast made them appear to be little more than the weathering of stone.

No wall space was unused, but instead was covered in small pockets indented into the wall. These pockets were in columns of two, each two feet tall by five feet wide. Separating the bottom row from the top row was about three inches of solid rock, with runes brushed onto the barrier. Two inches separated each column, and instead of runes, these barriers sported deep lines scratched onto the wall. The matrix was mirrored on either side, creating a common catacomb.

The ceiling and floor mirrored each other, made of dusty slabs of smooth stone, but they were by far the least interesting parts of the catacomb. The most eye-catching part was what lay in the matrix of stone: bodies, with no coffins in sight, each resting uncomfortably cramped in every crevice.

The pallid skin of the dwarves hearkened to the tomb of stone and chose to be alike to its color. They were dressed still in their chainmail, the same mail that to them was fur. Their black beards were covered in dust as if they had been dead for quite some time. The assumption was made that this was a place for the dead, but that assumption was soon horribly shattered.

"They breathe," Rose whispered.

The slow hum of breath was unnoticeable from the corpses and also indistinguishable from their armored chests. Yet still, it was true. The only thing that gave away their livelihood was the clink of their chainmail armor as their vitality gently bashed against it.

Viner lifted a hand and cut off his troops like they had been screaming. His fist, now closed, slowly descended, and he turned his head to snarl an order to his troops.

"Quietly," he ordered.

It was a miracle they had not already been discovered, but no accident. The dwarves were in a deep stupor. Rose did not know how long they would stay that way, nor how much it would take to wake them, but she did know that they had to use this.

"Move forward," she whispered.

Viner reached his hand out to stop them, but the army was already creeping forward like a centipede. None of the guards dared breathe. Most of them watched their feet, making sure that they were always placed firmly on the ground. Hera and Aaron had the easiest time of it, but they were nervous as ever. Henry crept next to his uncle, trying his best to imitate the guard captain's strength.

They lurked in the catacombs, inching forward ever so slightly. Perhaps they should have turned back, but what did they have to turn back to? This was the most uncertain any of the guards had ever been about a choice with only one answer. Dust filled their lungs, imploring them to cough, but none did, for if they were to cough, it would spell "death" in the ash. And like this, they crept forward for several minutes until Henry broke the silence.

"Look there, across the room. Spears, swords, shields, axes, and clubs. Some of the armor may even fit. With that, we can arm our people and keep ourselves safe," whispered Henry.

Viner thought quietly for a moment. The boy was right. Through a torment of twists and turns, this hallway was different. It led to an armory. This could solve multiple of Viner's problems all at once. What Henry had neglected to mention was the condition of the "guard". Laying across the floor was a creature that they had yet to see. Unlike the small stature of the dwarves, this beast was twice the size of Viner.

Humanoid and lumpy in shape, the pale figures of the dwarves were reflected on the hide of this leathery monster. It lay face down on the hallway floor, taking up a ridiculous amount of space. It was dressed in lumps of iron that seemed to have melted into its body. It had the ears of a pig and the snout of one, too, making it look like a giant hog. Its hands were gnarled into talons, and its feet were cloven. It looked bipedal, but no one could be sure. They did not want to find out.

Viner spoke quietly "I would very much like that weaponry, but it would be impossible to move it all without waking that beast."

"We can slay the beast," Henry whispered.

"It will squeal," Rose interjected.

"Some weapons are better than nothing," Henry insisted.

"Agreed."

She turned to look at Viner whose frown was growing ever larger with every passing moment.

"You know the best course of action," Rose said.

"I do not accept," Viner responded, a gruff tone entering his voice.

Rose turned to the nearest guard and hissed in his ear, "Bring the thieves here."

"I cannot let you," Viner started.

Rose glared back, "They are in as much danger as any of us."

Chapter 20
The Hob

Hera and Aaron were put in what they would call a tough spot. Of course, they did not want to carry heavy cargo stealthily across a rather long hallway with a hostile goliath restlessly snoring in the center of it, but they could not refuse. They would have refused if they could.

With a poke and a prod, they took the first creeping step, dizziness sweeping through them as adrenaline coursed through their veins. Their minds seemed to turn against them. Aaron's breathing was labored, and he tried to make it softer. Every step Hera took felt like a clanging cymbal, and the harder she tried to be quiet, the louder it became. A noise from Hera's left almost made her jump. A shuffle, they'd been found! But no, it was just another bump in the dark as the restless guards wiggled in their stone beds.

When they came across the hob, it smelled worse than a dead body—a smell they knew all too well. Its human-like flesh stretched with every breath, and the plates of metal cruelly welded into its back scraped against each other with a low screech. If the dwarves on either side did not sleep so deeply, Hera and Aaron would fret that they would be awakened at every breath of the hob.

Aaron and Hera did not say a word to each other. Aaron did not want to touch the wall or the hob, and Hera felt much the same, but the creature was dead center of the tight hallway with little wiggle room between it and the dwarves that lined the catacombs. They both sucked in their stomachs as much as they could and crept between the beast and the stone, too afraid to brush the wall and too smart to brush the hob. One completely trusts their ability to walk until they walk along a cliffside; only then do they fear a stumble. It was much the same with the hob. Aaron and

Hera knew that they had space to sneak by just fine, but the extra stakes made it nerve-racking nonetheless.

They were a few feet past the beast before they let out a labored breath. They wanted to gasp, but to do so would be suicide, so instead, they sizzled out breath as quickly and quietly as they could. They did not stop moving; they continued creeping down the hallway. At this point, they were closer to the armory than the exit. No point in turning back now.

Finally, after measuring each and every step, they reached the end of the hallway. The armory was larger than Aaron and Hera had previously perceived. Though there was no door, the room was distinctly differentiated by the lighter shades of stone. A large door frame could have fit in the barrier between the wall and the armory, but the space was empty, functioning instead as an unnecessary archway.

The armory was eerily similar to that at Great Neighbor, the main difference being its shape. Weapons and armor of all kinds were displayed on racks. Surprisingly, there were more than just axes and chain armor, even though it appeared that axes and chain armor were all that the dwarves used. The armor came in different sizes, too. A lump in Hera's throat formed as she thought of the implications of this. Either the dwarves had stolen this armor and kept it for who-knows-what reason, or there were more than dwarves in Hiver's army. The hob was indication enough of the latter, but they could not be sure.

Aaron strapped as much equipment as he could to himself, favoring smaller weapons over larger ones for obvious reasons. A gnarled knife caught his eye. Serrated at the edge, the metal was jagged and bronze. It shared the same half-sphere hilt of Hera's gladius, making the two weapons appear similar in design. Aaron recognized the serrated edge as a definitively Goldenhill design. It gave the weapons the appearance of one thousand shark teeth ready to catch a hapless fish, and the thought of stabbing someone with it made Aaron sick. He decided to leave that one behind.

Hera also gathered weapons, giving her the appearance of a metal porcupine. But the over-encumberment did not stop her or Aaron from turning to make the trek across the hallway again. This time, with a full load of weapons in their possession, both rouges doubted it would be quite as easy. Not that it was easy before. At no other point on this journey were they as resentful of their situation. But at death's door there was serenity; without Calm this would not have been possible.

Henry watched the two do their silent dance with wide-eyed worry. He could barely see their heads over the resting hob. He feared for his friends' lives and had to do everything to convince himself that they were truly the best for the job. He couldn't help but blame himself that they were in this situation. Was it not him who pointed out the weapons?

Aaron's palms started to sweat before he even got near the hob. His palms were the last part of his body he wanted to get slippery. This sweat on his palms was something he had never felt before—a sweat of fear, an exertion that only made him colder. He closed his eyes for a moment, yet when he opened them, he was further forward than he had wanted to be. It was not that his pace had quickened nor that he had made a mistake in judging the distance of his movement, but more that he didn't want to move forward at all. He was afraid, yes, but when he turned to his right to see Hera's determination, he couldn't turn back.

Hera sucked in her stomach to again go around the hob. Had it moved? No, her imagination. But it was rather tight. It felt faster than last time, sneaking past the beast. Her breath wasn't quite as labored. She could do this! But alas, the world has a way of throwing challenges in the face of those who dare claim to have mastered them. Aaron barely got past the hob before his sweaty palms could not hold onto one of his many swords any longer. Traitorously slowly, it started to slip. He knew he couldn't stop it, but he also knew it wasn't going to happen immediately, so he did the only thing he could.

"Hera, my sword," he breathed.

With a slip, the sword started to fall. Every onlooker inhaled quickly, looking at the sword that was prepared to kill them faster than it ever could have had it been used as a weapon of war. Hera knew what she had to do. Aaron always had her back, and she always had his, but she had only a moment to prepare. The sword began to plumet to the ground and as it was about three-quarters there, Hera caught the flat side of the blade with her foot. It swayed hilt-ways, but Hera shifted, compromising her balance to do so. With a hop, the sword was in the air again, and Aaron caught the pesky sword with his newly emptied hand. Hera shifted her feet with a spin, landing just barely upright. They looked at each other, each panting with panic. Aaron looked mortified, but Hera smiled and almost giggled. That made Aaron only look more mortified.

Halfway down the hallway, Aaron and Hera were on the final stretch. It was not particularly difficult to walk down the hallway, but doing so without making a sound in a completely quiet room was a challenge in its own right. Even so, the weapons gathered were measly in comparison to what was required for the entire army. They needed more than a thousand weapons for their citizens, not only those from Great Neighbor but all across Malue. A tall order, which meant that the two needed to make many more trips. So that is what they did. Over and over, Hera and Aaron risked life and limb to make sure the newest conscripts were stocked. They despised their job and despised Rose who tasked them with it. Every second was a hardship, but in that time between a second, that one offbeat of the human heart, they knew deep down that they were important. They feared death, not because they had already died, but because they lived. That was a gift.

The armory wasn't anywhere near depleted when Viner lost his nerve. He made the executive decision that since most citizens were now armed, any further expeditions would be more risk than benefit.

"I would have preferred a more professional selection, but these will do," Rose said.

"We did what you asked, and we succeeded. That is more than enough," Hera responded.

Rose nodded sharply, agreeing with Hera. Hera was surprised that Rose had been able to so easily ignore the disobedient tone. In turn, Rose was thankful that Hera thought she had ignored the disobedient tone. The weapons were distributed evenly among all unarmed citizens. Most did not know how to wield a weapon and were given the leftovers, predominantly small hand axes. It took hours to get the weapons into the citizens' hands, but they were glad that no dwarf had stirred. Even with the success of stealth, the army was nervous, and their guard was far from down.

Hera and Aaron's was a fantastic feat, worthy of song. So, a song was written and sung by a muse named Jackson. For whatever reason, Jackson insisted on spelling his name Jaxon. This caused no issue besides being minorly irritating to scholars trying to recount the details of his sung exploits. The song he wrote about the two thieves had a quiet tune, simple and light, with a whispered voice to properly sing it and a gentle harp to properly play it. Only in the dead of night could it be heard, and only with the crowds half asleep. When trying to recite it, one often finds they do not know the end because they had already fallen asleep before the bard had finished his song. They would ask if it were not that the bard had already left by morning. And for that reason, the quiet tool was quite the tool for a questionably credible performer.

The army mobilized again, this time with more equipment to haul. In their rush to arm their citizens with weapons, Henry, Viner, Hera, Aaron, and even Rose had fallen victim to a dastardly oversight. Simply put, one who cannot use a weapon cannot hold a weapon.

The clanging sound of metal on stone rang out through the dungeon, and the army froze. For a moment, it looked like no dwarf had reacted to the loud clattering of metal against stone, but this nightmare was not so merciful.

The hideous dwarf that stirred had eyes that did not fit well in his head, and when they opened them, the whites glowed a dim gray. Those eyes took a long, fixed stare at the nape of the unfortunate axe dropper's neck. The dwarf was a cruel creature, and creative enough to know the best way to raise the alarm. This dwarf was the smallest amongst them and the most primate-like. It jumped on the back of the hardly-soldier and sank its teeth into their neck. The screams were loud enough to wake the dead.

"I want a shield wall down this hallway! Get it done!" Viner shouted.

Viner did not expect the level of discipline he received from his soldiers, but they were ready. Down the line, soldiers repeated the formation orders.

"Shield wall!"

"Watch your sides!"

"Here they come."

"Forward, move it!"

"Shields, now!"

Within seconds, the army was ready for battle.

The monkey-dwarf stood only three feet off the ground, short even for a dwarf, but this did not stop him from being a lethal foe. To the dismay of those nearby, the sharpened teeth of the dwarf dealt a mortal tally to its first victim. The soldiers that saw their fellow warrior fall could only hope the neck was broken quickly. The monkey cared not; it bounced backward off its first victim into an upper coffin slot. From there, the monster jumped down and started wreaking havoc on the troops below it, using teeth and claws as well as a small axe to hack away at as many soldiers as it could. This devastation was but the first taste as to what could happen if the shield wall failed.

The army covered lots of ground, but they were surrounded. Even the walls came alive with small hands clawing at the faces of the soldiers that did not react quickly enough to deal with them. The dwarves slept with their weapons, which disgusted the army, yet now it proved a useful decision. The dwarves who slept near readied soldiers drifted into wakefulness just to be slain soon after. The ability to kill dwarves before they were awakened provided an unforeseen advantage to the human fighters if they were fortunate enough to capitalize on it.

The archers had already drawn swords to deal with the dwarves that had been awoken, but when they stepped back, they found themselves back-to-back with soldiers wielding shields. They steadied their courage, realizing that they had a bigger job than protecting themselves. They fought alongside the rest of Great Neighbor and Great Neighbor's allies. Bows were drawn and arrows were nocked. A shield wall was formed, not just with the heavy kite shields but with the bucklers too, and the deadly tips of arrows dotted behind the wall. The dwarves crawled like centipedes desperate for a drink of water, a tidal wave surging over the tops of shields.

Calessa used her claymore to slash a dwarf off the shield of one of her fellow guardsmen. The dwarf fell upon its own ranks and was used as a stepping stone for a forward attack. Before her very eyes, the kite warrior, overtaken by a mountain of limbs, was shredded into a gory mess. It took all her fortitude to not be sick. She felt so alone on the battlefield, with dwarves surrounding her from every angle. She looked to Rose, who was wildly swinging her cleaver. Dwarves crawled over her too, but they soon died, and Rose appeared unintimidated by their attack.

Calessa tried her best to swing her weapon like Rose did, to slash an area big enough to keep herself safe, but she was not her commander. Dwarves soon overtook her. The monkey dwarf that had been ravaging the inner ranks smelled weakness in the air, and jumped on her back, starting to tear open her plate armor. A nock of a bow and a thwip of an arrow, and the pesky dwarf fell into the abyss of bodies.

Tython was firing his bow as quickly and precisely as he could. He used his comrades for protection, and in return, he protected them. Calessa suddenly didn't feel as alone and looked to the Great Neighbor soldier she had watched fall. She dropped her greatsword onto the ground and picked up the kite shield that failed the soldier. In moments, Tython was at her back, firing arrows like a storm of sharpened hail.

A dwarf threw itself on top of Calessa's shield, ready to tear it to pieces. Little did the dwarf know that this was just what Calessa had planned. Tython strummed his shortbow, quick as the cord of a lute, and the arrow landed true in the dwarf's forehead. Together, with a shield and an arrow between them, Calessa and Tython were unstoppable. The dwarves felt not only the taste of steel but the wooden shafts of a well-placed piercing shot. Even if an arrow hit only chainmail, the sundered armor chainlinks would cause lethal damage to the warrior it was trying to protect.

"Forward!" Viner's command rumbled through the crowd.

The army started to progress forward, inching down the hallway slower than a crawl. The area in front of them was thick with dwarves, and the area behind them even more so. The heavy infantry could dispatch the dwarves in front, and the archers got ready to end the ones in back. Once the army had gotten its footing, the dwarves were sustaining losses ten times greater than the human force, but still, they approached, for they had more than enough flesh to spare.

And the dwarves had something more: a beast.

The commands of the humans were drowned out by a guttural noise. One that they did not, at first, recognize. A sort of chortle filled the hallway, the noise of laughter. The sight of dwarves laughing, dark-eyed and frowning, as they were pushed aside and slaughtered by a great beast was something Hera and Aaron would never forget. The hob, the creature that had guarded the dwarven armory, had awoken.

It barreled down the hallway, squealing nightmares. Its gray flesh ripped red with the exertion of its muscles against the plates of metal that were attached to its skin. It gnashed its teeth, bit its lips, and looked like it might injure itself beyond fatality before it even touched a human. Still, it bore forward, killing hundreds of dwarves before it could reach the rear shield wall. At least the lives of the dwarves were significantly slowing the monster's advance.

The pace of the humans quickened. The dwarves behind them had completely given up attacking. All efforts of the humans shifted to moving forward.

"Go, go, go," they cried, urging those in front of them to run as quickly as possible.

Cutting through the dwarves became easier with the combined might of the heavy militia and the archers. The entire army quickened in speed, but it was still not fast enough. Not only did they have to kill the dwarves, but they also had to walk over the mountain of corpses left behind. Some soldiers were trampled in the rush forward.

Slowly, the forces of the dwarves thinned. It appeared that the human army had traveled far enough through the catacombs before being found, as a well-lit staircase was becoming apparent in front of them. Viner had no desire to march blindly headfirst into an unknown room, but he had even less of a desire to meet the hob. With the dwarves behind them cleared, the hob started to rush at breakneck pace. There was no doubt it would make it to them in no time. Viner did not stop at the foot of the stairs and started clambering up them, like a bear up a tree. Then he heard a voice that he would remember until he died. The voice of the militiaman that Hera had spoken to.

"Goodbye."

Before anyone even got a glimpse of the soldier's face, the army member was gone. It was like rain suddenly appearing from a blue sky. When Viner glanced over his shoulder, he saw a faceless warrior, shield and spear in hand, standing alone before the hob. Viner shouted in anger, commanding the soldier to get back in line, but instead, his shield was knocked from his hand, and his spear rendered useless in the knee of the hob. Worst of all, it would not be enough. Despite the sacrifice of the soldier to slow down the beast, the army would soon be overtaken.

The humans climbed as quickly as they could up the stairs, even faster than their mad rush out of the white void.

But still, the hob climbed faster. That is when Viner heard it, a word he did not want to hear now and would never want to hear again, "Goodbye."

"No!" Viner cried.

But his plea was too late. Another soldier turned to stand against the pig-like beast, alone. Another soldier, another victim of the hob, and with the blood still not filling the stairs, another 'Goodbye', and with that goodbye, another sob, and with that sob, another death, and with that death, another minute and in that minute, another 'Goodbye'. It turned round and round. Men, women, young, old, soldiers, citizens, one after another, eight different souls ventured to face the hob, alone.

Viner's shouts were not the only ones in agony; plenty of soldiers cried out at those brave heroes. Viner wanted so badly to do something. Perhaps he, too, should give up his life in the line of duty. Viner started to turn toward the hob, to die with his men. He could not live with himself if he didn't do something. Then, his misty eyes caught Henry. He was not done yet. They had been given the gift of time, and now they would make it count.

The next room was massive. Not even close to the size of the white void, but still larger than Great Neighbor Keep. The floor they stood on was made of stone. It was reinforced with darker stone that curled like hinges over the other rocks. At their feet, rivers of molten iron dubiously flowed, crawling over itself with bulbous bubbling shapes. The walls were covered in textured marble, a relief in comparison to the previous form of marble they had witnessed. Giant pots of bronze, steel, iron, silver, and gold filled the entire room, numbering in the hundreds. The room was, unsurprisingly, boiling hot. The fonts of molten metal that circulated the area filled every crack and crevice they could find, almost overflowing onto the platforms on which the human army now stood.

"The iron, pour it on the beast!" Viner commanded.

The command was easier said than done. The thought had struck many soldiers, but the means to do it were more sparse in number. But with Viner's leadership and much gritting of teeth, they realized that the only way to get it done was the hard way. Their swords blunted against the stone pots, but they did not care. Great war hammers bashed against an even greater cauldron of molten metal. The one closest to the door, and to the hob, was chosen as a prime target.

The pot started to crack relatively quickly. A great fissure rounded the base of the smelter. Rose took the opportunity to land a critical blow. She dug her cleaver deep into the rock, splitting it like her cleaver was a pickaxe. Two soldiers with real axes followed her lead and started prying it open. The cauldron cracked like an egg, with Rose's cleaver being the final straw. As soon as the lava started to creep out of the opening, Rose dashed to safety.

"Use your shields to guide the lava!" Rose shouted.

Those with kite shields obliged without hesitation; they plugged the holes in the floor that would have directed the lava elsewhere. Lava lapped against the turtle crests of their shields, ruining them and singeing the brave soldiers who dared put themselves so close to such heat. The blisters would never heal. Calessa gritted her teeth and let out a scream as the heat rushed across her shield. She made sure that as much metal was between her and the lava, but still, it singed her arms and part of her face with painful burns.

"It's here!" Aaron yelled, but few heard him. They were distracted by the object of his revelation.

The hob crested the top of the stairs, peering over with its small, ugly eyes. It glanced at the molten composite of metals slowly gushing towards it with not even a moment of recognition. The soldiers stood, either holding back waves of lava or cowering behind a furnace. The beast let out a small squeal and lifted its foot onto the stone ground of the smeltery. Two spears and three swords were sticking out of its left knee. It reeled back when it put its weight on the injured knee, but something about its motion did not seem to convey traditional pain.

It took another step forward and made contact with the lava. It reeled in agony, but still, it took another step. Its right foot lapped lava against the other, causing it to stumble. The lava finally made it to the stairs and started cascading down.

"Release and run!" Rose ordered.

Calessa was more than happy to let go of her kite shield and did so as soon as the order was given. She wasn't going to take the metal heap with her, so she unstrapped it and rushed back. She watched her borrowed kite shield, as well as the kite shields of her fellows, become engulfed in molten steel. The lava started spreading towards them, but Rose was right; it now preferred the path of least resistance down the stairs.

The hob fell to one knee, using its hand to catch itself. It squealed in pain and quickly took its hand out of the slag. It had been burnt to the bone. The eyes of the hob dilated, but something else happened, too. The lava started to dance. It grew in place, defying all laws of gravity, crawling up the arms of the hob while the creature squealed.

The molten metal withdrew from the soldiers and formulated onto the arms of the hob. The bronze leaked from the floor, making its way up the beast and off the ground. Then a deep, slow, ominous voice with a subtle conglomerate of accents flowed through the lava as well.

"You are not worth the blood you hath reaped," the voice said. "You have ripped a red scar through my glorious white in a week. You have cost me great dishonor. I am Hiver, potentate of Disus, potentate of Dessees, conqueror of Malue..."

Chapter 21
The True Champion

The room rumbled, and the army cowered further back still. The lava wrapped itself around the hob and formed into an image. The face of the pig became shrouded in a plate of molten iron. It took the shape of a helmet, smooth and unopenable, with no facial features or eye holes. Horns of bronze blazed out of the back of the helmet creating a ram-horned headdress. The molten metals flowed down, silver lining the vague shape of a body, with armored arms and a cape that draped to the floor. No feet were formed from the molten inferno and instead, the creature's lower half melded into the cape creating a messy collage. Finally, as the creature was in full height and all the gray hob-hide was hidden, the image added detail to its previously vague gauntlets. Blooded steel lined the tips of the fingers forming talons, and the knuckles became sharp and jagged with gold. The new metal monstrosity they faced was several times bigger than the hob and towered to eye level with the smelters. If legends were true, this was a tevnal.

"So, if lava be your weapon of choice, then die by its hand." Hiver lifted his riveted gauntlet into the air and slammed it against the ground with a rock-shattering shake.

Hera and Aaron were suddenly thankful for their former selves' desire for mobility when choosing which armor to equip. The molten metal man was too much. The entire army lost focus and scattered throughout the smeltery. Hera and Aaron bounced from stone tablet to stone tablet over rivers of swaying molten metal. The moans of the gargantuan titan of melted mass rang like tremors throughout the entire smeltery, causing the stone to ring and the metal to vibrate. The sonic incursion was unpleasant, to say the least, and not only struck fear into the hearts of those who heard it but also caused pain in their ears.

"Why do you run?" Hiver bellowed. "You aren't supposed to run..."

A gushing fist of lava consumed two soldiers near Hera and Aaron, killing them instantly. The rogues pivoted around the next smelter and circled it counterclockwise. Their feet shook beneath them with the noise of metal against metal. They looked up to see the molten monster crawling over the top of the giant furnace behind them.

They did not stop running but instead made their way around yet another furnace. Hiver slithered like a serpent from this furnace to the next, growing larger as he absorbed the alloys contained in them. But the thieves did not care about the metal components present in the lava monster; they kept running as fast as they could. Hiver slithered forward, and Hera and Aaron turned again around yet another smelter. Dodging and weaving, they moved through the smeltery. Hiver accidentally slammed into the side of a furnace while trying to pursue his targets, but Hera and Aaron did not look back.

The two rogues felt a prickling heat on their backs and took a mad dive out of the way before Hiver tried to douse them in slag. The evasive thieves were quickly becoming more trouble than they were worth, and Hiver lost interest in eradicating them. The metal monster slowed down his pursuit and gazed over the smelters to find other prey to slaughter. But as he gazed over the sea of lava, he did not see where the other soldiers had gone. A burst of fire licked around the edges of the stone, and Hiver let out a great bellow from the deepest anger in his raging lead heart. The fire burst forward and moved faster than a galloping horse toward Hera and Aaron.

Viner was several rows of smelteries away, guiding the army in any direction that did not lead them towards the tevnal that they faced. He assessed his troops seeing that most of them were with him. But if all the troops were here, what was the lava monster fighting? A cold chill ran down his hot back.

"You useless peripherals," Hiver yelled down to Hera and Aaron. "You've been separated…"

It was true. Hera and Aaron did not run forward as most of the army had. Instead, they ran as far to the right as they could.

"If soldiers can die fighting a pig monster—if they can hold back lava with their hands—we can lead you away from them!" Aaron said.

They were no match for Hiver's great speed. He caught up to them in a moment.

"You did not sacrifice yourself." He coiled around Hera and Aaron, intimidating them to near death. "Don't take credit for playing the hero. You could not have known I would follow you of all people…"

Hiver stopped in his tracks for a moment. He seemed to be lost in thought. Hera and Aaron were sweating profusely from a combination of fear and fire.

"No…" Hiver started to laugh. "You're breathing me air… Maybe I should have given you more credit."

Hiver's head stayed stationary, but his liquid snail-like body flowed into his petrified torso, and he formed into a denser array of molten flesh. He pressed himself to almost human size, though he was still gigantic. He made a motion with his flat face and a sniffing noise, like he was smelling though he didn't have a nose.

"You… champion?" Hiver's tone was painfully curious.

Hera and Aaron looked at each other, wondering why everyone was always calling them champions. Hera took

Aaron by the arm and ran to the left, but she only found cold stone and Hiver's coiled lava. Hiver laughed gently.

"You are... aren't you?" he growled. "You have taken that from me?"

Aaron did a full three hundred and sixty-degree turn, looking for any way to escape. Hiver's face, if it could be called that, followed Aaron's gaze, keeping perfectly aligned to wherever Aaron looked. The lava tevnal cocked his head in a delighted way, yet when Aaron drew his eyes down from Hiver's arm all the way to his golden-red hand, it was clenched tightly, condensing, growing sharp.

Hiver spoke still. "You know nothing... do you?" His head snapped to Aaron and Hera suddenly and swiftly. "Feel weak!"

He was on them, his ember talons grabbing them both by the neck. The wave of heat was unbearable. It was the worst pain either had ever experienced. Pure hot torture. The melted hands had compressed into solid metal and held strong against Hera's and Aaron's necks, not killing them but threatening to.

"You can blast your way out with ice or you can consume the heat. Alternatively, you could let the heat consume you and become one with it. There are so many options available to you; you just haven't seen them yet," Hiver declared to them both.

Hera and Aaron both said nothing and kept on writhing in his grip. Aaron tried to grab at the hand around his neck, but soon his own delicate hands flinched away. The heat was too blistering. Hiver held them for a moment more, completely motionless. Then, he dropped them to the floor. Hera and Aaron clattered to their knees before the pontiff of fire. Hiver stood above them, his lava-flow body still curling them into his grasp. He tightly crossed his arms and looked down at them, fiery horns returning to a more normal shape.

"The world is beautiful, and you disgrace it by not realizing its true beauty." Hiver said with bitterness in his voice. "When magic came to me, I was nothing—a small shadow in the wake of our great empire..." Hiver looked around, and with an exaggerated motion, he spat lava on the floor, "*Republic!*" For a moment a mouth formed out of the metal but was soon consumed by magma. "A lie... a lie."

Hiver bent down close to Hera and Aaron. They flinched, fearing his scorching embrace. He looked at them back and forth, like a teacher excited to reveal a groundbreaking truth. And so it was that Hiver did.

"A lie that I believed until the stars told me otherwise... this world, Liax... there is only one objective. Magic. So, you must know... your life is meaningless without it... let me show you."

The tone Hiver took was one of endeared longing. Like the hand of his lover was slipping out of his. No something older, perhaps it was closer to the inflection one has when he realizes he is missing the last trinket left by a lover that has been lost, but hasn't quite given up hope that it is there.

Hiver bent away from the rogues and brought forth his hand. He was not offering the hand to them. However, he was quite obviously offering what was in it. This was especially strange because there was nothing in the hand. Until there was. Hera and Aaron couldn't say they were even remotely surprised by a fireball emerging from his palm, but still, they flinched.

"Look... you can hold it. Please take it. It won't hurt you..." Hiver mused.

He bent to hand the fireball to Aaron.

"Here..." he said, in that same slow, accented, dread-filled tone. "One for you, too..."

Hiver created a spike of ice in his left hand, and with that one, he gestured toward Hera. Hera and Aaron looked at each other for a moment, but they could not look away from the fireball or ice-spike for long. Fearing Hiver's wrath, Hera reached out her hand to 'take' the ice-spike.

"Don't touch it," Hiver interposed quickly. "Let it float above your hand."

Hera, using both hands, tentatively adjusted her angle to cup underneath the bottom of the ice-spike. After seeing Hera take the first step, Aaron did the same. A tear of pure terror let loose on Aaron's cheeks, and he was not alone in the feeling, for Hera too was about to cry. The pain on their necks was agonizing, their vision blurry. Hiver did not seem to notice. Instead, he chided them forward, delighted to let them experience his magic.

"See oh- see..." Hiver stuttered. "You can bend it- control it."

Hera and Aaron now cupped in each of their hands a powerful elemental entity, like nothing they had ever seen. It was true. They now held, under their own power, the fireball and ice-spike. They floated above their hands, up and down, with the shake of their arms. Hera and Aaron stopped panicking for a moment to witness the pure wonder unfolding before them.

"Now that you have seen it happen, you believe it is possible. With that understanding, you can now recreate the spell yourself. Try it; strike me with your weapon," Hiver chided.

The two stared at him, completely petrified in fear. They searched in the flames for any semblance of a face, but the only thing they could find was that blank plate of melting metal, showing no emotion.

Oh, the fire was so hot. They would faint soon. The realization hit them harder than the wave of heat. If they fainted, they died. Sure, they would die anyway from the burns on their necks, but some chance to live was better than none.

Hiver looked as if he was about to speak when Hera and Aaron both flexed their hands at the same time and sent their element into Hiver's faceplate. The ice made contact with Hiver's head and immediately melted. The fire also made contact, but was absorbed. Hiver did not pull his head back, nor did he roar. He only looked at them and spoke again.

"Well done," he applauded. "This time, conjure yet another spell. Reach into your soul, will the phantasmagoric energy into your line of sight and cast your strength into me."

Hera looked to her blistered hands and swallowed. Another set of tears burst through to her eyes as the pain on her neck flared. She reached into herself and did as he asked. Was it so easy? It could be done, but how? She didn't quite think about it; it was like moving a phantom limb. It was definitely mental, but more focused on creativity than anything else. She could not comprehend it, she could not explain it, but somehow, someway, a black star floated out of her hand. She knew it was there before it was. It was like time had stopped for her.

The army was elsewhere in the smeltery. They were moving quickly across the hot ground. But something was dawning on Hiver. He didn't know where Hera and Aaron were. It made sense now, Hera and Aaron were distracting that molten monster. Viner stopped in his tracks.

"Where are the thieves?" Viner asked aloud, "Where are Hera and Aaron!"

Rose heard his call. "You've lost them?"

Viner's face was stone cold, "And I need to find them."

"I'll go with you," Henry was by Viner's side.

"No—" Viner started.

"I'll lead the troops," Rose said, "—With me!"

Rose ventured forth with the soldier's guiding them as a shepherd does to sheep. Viner had sworn an oath to protect Hera and Aaron, and if that meant marching into the claws of evil, that is what he would do. Still he would have rather Henry not followed him.

Hiver still grasping him by the neck, Aaron too reached inside himself just as Hera had. He searched deep but found it hard to find the belief that he could do it. He looked over to see Hera holding a black star. He looked back at his hands without realizing the magnitude of what Hera had done. Suddenly, the power Hera radiated hit him, and he looked again at Hera's black star. He was awestruck by the radiant energy bursting from her hand. He looked at Hiver, who was leaning ever closer in. Something was odd about Hiver's body language, an oddity that Aaron couldn't place without view of a visible face.

Aaron looked back at his hands and, with a burning passion, tried his hardest to replicate Hera. He tried once to imagine that black star in his hand. Hiver started to say something, but Aaron didn't listen. He was completely focused on harnessing this new power. For a moment, Aaron visualized the star rising from his palm, and for a moment he saw it there. Excitement rushed into his body, but before he was sure if it was real, he lost it.

"My guiding star... would thou lead me astray?" Hiver said, though neither rogue listened. "Did you not always promise to be in the north? Though you are as black as the night sky, I could always see you clearly."

Aaron tried harder, in vain, to create a star of light, to replicate that soul energy that came so easily to Hera. Hera excitedly patted Aaron on the shoulder, trying to show him her power. Unbeknownst to both of them, Hiver tightened his circle of fire. It was a sign of the empyrean energy's intoxicating grasp that neither Hera nor Aaron noticed the blistering heat of Hiver's action.

Hiver continued his rant without pause, "But now here you are, not where I left you... What are you saying to me? Am I not the chosen? These acolytes, do they exist to tell me your bidding? So, shall I let them live?"

Finally, Aaron mustered the power. He had no bend or sway, only through extreme force was he able to conjure a ball of pure white light. It was beautiful, seraphic energy. The white light made the stone floor appear similar to the white void in which the army had been previously entrapped. It overpowered the red of Hiver's fire, and for a moment, it added the glint of an eye into the swirling molten core of Hiver's flat face.

"The stars... even in Dessees, they speak to me."

Hiver did not disdain the great light; if anything, he wanted to touch it. Hera looked over to Aaron's hands, and with a smile on her face, she looked up into his eyes. Tears and sweat still glistened on the thieves' faces, and their necks were still blistered to near death, but still, they smiled at each other.

Hiver reached out his hands, trying to touch both their lights. Hera and Aaron did nothing to stop him. Their dire situation flooded back to them. They were going to die. What was this tevnal's plan? Was he torturing them? Was he showing them hope so he could crush it? They were petrified by fear yet again, so they did nothing to stop him.

Hiver's fingers of fire prayed closer to both stars at the same time. All in a second, Hiver recoiled several feet. They weren't even sure if he had made contact with either magical entity, but now he was roaring with some emotion they couldn't distinguish. Was it pain, was it rage, could it even be sadness?

The lava surrounding them started to reenter Hiver, expanding him, making him grow gigantic again. With his seemingly uninjured hand, he latched onto the side of a furnace and started to be sucked into it.

Hera and Aaron weren't ready to accept victory yet. They stayed motionless, watching Hiver retreat into the furnace. They stayed a moment more, on their knees, balls of light cupped in their hands, making certain that he did not emerge again. Hera and Aaron were not acting out of reason, but pure fear that he would emerge again. They stayed for a long time without speaking or moving.

Hiver had left his battle scars on the stone floor. Hera and Aaron were surrounded by the glint of thin bronze metal that had melted into the floor and hardened there. A trail that Hiver had wrecked through the smeltery was clearly visible behind the two thieves.

"Can we still talk?" Aaron asked.

His voice was cracked, aged a thousand years as if all the metal of the smeltery had rusted into his neck and an ancient voice was now his only form of communication. It pained him to speak and blood came up his throat as well as words.

"What would we say?" Hera said.

She, too, could barely speak. She sounded worse than the noise of twigs snapping under her feet in her most desperate moment of stealth. No blood came from her mouth, but blisters boiled and split. The pain was too much to bear, so she didn't. She sat there motionless like she didn't feel the daggers being shoved down her throat.

Aaron was first to rise, and consequently, first to fall. He pushed off his knee, but though it passed the first test of strength, it was not capable of holding his body. He clattered to the ground, sprawled on all fours, blood spraying from his lips.

To this, Hera did react. She did not get off her own feet, but she crawled on her knees to reach him. Her ball of dark light hit the ground and started bouncing over to where he lay. It bumped up gently against his side and was followed by Hera fussing over him. Without saying a word, she prodded him gently on the shoulder, urging him to be alright.

Aaron reacted by looking up. He saw that his ball of white light now lay on the floor in front of him, in a pool of his own blood. Red had started to taint the innards of the energy star. For some reason, that bothered Aaron, so he attempted to pick it up. He only added more blood to the pool. He fell onto his side, a ball of light grasped in his hands, looking at Hera while she gently caressed his arm.

"If they find us..." Aaron coughed up along with blood. "Will they find us dead, laying face first in our own blood?"

Hera shook her head in denial, tears staining her eyes.

"What's the difference dying here and dying in Great Neighbor?" The act of speaking only spit up more blood from Aaron's mouth. He was obviously damaging himself by speaking.

Hera knew it would hurt her, but she spoke anyway. "Stop talking."

"There is none," Aaron answered himself. "We didn't die then; we won't die now. I don't know what magic can do, but if it can't do this, it can't do anything. Because this is everything. This is the only thing that matters. You being alive."

He pushed the ball of white light into Hera's neck. Hera tried weakly to push it away, but she was too slow. The warmth of the light spread from her throat through the rest of her body, following her blood flow. Suddenly, she took in a breath not burdened by burn. She had not known how clogged her throat was, but now it was clear.

"I..." she tried to say, but before she continued, she stopped herself and immediately took her black star into her hands. Blood from the floor swirled into it, but she hardly noticed. She shoved it with too much force into Aaron's wounded throat. He gasped and swallowed a mouthful of blood, but regardless, felt relieved. He choked down the blood and smiled up at Hera, his mouth still drenched in the remnants of red. His teeth were stained with blood and he looked ridiculous with such a goofy grin. Hera laughed down to him, finding Aaron the butt of his own joke again. She didn't move and neither did he. Perhaps it wouldn't be too bad to be found lying in a pool of their own blood, assuming that they weren't dead.

After a while, Hera heard a noise. She startled to attention, looking in the direction it came from, but Aaron looked none the wiser to the sound. Her panic turned to excitement when she saw Henry looking down on them. He was standing next to his uncle, the remnants of his worried face turning into exuberance.

"You're alive!" they exclaimed.

Viner smiled broadly and clapped his nephew on the back. He took a step forward and let out a hardy laugh, his arms extended for an embrace. Viner's mistake was not running in a full sprint because Henry was already on Hera and Aaron. His arms were clasped around both of their necks. His armor chafed Hera and Aaron's burnt necks. They flinched, but they could stand the pain.

Henry put his hands on their shoulders. He looked them over, and his bright smile turned worried when he saw their necks. Blood covered Henry's knees, and it appeared that

Hera and Aaron had more blood on the outside than the inside.

"Are you okay… your necks—" Henry said.

"Looked worse a few minutes ago," Aaron finished. "We will be fine… probably."

Hera looked down at him with a little bit of worry. She wasn't quite sure they would be 'fine' and would rather get help before it was too late. Aaron still had a scar on his neck. It looked to be little more than a discoloration and inconsistency in complexion, but still it was there, and the internal damage was unknown.

Viner's loud boots stomped against the stone, making sure that his approach was not subtle. He placed his gauntlet around Henry's backplate. Henry's eyes widened in surprise, and before he knew it, he was pulled onto his feet, much of the blood on the floor following him.

"Look at the mess you've made," Viner scolded, gesturing to his blood-stained gambeson.

Henry looked away sheepishly. "Hera and Aaron did it…"

Viner gave Henry a deadpan stare until his nephew couldn't help but look at him in the eyes. "Hera and Aaron… were attacked… by a giant lava monster… and now they are bleeding to death."

"I still don't think we are going to die. We will probably just be sore for a—" Aaron interjected.

"Now you blame them because you kneeled in their blood!" Viner shouted.

Henry stepped back, ironically placing his foot in more blood. Viner started waving his hands around, wildly gesturing towards the new mess he had made.

"M~m~mop it up!" Viner growled.

Henry desperately started searching the surrounding area for a loose mop. Unsurprisingly, a small wooden mop was not present in the dwarven smeltery made completely out of stone and metal.

"What happened?" Viner knelt down next to the rogues, getting his feet wet with blood. "I saw you lead that tevnal away; then I saw it retreat into a smelter. Are you okay?"

Aaron gritted his teeth and nodded, but Hera was tired of his assurance that they were fine.

"No, we're not okay," she said in a hurry. "That was the most..."

Hera looked down to Aaron. She could tell Aaron was of the same opinion as her. They were not sure if they should be ashamed or frightened, but one thing was certain... they were done being lying thieves.

"That was the most spectacular thing I've ever seen."

Chapter 22
The Restless Library

Viner and Henry escorted Hera and Aaron to meet the rest of the troop. Every soldier was exhausted from exertion, but none more so than the two rogues. On the way, Hera relayed the entire story in its fullest to Viner and Henry. Aaron only interrupted to make sarcastic remarks about how her voice seemed to have healed nicely.

The army was hard to miss. They crowded next to a spiral staircase. It was identical to the one they had used to escape from the white void. Hera and Aaron were shocked at the noticeable difference in numbers due to how many had been lost. They didn't realize until now that the army had been decimated by the back-to-back assaults of the dwarves, hob, and Hiver.

The sun rose on one of the soldiers' faces when they saw Hera and Aaron's approach. They pointed over at the two esteemed rogues and cried in delight. Guards whispered among themselves, "Hera and Aaron are back", "The two thieves, they live", and much of the sort. It seemed that Hera and Aaron had become icons.

They were rushed by a paparazzi of excited guards. It was perhaps the slowest, most drowsy flash mob in all of history. Though the guards wanted to pay their respects to Hera and Aaron, they were simultaneously out of breath and in need of sleep. On the plus side, some of the militia members had gotten thirty or so minutes of rest. However, this proved to only make them more tired upon awakening.

Aaron was happy to be praised and surprised that two thieves had suddenly become so valued. Evidently, many of the guards had seen the duo lead away the lava beast, not to mention many of them owed their weapons to the duo. Henry liked the feeling of being beside his friends while they got a well-deserved commendation. Hera, on the other hand, would have rather had some sleep. But she wasn't necessarily bothered by the paparazzi's existence either.

While Aaron basked in his glory, Hera started to shove her way through the crowd. She looked back to see Aaron being hoisted onto the shoulders of a guard and smiled. Her own smile was only a dim mirror's reflection of the gigantic grin on her friend's face. She turned back to look ahead of her. The crowd parted unnaturally, and as the sea split, she saw him—a man in white. A black star hovered above his right hand, and a white star hovered above his left. Hera frowned and nodded to herself. Though she was surprised by the image, oddly, she couldn't help but stay calm. She continued on to find a place to settle in for some much needed rest.

"Hera," Rose's voice was behind her.

She turned to see Rose looking at her with some level of admiration.

"W- Well done," Rose said. "Not only did you survive an encounter with that monster, did you see what happened when we diverted the lava down the stairs?"

Hera shook her head, "I don't know what you're talking about."

"You've dealt us a winning hand. The lava flowed down into the sleeping quarters of the dwarfs. You're lucky you got out with a burn on your neck, the dwarfs are dead."

"I—" Hera began, but her voice caught in her scorched throat.

"Isn't this wonderful?" Rose asked, "You've met the master of this castle. Now he has no army to boot. You, Hera, and your friend Aaron too, were a worthy deal indeed."

"Deal?" Hera asked.

Rose looked blankly back at her, "But I must take watch now. The army has earned a few hours of rest. You should take it."

It was dumbfounding really, that despite evidently not sleeping for the past week, running a full sprint several miles, fighting a full-scale battle, making a run for her life, and surviving an assassination attempt, Rose stayed awake to take guard. And all the while, she smiled to herself, replaying the moment when the army diverted the lava down the stairs and turned the entire dwarven army below into ash.

"I think you may have saved my life," Calessa grinned down at Tython.

They had set up camp under the giant stone stairs. The entire army sprawled across the smeltery, slumped against any odd stone formation they could find. It was dreadfully hot and difficult to sleep, but the exhausted crowd expected to manage.

Tython shrugged. "You had it under control."

The militia had not bothered to set up shelter. All they wanted was to fall asleep. Viner and Rose were a trifle uncomfortable with the decision but didn't have the heart to enforce a mandate. Tython had joined Calessa and her family for the resting period. They sat close to the foot of the stairs, trying their best to get at least some sleep. But Calessa thought it important to let Tython know she was grateful for his help. She could spare a few minutes.

She laughed silently. "A small axe-swinging rodent was attached to my back. You saved my life."

"Well, I don't think it really was a rodent, I mean..."

The smeltery was as bright as ever, and the guards were starting to long for the night sky as much as they longed for the sun. Even with the unfortunate sleeping conditions, no one had yet stirred at the archer and the soldier's conversation.

"That's not the point," Calessa said. "Stop being so coy."

There was a slight shuffle from behind Calessa, one not out of the ordinary, and Calessa's father opened his tired eyes and looked around hazily.

"Coy?" Tython asked.

Calessa's father shuffled to his feet in a motion that was all too loud for his wife. He lumbered over and around the foot of the stairs to peer at his daughter.

"Who are you talking to, Calessa?" He whispered.

"Tython," Calessa said.

Calessa's father was a short man. He looked like he was, as one would expect, an Aerokitian. Besides that, he had balding hair and a strong but not attractive build, but he still came off as a gentleman. He nodded to himself and pointed at the boy.

"I like that boy," he said.

He turned to rejoin his wife and go back to sleep. Tython laughed jovially and informed Calessa that he liked her father, too. Calessa rolled her eyes, and after some of the first small talk in a while, she went to sleep. Tython waited a moment and made sure she was asleep before finding his own place of rest.

***

The journey up the stairs was one all too familiar to the guardsmen. Rose had finally let them have a full eight or more hours of sleep. Even she was not too cruel to deny that the army had gone through much. The twin thieves, as Hera and Aaron grew to be called, became a symbol of hope. From the moment they had awoken, guards had tried their hands at addressing them, going as far as asking them for marching orders instead of Viner. Aaron and Hera were perfectly content to differ to Viner and talk to Henry instead. Henry gushed about how they fought like the Great Warrior himself.

"Who's the Great Warrior?" Hera asked.

Henry sounded aghast. "How do you not know who the Great Warrior is!?"

Hera shifted uncomfortably on the stone floor they sat on.

"I don't know; I just haven't heard of him," Hera said.

Henry looked like he didn't believe her, but he was happy to continue. "The Great Warrior is the best fighter in the whole world. He protects Goldenhill from all invasions, and he single-handedly convinced Ironforge to join Goldenhill's army. They were afraid that if they didn't, he would kill them all."

"He sounds despicable," Hera said.

Henry didn't like that either. "Not true," he insisted. "He can make golden crop grow all over the hills of Goldenhill. The land would be too rocky to farm without him. When there is a good harvest, it's because of him."

Even Aaron wasn't quite convinced. He shook his head with a smile on his face and looked down at the ground. No one from Goldenhill would be that great. Even if it was true, it would be his fault that Witshore was going downhill. Without Ironforge's support, Goldenhill would never dare be so tyrannical.

"Somehow I doubt that," he said.

"No! He's as agile as the wind, as strong as an ox. If he was here, that Hiver would already be dead."

"Henry, I thi—" Aaron started.

But he was interrupted by Rose walking up next to him. He closed his eyes and shuddered at the intimidating presence of the lieutenant. Rose extended her hand to him.

Aaron opened his eyes and looked up at her with distaste. He got up by himself instead.

"Henry, you stay here," she said. "Hera, Aaron, come with me."

Rose tried to pull Hera to her feet, but when her hand made contact with Hera's arm, Hera shoved her off. Rose acted like she didn't mind. She walked them away while loudly congratulating them on saving the army. She turned the corner around the second nearest smelter, and her voice suddenly hushed.

"The people think of you as leaders now," she told them. "It's all right; I'm not angry."

It had not occurred to Hera or Aaron that the turn of events would upset Rose. They had assumed Rose had come to term with the fact that everyone hated and feared her. Hera immediately wanted to leave the conversation.

"You must play into the role," Rose told them.

"Why is that?" Hera snapped.

If Viner had told her to "play into the role," she would have had no issue with it. The fact that Rose was giving her the order made it seem wrong in some way. Besides, she wasn't going to let Rose just push her around.

"Because if you don't, the brigade will fail," Rose said, emphasizing the last words.

"That's not our responsibility," Hera scowled.

Rose scowled back and leaned close to Hera's face. They were around the same height, but it could not be mistaken that Rose was stronger, smarter, and faster. Hera hated that.

"You don't know your potential," Rose scorned her.

Aaron gestured them apart but didn't dare touch either. "Woah, woah, back off."

Rose turned to confront Aaron, keeping the straight face she always held. She looked to the ceiling and slowly circled in place. She looked as if she was trying to find any patience in the world around her. Everything about her body motion conveyed rage, but her face was stone cold as ever.

"You don't know me," Hera snarled.

Rose pivoted back into Hera's face again. Hera took a surprised step back.

"I am you," she said shortly. "Now, get to the front of the marching order, tell Viner I sent you, and lead the troops up those damn stairs."

Hera looked like she was about to say something, but Rose cut her off with a blank stare that was worse than any real sign of fury.

"That is not just an order from your superior. I hold your life in my hands. As far as you are concerned, I am your queen."

Hera bit her lip and turned on her heel to follow the order, but not before uttering under her breath, "Not my queen."

"I can still hear you, Hera," Rose said over her shoulder.

Hera turned red with rage and kept moving. Aaron took one final, semi-apologetic look at Rose and moved to catch up with Hera.

Viner was organizing the troops, making sure that all weapons and soldiers were being deployed to their best advantage. The look on his face said it all. He was focused on observing and preserving, all while maintaining efficiency. As soon as a battalion was prepared, he sent them off, up the stairs in triple file, leaving ample space for him and others to climb the stairs alongside and past the army. The army was more disciplined than ever and did not struggle to follow the orders.

"At this rate, we might come out of this with fewer people than when we started," Viner whispered under his breath.

"Don't talk like that," Aaron told him.

Viner shook his head with an exasperated laugh. "You're right. If the troops heard me saying that..." He trailed off.

Viner clicked his tongue, observing the troops pass by.

"Axes, axes, axes," he said. "We are practically out of shields at this point, but I made sure to get one into Calessa's hands. The girl's a single person fortress with one. I'm glad she gave up on that blasted greatsword."

"We were sent by Rose to..." Aaron stopped and grasped for words, "motivate the troops."

"Yes, that's nice," Viner nodded, dismissing Aaron's statement. "Do you see how a majority of citizens who were previously unarmed had the sense to pick up discarded weapons off the ground? I'm not sure I would have thought of it at the time. We were being chased, after all, but now people are at least armed. Would prefer weapons other than axes, but still..."

Aaron nodded in agreement. It was of no use to talk to him about anything other than his army right now. Aaron occasionally observed Viner making solemn eye contact with an individual soldier. Two weeks ago, Aaron would be unable to discern the foundation of Viner's perception. But now he knew that behind that controlled, commanding look was the gravitas of a general who was hoping beyond hope that every last soldier would make it out alive.

"You better get up there then." Viner smiled sadly. "They need you now as much as they need me."

Aaron nodded in response and adjusted his rucksack, making sure it fit properly. He gestured for Hera to follow him. She was still sulking about how Rose had spoken to her. Hera walked over next to him with slow, deliberate motions. They walked up the stairs on the right side, trying their best to avoid looking down. The heads of the conscripts turned to follow their ascent, obviously excited to see the twin thieves moving past the ranks. Hera ignored them, and Aaron smiled awkwardly. He tried to wave but gave up halfway through.

In no time, Hera and Aaron were at the front of the troops, leading them up the stairs. They were glad the path was so linear. If it forked, they might have had to do something other than walk slightly ahead of everyone else. Aaron didn't feel like straining himself up the stairs, so he meandered relatively comfortably instead.

Walking up the stairs made the rogues realize just how sore they were. They had been moving non-stop for several days, and though they were now physically stronger, they were tired, and their throats were still sore inside and out. They had been left with a slight dark discoloration on each of their necks. Unfortunately, the burn vaguely resembled the shape of a hand. The skin was rubbery, and it hurt to swallow, but other than that, they were fine.

After several minutes of climbing, the loud shuffling of Viner's heavy armor caught up with them. A soldier let out a hearty laugh. Seemingly, it was in response to something Viner had said on his way up, but the rogues didn't hear the joke. Viner took his position on the right side of Aaron, who, in turn, was to the right of Hera. It took a moment for Viner's face to fade into a more business-oriented expression, but soon it did, and he addressed Aaron and Hera.

"Not too long to go," the man gruffly said.

Hera and Aaron nodded. Viner started to get slightly ahead of the two, so they quickened their pace to match his. Within minutes, they reached the top.

The room before them was still too cramped for their liking. It was not as spacious as the smeltery, but not as tight as the catacombs. It was lit by dim candles that hung on the ceiling, threatening to fall off chandeliers. This room was made out of dark wood, or perhaps the wood itself was a syrup brown, and the lighting just made it appear dark. Either way, wood was used for the first time in the tower, and it was used in abundance.

The room at first appeared taller than it was wide, but this was only because the army's view was sliced by a giant bookshelf. In fact, several giant bookshelves dotted both the corners and the center of the room. It was eerily similar to the king's study in that every wall was covered, from top to bottom and left to right, in books. A second story menacingly loomed over the first, rickety railings holding up a thin path next to bookshelves that grew taller than even the tallest human could reach.

The shelves formed a maze, placed in the room in ways that did not make sense. The shelves were too large to not have been built on-site. The carpenter who built them had to be crazed. Unlike the former king's study, the books on the shelves were neatly packed together, and though they looked old and worn, they were not abused.

"My, oh my," mused a familiar but almost forgotten voice.

Aaron turned to see who had spoken and saw the tall, gaunt figure of Filius admiring the books. He was wielding his knife and running his fingers across the spines of several of the books, admiring them as if they were fine silk.

"This library... it's a vessel for extraordinary enlightenment..." He thought for a moment, and then thought for a moment more.

The last time he had spoken, it had been important. For that reason, the people in his vicinity went quiet. Filius did not disappoint.

"Do not open a book," he said emphatically. "Your minds are too wandering and weak. One book opened and you will be corrupt and consumed."

Hera scrunched her face in disapproval. It was offensive to call someone's mind too weak for a book. If she hadn't recently become intimately acquainted with magic and what it could do, she would have had no fear of opening a book and seeing what all the fuss was about.

"They're cursed, aren't they?" she said loud enough for all around her to hear.

Filius grimaced. "In a wastefully wicked way."

"Then I agree," Aaron butted in. "We shouldn't open them."

The two's suspicions were all but confirmed when they glanced at the names of the books. Most were unlabeled. Of the few that were, most were labeled in a different language, but of the fewer still that were in Northern, almost all had a word in common: Magic. "Isolating Magical Tendrils", "Ritual Magic, What is it?", and "Blood Magic vs Soul Magic".

Filius completely lost interest in the conversation as soon as he had said his piece. Contrary to his previous statement, he reached for the nearest book. The book was brown and labeled in Ike. Neither Hera nor Aaron knew how to read the title.

"Didn't you just say not to read the books?" a soldier asked.

Filius looked up at the soldier with his mouth open and a dreary look on his face.

"Hmm?" he asked. "Oh yes... I said *you* shouldn't open them. I, however..." He turned his attention back to the book and read a little of it with his mouth still agape. "Am more accustomed to such things."

The soldier took a step forward in indignation, but Filius was already back to reading. There was no use in prying the man away from the books; it would just make him angry.

Viner walked right past Filius without a second glance. He huffed his great chest, seemingly more on edge than usual.

"Another blasted maze!" Viner exclaimed through the shelves.

The shelves did not quake. Why would they? They were so much greater than even the smelters in the room before. So much larger than the catacombs. So much fuller than the void. So much.

Few of the guards cared to read the books. If it had been just Filius who told them not to, surely at least some conscripts would have taken a look. But because of the twin thieves' warning, they avoided the temptation. The guard that got closest was Vanessa. She spotted a book titled "Vampirism and Lichood and How Not to Do It". The book itself was red at the bottom and blue at the top, with a strange color mixture into white at the center. It would have looked ridiculous if aluminum rigging didn't sinisterly clasp the book shut. With the addition of aluminum rigging and the handwritten font, it looked eldritch and evil.

She reached her hand out to touch the book. Dust particles lightly attached themselves to the tip of her finger, just a little more than the average amount that hung in the stuffy air. Just before touching it, her stomach lurched, and she backed her hand away quickly. She shook her head at herself and realized that perhaps it was better if she didn't touch the book after all.

"Can't be helped..." Viner sighed. "Stick together and find the way out of here."

Before most of the soldiers had even reached the top of the stairs, Viner started moving. He took a quick look around a bookshelf that would have been against the wall had they been a floor below. Sure enough, the wall was a short walking distance from it. At least this room's layout was consistent with the previous room. Unfortunately, they were on the opposite side of it.

Once they were set, Viner led the army on as straight a route as he could. The bookshelves didn't create complete walls, so it wasn't quite a maze, but they did restrict vision and space. Often, soldiers would take the path of least resistance and go around the bookshelves, rejoining the army after a short detour.

Viner himself kept trudging forward, the dim light keeping his eyes heavy, the noise of his metal boots against the wood floor keeping him awake. The walls were lined with every assortment of books. Some of the Northern titles were "Fire and its Natures", "How to Expand Your Soul", and "Everything to Know About Blood", each of the books as old and large as the last.

"I know we just woke up, but I already want to go back to sleep," Aaron whispered to Hera.

Hera nodded, "I think it's been a few hours actually."

"Are you hungry?" Aaron asked.

Hera shook her head.

"Me neither," Aaron said.

A fine mist that may or may not have been there before made it difficult for the soldiers to see their own shoes. Vanessa kept her head up while walking through the library, making sure to not tempt herself with any titles of the books. Her friends attempted to speak to her, but she did not respond. This wasn't unusual for her, so they let her be.

Eventually, she came to a place where the marching line had become too packed for her or her friends' comfort. They did what they had done many times before and moved around the bookshelf to not clog the flow of traffic. Vanessa didn't remember putting her hand out, but suddenly she had a book almost in her grasp. It was titled "The Name of Everything".

"Read it, Vanessa."

She jumped and looked around for who had spoken. She didn't see anyone. At first, she didn't think anything was wrong with that. Then she remembered that just a moment ago, she had been surrounded by people.

"You call me Horror, but you do not know my real name. I am…"

Vanessa started to panic. She threw whatever book was in her hands onto the ground and started running where she thought the army must have headed off to. Yes, yes, she heard them now. Tython was playing his ballad to home.

"Even if my footsteps are new," she could almost hear him singing. Almost.

"The Restless Sleeper," Horror finished.

She couldn't help it. She opened the book in her hands. It was at that moment that she remembered that there was no book in her hands. She read it anyway.

"Dragons Now" was the title. The book seemed to assume that she had knowledge that she didn't. It threw her immediately into some narrative about dragons in Disus, mentioning Liax and other strange words she was only vaguely familiar with. It wasn't all that ground-shattering, just confusing. It told her a story of dragons flying solitary in the sky from island to island. She wondered if they had ever visited Great Neighbor.

She remembered herself in a panic, looking up and seeing that she remained alone, but somehow it was quieter than before. She looked back down at her book and saw that the handwriting had completely changed. The subject of the book had changed also. It now talked about medicinal herbs and other things of the sort. She flipped to the book's cover and saw that it was titled "Magic and Healing".

"Did you have a nice rest?"

Vanessa couldn't help but jump at the voice again. Her bent back cracked under the sudden movement like she had been sitting in this uncomfortable position for ages. Despite the voice's insistence that she had rested, she was more tired than ever. She got onto her feet, but before she could understand what was happening, she was on the floor again awaking from some sleep. She gripped a new book titled "Water Flows Up". Her eyes were so heavy. She closed them to go to sleep again, but as soon as she fell asleep, she awakened.

"Don't resist. I am not cruel."

Vanessa was struggling to believe the voice. This felt cruel.

"It's not all a burden," the voice insisted. "Consider everything you know now. What herb cures the common cold?"

Vanessa didn't remember learning anything about the common cold, so she said: "It's not an herb, it's a fungus. It's called the nasopharynx remedium truffle. N, a, s, o, p, h—"

"Where does magic come from?"

Vanessa hadn't believed in magic until a week ago, and even then, she was skeptical. "The soul," she answered.

"And?"

"The blood."

"Don't you see? Look at how much of the world you have experienced." The Restless Sleeper sounded like he was trying to convince himself more than anything.

"I know we just woke up, but I already want to go back to sleep," Aaron whispered to Hera.

Hera nodded, "I think it's been a few hours actually."

"Are you hungry?" Aaron asked.

Hera shook her head.

"I am," Aaron said.

Chapter 23
The Sleeper

"We should probably make camp," Viner yawned.

Rose stared at him in her usual angry way. Surprisingly, Rose was the only person acting normal. Everyone else was horribly tired. Calessa thought she might have tripped once or twice, but she couldn't quite remember. Henry had all but forgotten that they were even in a library.

After a while, Viner slurred out a few more sleepy words, "I see that no one has any objections."

Hera and Aaron both looked tentatively at Rose, making sure that she, in fact, did not have any objections. After several moments of Rose staring blankly at Viner, his gaze awkwardly flicked from the floor to her and back to the floor.

"Alright. Get some rest. Set up a watch system. Make sure that we have a line of sight on everyone," Viner ordered.

The position of watchman was particularly unpopular during this resting hour. The only one who seemed to have any energy for it was also the one who had not slept once on this adventure. By now, it was downright unnatural. Rose showed no signs of fatigue. She seemed to have transcended the need for sleep completely.

She gently lowered herself to her knees assuming her usual meditation posture. Perhaps her alert meditation was a substitute for sleep? All that Viner knew was that it unnerved him ever so slightly. He only hoped that he had been the only one to notice. It wasn't like Rose jumped up and down and rudely insisted on taking watch; she just always stayed awake, and no one argued.

This rest, several people were keeping watch as there were several thousand to watch over, a task made difficult by giant bookshelves interrupting the view. Those who took watch considered having a pleasant read but heeded Filius's rude warning and decided it would be best to keep alert in other ways that were less distracting.

"On that note, where is Filius?" Aaron asked.

Hera sleepily looked to him, "On what note?"

"I don't know," Aaron said. "But I also don't know where Filius is."

Hera shrugged. "He's skulking probably. He's kind of a creep."

"That's a little mean." Aaron yawned.

Hera laid down on her sleeping mat. "He's a little mean."

Aaron chuckled softly and went to sleep. But he didn't. He had the sensation of falling asleep—the closed eyes, the drift into nothingness, even grogginess as if he had just awakened—but he had not been asleep. He turned in his bed and found that he was indeed fully capable of doing so. Was he in a dream? His supposed dream self didn't want to bother anyone, and his lucid self agreed. So, he semi-consciously reasoned that he was either experiencing the most boring dream possible or that he was simply tired and about to fall asleep.

Aaron closed his eyes and went to sleep. But he didn't. Instead, he remembered that, though he had closed his eyes, he hadn't opened them since the last time they were closed. Yet here they were now, completely open. But hadn't he closed them? That didn't make sense.

"Am I—" Aaron whispered aloud.

"Me, too," Hera whispered back.

They went to sleep for a moment more. This time they got some good rest. At least until they remembered that scanning the bookshelves for books to read did not qualify as good rest. All at once, they remembered themselves, and all at once, they sped off to Viner.

"Viner, something's wrong; we can't sleep," they said.

Viner turned to look at them and squinted open his eyes. "I can read you a bedtime story if you'd like."

"No." Hera glared. "Something is wrong; can't you feel it?"

"I feel a little odd," Viner confirmed. "But nothing a little..."

He stopped for a moment to let out a huge lion-like yawn. He continued speaking halfway through the yawn, affecting his inflection greatly.

"—rest can't fix," he finished.

Hera grumbled her disapproval and Aaron looked at her weakly. There was nothing for it. Hera and Aaron weren't certain that something was really wrong, and though they were uneasy, they weren't going to cause any trouble. They went back to their sleeping mats to lie down and fall asleep yet again.

Unsurprisingly, they still couldn't fall asleep. Now that they listened closely, they noticed that there was a slight murmur, one that was strange for a sleeping crowd. Additionally, there was a distinct lack of snoring across the army. They couldn't be certain, but the crowd must be awake.

Unsurprisingly, they still couldn't fall asleep. They again noticed the slight crowd murmur and the distinct lack of snoring across the army. They thought the crowd was quite possibly awake.

Unsurprisingly, they still couldn't fall asleep. The crowd was definitely awake.

Half an hour passed without much of a fuss, but the tranquility was soon broken. With a crack and a creak and a tired, irritated murmur from the rest of the guards, one took the initiative of informing the other guards of their quite obvious predicament.

"I can't sleep!" the guard yelled in a panic. "My body is weak, my eyes can't stay open, but still, I can't sleep."

The worry was obvious in the guard's voice. Hera thought that the sudden panic was unnecessary, but Aaron could see why they were so distressed. He would also panic if he was put in the same situation. While this thought crossed his mind, he realized that he was actually in the exact same situation, and he was not panicking.

The militia was grateful that this unfortunate soldier had the gumption to announce the common problem before any of them, but that didn't stop them from being irritated with their outburst and they chastised the rude soldier. Then the sleepy crowd got up and stretched. Their bones cracked as they moved their arms, hardly a healthy noise.

"Me, too," another guard confirmed.

"Aye," added another.

Viner got to his feet like a lumbering giant, "I'm sure that—"

"This place is cursed, and we must keep moving," Rose interrupted.

Viner looked over at her. By now, the captain of the guard had completely lost patience with Rose's outbursts. He considered informing her that he outranked her but then remembered what she had done to the King. The memory only filled him with more rage. He took a moment to balance himself, remembering the time he had spent with Mordecai and how much he missed his old friend.

"Sir, I think this is a good time to tell you," a tentative voice said. "We have lost track of Vanessa. We haven't seen her for a long while now."

"A long while?" Viner inquired sleepily.

"Yes, sir." The militia member yawned. "Two hours at least."

"How good is your sense of time?" Rose asked.

"Not good."

Rose's face was somber. "Yes, well. It hasn't been two hours since we entered the library."

The sleepy soldiers chuckled. Of course it had been two hours. What was Rose getting at? They didn't even remember what it looked like outside of the library. Rose was a strange legionnaire indeed, speaking such nonsense at a time like this.

"That doesn't sound right," a soldier grumbled.

Rose's tone remained level. "Really?"

She walked forward a few paces to get into the face of a guard that may or may not have believed her. "Would you like to fetch the book "Ritual Magic, What is It?"? It should be a five-minute jog. If you still don't believe me, count the steps back."

They shook their head in disagreement, under the false impression that Rose's request was optional. Rose considered punishing the soldier, but she thought better of it. She turned her back on the conscript and commanded the army as a whole instead.

"Run down the line and fetch "Ritual Magic, What is it?". You should find it on the second bookshelf to the left of the staircase. Three shelves up and twenty books to the right," Rose ordered.

Her orders were followed. Her message was sent word-for-word down the line until it reached the stairs. The stairs that had just then, after what felt like two hours, been crested by the final soldiers in the march. Just then, did that dreary feeling of uncertainty rest on the heart of the soldier last in line, and just then did they get the message to fetch the book.

The soldiers who were given the task thought little of it. They had not heard Filius's warning, nor had they felt that any substantial time had passed. They grabbed the book from its shelf with little difficulty, and it was passed up the line.

The book had never been touched by so many hands and so many warm fingers. It would have smiled had it a mouth to do so. It would have been blissful if it had the childlike heart to be so. It would have been grateful if any words contained in the book had not been wrought with sorrow. All of these things it was, despite being unable. The book did smile, and the book was blissful. Most of all, the book was grateful to be taken from its prison.

Rose was handed the book, and with that handing of the book, the hearts of the citizens of Great Neighbor dropped. Rose was not happy to be proven right, but she had known it would be in her hands soon enough. So, when it was, she was not disappointed.

"We've been going in circles..." Henry hissed through his teeth.

Rose shook her head, "No. We haven't been moving at all. We just feel like we have. Even I was not immune to it. We've been asleep a majority of this time. We've been walking down the same hallway over and over in our dreams."

Viner called the bluff. "That is quite the claim. Do you have any evidence to support that... theory?"

Rose was not looking at him when she said, "I can tell when it happens."

"Why? What makes you so special?" Hera interjected.

"I haven't slept since the invasion." She said it as if that statement didn't lead to more questions.

The room was aghast in disbelief. What was Rose playing at? Did she seriously expect them to believe that she hadn't slept for two weeks? That was insane. Rose's plausible insanity crossed their minds like a shooting star in the night, a gleaming streak of possibility. Rose was insane. There was no doubt about it now. So maybe, and just maybe, she could do the insane.

"People are so focused on what their eyes tell them," a hissing male voice said.

Aaron spun to find the voice, "What? Who was that?"

"I—"

The room was now in complete chaos. Was the voice just that of a random guard in earshot, or did the voice speak in all their heads at the same time? Hera and Aaron expected the scrambling of armored warriors to die down at any moment, as soon as the speaker revealed himself as someone who had just spoken loudly. Yet the tone was a whisper, and though not deafening, it was audible above all other noise.

"Am.

"Your

"God

"Now."

Henry was falling!

No, his feet were planted on the ground. He could not see anything but himself and a white nothingness. He lifted his hand to shield his eyes from the bright cosmos but found that the white wasn't so hard on his eyes after all. Had he gone blind? He wasn't left wondering for long. Before he knew it, a wave of color painted a scene around him and he was in a different place entirely, all alone.

The white floor turned to white mist and engulfed Henry up the ankles with a cold, wet feeling. Slowly, the dim blue of a foggy morning sky became almost visible above his head. The warmth of the sun was a comfort against the cold winds that now wrapped around his body. He lifted his foot and felt the ground compress under his feet, a feeling he did not know he had missed.

Suddenly, the wind made up its mind about which direction to blow and split the fog before Henry. It brushed aside his hair and knocked him almost to the ground. He was grateful he had not fallen because the platform he stood on, though it was dirt, was not ground. It floated like an island in the sky, overseeing the land and water that grew before it. The choir was singing, and the strings were screeching, and above it all was the voice of that dastardly Horror.

"This is Disus..." he proclaimed. "Home..."

The island Henry was on was small; perhaps it could fit ten people comfortably. To his left, there were more islands and as the fog retreated further and further, the islands in sight became larger and larger. The wind on Henry's face made him uncomfortable. It looked to him like his small island rotated around a larger one. It felt like the cold air on his face wanted him to fall into the blue ocean below.

"But Disus is what it is. What you see is what it was— Liax. All three worlds as one."

Henry was filled with a combined sense of both fear and wonder. He looked down over the edge and tried to see all he could. He looked as far as he could, but all he could see was a deep blue.

Then there, he saw it. He could make out the tips of the Whitegold Mountains. Just barely, but still, he saw them. Even in their tiny scale, they were more grand than he had ever imagined.

The voice started to cry, but not only did it cry, it screamed also. "But did you think that this was a dream? Did you think that this is how it is, how it was, and how it will be? You are so focused on what your eyes tell you; you never remember what lies behind them."

The beautiful scene changed in an instant, gone like the gleam of the sun on the corner of a window's frame. The oceans burned, the grass died, the soil cracked. In a moment, it was night. The darkness was enveloping Disus, the skylands. As Dessees was the underworld, this place was the opposite—the skylands.

The ground beneath Henry's feet dissolved as quickly as it had come into place. This time Henry was actually falling, falling into that burning ocean. Henry shielded his face from the oncoming winds and approaching heat. He began to feel the scorch of the flaming ocean. He screamed as he fell from the sky, his tears like raindrops chasing behind him.

Right before he hit the ocean, it opened before him. The flames whipped away, leaving nothing but the dark of night, the moon, and the stars. He was grateful beyond reason for the unreasonably great miracle that had unfolded to save his life. The voice that spoke in his head still chided him in an angry but not so malicious tone.

"I am the Restless Sleeper, and this is your nightmare!" proclaimed the nightmare.

Henry floated in an ocean of stars, weightless despite gravity. Soon, his feet touched a white-sand shore and the smell of burning filled his nostrils again. The smell of Great Neighbor's siege.

"To me, you are a wasp"

"To me, you are nothing!"

The clashing and breaking of bones. Henry's father was fighting Horror on that desolate beach. This must have been his last moments of life. Henry could not look. He knew what happened next. Tears streamed from his eyes until he had none left to give. He scrambled onto the shore, desperate to get out of the water. Just as his feet left the ocean, the water turned to ice. Henry was pulled by the ankle like a rope had suddenly been tied around his leg. He was pulled across the ocean over frozen waves, stars passing before his starry eyes. Was one of those stars missing?

Each and every soldier in the army, including Hera and Aaron had experienced much the same event. The army rested on their knees in a great lecture hall filled to the brim with people. The hall was a half-circle in shape, each seat filled by another person, perfect in number. In this arena, the army seemed more like a small group than a true force of power. What commanded the eyes was the Horror that stood in the professor's spot.

Standing behind an expensive-looking mahogany desk, Horror, the Restless Sleeper was the same black skeletal figure that had led the siege of Great Neighbor. He had changed little. The only thing different about him was the layer of dust that rested on his moth-eaten toga and the missing tooth, almost unnoticeable in his tarry face and moon-tinted mouth. All four of his arms worked in tandem, pushing gently against the strange, rotting plank of wood tied to his back. He was as tall as ever and his desk had the same lean height.

The lecture hall itself was an elevated semi-circle around Horror, the Restless Sleeper. Much like the library, it was dim and constructed of wood. The ceiling was oddly shaped with several slabs of wood creating three massive scales that, taken together, created a whole rounded trapezoid. A warm red light that didn't quite make it to the bottom of the room glimmered between the scales. A dark fog made the dimness of the light evident and was only accentuated by the lack of any other source of illumination.

Most disturbing of all was that there was only one entrance and one exit. A window, circular in shape and fifteen feet in diameter, revealed a cavernous waste. The cave walls that the window led to were marble, gleaming with a thin sheet of water that appeared to flow upwards across the white stone. The marble was pure with almost no imperfections. Some of the jagged rocks lacked texture and were reminiscent of the white void, but other areas were shattered and sharp, reacting as they should to the light cast from the smooth marble.

This window must have looked outside of the Marble Tower and into Dessees. On the ceiling of Dessees, pools of clear spring water formed, defying gravity. The water had no sky to reflect, so instead of blue, it was white. The white was so rich that each massive pool looked like an ocean of cream. When looking into the cave, it was as if the entirety of the lecture hall was upside down.

Cold sweat dripped down Henry's face and nose. He was uncomfortably seated in an uncomfortable chair, clutching the arms of the wooden construct that his butt fought against. As soon as he understood his new surroundings, he immediately hunched over, breathing heavily. Many of the guards did the same.

Saltwater crawled down Henry's nose, creeping like an insect down his face. It did not drip. Instead, it clung there, itching Henry's nose as if challenging him to wipe the sweat away. The Sleeper turned to look at the crowd, and it felt like the whole room swayed when he moved. The chairs folded in on themselves. Could this be…

"What does it matter if it's real? It's real to you." the Restless Sleeper said.

It felt like Henry was the only one in the room. He looked to his right—empty. He looked to his left—empty. He knew it wasn't real. But then again, it was real to him.

"I don't blame you. You don't understand; you don't have to understand. All you need to know is that you are dying for a good cause. For posterity."

He didn't care what it was for. He heard he was going to die, and he didn't like that. He panicked, flailing for a moment, but he felt glued to the chair. He stopped in complete despair. What could he do? He sat there, empty-eyed and looked at Horror. And Horror looked at him.

The Restless Sleeper looked down at his clear desk. For a moment, he wished it was full of paper. It wouldn't matter when he remembered why he could not touch a pen. He felt the wood. He had not felt a polished surface in so long. Ahh. There it was—the reason he couldn't touch. The wood turned to rot faster than his thought. He did not react fast enough. In a moment, the wooden desk had lost stability and split in two.

He looked at his hand, stifling a scream at the boney complexion of it. He had to, didn't he? He had a purpose, more than they could ever know. With a sad glance at his desk, he moved forward, not bothering to go around it, letting the wood decay under his feet. The result was like walking through snow. His foot crashed through the desk with barely a crunch.

His thoughts raced. 'They recoil when I walk forward. Damn, could tears still well in my eyes? Maybe they would see a snarl. Let them see a snarl. Let them not know that I, too, am in pain. Let them think that I am evil. Let them never know. It is not their burden to bear. It is mine and mine alone. For my star.'

Horror crossed the floor, his teeth casting dark shadows onto the faces of the soldiers. Would they be enough? Without a doubt, they wouldn't. They had already damaged the dwarves too much. The soldiers couldn't help but wonder what he would do to them.

"Love, as I love. Remember that if you die, you die together," the Sleeper said.

He did not know his mistake. In those final words of kindness, in the moment before he sucked out their souls and used them in his book, in the moment before he drained their blood and infused it into his tower, he had made one grave mistake. He had reminded Henry of who he was.

Henry looked to his right—empty. He looked to his left—empty. He knew it wasn't real. But then again, it was real to him. So, he made it so. He broke the spell without even trying. He looked to his right again and Viner stood. He looked to his left again and there they sat, Hera and Aaron, their eyes on him. Finally, he looked to the Restless Sleeper and saw who stood behind him. His father's hand was on Horror's shoulder. A sly smile and hair blazed red.

For one last time, Henry looked at his uncle. He remembered how much his uncle loved him and only wished they had spent more time together. He leaped over the chairs that were in front of him and landed with a crash on the floor. It crippled him, but it wouldn't stop him. He got back on two feet. Then, he rushed forward using his offset balance to move faster than ever.

The Restless Sleeper took one step back in surprise. How was this boy moving? His black eyes narrowed and darted to the boy's face. Disheveled blond hair, borderline malnourished, and a face that could take on the world.

"Henry?" The Sleeper asked in surprise.

Henry continued running forward and tried to tackle Horror at chest level. Horror backed away in a hurry, careful not to touch the boy. Was this child an idiot? Did he not know that the Restless Sleeper killed with a touch?

"No, get back," the Restless Sleeper said.

Henry did not. He landed on his feet like a cat, and with another lunge, he punched Horror in the gut, pushing him back a few steps. The Restless Sleeper swiped at Henry, but

Henry did not recoil. Instead, a black slash was left on his chest. Henry's eyes remained dead set on Horror. He lurched forward, and the Restless Sleeper took three steps back. Henry reached back for a punch and hit Horror in the abdomen, forcing him to take another step.

The Sleeper was tired of these games. Somehow, he knew this soldier, but he didn't know from where. He had to die. The Restless Sleeper lifted his arms, ready to end the boy's life. He started weaving a spell that would snap this foolish child's neck. His right arm slashed into thin air like a conductor's stick. He harnessed his own soul into his hands and prepared a potent spell. He weaved together the web that was power. Until finally, Henry socked him in the jaw. The spell was easily interrupted, and the Sleeper took one final lurch back and felt his upper back compress against glass. The glass window that the Restless Sleeper had so lovingly crafted now cracked beneath his body weight. If it weren't for the wooden plank against his back, it would have decayed through.

Henry had no choice then. He could risk it, sure, go for a normal push and hope that it was enough to break the window. But Henry wasn't going to do that, not the way he was thinking. Even now, Horror was getting back up. So, Henry ran full force against the Sleeper. For a moment, it looked like the window would not crack. Then the moment passed. Like ice thawing from a shelf, the glass cracked, not with a shatter but with a crunch not too different from the crunch of the desk under Horror's feet.

The Sleeper's hands curled around Henry like a dying spider in a final embrace. Henry's hair decayed, but his honor was preserved. Before anyone could see the boy's tattered complexion, he was out the window, locked in a seemingly warm embrace with Horror.

Viner had already crossed the room. He was slower than he wanted to be, and it was only after Henry's second attack that Viner was able to release himself from Horror's hold. He moved quickly. But not quickly enough. Viner's fingers were a second away from Henry before he fell. Viner did not catch him. Henry's uncle flung himself at the window.

"NO-NO-NO-NO! Henry-NO! NO Henry-PLEASE NO!" he sobbed.

Viner gazed down at his nephew falling into a sea of white. The floor of the marble cavern was not too different from the walls. When he looked out the window, he hardly noticed that they were in a tower made of pure marble, the same that filled the white void. Cascading down its side was the silhouette of The Sleeper and Henry, falling, falling, falling, until they became little more than dots.

Viner's face was completely empty. Tragically, he was the only soldier with the courage and, perhaps, strength to stand up to save Henry. During the entire fight, all that the people of Great Neighbor could do was sit and watch. They did not know if they were still stuck to their seats, but they didn't bother to check. They were shocked, shocked about all of this, about what the Restless Sleeper had shown them and how Henry had died to kill him.

So it was that bravery killed Horror.

As for Rose, she was not present in the Restless Sleeper's twisted game. From her perspective, the entire army had fallen asleep as soon as they had heard Horror's voice. Hera, Aaron, Viner, Calessa, Tython, the entire army, their corporeal bodies were still with her, sleeping in the library. All except for Henry's. With a sigh, Rose drew her cleaver and crept towards the bodies.

Chapter 24
Blood

The troops had no purpose without leadership. Viner spoke to no one. He did not cry. He sat on the floor, seemingly meditating. Hera and Aaron were the obvious next choices as leaders, but they were only popular and little more. Although Hera and Aaron were being looked to for guidance, they had no idea what to do. No one among them knew that they were within a dreamscape.

Hera tried her hand at giving orders. "Find a way out of here," she said hesitantly. "There must be some entrance."

The soldiers tried their best to follow her command to the letter, but the room provided little for the imagination. The walls were blank and flat; the floor equally as uninteresting. The only exit seemed to be Henry's, and no one wanted to follow him. The order only led to citizens tapping the walls, trying to find hollow spots, of which they found none. It felt like this might be where their journey ended. They had made it to the castle, defeated the sorcerer at its top, and now their story was over.

For a long time, while Viner sat on the floor, seemingly meditating, Hera and Aaron brainstormed for a clever solution, and the rest of the soldiers tried every brute-force way they could think of to escape the lecture hall. They resorted to using axes as pickaxes and tried to tear apart the wooden walls, only to reveal the marble structure behind them.

Their progress was interrupted by a rumble.

The ground beneath them growled like the stomach of a hungry, fat bear. It was not unlike the Potentate of Dessees's grand entrance. The wood beneath their feet seemed to crack somewhere deep, deep below them.

"The tower is falling, isn't it?" a soldier asked.

The soldier's eyes were empty, not filled with fear or rage, just a despairing woe. The question was directed towards Hera and Aaron, and truth be told, they did not know if the soldier's wager was right or wrong. A majority of the army believed that the soldier had hit the bullseye. It would be a common reaction to run, to scream, to cry. But this was an uncommon situation. Most instead sat on the floor, blank faces and pale cheeks.

That is when Rose fell into place.

Despite the initial reaction, a scream did end up shooting its way through the crowd, one of surprise and pain. A blood-curdling scream, followed by complete silence. The crowd parted, and lying on the floor in its center was a guard with a large scar down thier torso. It looked like a stabbing wound, but the scar was thicker than any normal spear or rapier. Hera and Aaron had little time to gawk before the same thing happened again.

A scream of pain and fear shot its way through the crowd. Hera pivoted on her heel to see where it had come from, and sure enough, another identical scar on another lifeless soldier. The piercing went straight through the body; it was clean and was, apparently, quickly lethal. The blood looked as if it was draining onto the floor and then rapidly evaporating.

Another scream shot its way through the crowd, this one of pain and realization. This one died a few meters in front of Aaron. Aaron moved forward to try to catch the body falling face down, but it was too far away, and he was not quite fully invested in the gruesome venture. Another scream and another thump. Everyone looked around wildly for the assailant but saw no one. Soldiers rapidly started falling, and the only one who wasn't panicked was Viner, who sat on the floor, seemingly meditating.

In the next instant, Hera's eyes were opened, as if she had awakened from a dream. She was laying on her back and Rose was standing above her. When she looked down at her torso, she saw that Rose's cleaver was plunged into her chest. Rose grimaced as Hera awakened. The king killer removed her cleaver from Hera's chest and moved on to the next hapless victim while Hera bled out on the floor. The pain was equal to that of when Hiver had grabbed her by the neck. She reeled from it, unable to see clearly.

"They need to be awoken," Rose said.

Rose's method of awakening her victims was to allow their blood to spill onto the ground in as much of a mess as she could without instantly killing them. When each soldier awoke, they found themselves back in the restless library, but this time there were a few key differences. The library was far brighter. Real chandeliers hung from the second story. The grand and neatly organized bookshelves did not look nearly as sinister with the addition of light. The bookshelves curved in ways they hadn't before, a more ornate picture in a more ornate place. If anything, it looked like an evolved continuation of the place they had been in before falling into the nightmare.

But of course, the strangest addition was that of Rose. She had systematically dealt a large wound to each and every soldier near her. She seemed satisfied with whatever bizarre ritual she was doing. Now she stood with her cleaver embedded in the ground surrounded by five books:

"How to Expand Your Soul",

"Isolating Magical Tendrils",

"Vampirism and Lichood and How Not to Do It",

"Everything to Know About Blood", and

"Ritual Magic, What is it?"

Strange blood markings were written on the ground, and blood seeped from the bodies of the soldiers that lay around Hera, siphoning into Rose's cleaver.

Hera tried to get up quickly but found that she was weak. She looked at her fingers and saw that blood was weeping from them, oozing toward Rose. Hera panicked and looked closer. She saw five bodies around Rose, evidently stabbed by her cleaver. Rose had some sort of magic coming off of her that was summoning the blood from the bodies of her fellows.

So this was blood magic. It was the most evil thing Hera had ever seen. Was it possible that Rose was doing this on purpose? Hera looked intensely into the legionnaire's face. Stone cold, no fear, no anger, only a deep desire.

"Rose, stop..." Hera said weakly.

Rose looked down at her, but her face did not change. Blood from the soldiers made contact with Rose's armor and clung there like honey to its comb.

"The tower is falling apart. I've searched this whole library. If I am going to kill Hiver, I need to make my own entrance," Rose told her.

"What are you talking about? This is crazy!" Hera's vision was blurry and she was barely able to stay awake but still she continued, "We barely even know who Hiver is."

"I know he must be stopped. At any cost," Rose said. "I either kill him now or he kills us later."

The tendrils of blood floated into Rose's face, forming veins outside of her skin. They picked up the books on the floors like riptides pulling dead seaweed into a wine sea. The books started to swirl around Rose, moving like a rowdy wind. The maelstrom bent and curved, twisting into a wall of swirling blood, the books sailing the wall like the overboard bodies of a wrecked ship. The blood formed into a wave of white and red. It crested, and in the eye of the wave it revealed a black figure, draped in a long red cape. The figure was bent over what looked to be yet another dead body. The books made a portal out of blood into another room.

"I'm sorry, I really am." Rose heaved her sword up to her face and held it there, examining the gleaming red of the bloodied blade. "But I've waited a long time. Too long for any one person to mourn. Hours awake. But now, I am become Nemesis."

With her words of recognition, more to herself than to Hera, Rose turned to walk into the portal. She had barely taken a step before she was stopped by a laugh. She indignantly lurched to a halt as soon as she heard the blasphemous noise. The cape clad figure looked over its shoulder. Instead of a face, there was a black void. This figure was the corporeal body of Hiver.

"'I am become Nemesis,'" Hiver mocked. "Cute." He turned completely to present himself to Rose.

He was no less than nine feet tall, but unlike Horror, he did not look skinny because of it. Black armor melded onto his body perfectly, like it was designed specifically for him. It showed no definition of muscle and instead favored a single smooth mold. He looked less like a man encased in metal and more like a man made of metal. The only decorations he had on his armor were ram horns on his head, giant smooth metal plates mounted on his shoulders, and jagged gauntlets encasing his hands. The gauntlets were black like the rest of his armor, but tinged red ever so slightly on the tips, making it look like his sharp talons were forever stained in blood.

"Welcome Nemesis; I am Vetur," Hiver said.

The red velvet cape he wore extended to the floor, sprawling like a wedding gown. It looked all the more intimidating in front of Hiver as he turned, laying across a white ground, enhanced with runes dramatically revealed by the light. Per usual in the Marble Mirror, the room that this portal led to was strange, and though light was cast down from the ceiling, no light source was visible.

"Please, come in," he roared.

Rose did not go through the blood portal; rather, it consumed her. She only took one uncertain step before it completely surrounded her. She forgot about positioning her blade in an intimidating stance. It fell to her side, and she bent her knees into a defensive plié.

The walls around her were domed in a rose quartz crystal. Behind Hiver was a bed, plush and big enough to fit three of him. The room itself was very large and very empty with the only thing of interest, besides the bed, being the body that rested on the floor. It had a purple gilded knife stabbed into it.

Rose did not get the chance to strike before she met Hiver's gauntleted hand. It was unclear whether the room moved to bring her closer to Hiver, or if Hiver had imperceptibly darted across the chamber. His cape fell to the floor behind him, dislodged by whatever change distorted the light.

"I've lived three times your life and never did I waste any of it," Hiver growled.

His sharp claws dug into Rose's stomach and with a heave, Hiver lifted her off her feet. With Hiver almost double her height and more than triple her weight, he had no issue forcing her to the ground. Rose made a decent strike against Hiver's side as she fell, but the cleaver only bounced off of his armor, doing nothing.

Hiver mauled her like a tiger, ripping and tearing into her, and after three rakes of his claws, Rose fell still. He slowly got up and backed away. His chest moved up and down and the noise of metal against metal indicated a sort of strange breathing. Rose was covered in scratches, and the armor around her stomach where Hiver had struck was in tatters, but something was odd about her.

"No blood..." Hiver awed.

Rose twitched on the ground. Hiver did not react, but watched, shoulders hunched, as Rose got to her feet. She wiped away the blood that was not there and kneeled to take back the bloodied cleaver in her left hand. With her right, she started working the straps of her armor. With a clank, the shattered metal fell to the floor, and she was left with a gambeson torn at the stomach. Even Hiver was surprised at what he saw. Two massive gashes pierced her through. The gashes were wide enough that you could see straight through Rose to the other side like windows. One hole was over her heart, and another in her stomach. It did not match Hiver's claws. It looked instead like two separate spears had pierced her entirely.

***

The night when Great Neighbor was attacked, Rose had died. It was all a big mistake. But that night, she had a job to guard the gate and that is exactly what she did. It didn't matter what the king said, she would save her husband and the rest of Great Neighbor.

She had turned to look at the gate and had seen blood spewing in every direction. Limbs and fingers flew as axes glinted in the crimson, setting sun. The raiders had gone mad and were killing everything in sight. Tears streaked down Rose's face. It took all her might to not let go of that gate. She would face down the crazed hoard if she had to; she wouldn't lose him. But she feared it was too late. For a moment, she was filled with hope. Could it be true that the dwarves were retreating? She waited a moment more, and yes, they were walking into the ocean! It was just then that a piercing pain split her armor and flesh. She looked down at her stomach, and to her shock a spear was poking two feet out of her. She would have died. She should have died. But she was held by hatred.

The spear slowly withdrew from her stomach, making sure to hurt on its way out. It took its pound of flesh with it. Once it was out, Rose fell to her knees and turned to look at who had stabbed her. He was dressed in armor, but he was no guard. A gruff beard hugged his face. Everything about him was black—his armor, his beard, even the ridiculously oversized flail he held in his right hand—all a deeper black than the night sky. All except his eyes. Pure hot, blood red.

"Hey there little one," he said.

Rose couldn't react. Her mouth was agape, and her eyes looked sadly at her killer. She had seen the face of almost everyone in the guard force, but this wasn't a guard. She had never seen this man, not in the market nor roaming the streets. She groaned a noise of pain and looked down to the hole in her stomach. It was a wonder she hadn't passed out yet; a good chunk of her had been taken out by the spear.

"What?" Rose asked.

"There, there," the red-eyed man said. "I'm sorry about this... the others can't know about you. So, we have to go through a slightly different process. Consider it a right of passage."

"I don't—"

The figure hushed her, "That's all right, you will, you will."

Her eyes went dark. She didn't see that man again for some time. Though he had promised she would understand, she didn't. It was all so confusing. She had woken with a hole in her stomach and no blood coming out of it. She didn't bleed, she couldn't sleep, she could hardly feel anything. If she had been unfeeling before, now she was completely feelingless. At least, physically. Though she didn't taste the softness of bread or feel the air on her face, she did feel one thing inside of her.

A resentment festered in her stronger than any emotion she had ever felt. She had been angry before, but not like this. She hated everything she saw. She hated her old friend Viner for how little he cared about anyone else's pain but his own. She hated the king for how poor of a ruler he was. She hated the dwarves for what they had done to her. But most of all, she hated the red-eyed man. Not only had he taken her humanity; he had taken something else. If it wasn't for him, her husband would have lived.

***

"I see you have another scar."

Rose pulled herself free from Josephine's spear. The cold stupor that she had put herself in during the battle was all but gone. On hearing that dreaded voice, her spine snapped into place. She turned around faster than ever before to look at the man that had taken everything from her.

"You!" she shouted.

"Aye," he said back.

He was sitting on the marble floor polishing Rose's discarded cleaver in his great hands. There was some fleshy thing in his hands that he was using to do it. It left a red gleam across the entirety of the blade.

"This weapon," he said. "Is it special to you?"

Rose only glared at him. She paced back and forth looking at the giant man, figuring out the best way to retrieve her cleaver and slice his thick neck. She wasn't sure if her cleaver would cut through such thick armor. She wasn't even sure if it would cut through such a thick neck.

The dark-armored warrior saw her pacing and grunted softly. "I suppose it would be. This must be custom. The only black smith that would forge this would have to be..." He stopped for a moment, picking his next word carefully. "Mad."

Rose continued to stare at him. That armor had to be heavy, and it looked like his best weapon was her own cleaver, unless he had something hidden. He would tire very quickly in a fight. But would it be quick enough? Rose was already fatigued from her last encounter. She had also only been able to guess that she wouldn't be able to die. She didn't realize how much it would hurt even with her dulled sense of pain.

The brute laughed a roaring laugh and surprised Rose. "I would want to kill me, too."

"Why did you do this to me?"

"Because I wanted a little bit of Mayhem." His voice dropped at the word 'Mayhem'. "Calm wasn't going to have a good champion; I needed someone who would get things done."

Rose gestured around angrily. "So this is all fun to you? 'A little bit of mayhem.'"

"No." He shook his head.

"What do you mean no?"

He shook his head firmly again and rose to his full height. "You're saying it wrong. It's 'Mayhem.'"

Rose glared at him. "You're just saying the same word with a deeper voice."

"No, I am not. 'Mayhem.'"

"I'm not saying it like that."

He looked at her angrily. "Understand this—Rose daughter of Diane, daughter of Dane, daughter of Wendis, daughter of Lane—I am your god. I am Mayhem. An animal trapped in a snare succumbs to madness in its final breaths. All my followers are snared. All of them succumb to me. Even if I do not ask for them to fight by my side, I cannot deny them. Josephine was my adversary until the end when she succumbed to me, my Mayhem, my being. At that moment, she was my daughter, just as you are to your lineage, just as you are to me. I could not help you then, but I can help you now."

"Is all this to tell me your name, brute? Mayhem?" Rose asked.

"It is to tell you who you deal with, what you deal with. Power, Rose, power. To avenge your husband."

Rose had enough. She screamed at him in rage, spit flying from her mouth. She ran at him as quickly as she could and threw her body against his. Her head only came up to his abdomen. She punched as hard as she could against his armor, but only served to leave scars on her own hand.

"Don't talk about him. You killed him. You killed him," she yelled.

"You are weak," Mayhem roared.

He took the cleaver in one hand like it was a short sword and used the back of his gauntlet to send her flying across the white wasteland. Mayhem stepped forward, his armor clinking like the chiming voices of a thousand souls.

"This is your weapon," he said.

He threw the cleaver at her feet. It oozed with blood, unlike it had a second before, and stuck into the ground.

"I have gifted it with the curse of Darkred, the same curse that imbues my weapon."

He lifted his hand to the sky and in it was suddenly a black star. It morphed into something else before Rose's very eyes—a flail and chain. It was similar in proportion to her cleaver, but with the chain, she didn't know if even she would know how to manage the unwieldiness of the weapon.

"Mourning Star," Mayhem announced. "In it is the soul of my greatest adversary—the Seraphar, Isiah Darkred. It is he who created this curse. In each person are several core humanities. I took one from you and stored it in this."

He threw down the bloody mess of flesh he had been using to polish her sword. It sizzled into the floor and left a red dye on the marble.

"In your body, you no longer bear any lineage to the ame, those born red, not unlike yourself. Now the cleaver holds all that power. Your soul, too, is mine, thought that I cannot show you."

Rose didn't know what any of this meant. She had heard tales of her ancient ancestors, the ame, but she didn't know what that had to do with anything. She wanted to fight this monster but deep down she could tell she stood no chance. She looked at her cleaver and made her decision. She started to pull it out of the ground. It slid out easily, at least as easily as such a heavy weapon could.

Mayhem spoke again, "I didn't order the invasion, Rose. You didn't come all this way to kill me. Your journey isn't over. Hiver is your enemy, Rose, not me."

Rose yelled angrily and sprinted forward again with her cleaver ready to swing up and crash down on that stupid armor.

"I will kill you, child. If you fight me, I will kill you," but he couldn't hold back a smile. "Still, you wouldn't be my champion if our metal did not clash!"

Rose was so close to chopping straight through the armored leg. It would have been the perfect strike. But just as she had done to Mikil, her attack was parried. Mayhem thrust Mourning Star down on the cleaver completely shattering it. Rose felt a tug in her chest as she watched her cleaver shatter. It wasn't a tug of sadness for losing a precious item. Rather, it felt like the cleaver had been part of her and that part of her had just been destroyed.

"Now that part of your life has been killed," Mayhem told her. "I told you I would kill you. Because you lost. You lost against Josephine, and you lost against me. That is why you have two scars on your body, and you will always keep those scars. And in three days' time, those scars shall be your end. Because you lost."

Fury was in his voice, but Rose could only look slack-jawed at her cleaver the same way she had when she had been stabbed through the stomach. So all he said was true. Her lifeforce really was in that cleaver. And now, it was on the marble floor.

Mayhem sighed deeply and looked at his failure of a champion. "Mourning Star shall be your cleaver now. When you die in three days' time, I shall take it back. For now, it shall take the form of your cleaver. It shall be lighter and faster than ever before, just as I made you when I took away your blood."

Rose hardly noticed as he put a new cleaver into her hands. She fell to the floor with it by her side. She felt a little tug at her heart toward the new cleaver, but she wasn't attuned quite yet.

"This shall be called the Bloody Cleaver. A fitting name," Mayhem told her. "Rose, you would not have your vengeance without me. Your instincts are the instincts of an animal. Their source is from me, not you. All your power is my power now. Your soul is in my hands, and in yours is mine."

"So how?" Rose asked. "How do I get vengeance?"

"I shall guide your hand. What you must know is that Hiver is a machination created from metal and given an automaton's heart. In some languages, this creature is called a daemon. Yes, the creature that your people think of as ultimate evil. But in our tongue, he is called a tevnal. The tevnal, a being of artificial life, were created from the Curse of Darkred by seraphars. Ironically, your people think of the seraphars as the ultimate good. How you came up with such nonsense is beyond even the gods. The point is, he is made, not born. He has the heart and soul of a dragon, but his skin cannot be broken. However, with enough lifeforce, enough blood, the curse of Darkred can undo its own creation."

"That doesn't mean anything to me."

"That's the beauty of it. It doesn't have to. Just go on and kill him. Break his shell with the curse. You don't have to know who created what, when, where, and why. You just have to climb up a tower and kill the king at the top. You're a champion, it's what you do." Mayhem chuckled softly. Then he leaned forward and held out his palms to Rose. "Your hands, let me heal them."

She looked down to her hands. She could see bone. Just a few punches, and she had been scarred down to bone. She would have thought it was because she was strong, but now she knew better. Mayhem was strong. She was a puppet. But if she was going to be a puppet, she would get what she wanted. Hiver would die.

Mayhem wrapped his giant hands around Rose's. They were so large that they could hold them completely. From out of the armor came a trickle of blood. When Mayhem removed his hands, Rose saw that the skin had been repaired and some color had returned to them.

"Can you heal the spear marks on my body?" She already knew the answer.

"They are your failure, Rose. I shall not erase them. But the day you wear them proudly shall be the day that they mark my power."

***

Rose lay face down on the floor of Hiver's throne room. A portal leading to the restless library was far out of arm's reach and the people of Great Neighbor's army were dying useless on the floor, only able to watch Rose fight for them. But she was done being a fool. She had marched an entire army into a void of nothingness with no plan. Despite all her intelligence, she had been made the fool. But not this time. She had a plan. The curse of Darkred held all the power of Great Neighbor. And she was held by hatred. It had to be enough.

So, when Hiver saw her rise from the dead, she dared him to attack her. She pinned each arm under the other in turn to leverage the metal gauntlets off, discarding them on the floor. She rotated her cleaver in one hand, wielding it as easily as a dagger.

Hiver took the dare, and again, he lunged forward with both hands outstretched pouncing like a lion. Rose's cleaver met the five metal talons and parried him aside. He fell forward. Hiver was shocked that Rose was able to fight with such expertise. Hiver's deflected claws left white scars down the side of Rose's bloodied blade. Even with the scratches, the cleaver would cut just the same.

Hiver slid across the ground on all fours. He lifted his great taloned hand and swiftly lunged toward his enemy.

Rose shifted her weight and moved her cleaver up to meet Hiver's hand. But the potentate was finished underestimating Rose. As soon as Hiver's claws made contact with the blade, his fingers curled around its sharp razor end. The tungsten hand and cleaver moved as one. Hiver forced Rose's own weapon up and over her head. Rose held onto the hilt as hard as she could. For a moment her feet hovered above the floor.

Then, with a crash she landed against the marble ground and fell backwards. Hiver assisted the fall and pushed her to the floor, with the cleaver being the only barrier between her and Hiver's deadly talons. Hiver pushed the blade hard against Rose's face. The contest of strength was one Rose knew she could not win, so she scrambled to the side and let Hiver push the blade to the floor.

The claws of evil were not so clumsy as to let Rose escape unharmed. They released the cleaver quickly and took a swipe at Rose. He slashed her down the scalp, leaving four white scars where hair used to be. Rose fell forward with the attack, and Hiver used the moment of weakness to grab her with both of his hands and lift her over his head. Hiver threw her back to the ground, and she slid to a stop next to her cleaver.

Hiver took a step back and roared like a dragon at Rose, demanding that she stay down. His entire body shook with the roar, and he was furthest from human any of the onlookers had ever seen anything be. Rose did not witness the show of strength, her eyes were focused on one thing— the cleaver. She was already a mostly destroyed mess, but she hadn't lost any limbs yet, only broken a few bones. She almost felt the pain, but she was held by hatred.

The cleaver was back in her grasp in an instant. She crouched, ready for another barrage of attacks. The tip of the cleaver rested against the ground, but the handle was firmly clasped in both of her hands. Hiver stopped his roaring to examine the scene before him. He cocked his head looking at her.

"Ahhhh..."

Hiver was still euphoric from his roaring session, and he shuddered with a sudden realization. Battle hysteria was gripping him, and his voice wavered with laughter.

"That's not allowed, Mayhem..." Hiver chuckled. "You always were a rule breaker."

Hiver slid forcefully across the floor, his hand pointing forward like an arrow. The power radiating from Hiver's attack caused his discarded cape to lift ever so slightly off the ground. Hiver struck Rose, but this time, Rose struck him back. Her great cleaver swung to hit him on the side. If Hiver had been a normal man with normal armor, he would have been dead before even touching Rose. Instead, Hiver only flinched a little to the right, not nearly enough to interrupt his vicious attack.

It was impressive that the strike caused any movement at all from Hiver, and Rose was proud of the blow, if only for a second. Rose's victory was cut short when five of Hiver's talons dug deep into her shoulder. Though her likelihood of survival, much less victory, was miniscule, Rose was held by hatred.

They were both on the floor, with Hiver in a far more opportune position. While he grappled her, Rose took her bloodied cleaver and smacked the blunt side into Hiver's flank right where her last strike had been. Hiver recoiled at the attack, but not enough to give up his hold. Hiver pinned Rose to the floor with his right knee while he readied his claws. Before Rose could establish any further attacks, Hiver was ripping at her head and neck.

It was a brutal attack, but no matter how hard Hiver tried, he could not draw a drop of blood where there was no blood to be drawn. Rose twisted her blade to get it in between her and her attacker. Instead of using the predictable blocking maneuver Hiver had expected—and that any reasonable warrior would use—Rose slashed at Hiver's neck, hoping to find a chink in the armor.

Hiver drew back for a moment, the impact on his neck obviously startling him. The barrage of attacks suddenly stopped as Hiver took a moment to place his hands on his collar. He rubbed the smooth metal before removing his hands and looking down at his open palms. He was disappointed to see nothing but a black void cupped in his moon-tinted gauntlets. He clenched his fist and looked back down to Rose. She was a mess, barely recognizable as human anymore, but still, she was alive.

"Even if..." Hiver got to his feet and let Rose up.

Rose followed him, cleaver in hand. Hiver stood still while Rose launched an aggressive attack against his legs. He didn't even acknowledge that he was being attacked. Rose did not look remotely upset by the fact that she was doing no damage and instead continued attacking with the same ferocity, the blood of her cleaver seeming to mold into his armor with every strike.

"If I must tear you to pieces—" Hiver growled down to her.

He picked her up by the neck in one swift motion that she could not dodge and threw her across the ground. Her landing shattered the runes that labeled the ground, but never did she let go of her cleaver. She tried in vain to steady herself while still moving across the ground. It was only when she came to a complete stop that she was able to get to her feet again. Hiver was already walking towards her.

"It will not be the worst thing I have been forced to do."

Rose ran at Hiver, and Hiver walked to meet her. The reunion was a clash of red. But the only blood being spilled was that which was coming off of Rose's cleaver. Though Hiver was hit more than Rose, the rumble of combat ended with Hiver slicing off Rose's arm with his sharp talons. After accomplishing the task, he tried to compose himself for a moment. He looked down to see Rose look at her severed arm. She seemed more annoyed than anything.

"You've been bested yet again," Hiver said.

Rose said nothing. She walked calmly to her lost arm and bent down to pick up the cleaver she had dropped. Hiver prepared to berate her, but was instead met with Rose's continued barrage. Despite having an arm sundered, Rose was still able to attack, holding the cleaver in only one hand, held by hatred.

A slash up Hiver's back, a siege on his hamstring, a slice on his neck that had so easily killed the king... nothing hurt the metal goliath. Hiver switched battle stances, and instead of taking the position of a cat, he now looked more like a bear, standing proud and tall against Rose's attacks. The next thing Hiver destroyed was Rose's cleaver. He caught it in his left hand, and as easily as breaking a branch, the cleaver was snapped in two.

A wave of blood burst from the cleaver and consumed both Rose and Hiver. Hiver roared in panic like he was a child. He reared back from the avalanche of blood, but the blood pursued him and Rose. Tendrils started to latch onto Hiver's armor and Rose's demolished face. Rose laughed gently to herself, the faint remnants of a smile playing at her lips.

"I knew I would destroy you at all cost," she croaked. "Even my own life."

For just a moment, color returned to her features. Her body was rejuvenated. The gaping holes in her stomach and chest were closed. She let out a scream that was all the pain she had gone through in the last few weeks. Her eyes burned like a bright fire, and she gritted her teeth, shutting down the scream. Her face was still enraged when memories of sleepless nights suddenly came back to her all in a blur. She started to drift into a dream. Her eyes closed, and she fell unconscious. The blood drained from her body and started to worm its way toward the crowd that had been watching the battle unfurl; it seeped through the portal from which it came. The crowd would have run from their own stolen blood had they the energy to do so. But debilitated on the floor, the blood could cross the portal without issue. But the fallen soldiers were not the only destination for the blood. A large portion covered Hiver and more still was climbing up his body.

The blood decorated his armor for a brief moment, before going through it. Hiver shuddered in what seemed to be pain. He groped at his chest, struggling for air. He fell to his knees. And then he breathed a grating metal sigh. He panted on the floor for a long minute. What was happening to him? What had Rose done? Was this it; was Hiver going to die to some sort of bloody poison? Then, he struggled to his feet. No, not he. He, Hiver, had died once before and this was not what it felt like. This was likened to a sore throat in the morning. Annoying, certainly, but hardly fatal.

Hiver survived. Rose failed.

The armored man ignored Rose's body completely, as if the fight had never happened. Rose's dream was a permanent one. She was dead. Hiver took the dagger from the other body and resumed what he had been doing before being interrupted.

Chapter 25
The Claws of Evil

Hiver completely ignored the army behind him as he began working on the corpse. The blood coming from Rose inched forward, returning to its source. Hera and Aaron had been watching the battle unfold, not entirely sure if they really wanted Rose to win. On one hand, Hiver was an evil god, and on the other hand, Rose was just the worst. But, of course, they mourned their loss. All of Great Neighbor was doomed to die, betrayed by their leader with nothing to show for it.

The entire army was drained of most of its blood. They weren't quite dead, but they were left weak. Perhaps it was some semblance of mercy that allowed Rose to let them live. Or more likely, it was a plan. Hera and Aaron groaned painfully to themselves. Luckily, the two had fallen asleep near each other and had the comfort of the other's company while they waited to die.

The blood of Rose's cleaver made its way through the portal. For a moment, it looked like it would coagulate and become part of the portal, but soon that proved to be false. The blood pushed its way through the tear left in the wake of Rose's sanguine ritual and into the restless library. The blood seeped slowly back into the bodies from which it came. If that process terrified the victims, they were too weak to do anything to stop it.

It floated in a crimson mist. It was clear that not all the blood had returned from its venture into the portal, but still, it rejuvenated Hera, Aaron, and the rest of the army. It closed the wounds in their stomachs as if it had never been there at all. They did not realize how sore the rest of their body had been until they got to their feet. On the bright side, the agony of such a vast wound was now a painful memory. The rogues were two of the first to rise from the brink of death, but soon after other soldiers rose, too. It was only a matter of time before all the warriors were on their feet. All except Viner.

Viner did not move. He wished he had died from Rose's ritual. No, even worse, he didn't care about Rose's ritual at all. Another betrayal from the betraying world. Henry was dead. He looked around for a moment, trying to see if he could spot his nephew. It was of no use. His boy was nowhere that he could easily see. He was ashamed of not looking harder, but he hadn't the strength to do it.

Calessa first made sure that her family was okay before going to reunite with Tython. It didn't take her long to find him. He was wandering around the army with a confused look on his face. The furrow in his brow made him look like he was lost.

"Tython," Calessa called out to him.

He looked around for her, and Calessa was practically right next to him by the time the short man could find where she was. Calessa placed her hand on Tython's shoulder, and he smiled up at her.

"Hi!" he said cheerfully.

"Listen, we are about to do something very dangerous. Look around." Calessa beckoned around the room.

Now rejuvenated with their blood returned to their body, the army was meandering in circles around the restless library. None of them had any clue what to do. They didn't want to fight Hiver, and they didn't want to turn back. Hera and Aaron were fixated in place, and Viner was sitting alone, dead in the face.

"They don't have a purpose. You need to remind them of who they are," Calessa said.

"Where is this coming from?" Tython asked. "Why me?"

"You are the only one who can."

"But I am not one of you," Tython argued.

Calessa laughed in his face. "You are the best of us."

Tython took in a breath allowing himself one last uncertain look around the room. Then he fixed his eyes on Viner. Calessa believed in him, he would do this. He started walking over to the man. He was almost knocked over by a destination-less soldier, but he did not care. He pressed forward. The captain of the guard sat on the floor. His back was hunched, and his weapons were laid out before him. His armor looked like loose skin.

"Captain," Tython said timidly. "What do we do?"

Viner didn't even shrug. So early on Tython had already been stifled. But he wouldn't give up, not with what was at stake. Viner was the man they needed.

"Viner, we need orders," Tython urged.

Viner seemed to shrink further into himself, a shadow of the man he once was. But how could he be expected to be strong now? This was his weakest hour, could he not be granted a moment of grace?

"Go away, Tython."

Tython did not obey. "We have to go home," he said.

"Then go home."

Tython turned red. "Is it all for nothing?"

"Yes."

This wasn't the Viner Tython had known. This wasn't the Viner that had trained them all to go to the depths of hell and retrieve their families. This wasn't the Viner who broke the first lock with nothing but his shield and one mighty blow. He didn't believe it

Tython shook his head, "Come on, we still have lives to live."

"No, we don't."

If his words alone couldn't reach the Hand of the King, then perhaps the dead could. In Viner's mind, he had lost, but he didn't fully grasp what he had lost. What did Henry really mean?

Tython took a step back. "He doesn't want you to die, Viner."

"Didn't stop him."

"Yeah," Tython laughed bitterly. "He got it from you."

Viner looked up angrily into Tython's eyes. "You think I don't blame myself already?"

Tython's face drained of color. He looked to the side nervously. It was a foolish thing to say, perhaps foolish enough to lose him the argument. But Calessa believed in him. He had to keep trying; he wouldn't give up.

"Would you love him any other way?" Tython asked.

Viner clenched his fist and gritted his teeth, but he gave no response.

"Do you love him?" Tython yelled.

And Viner rose to his feet. Tython scurried backwards as best he could, falling on his backside. The menacing figure of Viner looked great and powerful, more imposing than Horror ever did. He raised his fists in anger, his teeth bared. The man who had led his people to freedom stood opposite to Tython. This man had smashed the locks. He had conquested into Dessees itself. But the death of his nephew had broken him.

Viner roared like a great gorilla, "With everything I have."

"Then—"

"Leave!" Viner roared.

Tython scrambled to his feet, "Viner—"

"Leave now!"

He took one last look at Viner and then turned on his heel. He cursed himself for being so stupid. 'He got it from you.' What an offish thing to say. Tython's face burned with shame. He had tormented a grieving man. He walked five paces away before he felt a tingle on the back of his neck. No one had touched him. Viner probably wasn't even looking at him. No, this tingle was an instinct. He turned around to see Viner with his head in his hands. He looked to the ceiling and started to remove his gloves as he began to sing solemnly.

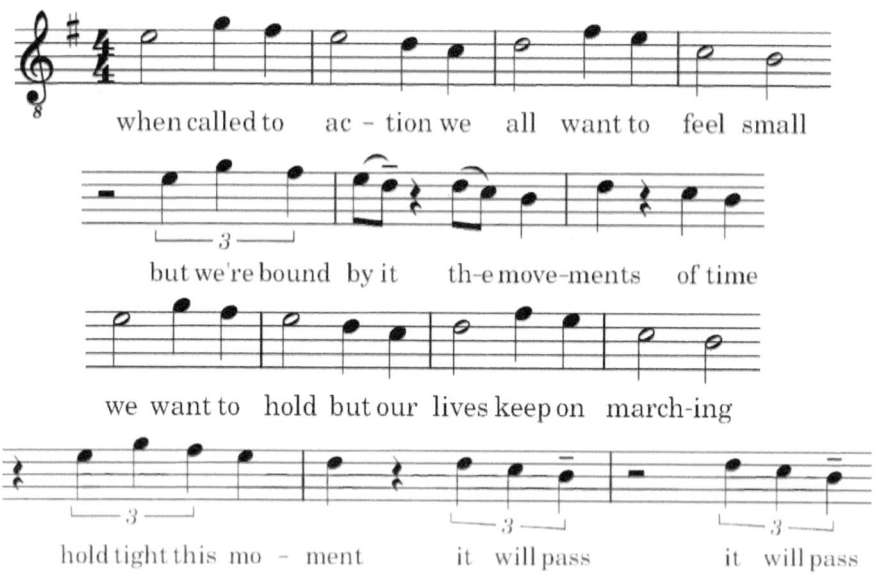

when called to   ac – tion we   all   want to   feel small

but we're bound by it   th-e move-ments   of time

we want to   hold but our lives keep on   march-ing

hold tight this mo – ment   it will pass   it   will pass

"Tython, what are you doing?" Viner asked "Don't sing to me now. Not here."

But Tython did not listen. He kept his voice steady and loud. Calessa smiled to herself. A bold move on Tython's part. Not something that someone should usually do for a grieving man. But if it was the only thing to get Viner moving, it would work. It had to. She walked behind Tython and placed her hand on his shoulder.

our path is blocked by the dusk turned to night-fall

we've lost our spir-it o-ur com-pass points dark

win-ter is com-ing our days be-come shor-ter

hold tight your blan - ket   it will pass   it will pass

"Damn it, Tython," Viner said.

His eyes were red. He started to weep. Any soldiers who had been watching the spectacle averted their eyes out of respect for their captain. Tython spoke of sadness and of longing. Tython did not let Viner hide from his grief. The sad tune of his voice was not meant to lift Viner's spirit. No, Viner would grieve as is the way of things. He would not be denied that humanity. But Tython would put into words that pain. Calessa, a soldier after Viner's own heart, took the last lines.

brave are the peo-ple in light of a ga - le

who steal their cour - age   and pre-vail   we'll pre-vail   we'll pre-vail

Viner crumpled to the ground. He couldn't control a single muscle in his body. His face spasmed and his limbs curled. He had felt like nothing would ever be the same again. But his boy was brave. Maybe he could be, too.

"Go talk to Hera and Aaron," Viner commanded. "The people trust them. I trust them. When the time comes, I will be there."

Unknowing of the sweet words that Tython of Dimfir and Calessa of Great Neighbor sang to their guard captain, Hera and Aaron huddled together spying on Hiver. Their faces were pressed close and their eyes tried their best to penetrate the metal coating of the dark lord.

"He said something about the knife being enchanted. Did you hear it?" Hera whispered to Aaron.

They had been listening to Hiver mutter under his breath at the edge of the portal. The metal man was clearly casting some sort of spell, and it took both Hera and Aaron to be able to distinguish any exact words. But in the end, they heard enough.

Aaron nodded to Hera. "Learn to walk again, learn to sleep again," he repeated.

"This knife was once able to cut the fabrics of reality and move a man from one place to another as you enchanted it so," Hera repeated what Hiver had said.

"Now it takes a different course," Aaron continued for her.

Hera took her part in recounting, "You shall go to the Inbetween and be stuck there never-dying just as I am stuck here never living."

"You shall be released from the needle and thread when you can offer Despair the blood of Malue," Aaron finished.

Tython had a fearful look on his face when he announced his presence. "Well, that was weird."

Hera and Aaron were both startled by his words.

"Oh, Tython, sorry," Aaron said.

Looking at Calessa, Hera added on, "And Calessa, too."

"Yes." Calessa nodded. "We are here for orders."

Tython finished for her, "Viner says he trusts you two to give them."

"We never wanted that," Aaron said.

Calessa responded quickly, "That's what makes you good candidates."

Hera and Aaron looked at each other. They knew she was right. They looked back to Hiver. They were not surprised when the body rose from the ground. Hiver gently handed the figure the knife, and the figure took it, looking confused. Aaron saw a glimpse of purple in the figure's eye and was hit with a sudden realization. Filius, that fool. He must have gotten lost in the library.

Filius slowly walked a few meters away from Hiver, like a marionette with no strings. He took the knife that he valued so much in both hands, and he split a tear in the air. It was like he was severing the fabric that weaved together the wind. It didn't look physically effortless, but it didn't look hard either. The cut was clean, and the other side of the tear opened into a purple mess of color. With zombie-like motions, the man walked into the void and was gone.

"We can't turn back?" Aaron said.

It was a question, not a statement. He genuinely wanted an excuse to turn back. But they didn't know how to get out of Dessees. They didn't even know how to get out of the library.

"I think we would know by now if we could," Hera answered.

"We have to fight. We can stop him," Calessa said.

Aaron nodded and turned on his heel to address the crowd.

"Do you hear that?" he called.

The army recognized his voice. Viner was right; he had sway, and the army responded well to it. The room they were in was big enough to provide a clear line of sight to all in it as long as the book shelves were avoided. They packed in close to each other to listen to what Aaron had to say. Aaron did not wait.

"We've come this far," he said. "But this has ended up being bigger than ourselves. It is true, I do not want to step through Rose's portal and face the metal beast that lurks on the other side, but we have been granted a chance to live. To do the right thing. I will not hold it against you if you leave now, but know that if you do, you will forever regret it. He calls himself Vetur, which means winter in Ike. Let us show him the sun even when it does not shine on our face."

It would have been beautiful if the army rallied. They did not. They stared up at him, dead in the eye, dead in the heart. Was this the same crowd that had been so full of life two days ago? It didn't feel like it. Something in the air was different.

"I'm waiting..." Hiver called through the portal.

Hera turned first. It was true. Hiver was a few steps closer to the portal than he had been a moment ago. The body of Filius was gone and replaced with the body of Rose, ready for another strange ritual. The army cowered at his words. Any semblance of morale that they held before was shattered by Hiver's simple statement. Hiver was not done speaking, however.

"They don't seem as excited as I. Maybe they should know what they die for!" Hiver boomed.

The portal of blood again attacked the army. It grew, engulfing them the same way it had engulfed Rose. In a moment, all the soldiers' regrets came to them. One more moment of sunlight was all they wanted. It was what they were given.

"I am Hiver," he cried.

And he did cry. His voice held the same pain as the soldiers'. The ten-foot-tall man took no pleasure in this moment. All bravado fell from his voice. Not only that, but also it cracked. The world around the soldiers changed, too. They were not in the underworld. A beautiful sun was now over their heads.

The ground beneath their feet was snow. The sun in the sky shone a beautiful, crisp white light through the cold air. The air was thin and at a much higher altitude. The soldiers recognized this place. It was Disus. Heaven. Small floating islands were visible in the clouds above. A few of them cascaded down trickles of weak waterfalls.

The terrain was decently flat. A few trees with no leaves dotted the surrounding areas, but mostly it was barren. Hiver stood, arms extended, appraising the area. He leaned forward, taking in the scene as much as anyone else.

Hiver spoke to the crowd, still sobbing. "This place was once filled with life. It is more beautiful than anything in Dessees, more beautiful than anything in Malue, and it is kept locked away. Even now, we are not truly here. It is only by magic, also locked away, that we can ever see the true meaning of life."

He let his arms fall, and he looked sadly down at the ground. The illusion faltered. Soldiers tried their best to catch the air and keep it for themselves, but it was gone a moment later. They found themselves in a new location yet again, a giant gray cave with a tower of white marble far in the distance. The tower was huge, but not as massive as Hera and Aaron knew it was on the inside. This was what Dessees was really like outside of the Marble Tower.

The tower loomed over them, cracking at the base, threatening to fall at any moment. If it did fall, it was still close enough to fall near or on them. It was the only thing of interest in the cave. Despite its evil, it provided an eerie beauty to an otherwise desolate and empty Dessees.

"Long ago, Disus was plagued by great evil. One I tried and failed to destroy. Now, it is empty, and there are those among you who seek to serve that evil. With your blood, I can break my curse and reclaim my home. That's the key difference between your twin thieves and I."

Hiver snapped his hand to the side, creating a scythe out of blood. The blood was not crystallized, but a smooth liquid that retained the shape of the tool despite gravity. He held the scythe not like a weapon or a tool but like a long walking stick. Still, it would not reach the ground with Hiver's great height.

He walked comfortably towards Aaron. The distance between them shrank unnaturally quickly, as if Aaron was sliding across the ground towards the pontiff of metal. About a meter away from Aaron, Hiver tried to make a grab at him with his free hand. Aaron was nimble and dodged to Hiver's right, but he soon realized how unwise the action was once he became uncomfortably close to the pommel of Hiver's scythe.

Hiver thrust the pommel into Aaron, but it did not strike him. Instead, it thrust against his chest with a slight amount of pressure, but nothing that could be mistaken as an attack. Hiver shook the scythe, commanding Aaron to take it without words. Aaron looked up at Hiver, distrust in his eyes, but after another vicious shake, he took the scythe.

"Strike me with it, and kill me," Hiver growled down at him.

Aaron obliged within seconds, taking the scythe into both of his hands and preparing a lethal sweep, just like a farmer about to reap his crop. It was too easy. There was no way Hiver would leave himself open like this. Did he seriously think that Aaron wouldn't kill him? He had to be joking. Aaron had killed before; he could kill again. So, he swung the scythe.

The Scythe was about to plunge into Hiver's neck when Aaron stopped. He wasn't sure he wanted to kill someone who wasn't an immediate threat to him. He pulled back the scythe again, playing off the stutter as a flinch test or a test swing.

His feet moved with the ground, reacting to the force of the scythe. Regret coursed through Aaron's veins. Hiver would kill them. He had said it himself. But if Aaron took Hiver's life, there was no giving it back. Would he be so quick to steal something he couldn't give back? Wasn't he done being a thief? He noticed how the scythe was serrated on the edge like the Goldenhill knife he had seen in the hob's armory. A weapon that was cruel for cruelty's sake. Again, the thought made him sick.

But, he had to. He had no choice. He upturned the scythe and it glinted sanguine in the sky. Did a choir sing of its blood red curvature? Was it this scythe that banished the sun under the horizon? Aaron plunged the sun-setter into the side of Hiver's neck. Hiver tensed around the scythe and growled in pain. The great tungsten man roared and lurched backward writhing with small movements like he was covered in chains. Aaron stepped back, letting go of the scythe, his mouth and eyes opened in aghast dismay. He was shaking from a surge of adrenaline stronger than he had ever experienced. But he had to; it was the right thing to do. The right thing.

Hiver's knees fell rigidly to the floor, the scythe still stuck in him. The giant's fall shook the cavern creating a deep rumbling tremor. With its master fallen, the tower could not stand. The marble creaked just a moment before it started to tip. The knees gave way and the metal body hit the floor.

The ground rumbled, and the tower couldn't help but topple with its patriarch.

It crashed down only a few meters away from the closest soldiers. It would have been a far better story had they survived, but the shrapnel from the falling tower had other plans. As it smashed against the dust, a mixture of marble and gray stone flew upward, impaling three soldiers.

Simultaneously, the scythe embedded in Hiver's side started to shrink. The blood was moving through Hiver's armor and making its way into his body. The scythe shrunk like a worm into a hole, a disgusting sight. The grim visage was accompanied by Hiver's renewed breath. Aaron watched in horror as the blood rejuvenated Hiver. Hiver got to his feet, that old bravado back in his step as he presented his claws to Aaron.

"That's the key difference between the twin thieves and I—when they take life, they think it is permanent!" Hiver roared at the failing brigade.

He raised his metal talons into the air and praised the stone above. The Marble Tower, now fallen, started to shake with a rumbling call obviously coming from the Potentate of Dessees. So it was that his power would remind the world yet again of what can happen when balance is lost. So it was that Hiver, Potentate of Disus, would rise to right the wrong. So it was that Hiver would become Conqueror of Malue.

Hiver announced with Pride to the world, "We know better!"

The Marble Tower cracked like a nest of spider eggs. The children that crawled out were not spiders but the deformed bodies of dwarves. They were missing limbs and covered in casts of metal. The half metal dwarves trudged forward, slowly creaking along the ground as they struggled to stand. The lava seemed to have done its part in obliterating most of their bodies, but apparently, Hiver didn't need a body to reanimate someone. All he needed was a little blood and a little soul.

The dwarves cascaded forward like clockwork toys. Most could not wield a weapon, and none were nimble, but still, they moved forward, moaning in pain. They were not meant to be alive, and their bodies knew it, but Hiver's will was much stronger than their bodies.

It felt like slow motion. The army of humans turned their shields on the dwarves, creating a defensive circle as quickly as they could. Had it been that the dwarven army moved any faster, the brigade wouldn't have had the time to ready themselves for the onslaught. Aaron was struck by Hiver right in the chest, forcing him painfully into the ground. He skidded across the stone a distance more than twice Hiver's height.

"Bare witness to a true champion of old," Hiver's voice was a cascade.

The army divided into sections. A majority were focused on stopping the dwarven invasion, but still, a great number attacked Hiver. Hera rushed to Aaron's side and looked him over. Aaron had left a long streak of blood across the ground, and he was gasping in pain.

The soldiers charged Hiver, blades in their hands and war cries in their hearts. The bravest and fastest were the first to meet Hiver, so the bravest and fastest were the first to be grabbed by the throat and choked to death. Hiver stood at his full height, picking guards off the ground by their heads and snapping their necks effortlessly. He was disappointed that none of them could face him the same way Rose could. He took a limp body into his hands and threw it at the nearest soldier, toppling them to the ground. He scoffed to himself, noting how none had even landed a blow before being pushed back.

He pounced on the next guard and forced them against the cave's stone. Like a wolf, he tore at them while they were helpless on the floor. Slash after slash, he tore at the guard, more animal than man. The superstitious could have sworn he was a werewolf. Hiver was no wolf, however, and was as skilled with the blade as he was with his clawed gauntlets. He turned to the next swordsman, and before they could even land a single blow, he grabbed the sword by the point and yanked it out of their hands. He pivoted to the next attacker and tore the tip of the stolen sword up their spine.

Hera knelt over Aaron, panicking. He had been smashed twenty feet across the ground, tearing the floor and his flesh in the process. Perhaps Rose could have survived the attack, but she was a revenant. Aaron looked as if he was going to die. Hera tried her best to shake him to life, but no matter what she did, he only responded in groans. Tears started to fill her eyes when she heard a voice in her head.

"Oh dear, that was not supposed to happen," the voice said.

The voice was old but consistent. It did not crack or break; it was confident yet worried. Hera looked around for the voice, and it laughed gently at her.

"I'm not by your side yet, but I will be soon," the voice said. "It's me, Calm."

It still took Hera a moment to comprehend what was happening. She usually didn't have powerful beings whispering in her ear. Calm had come to save Aaron. He had known they were in danger, and he had come to save him. Hera was eternally grateful. The tears that stained her face turned a color less blue.

Hera didn't think; her hands just moved and she believed Aaron to be healed. The world obeyed. Aaron's groggy eyes flickered to life. The blood rushing from the ground back into his body was not a pleasant feeling, but he was alive, so he didn't mind all that much. With an involuntary flexing of his muscles, Aaron started to writhe off the ground. After the spasm passed, he rushed to his feet, using Hera as support.

Hera moved to his side to help him up. Blood splattered the side of her face, and her pupils dilated in fear. She looked to her left to see Hiver holding a sword in the air. Specks of blood spewed off it. It was terrifying. She would never get used to watching people die. It was a horrible thing to see Hiver slaughtering the army.

The conscript who now lay motionless on the ground had been killed without a second thought, but forever Hera would remember him. She would remember all the people who died even if she never knew their names. She still remembered watching the apple stand owner getting dragged away by the dwarves. She was filled with a sad rage, an all-consuming despair that only propelled her to react on instinct.

Hiver climbed atop a chunk of rubble from his tower and walked forward with the slow metallic drum of his feet against the engraved marble. "You have been given strength that is not yours. It may be intoxicating now, but it is a burden. I am sorry, champion. You must die."

Aaron pulled Hera behind him, and Hera tried to do the same to Aaron. The result was two people foolishly tugging on each other, trying to pull the other away. Aaron remembered Henry. He knew it was time to be brave. All his life, he had been a stain on humanity. Now, he was going to prove himself.

Aaron mustered all the courage he had ever had and pushed himself away from Hera. He spread out his arms in a taunt. Once his hands were in the air, he noticed he had forgotten something important. His sword.

Hera hissed over to him, "What are you doing? Are you crazy?"

"I have a plan; I always have a plan," Aaron responded.

"Since when have you had a plan?"

"You will know what to do."

Viner laid on the floor, barely comprehending what was unfolding before him. The more he watched the battle unfold, the more ashamed of himself he became. He couldn't let his army do this without him. Even with that thought in his mind, he did not have the strength to stand. So he laid, a battle raging around him. Perhaps he had been ignored because soldiers thought he was dead. He looked the part.

Aaron didn't stop moving towards Hiver. For a moment, it felt like the entire army, metal dwarves and all, had stopped to witness what was happening. Aaron circled Hiver, making sure that no side of him was exposed. Aaron's knees constantly faced Hiver as he shuffled from side to side. The regard for safety ended up making the show of strength look more like a nervous attempt at escape.

Hiver moved in the exact opposite way. He stood tall, pivoting in place and nothing more. He made sure that he was always staring directly at the scared boy. It was not long before he read Aaron like a book and knew he wasn't going to attack any time soon.

Hiver gloated, "A child to face a god."

He delicately flexed his claws, then suddenly ran at Aaron. Aaron hastily jerked away, running back into the crowd of people, all too nervous to charge. The crowd rushed to escape, and for that Aaron was grateful. He didn't want to put anyone else in danger. Aaron was right; Hera did know what to do.

As soon as Hiver moved past her, Hera jumped onto his back, an act of bravery that cannot possibly be overstated.

She crawled up his spine like a monkey. She had not known she was able to climb so quickly.

Hiver reacted by stopping in his tracks, which was exactly the wrong move. He reached behind his back attempting to grab Hera, but he couldn't quite reach her. She barely flexed in and out of his grasp, only leaving Hiver clawing at his own back, gray streaks trailing his talons. Hiver became beyond irritated in only a few seconds.

Viner's eyes started to glaze over. In a moment, he would lose consciousness. Just lie down and die. But there was one thing he saw. A man of metal wreathed in fire. Viner saw Hiver. He saw his claws. He saw his cruelty. And he saw Aaron and Hera. And he was watching them fight to survive. Viner struggled to remember himself but was met only with regret. He had put them in this position. It was because of him they were drafted. He had sworn to them that they would live to be happy, and that hadn't happened yet. Was he an oath-breaker?

Aaron was not done yet. Hiver had made the foolish decision to stop pursuing him, something Aaron intended to exploit to the fullest. Aaron flanked the metal man positioning directly behind his right leg. The rogue cocked his arm for a punch and with all his might, he struck the metal plate that protected the backside of Hiver's knee. Pain shot through Aaron's hand and up his arm. He roared with the paralyzing sting of metal against bone, but his strike was not in vain.

Hiver's knee buckled, and he toppled to the floor. Aaron was not alone in his pain. As Hiver's knee hit the floor, a flair of affliction coursed through his veins too. Something about the blow felt different to Hiver. Maybe it was just well placed, but a pang of worry started to flow through his blood. Hiver still had the rogue on his back to deal with, and with the new vantage point, maybe he could catch her off guard. The knee cripple was by far the most effective strike that any of the soldiers had yet to place against the metal behemoth. It had left him open on the floor, open to attack. Aaron took the opportunity to charge forward but was met with the swift motion of Hiver's claw, bidding him away. Aaron skittered back before the rampaging metal could cut him open.

Viner moved for the first time, but only so he could bury his face in the floor. Tears freely streamed down his nose, but he made no noise. The captain of the guard realized something then. It wasn't some silly oath that held him to Hera and Aaron. Aaron and Hera were naive and misguided. In essence, they were young. Viner knew that he couldn't abandon them. They had no one. He had no one. Why couldn't they have each other?

The momentum of Hiver's fall shook Hera partially off Hiver's back. In a panic, she tried to clamber her way back to a safer position. Just as she thought she was safe, Hiver's claws raked against Hera's leg, surprising her to say the least. She yelped in pain before being dragged off half a second later. Aaron charged at Hiver, but he too was thwarted. Hiver had the training of years on his side, and it was only a matter of time before the rogue's tricks ran out. Hiver reached out his arm to grab the boy by the neck. Aaron was unable to turn his charge into a retreat, and Hiver used his massive reach to easily seize him the same way he had captured him when last they met.

Hiver spoke quickly, indignant and irritated, "You seek to kill me while I kneel at your feet? Do you not understand who I am? Nothing can wound me. I am impenetrable, I am unbreakable, I am Hi—"

"Put those kids down," a man shouted.

Then, he charged, spear in hand, tears and spit flying off his face. He was Viner, Captain of the Guard. His brother Fredrick, Hand of the King, had died fighting Horror. His nephew Henry, the bravest man Viner had ever known, had died killing Horror. Viner would be brave; he would do the same if he had to. He didn't have a shield, but he didn't need it. All he needed was to strike true. Hiver? Impenetrable? He would see about that.

For one reflexive second, Hiver was afraid. Just before the spear made contact, he saw its pointed tip about to pierce his stomach. But what did the god among men have to fear? His armor was unbreakable—

Hiver's thought was cut short when the spear struck his tungsten stomach and shot the wind from his inhuman lunges. The spear stuck there for a moment, just on the surface of his armor. Hiver breathed a wheeze of relief; it hadn't gone through. Why would it? His metal flesh had never failed. But Viner was not done yet. The spear was stuck, so that meant it hadn't glanced off! Viner took in a breath, and with all his strength, he pushed harder. The metal screeched and blood slowly oozed out, blood that was not Hiver's. Hiver's imageless head slowly looked down. The armor creaked, then it grated, and all of the sudden it gushed blood, as if the metal had melted into wine.

'Ah...' Hiver thought, 'I've been bested. Damn that champion. Her blood is as potent as the red of her hair. I see now. She broke my shell. That was the spell... she broke me.'

The spear plunged deep into Hiver's stomach. His hands reflexively opened, dropping Hera and Aaron to the floor. They clattered to the ground and spiraled out to look at Hiver. Hiver crouched, touching the ground with his left hand while, with his right, he grasped the spear. Viner looked into the faceless void that was Hiver's mask. The Captain of the Guard gritted his teeth and pushed the spear deeper into Hiver. Viner pushed his gauntlets up against Hiver's stomach and the spear sundered the dark metal on the other side of the potentate's body.

Rose's final cantrip. She knew she couldn't defeat him, not with that armor. So she cast a spell. She didn't know she could, but she did. Rose had gotten her revenge even after her death. It was her blood that imbued Hiver's armor, her blood that weakened it. The curse of Darkred.

"The next world… you must free them… don't let them live under… a false god…" Hiver gasped his final breath.

The dwarven army fell to their knees, replicating the motion of Hiver. The soldiers were surprised to see that they were weeping. At least those that had eyes. The dwarves begged the soldiers for forgiveness, but before any of the dumbfounded soldiers could respond, the dwarven bodies grew stiff and still. His army was finished, Hiver was dying. He sputtered on the ground, trying his best to come to life like one of his necromantic puppets. He could not. He laid there accepting his fate. His death would not be a quick one without intervention; his artificial body was too strong to allow for that.

Then it all ended happily ever after? By some magic or other, Hera and Aaron returned home, living with Viner for a time before making their own life on Great Neighbor. At least, that's how the story should have ended. But that's not what happened.

Epilogue
The Limits of Love

Horror, the Restless Sleeper, would not take his final rest. He was cradling Henry's body when his eyes opened. He was laying in a pool of water no more than a few inches deep. The water was cool against his skin and still, apart from his breathing. When the Sleeper looked to see the boy in his hands, he recognized him. The child he had heard so much about but had only seen once before. A cold panic filled the place where his heart would have been, but Henry's death was only the first of his realizations.

"Henry—" he said. "Henry, oh Henry, no, what have I done?"

He looked around, and through his dark eyes he saw something he had hoped to never have the displeasure of seeing. The Marble Tower had fallen, and out of it crawled dwarves, the army that Horror had raised. Oh, his pride was folly. Now, not only did the Marble Tower come crashing down, but also his sins. And who to punish, but those he had wronged. Dessees was not a hell before, but now all those who had ever met the Sleeper would feel hell's wrath. All of that suffering just to punish one half-man.

His heart bled on the floor before him. "What have I done?" he wailed. "It can't be for nothing."

The memories of all the Restless Sleeper's mistakes came flooding back to him all at once. He had been a mindless skeleton before, but now he was fully sentient again. To remember so much pain was a vile torture that should only be given to the whole-heartedly evil. Yet the irony was that the only people immune to dishonor's torment were the whole-heartedly evil. So even with his heart on the floor and an empty chasm where it had leapt from him, the

Sleeper knew that there was one light that still guided his memories.

The Sleeper must have looked ghastly—mouth open, black gnarled teeth slowly growing into fangs as he gawked at the expanse of his mistake. If he had the time, he would have buried Henry. But he hadn't the strength, let alone the time, because with each memory, a new wave of sadness engulfed him. He still could not comprehend what it meant to have killed Henry.

He screamed so loud that he was deathly quiet; he ran so fast that he did not move at all; he was so strong that everything about him was weak. One step forward and then the next. The Horror no longer disintegrated the ground but disintegrated himself, collapsing under his own weight, like wet clay forced to walk. He sobbed forward, but he had no tears to give. He was not man; he was not magic; he was a black endless vat of regret with one thought on his mind— 'It's too late to turn back now. If they call me Horror, Horror I shall be.'

***

Viner looked into the place where Hiver's eyes would be, and Hiver looked up at him. The potentate of Dessees had to admit to himself that he was going to die and that his reign was at an end. But there was always that one hope, that hope that would forever guide Hiver deeper into darkness no matter if he was about to die or about to feast. That one entity, that power, the purpose to his bleak life, the faith. The Black Star.

A wave of dark energy burst across the crowd. A dark light that snaked its way through the air, leaving a trail of cold embers. Viner held steadfast to the spear, but the magical power was too much for him. His grip slowly slipped, forcing him away from the weapon and, in turn, away from Hiver. Horror walked forward, his face changing, gray color being added to his flesh. The nose that dilapidated against his face started to elongate to an unnatural length.

"I will banish you home. All you must do is let me!" he boomed.

With his four hands, he weaved a spell, and this time Henry was not there to stop him. He blasted out strings of light that bounced from person to person. The light tore through the remnants of the dark energy, not dispelling it, but consuming and reusing it. The strings of light raced towards the army, and each person they hit disappeared. Hera and Aaron's eyes widened before the string of light hit them. Aaron started to run, but it was too late. He was struck. But nothing happened. He breathed heavily before making eye contact with Hera.

Calm's voice rang in Hera's ear, "Let's not be hasty... I will teleport you out if you must leave."

Hera trusted Calm and nodded resolutely. The light hit her, and nothing happened. She looked down to see Aaron using his knees to support his wheezing. She hoped that the Sleeper was being honest when he said he would "banish you home" and this wasn't some sort of trick. She pushed the thought aside. It was possible that she had just watched everyone die, but she did not know that. She could not know that. All she knew was that this monstrous Horror had killed Henry and now it had the audacity to live.

Viner's psyche should have been crushed by the knowledge that the Restless Sleeper had lived. But instead of it filling him with rage, it just made him sad. He fought back tears that stung his eyes, looking at the beast that had killed his nephew. The Sleeper looked back at him, and out of those cold black eyes radiated a warmth that echoed

Viner's emotion. Viner's face quivered, trying not to cry. Something about him felt betrayed, and the Restless Sleeper felt like a betrayer.

The white zap hit Viner in the side of the head and was sucked into his temple. But he did not disappear. The cave was suddenly dark, with Viner being the last to be struck by the line of white. The army was gone, no one had chosen to stay except for Viner, Hera, and Aaron. The Sleeper nodded sadly, slowly at first, then quickly, as if he was staving off tears that would never come. His head snapped quickly to Hiver.

"My son," the Sleeper said.

Hiver did not look at him. His face was still clouded by tungsten. When the thieves looked at his wound, they noted something strange. Hiver did bleed, yes, but what was under his armor was not flesh. It looked nothing like flesh. It looked like more bits of metal haphazardly entombed in a stronger metal prison. How could this despicable man have a heart made of gold?

"You," the gold heart said.

The tone was flat and, if anything, annoyed. If the Sleeper was hurt, he did not show it. His long legs quickly took him to Hiver's side, kneeling next to him. He started fussing over Hiver's wound, touching it madly. He snapped the two sides of the spear as if they were twigs, allowing Hiver to lay on the floor. Hiver looked away while the monster worked on his fatal scar. The Sleeper suddenly stopped using his secondary arms to attend Hiver. They became stiffer and the fingers became webbed. On top of that, gray color started to pump through veins that now protruded through the thin flesh. It did not stop Horror from doing his job.

"I won't let you die, my son," he hummed while trying to assess the damage.

Calm's voice cut through the commotion, "Old friend... please?"

This time, the old wizard was not in Hera's head. He was standing behind her, his hand on her shoulder. Hera had not felt him place it. It seemed that somehow, Calm's hand had always been on her shoulder. Calm was tall, but both Horror and Hiver dwarfed him. At his side stood Fear, black and red robe and all. He couldn't help but look creepy in the darkness that was cast by his wide-brimmed hat. Calm had a gentle frown on his face, looking over at the Sleeper.

"I know he is your son, and I know you love him, but you have to let him go. He is gone," Calm said.

"My son is right here, and he is dying," Horror hissed.

He smashed his hand into Hiver's wound. Hiver roared in pain, his faceless mask darting up to look at the Restless Sleeper. When the Sleeper removed his hand, a large black mark was left on Hiver's stomach, sealing the wound closed.

"He is evil," Calm said.

The Sleeper was getting angrier by the second, "He is not! He is my son!"

Fear looked to the floor, shading his eyes from Hera and Aaron's view. A despicable smile crept across his face. He was looking directly at Hiver.

"We must put him down," Fear grinned.

"Put him down?" Horror asked.

The Restless Sleeper jumped to his feet. All six stood in dazed silence for too long of a time. Hiver slumped against his own leg, doing all he could to not pass out. Hera and Aaron held hands, afraid of what was to come. Viner seemed to be coming to a realization, his head shaking viciously from left to right, his eyes turning red. The Sleeper gritted his teeth, seething at Fear's statement.

After a moment, he regained his composure. "I've given everything for my son. Do you think I will stop now? I used to be the highest of Disus. I had everything, but I gave it to my son because I love him. You would never understand, Fear."

Viner's eyes shot up to look at Horror. The great man was brought to tears on seeing his face. The highest of Disus. He knew the highest of Disus. Where the Restless Sleeper stood, stood too another man. His face was snakelike, small wings grew from his sides, his scales gray and laugh lines dotted his sad eyes.

"No—" Viner whispered, hoarsely.

"I am Mordecai, the Restless Sleeper."

Calm looked down at the floor sadly, "I should not have let you see this…"

"I was elected the lord of Disus, and my reign marked the end of democracy among the dragonkin," Mordecai announced with sorrow.

The wilted body that had once been Horror was now the skeletal mass of Mordecai. While his mind was trapped within the confines of the marble tower, his body remained living but defiled. The secondary set of arms was not arms at all, but instead a pair of long-discarded wings. With flesh now on his body, Mordecai looked like a hideous mix between a man and a dragon.

"How could you!" Viner shouted, spit flying out of his mouth. "You killed my nephew! He was like a son to me!"

The Restless Sleeper frowned genuinely. "I am sorry, my friend. I was not aware of myself. To create the Marble Tower required giving up a part of myself. And to make something so large and powerful required a potent sacrifice. My consciousness brought me nothing but pain and regret, so I used it. I had no idea what my empty body would become."

"You're a killer at your base," Viner denounced. "You told me your own failures as a father in that year we spent together. Because you could not have it, you took fatherhood from the only man who cared about you. The only man who took pity on you. Henry was more than my nephew, he was my purpose!"

"I couldn't control myself," Mordecai begged.

"I don't care!" Viner lunged toward the Restless Sleeper. He had no weapon in his hand any longer; his spear lay discarded next to Hiver. But it didn't matter to him; Viner would eliminate this uncouth creature. He hit the tall lizard squarely in the neck with a right hook, going straight past him in the process.

"You debauched filth!" Viner cried.

Mordecai staggered back, completely unprepared for the assault. Viner appeared to be set off-balance by his rigorous punch. He toppled to his knees beside Hiver. Hiver cocked his neck. Was he entertained by this?

"I will not fight you, my friend," Mordecai told him. He reached his hand out to help Viner up.

But Viner's stumble has been merely a deception. Viner had not lost his balance but instead purposefully descended to the floor so that he was able to pick up the discarded spearhead. He twisted his body back towards Horror and stuck the small tip into the palm of his outstretched hand. If Viner had been looking, he would have aimed for something more vital.

Mordecai hissed in pain. He held his hand to his chest and stepped back. But he was not far enough away before the shaft of the spear was in Viner's hands, and he struck Mordecai across the face. The giant serpent went tumbling to the floor, coiling around himself as he did so. He did not look like a dragon now. He looked like a weak old man. He was not.

"This madness must stop," Calm proclaimed, "Please, Mordecai, your body is not well. You must move on."

The place where Mordecai had been struck was turning ashen. Scales were disintegrating from his very bones. But this time, his corpse would not live on without him. This reuniting of the soul and body that had occurred when both had died was only temporary. With a firm resolve, Mordecai knew he had to take what he had.

"Hera or Aaron, have either of you heard of vampirism?" Fear asked the two.

Hera and Aaron were frozen to the spot, unsure of what to say to the creepy old man.

"No?" Fear asked.

Calm interjected, "Fear—"

Fear ignored him, "It's a way in which powerful entities gain immortality at the cost of the blood of another. Would you like to try it?"

Calm looked down at the two young adults. "He's only joking. Aren't you, Fear?"

The two wizards shared a smug smile for a brief moment. For now, Viner had stopped attacking Mordecai, who was still on the floor, clutching his face. After a moment of silence, Calm's bearded face lost some of its soul, as if his skin had turned to ceramic and his eyes to glass. He gestured towards Hiver.

"Go ahead," he said.

Fear moved like a shadow over twilight. His cloak was wrapped around Hiver's body. Hiver vainly tried to push Fear away, only to be met with the clicking of the dark wizard's tongue.

"No, no, no, Hiver. You won't be strong enough to walk for a very long time," he cooed.

The metal arms of the automaton were no match for the strength of this outwardly weak old man. Fear interlocked his fingers with Hiver's and pushed his hands back to the ground. He shushed him softly before being interrupted.

"You dastardly snake!" Viner shouted.

Before Fear knew what was happening, he was being lifted off his feet by the neck. He gagged against the scrawny scaled hand of the Restless Sleeper. His legs flailed beneath him as he was lifted two feet from the ground.

"I've lost too much to lose," Mordecai said.

Calm sprang a spell from his sleeve. A torrent of chilled wind leaped from his white cloak, as if a desolate tundra was hidden beneath the folds of fabric and stitching. At the same time, Viner charged towards Horror yet again, with the broken haft of the spear raised above his head. Mordecai used Fear's body to push Viner aside and then threw the limp wizard into the icy wind, practically dispelling the evocation.

"I'll kill you," Viner roared.

"I am already dead," Mordecai answered.

Viner tried to swing at Mordecai again, but this time the stick was caught in the lizard's wounded hand. Mordecai did not wince as the metal spearhead wiggled out of his skin and clattered on the floor, spilling blood onto the ground. A dribble of blood poured down Mordecai's hand and created a puddle on the ground. From that puddle rose a mist of purple fume.

"When you awaken, my friend, you will be home again," Mordecai said softly.

"I did not allow you to banish me before. I shan't allow you to banish me now."

"We all wake up from our lies eventually."

The smell of poppy flowers was on Mordecai's breath as he said those final words to Hiver. The purple fume of his blood was intoxicating, causing even the stoutest of hearts to be unable to stay awake. Through nights of torment, it was always easy for Mordecai to put others to sleep. Viner collapsed in his armor, not completely passed out yet. But his knees were too weak to hold him, his eyelids too heavy to keep open.

"But what do we wake up to?" Viner said before his head nodded into his chest, and he fell asleep.

Hera and Aaron ran to the man's side. Mordecai watched them out of the corner of his eyes. The lizard backed away to allow the two to be beside Viner for a moment. Aaron looked back at Calm, making eye contact with him. Calm shook his head. With a wave of his hand, the wizard sent Viner to Great Neighbor, fated to awake in his own bed. Fear appeared over Calm's shoulder. He was still shaking violently from the powerful spell Calm had accidentally inflicted upon him.

"Hera, Aaron, you are chosen by the very gods to kill this half-man," Fear said disdainfully.

A shiver ran down both of their spines. They felt out of place among all these powerful people. Mordecai seemed like a cornered animal, unwilling to allow anyone to come near but not desiring conflict. Neither Hera nor Aaron were sure they liked what they were being asked to do, but these two wizards had always been good, and they trusted them.

"Concentrate, keep the image of something phantastic in your mind. Channel it into magic," Calm told them.

"Do they know what they are being trained for?" Mordecai asked.

Aaron tried vehemently to imagine a massive fireball at his command to be hurled at Mordecai. A fireball would serve him right for all the pain Horror had caused. Aaron could visualize that fireball gently spinning towards the lizard, licking at the air as it did so. He imagined the displacement of the atmosphere around the blazing inferno. He would burn this lizard alive. But try as he might, such a violent request didn't feel right to Aaron. He could visualize it happening, but not him doing it.

"Learning takes time," Mordecai said.

"So you're going to let Hiver get away with this, Mordecai?" Hera asked. "After all he has done? You're going to let him mindlessly kill everyone?"

Mordecai frowned down at the four. "One day you will understand, Hera. I believe with every fiber of my body that what Hiver is doing is wrong. But he..." Mordecai looked back to the crumpled body of Hiver on the floor, still reeling from his wounds, "He believes."

"It's true," Hiver coughed.

"Hera," Calm whispered hoarsely in her ear, "immobilize Mordecai, he has clearly lost his mind."

"I take no revelry in the deaths of others. But I have been cursed," Hiver sucked in a deep raspy breath. "While my soul is being consumed, I cannot escape Dessees. I wish only to be free of this eternal hell. Mortal flesh was a small price to pay for the return of my people. And once their bodily power was consumed, their souls would be free from the influence of the false gods." Hiver lurched forward. "They would be under the safety of my vast talons, like eggs in a hawk's nest."

"So you see," Mordecai said, "My son believes in what he says. Yes, I know it sounds crazy. But it might work," He begged them to understand. "I may not agree with him, but I trust him."

Hera could clearly visualize the rubble of the marble tower rising to pummel Mordecai and Hiver into the grounAd.

She would not let this madness stand. Blind loyalty to a false ideal. Hiver was a serial killer and a madman. His tyranny could not be tolerated.

Mordecai scowled, "But even now you rise against us."

A chunk of marble levitated off the floor. It was larger than ten men and must have been heavier than even more. But it flew, along with others. All the destroyed pieces of the marble tower were radiating with energy. It felt to Hera like she was connected to the marble in some way. It was incredible, euphoric even. Hera shook with new energy she had not felt before.

The giant boulder cast a shadow down on Mordecai's head as it blocked a nearby vent of light. Then it started to fall, surely crushing him. But Mordecai would not so easily kneel, he flicked his tongue out of his mouth like a snake tasting the air and the boulder changed course towards the wizards and their warlocks.

The chunk of marble would have crushed both gods and mortals had Aaron not cast a spell of his own. He stood in front of the enormous mass and covered himself defensively, unable to comprehend death. Only a few feet away from the group, the boulder lost momentum and shattered into the ground. Mordecai, Fear, Hera, and Aaron were all pushed back from the shockwave, leaving Calm as the only one standing.

"Even an apprentice can stand against your juvenile sorceries," Calm boasted. "Now face the wrath of the god of war."

A shockwave of sound blasted from Calm's mouth towards Mordecai. The sound caused Mordecai's horse mane white hair to flow behind him. Soon, he had lost his footing and was forced behind Hiver. Calm walked forward slowly and conjured a blade of light in his hands. Calm stopped above Hiver's body and clutched the sword in both hands. He raised it above his head and aimed it at Hiver. The tevnal's face remained emotionless.

"No!" Mordecai shouted. He conjured a bolt of lightning from the tip of his finger. The lightning zapped towards the white wizard, striking the sharp blade of the sword of light, and static absorbed into it. Calm's grip tightened, but the sword was somehow frozen in place. He grimaced and started to yell before the sword exploded thunderously in his grip. Calm staggered back, his face a blackened mess of flesh and bone. Hera saw her crippled master briefly on the brink of death before his skin stretched itself back together and his beard regrew as if nothing had damaged his perfect face.

"I have given up my very humanity once before." Mordeaci levitated from the ground and spread his wings before Hera and Aaron. "I shall do so again."

The Sleeper's claws grew to immense sizes, hard as steel and white as bone. He dove through the sky towards the two, ready to slice them to ribbons. Hera raised her hands and shot a torrent of ice through the sky like a comet. Mordecai's flight was thrown off course and he plummeted to the ground.

"You vile thing!" Fear shouted, "You'd give up your humanity twice? Cheat death and spit it in the face of Despair."

"His humanity?" Hera asked, "Filius described that as a living soul. Would he use one of those to kill us, even if it killed him?"

"He's already used up all of his humanities, I'm afraid," Fear said. "But he has them back now. He'll die soon anyway, might as well go out with a bang. First, he'll probably get rid of something small, like his sense of smell or individual memories. Then he'll move onto larger requests."

"Sounds like a lot to give up for a moment of power," Aaron said.

"Some actions last a lifetime," Fear replied.

Mordecai convulsed over something. He clutched at his left eye. When his claw was retracted, his eye was milky white. The marble tower began to shake. The chunks of stone began to float as they had when Hera cast her spell. But this time they seemed somehow liquid. Mordecai had used his eye to animate his creation, the marble tower, yet again; but now the marble conjoined into a new shape. A limb was formed first, a leg of some sort, like a pristine statue made out of porcelain. Then the torso and another leg. Finally, the arms emerged from the side of the goliath's torso. The creation was a headless mass with engravings of dragon's flying across its humanoid body.

"That's a single eye?" Aaron asked.

The arm of the creature came collapsing down on top of them. Hera and Aaron ran to the right while Fear and Calm dodged to the left. Mordecai came flying down upon the two young thieves, his claws magically elongated yet again. Aaron created a shield out of white magic energy that collided with the slicing claws of the once-dragon.

Hera hid behind Aaron's shield, but while she was keeled over she created a string of fire that licked at her skin. She was careful not to touch it, lest it attach to her, but she held it with her mind, her hand hovering just a few inches away. She struck Mordecai with it and the flaming whip wound around his arm.

The goliath bent down on its elbows and knees and pushed its hand out at Mordecai, Hera, and Aaron. The fingers of the giant hand streaked across the ground towards the three, pulling up rubble as it was hurled forward. Hera pulled at Mordecai, who tried to stop her from moving him, but with a feat of determination she positioned Mordecai around to take the brunt of the goliath's attack. Aaron put the shield between them and Mordecai and allowed the lizard to be pinned against his shield and the goliath's marble hand.

Hera and Aaron were struck hard, Hera felt her arm break and Aaron felt the uncomfortable popping sensation of his shoulder dislocating as they were thrown yet again on their backs. Mordecai looked even worse than the two, his back was bent at an impossible angle, and he was covered in blood. But he still labored a shallow breath.

On the other side of the goliath's hand, Fear and Calm were barred from vision of Mordecai. Yet still, the goliath attacked them. It swept its arm against Calm and Fear. Both wizards created a barrier between them and the giant marble arm as they were pushed backwards across the rocky landscape. At the same time as attacking Hera and Aaron, the goliath attempted to pin the wizards with its knee. Fear shifted the barrier above his head to block the assault, while Calm turned ethereal and flew away.

"Fear, you fool, the weight will crush you!" Calm shouted.

But Fear only laughed. "Not with this," he said.

He reached into the pockets of his coats and emerged a blood red ball. He looked at it with an almost hungry expression on his face as he lifted it above his head. A beam of red light shot up at the knee of the goliath creature, causing the marble to crack and shatter. Blood gushed from the beam and across the floor. Fear's arm became draconic while holding the beam and his eyes became fiery and lizard-like.

Meanwhile, Mordecai was recovering from his attack. His spine began to mend and his blood began to dry. Mordecai rose from the ground and shrugged off the wounds.

"The only memory I need now is that of my purpose," he said.

Hera and Aaron stepped back in fear. Aaron rubbed at his dislocated shoulder, trying to pop it back into place with magic. So far he only succeeded in providing himself with agonizing pain that even the spike of adrenaline could do little to stop. He and Hera slowly backed away from Horror. Hera was clutching at her arm and her hand was glowing, but little else was happening.

"The wizards only want to use you," Mordecai spat. "They hone your skills so that they can absorb your power. You're like a boar being fattened."

Mordecai launched a torrent of magic blasts at the two. Aaron flicked his working arm and redirected the attacks back at Mordecai. His shoulder slumped painfully as he let go of it and he winced in pain, causing his aim to be off and the blasts to go over Mordecai's head.

Mordecai watched the magic go by his shoulder. His eyes caught Fear fighting back against the goliath out of the corner of his vision. Fear was laughing maniacally as the orb of blood tore through the goliath's white marble like a heated knife through butter. Mordecai huffed out a breath of rage and reached his hand out as if to stop Fear from destroying his minion.

Hera took the opportunity to run forward. She conjured a sword made out of dark energy and with it, she slashed at Mordecai's outstretched arm. Mordecai's arm was sliced clean off at the shoulder and he roared in surprise and pain.

At the same time, the goliath was completely overtaken by red energy. The bloodless creature bled profusely from cracks in its stone skin. Its arms and legs fell off as if it had never been created in the first place. Fear stood victorious with a smirk on his ghastly face.

"That is my blood you use," Mordecai announced. "And I want it back."

With his remaining arm, he plunged his fingers into his eye and ripped it from its socket, much more viciously than he had blinded the other one. The effect of this spell was less subtle but as powerful all the same. Fear, as if by some act of clumsiness, dropped the orb in his hands. The very tides of fate were changed as it plummeted to the ground. Though normally, the orb would have survived the fall, now it was not so. The glass shattered on the ground. Fear roared.

"My orb," he cried. "Do you know what you've done? How many people you've killed? I'll have to harvest them all now, all because of you!"

"You won't stop will you?" Mordecai asked sorrowfully.

Hera could not let Mordecai off of the defensive now, not while she had the advantage. There he stood, his arm missing, completely blind, it would be a simple matter to dispose of him. She visualized Mordecai being attached to her by threads coming from her fingers, and with her will it was so. She extended her hand and ethereal blue threads, one from each finger, sprung out and wrapped around Horror, two around his torso, two around his remaining arm, and the last around his neck. But there was something new with this spell; she felt an exertion that had not plagued her before. Her mind became slow. She barely had time to react before Mordecai pulled the strings from her finger and caused her to stumble forward.

"Hera, are you okay?" Aaron was above her, she was on the ground and her vision was blurry.

Mordecai was saying something dramatic a few feet away, "If my voice fails me now, I have no use for it any longer."

Fear screamed; it was all very confusing.

Then, a man in white was standing beside Hera, looking down at her. "My champion, you can fight no longer, your soul is running dry."

"My soul?"

Calm turned to address Aaron, "My boy, the time has come for you to lend me your strength."

"Lend you my—"

"Enough of your incessant questions, yes, lend me your strength. I will take it from you if I must, even now Fear can last little longer. Mordecai will not cease giving away his humanities."

A growl rang from the cave ceiling. Long shadows struck over white and gray stone. Humanities flowed like water here in the cave, for not only did Mordecai give up his voice and his reason, Fear too gave something up, though it was impossible to tell what. The stone growled and claws streaked across it. Two wyrms of immense size were locked on each other's long necks. One of these wyrms, once Mordecai, had three legs and was gray in color, large spines stuck out at odd angles across the entirety of the lizard's body. Two wings shriveled to the sides of the titanic monster, once large and grand now too weak for flight. The other, Fear's new avatar, was quite the opposite. He was slender and sleek, with a black hide of slimy scales. Fear's gigantic wings were large enough to cocoon both reptiles in darkness.

Calm bent down to pick up Hera by the arm and hoist her on his shoulder. She was barely sentient as he did so. A swelling of dizziness overcame her vision and she felt sick to the stomach. Calm then placed his hand on the back of Aaron's neck and led him toward the dragon.

"Lord of Disus, father forthmost, I as god of war stand with two brave champions to warn you of your imminent death."

The two dragons seemed not to hear Calm's cry. But someone did. A metallic laugh graded against Aaron's ears. He looked over to see Hiver on the ground drumming his fingers against the floor, slowly convulsing in what looked like painful laughter.

"Do you see the state of that girl?" he asked, "Absorb her soul and she dies. Permanently."

Calm did not look at Hiver; he insisted on pushing Hera and Aaron forward.

"The dilemma," Hiver chuckled. "You can't possibly believe that this young boy alone has enough reserve in his soul to be able to single-handedly defeat my father, not when he is like this."

Calm looked like he was considering what Hiver had to say. Mordecai was on top of Fear now, and it appeared he was winning the fight even with a missing limb. Fear reared back his head and flame started to broil in his mouth. But Mordecai clamped his jaws down on his neck again, effectively putting him out of range of the flames. A cascade of fire burst out of Fear's mouth, only serving to char the ceiling and miss Mordecai completely.

Hiver continued, "There are so many options. But you gods always manage to pick the worst ones. Where is Love when you need her?"

Aaron was beginning to feel uncomfortable with the way Calm was looking at Hera and him. What was the old man thinking? Hera was almost passed out on his shoulder, but Calm needed her strength to kill Mordecai. But how was he going to use that strength? Was Calm going to have to let someone die?

"You can't kill Hera!" Aaron shouted.

Hiver laughed again, "Listen to the boy. But have you ever listened to anyone in the past? It was always about the greater good, wasn't it, Calm? Always about your family. Is Fear not your family anymore? One broken dish and the whole tree is uprooted?"

Calm looked down to Aaron and down to Hera. He had a frown on his face, one of complete and utter loss. Aaron hadn't seen much of Calm, but this was an expression unusual to him. What was he thinking?

Fear thrashed back at Mordecai, using all of his limbs to cut and scratch the hard hide of the dragon. It was evident now that even with a missing leg, Mordecai was winning. Perhaps he was just more used to being in a dragon's body. Whatever curse had bound him in his half man state must have been chastising. To be free of it was liberation.

Calm let go of Aaron's neck. He hadn't felt how tightly the old wizard had been gripping it until the fingers no longer dug into his skin. They left marks of pink on Aaron's scalp as blood rushed back to the spot where Calm had been holding him. Calm moved his arm to the boy's shoulder. He began to turn away from Fear. He walked in the opposite direction.

"Oh no," Hiver said jubilantly, "Not Calm running away. No, no. no, it can't be. At least slay me, Calm. Smite me down with all your godly righteousness. You can spare a few human souls for that can't you?"

Calm continued walking, with Aaron walking beside him and Hera limping along. They heard the sound of Fear struggling for his life in his fight against Mordecai. Calm was about to let Hiver get away with all of this. For what? Aaron thought about that for a moment. Rose had given her life to kill Hiver. Henry had given his life to kill Mordecai. But now their deaths had to be affirmed by Hera? They didn't die for her to die.

"But then again, you would never be able to kill me yourself. The moment you allow me access to the afterlife, I'll rapture all of them. All the souls you use to conjure your magic tricks would flow right between your fingers. A vast vortex in the pool of your power. Your little prison no longer, lich."

"There is always another way, Aaron," Calm whispered down to him. "But some setbacks aren't worth taking a step in the wrong direction."

***

Hours later, Hera and Aaron awoke. It was midday and they were lying on the beach of Great Neighbor. The water gently lapped against their feet, kissing their toes through their shoes. The sun glimmered its warm embrace down to them. It was hotter than when they had left. Was winter already over? Aaron sat up. Promptly, he fell back down.

"What do we do now?" Aaron asked Hera.

Hera didn't know what to say. She was still processing what had happened. She wondered how many good people had died.

"Live to be happy again."

Aaron searched within himself for any happiness, but all he felt was emptiness. Maybe it would come in time. Maybe he just had to live on a little longer. He placed his cheek against the shore, appreciating the soft sand. They laid there for hours, not knowing what to do until it came to them. They heard the shuffling of heavy feet, thankfully not armored.

"Hello..." Viner said timidly.

Aaron and Hera did not respond, they did not know how to.

"I have a place for you to rest... at least until you get one of your own. I imagine you'll be wanting a nice bed right about now," Viner continued.

Still, they lay motionless, not acknowledging Viner in the slightest.

"I was thinking that, after Calessa's wedding, we can go to Aerokite and have some… hot chocolate," he said.

Viner frowned when they still did not respond. He pivoted on his heel, the sand moving with his feet. Then the giant man started walking in the opposite direction.

Aaron and Hera practically talked over each other. "I would like that," they said.

Then they looked at each other, almost laughing at how they had both said the same thing. Viner stopped in his tracks, the waves lapping up against his boots. It was a surprise to him that the water from one of the waves had gotten all the way up to his left eye and now fell down his cheek. Hera and Aaron both tried their best to get up, taking more time than any healthy person should. Their bones cracked as they moved, worrying Aaron a little more than was reasonable.

"Calessa is getting married?" Aaron asked.

"Not yet, but that Tython boy isn't leaving any time soon," Viner chuckled. "It's only a matter of time."

www.ingramcontent.com/pod-product-compliance
Lightning Source LLC
Chambersburg PA
CBHW021845010726
47493CB00005B/1564